MONICA LA PORTA

ELIOS

WORLDS APART SERIES

To keep up to date with Monica's new releases and promotions
scan the QR code with your smartphone or mobile device.

To Dad.

TABLE OF CONTENTS

1

Fido moved restlessly around the small kitchen bathed in the morning sun. I looked out the window one more time before closing the blue shutters. My companion was susceptible to the heat and dust coming from the crowded street just outside the room. More than once, I found Fido repeatedly banging against the wall. Normally, I could easily reset its circuits by flipping the on/off switch until it started working properly again.

Resembling a small, compact air-conditioning unit on wheels, Fido was my only friend on Earth. If not for Fido, I would have forgotten how my vocal cords worked.

"Good boy." I patted the metal box. "Must go out. Stay put."

Fido chirped the four notes indicating it had recorded the command. A moment later, it went into standby and stopped near the corner. It always shut down at that particular corner. I knew its robotic actions meant nothing more than the sum of its programming, but after several millennia spent in solitude on this planet, I felt a sort of attachment to that piece of metal and regarded it as if it were capable of human emotions—or Solean emotions.

I looked at the clock on the wall. "Better get going before the sun is too high." On my way out, one look at the mirror facing the door reminded me I was wearing only jeans. I strode back to the bedroom, opened one of the chest drawers, picked up the first item of clothing I found, donned the white shirt, and sighed. I missed the loose fabric of the Ionic chiton, the linen garment so much easier to wear in summer's heat. Modern fashion was a nuisance. Once outside my small apartment, I was engulfed by the darkness of the communal hallway leading to the street. I breathed in the musky scent of the brick walls surrounding me and then moved forward to meet the Greek sun. White light and a pleasant breeze welcomed me just outside the hallway. I closed the metal gate behind me and looked for my car. Maybe a week ago, I had parked it somewhere south of my apartment complex. It was still there.

My car, a forgettable excuse for a vehicle—I had chosen the third- or fourth-hand white Fiat Panda because of its lack of appeal—was safely sitting under the shadow of a leafy tree. Once inside, I manually rolled down the front windows and readied myself for a new day of observation. I wished I could bring Fido along, but it wouldn't do to be seen talking to an AC unit. I started the engine and merged with the traffic. I had been living in modern Athens for a while now—close to ten years—and I'd come to appreciate those early summer mornings when the majority of the city was sleeping and the heat was still bearable.

I drove to the Agora and back. I didn't have a specific location in mind; observing was a task to be taken unhurriedly. After years of tumult, Greece was living an uneventful decade although I knew that was just a phase. Unrest was in the air. I had collected enough data to support my hunch. I had been ready to move for a while. I didn't want to be there when the first demonstration happened. As an Observer, I couldn't intervene, and it was painful to be relegated to a corner without being able to help. Human pain and sorrow were strong emotions to filter. I was relieved that I would leave Athens and Greece in a few hours. After just one last drive around town, I would go back to the apartment to pack my few belongings. India was my next destination, and I was looking forward to the change of scenery.

For no reason at all, I turned left instead of right at the corner between my apartment's street and the main artery leading back to the city center. And I saw her. Standing on the sidewalk with her nose in the air was a girl. For the first time in all the eons I had lived, I saw, truly saw, one of the subjects of my studies as a single entity. *I saw her.* Without thinking, I hit the brakes. She turned and lowered her eyes to me. She looked at me, not through me as she was supposed to do. After a moment of shock, I reacted—not in the way I should have, though. Without wanting to, I reacted to her. I attuned my senses to her aura. The rest of the city slowed down. The urge to exit my car and walk to her side became so strong I gasped for air. At the same time, life fast-forwarded to the present moment, and she turned to talk to somebody. I forced my foot to push the gas pedal, and I drove away. It took all my willpower not to look back, but I reached the end of the street, turned right, and parked in the first available spot. Unable to think straight, I turned off the engine and then laid my head on the steering wheel.

Her aura had called me.

I breathed. I didn't know what to do. I wasn't prepared for that. Observers never had contact with the population they were watching over. Doing so was strictly prohibited, not that the thought had ever occurred to me.

A small touch nudged my mind, a feather-light question mark ringing at the edge of my consciousness like a doorbell. I recognized the mental signature. Areel was calling me to the Astral World.

Not now. I closed the channel before my friend could ask me anything. Had he sensed my distress? *No, it isn't possible.* I made an effort to stabilize my heartbeats. Areel called again. I wasn't ready to talk to him.

Is everything okay? Areel's question reached me unprepared.

Just busy. I'll see you later. I closed the channel a second time. Then, instead of driving to my apartment where I could lie in the dark and meditate, I started the engine and drove toward the sea, following the residual ghost of the girl's aura. I reached the Aegean Sea in a state of confusion. I knew I had to turn around and purge my mind from that unwelcome feeling, but I wanted to see her again. Inexplicably, our auras had connected. I parked the car by the beach and walked to the shore. After removing my shoes, I fell on my knees and let the tide bury me in the sand. I stood there, not caring that my clothes were being soaked in salty water, not caring that my exposed skin was reddening under the sun. People walked by, but they didn't see me. They skirted my unmoving body as if I were a rock blocking their path—as it should have been.

Hours later, another mental call, this time from my friend Kam, awoke me from my torpor.

Care to come visit us at our place?

I wondered for a fleeting moment if Areel had warned Kam about my previous response to a similar request. Then I decided I was being paranoid.

Must go pack. Later. Normally, I would have never said no to a visit to the place Areel, Kam, and I had created for our entertainment. Observers, when on duty, lived in complete isolation, the only appropriate means of socialization provided by those trips to the mental realm of the Astral World. In the Astral World, we could meet friends and spend as much time as we wanted recharging our mental batteries. There, time had no meaning. Years in the Astral World could be mere seconds on Earth.

We are adding a room.

Go ahead. We had re-created the layout of the dorms we all had slept in back at the Academy. It was the one physical place we all had shared. Familiarity helped when creating mental spaces, because every mind involved in the process added personal details that made the experience more lifelike. At the moment, I didn't care if they added a whole new wing to our place.

Later, then.

Later. I summoned the strength necessary to uproot myself from the hole I'd sunk in and, I couldn't help but smile at the thought. Covered in wet sand, my pants weighted down by it, I was walking back to the car, when I caught the unmistakable signature of her aura. The wind had driven the multicolored gossamer rainbow close to me. I automatically drove away from the beach, following the tail of what was left of her passage through the city. In places, I could see her aura as if she was standing nearby, but when I stopped, she was already gone. In other places, its shadow was so faint, it was a wonder I could sense anything at all. I forgot my previous plans and spent the whole day tracking the girl's aura in and out of Athens. The sun set and the starry night sky replaced it, and I remembered I was due out of my apartment in a few hours. *One last mile.* I was incapable of turning around. And then, several one-last-miles later, I accepted defeat and headed to my place.

If it weren't for Fido, I wouldn't have bothered coming back. I had no attachment to the few items I had amassed throughout my decade of living in Greece. Objects could be replaced easily, and I didn't need anything more than the strictly necessary. Fido was irreplaceable. It had been assigned to me fresh out of the Academy, before I left for my first mission. My first task as an Observer had been on a small planet, Radesk, where life had evolved in a communitarian form. Radeskians had been a peaceful aquatic race. First missions were meant to be no more than dry runs to acclimate newbies to the tasks ahead. When I left for Radesk, one morning so many eons ago, I didn't know I shouldn't fear failure. Fido was there for me when I was mentally cut from the safety net of my friends' support system, and I confided my anguish to the robot. Once mental communication was restored—at the beginning of every mission, Observers weren't allowed to interact with anybody—and I reached Areel and Kam on the Astral World, several millennia had already passed. Fido had recorded every word I had spoken, and I had come to think of it as my confidant. In terrestrial terms, it was nothing more than a black box meant to be used to extract data if anything happened to an Observer during a mission.

"Wake up." I looked at the metal cube, and it chirped, its red light blinking in response. "Time to move on." I almost said out loud what I had done the whole day but thought better of it. Fido left its corner and wheeled closer to me. I absentmindedly patted it while the first rays of light filtered inside between the shutters' panels. I had already sent a check to my landlord—a burly man in his late sixties I had successfully managed to avoid for the last seven years. My rent contract would be terminated the coming week, but I had booked a flight to Mumbai for later that same day. I checked the clock on the wall. "Almost time to leave for the airport." I gave a last glance around the small apartment that had never felt like anything more than a place I occasionally slept, and then I closed the door, one backpack dangling from my right shoulder and Fido firmly held between my arms. "Home is where you are." Fido flashed a blue light.

The morning was cold. The sun was still young, and I had forgotten to wear a sweater. The brief exercise of hauling Fido to the car was enough to warm me up. I opened the trunk and lay Fido on the blanket I had previously removed from my apartment. "Here you go." I slowly entered the early morning traffic, my senses straining to catch any trace of the girl's aura. Nothing. I shook my head at the feeling of disappointment. The low sentiment was unbecoming for an Observer. I centered myself in the moment and breathed in and out. Driving usually helped me focus, but not today.

On my way to the airport, I stopped at the shipping company that would take care of moving Fido to my new address. I didn't trust the airline to safely handle my robot. I had already prepaid for the shipping company's services, and it took five minutes to drop off Fido and get the receipt from the sleepy clerk, who gave the AC unit a raised eyebrow.

Not even ten minutes down the road, I slowed down and parked by a rest station bordering a crop of wind-shaped trees. I got out of the car and sank on my haunches. *Just one more time.* I wanted to bathe in her aura, if only for a moment, and be done with that madness consuming my thoughts. "This is not happening."

Then, a hint of her reached me, a brief, feather-like nudge with enough residual power to take my breath away. My reaction terrified me. I was already driving before I took notice of what I was doing. The fading rainbow of her aura was a directional vector I followed without question. Instead of heading toward the airport where my flight was going to leave in fewer than three hours, I headed in the opposite direction. "I have time to go through check-in and board." I remembered a moment too late I was alone in the car.

Three hours became two, then one, then half an hour. Then it was four hours past my flight, and I had stopped once to refill the tank; there had been enough gasoline in it to reach the charity depot I had signed my car to. The original plan had been to hire a cab from the depot to the airport. I detoured through the Attica region the whole day, without eating or drinking water. The girl's aura was stronger around two or three spots, but I didn't catch up with her. The night soon arrived, and I realized I had missed my flight and had nowhere to go.

I parked at the closest rest area, where I found a fountain trickling warm, desalinated water. My stomach rumbled, but I was in the middle of nowhere and too tired to drive to town. I went back to my car, lowered my seat, and closed my eyes. Although sleep wasn't a necessity for me, once in a while, my human body needed the time to regenerate. I must have been more tired than I thought because I slipped into a dream state almost immediately. My Solean mind never released control, but I went close to let it happen.

When I woke the next morning, my muscles ached, and I wondered what I was getting myself into. My concern lasted only a moment. The next whiff of the girl's aura was the only reason I needed to be on the road again without a bathroom break. Hunger and headache fought with general muscle discomfort to get my attention, but I ignored them. I knew I could go days before I needed to take care of my body.

"Where are you?" The sun was low in the sky, late in the afternoon, and I had been driving back and forth on dirt roads after losing her trace at some point during the day. One glance at the rearview mirror showed me an unhealthy version of myself, the skin on my face too dry and my eyes sunken.

I was about to turn and look for the closest hamlet to buy something to eat and drink when the shadow of her aura popped out ahead of me, pointing at Cape Sounion. Bodily functions forgotten, half an hour later I sat on one of the natural seats overlooking the Aegean Sea, the temple of Poseidon at my back. The sun had already set, and I knew the girl had stood nearby, watching the yellow star disappearing into the sea. I had just missed her by a matter of minutes. Her aura permeated the whole place in a display of colors and scents no human eyes and noses could sense. The girl had one of the most beautiful auras I had ever met. I longed to be in her presence. "Where are you now?"

Walking back to the car, I saw the trail left by her departing and followed her to the Acropolis. "You are a tourist." The realization saddened me. She would leave Greece, and I would never be able to see her again.

By the time I joined the late crowd visiting the Parthenon, her aura was a recent memory embossed on the marble of the temple's columns. "That's it." I stood there while a sea of uncaring people walked by. Hunger and exhaustion were taking their toll on my body. My mind had succumbed to a malady I didn't have a name for. I went back to the car and resolved to take care of my physical needs first. Near the Acropolis were plenty of touristy traps, but I had never cared for food before, and I wasn't going to start now.

Water and anything edible would do. I drove down toward the city, noticing that the restaurants in the first row were busy, and not a single parking spot was to be found. I wasn't sure I could go another minute without a beverage, my eyes were playing tricks on me, and my head was pounding.

A magnetic pull made me slow in the middle of a crowded road. Sitting at an outside table at one of the restaurants facing the Acropolis was the girl. Her eyes locked on mine in recognition. An electric buzz singed my skin. I willed the moment to freeze and attempted to memorize the feeling that started at the center of my heart and radiated everywhere else. The emotion was painful and pleasant. I knew I would never share it with anybody else.

Her lips moved, and I read the question she whispered. "Who are you?"

I smiled, ready to leave the car and reach for her.

Hi. Areel's greeting startled me.

My left hand had already pushed down the handle to open the door.

What are you doing? Kam asked.

Are you still there? Areel sent me a stronger nudge.

I ignored the mental calls, but I was suddenly aware of what I was doing and froze in the act while still looking at her. Years of training rushed through my mind. My sense of duty pressed on my chest like a physical weight. She stood up, and I hoped she would do what I couldn't and come to me. One of the people at the girl's table, a woman to whom she had a striking resemblance, asked her something, and she turned for a moment.

The connection was lost, but I had made a decision. I left, terrified by my resolution.

What are you doing? Kam asked again.

Driving toward the airport.

I thought you were already in Mumbai.

Changed my plans. I'm booking the first flight to Rome.

2

"Today is the day I'm going to find her."

Fido moved around me, blinking its red and blue lights as it assessed my stress level. Fidos, when not recording every single word of their Observers, were also used to keep track of their owners' physical and mental well-being. It chirped a warning: I needed water.

"I'm fine." I walked to the single chair sitting in the otherwise unfurnished room comprising the entirety of my studio apartment. At the last moment, instead of sitting on it, I went straight to the window, which was open to a new Roman day. Outside, despite the early hour, pedestrians were already fighting cars for the right to cross at the intersection; elderly residents hurried to buy their groceries at the neighborhood market before the crowd woke up. Colorful tents had come out around five in the morning, and fruits and vegetables displays had been carefully arranged soon after. In a matter of hours, the place would be chaos. A flash of light ahead blinded me for a moment. I blinked and focused. The green water of the Tiber River flew unhurriedly on the other side of the bridge facing my building. Standing naked before the window and listening to an old couple only a few feet away comment on the May weather, I let my skin soak up the warm light of the late spring sun. Nobody ever saw me. In all the time I had been living on Earth, the girl had been the only one who had noticed me.

Two years after I had last seen her, I was still searching. When I had heard her mother talk to her, I had discovered where she was from and followed her to Rome. One of the advantages of being an Observer was that I had acquired knowledge so vast about humans, I could pinpoint the exact neighborhood she was living in by the slightest inflection in her Roman accent. Given the sociopolitical situation at that moment in Italy and her apparent age, I also knew she was still living with her family while studying at one of the universities in the city—most probably the Sapienza because of its geographical proximity—and that her parents came from the middle class. Had she lived fifty years prior, the third-born daughter to a southern family, she would have been a nun by now.

I closed my eyes to let the sun wash away my fatigue. Lately, looking for her aura all around Rome, I hadn't kept up with sleeping and eating. On a few occasions, I felt so close to her, I forgot to take care of myself for the excitement. I knew it was a matter of days. The day before, at the Termini Station, the public transportation hub that served millions of people from the whole city, I had sensed an aura strongly resembling hers, and I followed it from Termini to one of the turn-of-the-century buildings in the Trieste neighborhood. Eventually, I did catch up with a girl who resembled her but was much younger. Satisfied that I had found her sister, I waited around the corner the whole day and the whole night for my *girl* to appear. I pushed my physical limits until I could take no more and then went back to my one-room studio facing Saint Angel Castle to let my body rest. I wasn't able to shut down my mind, though.

Are you up for a session? Kam had the uncanny ability to check on me whenever my mental defenses were at their lowest.

I closed the window, stepped inside, and sat on the lonely chair. I breathed in and out and let the rest of the room disappear one item at a time: first the wall in front of me, then the one on my right, next the one on my left. A blank screen engulfed my vision. The mosaic marble tiles with their floral pattern followed the walls. I was sitting on a floating chair. Then I was simply floating, and the blank screen zoomed toward me. A slow-moving tunnel sucked me in, and I emerged at the other end to face a smiling Kam.

"You made it." He raised an eyebrow. "You look horrible."

"Thank you." The next time, I would be more careful in composing my mental appearance. I had been successful so far in keeping both Kam and Areel unaware of my inner turmoil. "Where is Areel?"

"Unexpected session with his Guide." Kam materialized the furniture in the astral room as he strolled toward the center.

I had to move out of the way to make space for a chair and two cabinets. "Why do you bother?" I regretted my words as soon as they were out of my mouth.

"You know why." He blinked, and the old, battered couch we had spent so many hours sitting on appeared before him. "I like our digs to be lifelike. It makes our shared time here all the more enjoyable." With a tilt of his head, Kam gestured for me to join him on the soft cushion he was patting.

The fabric let out a fine cloud of dust that reached my nose. I waved my hand to dismiss my earlier statement. "You're right, of course." I added the pillows and the rugs on the floor and went to lie there instead. "So, is Areel having problems again?" Our friend was still healing after the trauma of his first mission's end.

"It takes time to adjust to the idea you had to doom an entire species to oblivion."

Areel was the talk of the moment back home. Although to become an Observer was one of the greatest honors on Solo—only second to becoming a Wise—Areel's experience had caused a drop in the Academy's enrollment. Nobody wanted to watch over a race for the entirety of its existence and then judge it unworthy of saving. We were supposed to be impartial and detached, but it was a state of mind difficult to achieve on a first mission. "Our Superior Officers should've done a better job at pairing a new Observer with an unstable planet."

Kam shrugged. "Well, our superiors didn't know the planet was going to be unstable when they assigned Areel to Crome." He looked at the right corner, and our old dispenser of beverages appeared. "Do you want anything?"

"I'm fine, thanks. How is he doing?" I hadn't talked to Areel in a while.

"You know him. He's trying to act all rational." Kam walked to the beverage dispenser and filled a transparent cup with a foamy, amber liquid.

"I don't know what I would've done in his stead." I shivered at the thought. After investing so much time and effort in a species, it would be devastating to declare them unfit to reach the next step of enlightenment. The Solean credo was that every sentient race deserved to be remembered forever.

"You would've done exceedingly well, as our superiors love to remind us at any given occasion." Kam laughed.

I tried to hide my irritation, but I wasn't fast enough.

"You're Lex's favorite—"

"He's my Ancestor Guide." I stood up and went to the dispenser. "It's not my fault I was assigned to him." Lex was a Wise, one of the few Soleans who had survived the Dark and helped build a new civilization.

Kam took his time drinking from the cup in long sips and then looked at me, an eyebrow raised. "Rumors has it Lex *chose* you among all the cadets. It had never happened before."

He was repeating what I knew everybody back at the Academy said, but I had never liked to be the center of attention. "You should know better than to believe anything said about me or anybody else."

"I know that I would've reacted exactly as Areel did, but you would've never cracked under pressure. And that is why you are Lex's pupil and I am not." He smiled at me and then gulped the remainder of his drink.

"I don't even know how I would react. How can you be so sure?" I went to the dispenser for a cup of that foamy beverage. I wondered how Kam would react if he knew I had spent the last two years chasing after a human.

"You were the first at the Academy—"

On my way back to the rug, I raised one hand to stop him. "We were talking about Areel."

"He'll be fine. It was unfortunate he got stuck with an unworthy species, but he isn't the first one, and he won't be the last." Kam went for a refill.

"His words?"

"His words." He came back and instead of sitting on the couch, lay down beside me. "Cheers." He gently clinked his cup against mine.

"To Areel." I slowly drank the cold beverage that reminded me of a sour brew we used to order at the Academy cafeteria. Kam's memories of the drink were slightly different than mine. "Remember that game we played?" At the beginning of the Observer training, cadets had been given bodies to get acquainted with the physical realm. Interacting with objects was one of the first classes taught.

Kam nodded. "It took me forever not to pour the contents of the cup on the floor. The first time I managed to drink from it, I was so happy I wet myself."

I laughed, remembering that episode.

"They should give us bodies in our toddler years. It takes time to get used to being corporeal. I'd rather interact mentally than have to incarnate in a different body any time we are assigned to a new planet."

"So say we all." It was a long-standing conversation Kam, Areel, and I had. Up until two years ago, I had been of Kam's opinion and vehemently discussed the pros and cons of incarnation with Areel, who defended the necessity of it. Then, *she* happened.

"Are you okay?" Kam tipped my cup back toward me, and I realized I had almost showered him with the brew.

"Lots on my mind lately." I tossed back the drink and then went to put the cup in the sink by the dispenser. None of the actions we took were necessary—the cup would disappear when we closed the interactive channel, but we went through the motions to make it real. The Astral World was primarily an interactive class to help newbies acclimate to their bodies, but after spending countless hours getting used to the exercise, Observers came to like spending time there with their friends. Spread through the universes, sometimes separated for eons from family and friends, Observers could at least meet in the mental realm. Areel had sought the interaction daily, especially during the last phases of his mission. I had been avoiding our meetings with the same fervor. What if my friends asked me for a Share? They would touch me and absorb all my memories. I couldn't open my mind to them and let them find her.

"I can see that. Anything you want to talk about?"

"No, thanks. Nothing I can't solve by myself." I smiled. "Do you know where you are headed next?"

Kam was, like Areel, between missions. His had successfully ended with the race he was observing—a matriarchal society inhabiting the small red planet of Ura—reaching the next level. The Ureans had now joined the list of races that would be remembered forever. Soleans had created a pantheon for worthy souls.

"Still waiting. My Guide is assessing a few planets. We'll see if any of them is a good fit for me."

I was growing restless. Astral sessions normally soothed my mood, but not this time. "I've got something I must check."

Kam gave me a look and then nodded. "I'll call you as soon as Areel is free."

"Do that." A moment later, I was back in Rome. I checked the clock on the wall, one of the few items I had bought for my apartment in two years, and noticed not even a minute had passed. It took time to enter and exit the Astral World, but staying there wasn't regulated by the normal laws of time.

It was still early, barely six thirty in the morning, and I had the feeling I was wasting time already. I went to the corner where my bed lay unmade—I never took the time to straighten the linens and the cotton duvet—and I grabbed the shorts and the shirt forming a rumpled heap by one of the bed's legs. Ancient Romans, like the Greeks, had it right: a shirtless *tunica* for the comfort of the house, and a toga to cover it when outside. And when even the toga turned out to be too cumbersome to wear with its nine yards of material, the *lucerna*, a much simpler cloak, took its place. Wool for the winter, linen for the summer—I didn't need more than that and soft leather sandals. I gave the crumpled garments in my hand a disgruntled squeeze, but I donned them, ordered Fido to shut off, and left my studio apartment.

I strolled directly into the elderly crowd shopping for groceries inside the enclosed portion of the market, and I came out on the other side of the bridge where I had parked my car. I had chosen another non-descriptive Fiat that disappeared into the sea of similar vehicles. It was perfect, if not for the fact that sometimes I tended to confuse it with someone else's. At least it had an alarm, and I pressed the button on the key fob to find my car. It was just outside the market and close to the brick wall of the bridge. Inside, the driver's seat was cool, and I shivered when I sat. Exiting the parking spot without thumping against the other two cars mine was sandwiched between took me several minutes, and by the time I entered traffic, I was feeling warm.

I preferred driving early in the morning or late at night. In Rome, any other time of the day was an exercise in patience, which I had to spare, but lately my mind was easily distressed, and I didn't care for long calming sessions. My destination, the Trieste neighborhood, was half an hour north of where I lived. Two roadblocks—a Roman villa had been recently discovered under the subway nearby—doubled the length of my driving, and I was soon stuck in the middle of school-hours traffic. Between one red light and the next, I found a forgotten water bottle on the back of my seat. A sloshing sound had accompanied me on the ride, and I finally decided to check what it was. I drank from it and almost spat it out, but it was water after all, so I kept it down.

I reached my spot around the corner from *my girl*'s building and parked. I could see the complex's door from where I was and set out to wait until she came out of it. And I waited. I didn't want to leave my spot because I was worried the girl would come out the moment I left, but I had forgotten to relieve myself, and I had to run to the closest bar, where I ordered a tonic water just to use the bathroom. I ran back to the car and waited some more. The sun bathed the façade of the building and then left it in the shadow, and I was still there when the street lamps flickered on one by one. I hadn't dared exit the car a second time, and not only had my legs gone numb, but I also felt slightly dizzy and was having problems keeping my eyes focused.

A car stopped before the building. The driver, a young man in his twenties, didn't bother to look for a parking spot but left the car with the engine running while he went to ring the intercom. The door opened with a buzz, and he stepped back while an older man came out and greeted him affectionately. After hours of slipping in and out of a mental slumber, I immediately perked up. The older man's aura was very similar to the girl's aura. He was *my girl*'s father. I watched as he disappeared inside the building, and a few moments later, the door opened again, and a girl came out. *She* came out.

My girl.

Her aura was even more beautiful than I remembered. Two years had passed since the last time I'd laid my eyes on her, but that was a blink to me, and I was back in Athens. She walked slowly, her skirt rising slightly at each step, her hair moving like a wave from one shoulder to the other; her lips parted in a smile that wasn't meant for me. Then, I was in Rome. I watched as the young man embraced her and kissed her and then let her into his car before I could react. A sentiment I had never felt before took hold of my chest. Fingers wrapped my heart and squeezed.

I hadn't planned ahead far enough to know what to do once I saw her again. *I only need to look at her one more time*, I had said to myself time and time again. But now, I had seen her, and it wasn't enough. Pain seared my body at the thought of letting her go with that man. Nearby, rubble from the ground spiraled into an eddy, and the hair on my arms stood up. On her way to his car, the girl turned and looked toward my corner. For a moment that seemed endless; her eyes scanned the darkness shielding my hiding place… then she moved on.

I gasped and let out a choked cry. My empty stomach churning and my mouth dry, I doubled over the steering wheel. *I need help.* A moment later, I was following the car she had just left in. I knew I shouldn't have. I knew I was committing the first step toward breaking my oath of not interacting with the race under my watch. Until now, I had been dallying with the idea of her, but I was still carrying on my mission to the best of my abilities. Europe was on my list of places to check on; India could wait a decade or so.

I sped up and ran two red lights. The man was taking a leisurely drive around Rome, and I could keep up with him thereafter without breaking traffic laws. Later, when the car disappeared inside a private garage under an elegant building, I hit the dashboard and hurt my hand. The last image I had of the girl was of her head tilted toward the man's as if they were kissing. That man could touch her, and it enraged me that I couldn't.

Waiting there was useless, but I couldn't leave. She was on a date, and I wanted to follow her inside and convince her to come with me instead. A dull ache spread from my chest outward, and I pressed my hands over my heart. On the other side of the road, a trash can flew over a car and smashed its windshield. A chorus of alarms blared in the night. I breathed in and out and forced my thoughts toward a happier place. The nuances of her aura were deeply embedded in my mind, and it took only a moment to lock my focus on how I experienced them. I felt calmer. Outside, the whirlwind ceased wreaking havoc all at once, and the alarms shut off soon after. The trash can rolled to the end of the cul-de-sac and then lay still at the foot of a low brick wall.

Then, a vision stole my breath away. I wasn't in my car but was inside the building, somewhere, with her. I stared at her hazel eyes and saw in them a fire that burnt me. She was under me and smelled of flowers. My hands caressed her bare back, and I was stunned by the texture of her skin. I looked at her lips and lowered mine on them. My heart exploded at the contact. I drowned.

I opened my eyes, and she was gone. A strong feeling of loss pervaded me, but it wasn't entirely mine. My senses on alert, I scanned the darkness ahead. Something was happening. My heart thumped against my ribcage, and my head pounded. I lowered my window to let some fresh air in, but it didn't help me cool down, and I stumbled out of the car. I walked a few tentative steps, unsure of what should I do next. A car arrived at full speed and stopped by the entrance of the building I was observing. Almost simultaneously, I sensed the girl's aura from behind the brick walls of the building. I could see her racing down the floors until she reached ground level. From the big entrance door, she exited in a rush and entered the car.

The whole experience lasted less than a minute, but coupled with the vision I had just had, it left me unable to react. I barely made it back to my car when the other car left. My hands shook, and my legs felt boneless. I tried to turn on the engine, but I couldn't center the key. After several attempts, I lowered my head to the steering wheel, and with a strong sense of déjà vu, I let my body crash. I welcomed the peace darkness brought me. Several hours later, I came to and drove back to my place.

"I know I need help."

Fido had been beeping so loudly I was afraid the upstairs neighbor would come to knock on my door. People were unaware of me, but they could still hear noises. As soon as I had entered my studio, the robot had activated itself and wheeled toward me, its sensors already sweeping me and analyzing my wellness. I was found lacking.

"First things first." I went to the kitchen sink and filled my one glass with water. I drank the contents in one gulp and repeated the action three times before my eyes would finally focus on the present. I sank to the floor and patted the robot. "I'm going to be okay. No need to worry."

Fido wasn't of my opinion.

A strong nudge knocked at the edge of my conscious mind. I wasn't going to get out of that mental call easily, and at the moment I didn't have the strength to even try. *Lex, what a pleasure to hear from you.*

How are you, my pupil? Lex's voice was low and reflected his age.

My health-bot is overly cautious. There was no need to call on you. I know you are busy—

I'm never too busy for you. Lex summoned me to the Astral World with another nudge. As the depository of my mental signature, he was the only one who could transport me there without my permission. Not that he had ever had to, but doing so was in his power if necessary. My consent was a polite formality.

Terrified my Ancestor Guide would ask for a Share, I wanted to refuse his invitation, but that was never done. A Wise's call was an honor for an Observer—even more so if that Wise happened to be the head of the Wise Ancestors as well. The distant memory of the Initiation Ceremony, when I had freely offered my mental signature to him, came back to me, and I felt as scared as I had been then. Lex was the keeper of my most intimate thoughts, memories, and desires. At the moment, I would have preferred to be the pupil of a less skilled Guide.

Please. I closed my eyes and prepared to be transported to his retreat, an open space he had modeled after a beach on one of the planets he had visited. I normally enjoyed my time there. Lex's mental realm was composed of golden sands, placid violet waters, and fishes resembling majestic manta rays swimming lazily in the sky. That time, I dreaded the experience. I was already in the tunnel spiraling toward his place when he stopped me and sent me back to my body.

I am sorry, but I am needed elsewhere. Lex sent me a mental pat.

When I was younger, my Guide would make my day by just acknowledging my existence. I would feel content for a long time afterward. Had he abruptly interrupted a mental session, I would have been crushed. Not then. I hoped he hadn't caught my sigh of relief.

Lex waited a moment too long before adding, *I can still talk to you.*

Thank you.

Your health-bot sent me a worrying read of your stress level. Are there any problems with your mission?

I steadied my heartbeat. *I feel Europe is on the brink of substantial changes and Italy will struggle through it.*

Another long pause before Lex's next thought. *Is that worrying you?*

No. Given the data I've collected, Earth is due for another cycle of unrest and civic turmoil. The Americas are next. Parts of Asia are already uprising. But it will be over sooner or later. Humans are still in their infancy.

Then why do I read uneasiness in your words?

I banged my head against the kitchen cabinet I was resting against, and the glass I had put on the counter fell into the sink and broke. *I've been neglecting my body—*

Why? He closed the communication channel for a brief moment and then came back. *It's not like you to do something like that. You are always meticulous in following the code of conduct.*

It won't happen again.

Should we schedule an evaluation session? How long has it been since the last one? I don't remember.

Of course he remembered. I held my breath and then chose my words carefully. *I had my last evaluation soon after I came to Earth—not so long ago—but if you think I need another one…*

Not now, then. But be considerate with your body. You aren't due for a new one.

I will. Promise.

After a last nudge, my guide was gone from my mind. I was already on the floor; otherwise I would have fallen like a rag doll. My former self, the dutiful Observer Lex had depicted, would have been appalled by my current lack of control over my emotions. "I shouldn't have feelings for her."

Fido chirped in response.

"I shouldn't talk out loud." *When there is a bot around recording everything I say.* I took my head in my hands and sank it between my knees. "I must stop this nonsense."

Fido seemed to agree with my last statement and moved away from me to reach my bed. I contemplated the idea of getting some sleep on a bed—lying unconscious in a car wasn't a good substitute for it—but my conversation with Lex had been a wake-up call I couldn't ignore. My mind was wide awake, and I knew I couldn't rest even if I wanted to. "I'll go out for a walk."

Fido wheeled around the bed and came back to me, violet light blinking. I placed my right index finger over it and pressed. The light became blue, and I removed my finger. "Satisfied I'm well enough?" The bot stepped back and went to its corner. "See you later." It didn't chirp back this time. I closed the door behind me and went out, looking for a way to distract me enough to let me finally think about what had happened. I walked, and I walked, and I walked some more until my legs begged me to stop and my eyes weren't able to see anymore. I witnessed the dawn waking up Castel Sant'Angelo and followed the flat boats floating lazily on the Tiber River, starting their daily business. Young crowds passed me happily, going home after spending the whole night out. I felt alone.

I had never felt alone before in my life. Not even when I had gone through the Change and had to leave my Commune behind and become One. I had missed the mental closeness with my extended family, but we still had the Share to support each other with. I hadn't felt alone when I had incarnated the first time. Nor when I wasn't allowed to enter the Astral World at the beginning of my first mission. I knew it was part of the process and that I had to endure the discomfort of being isolated. I knew it wouldn't last forever. But I would never be able to share myself with her. And the pain resulting from acknowledging that truth was too much to bear. Before I did something regrettable, I ran back to my studio. Once inside, I longed to be outside again; the room was stuffy and not even opening the window helped me breathe more easily.

I remembered the broken glass in the sink and realized I had to drink from the faucet, and that made me laugh for no reason at all. Cleaning the shards proved to be more dangerous than I thought. For the first time, I spilled my blood. I looked fascinated as it swirled down the drain, and I was equally surprised by the stinging pain caused by the small cuts on my hands. Finally, I ate some leftovers I had left in the fridge and then showered. After the warm water relaxed my tired muscles, I went to lie on my bed and commanded my body to sleep. I didn't want to think anymore.

I opened my eyes one afternoon two weeks later and looked around, surprised. That wasn't the first time I had gone into deep sleep, but normally I decided I wanted to. I was out in the street not even half an hour later, looking for her. Fido had chirped a string of warnings, but I ignored all of them. I braved the afternoon Roman traffic, searching for her aura in the air, the mere hint of it. I thought I caught it before I entered her neighborhood proper, but it soon dissipated. I parked close to her building, but instead of waiting in the car, I walked around for hours. It was like déjà vu. As it had happened two years prior in Athens, I spent that day and the following ones moving from one spot to another, chasing her. Her aura showed traces of sadness, and where she had touched things, the rainbow color that was her signature looked marred by darker colors.

The whole summer passed uneventfully. I kept driving daily to her neighborhood, and I contented myself with glimpses of her aura here and there. At the end of August, I lost it for several days. The traces from her aura became faint and then disappeared altogether. I knew the whole city shut down in the month of August, and I didn't think anything of it other than she and her family were on vacation. I still drove every day to Quartiere Trieste, and then, at night, when I went back to my studio, I usually engaged in long conversations with Fido.

One evening, more than a week after the last time I had caught her aura, I felt restless. "You are a great listener." I looked at the inexpressive piece of metal and laughed. Fido's violet light blinked in rapid sequence, and I dutifully placed my finger on it. I breathed in and out. "Happy now?" The light switched to blue as I had expected. I should have felt guilty; I had deliberately slowed down my vitals and tricked my bot into recording a false reading. Lately, I had been practicing. My tricking the bot's sensors had started as an exercise to keep my mind occupied when I couldn't regulate my body temperature at night. Roman summers had become increasingly hotter in the last few years, and while during the day the asphalt on the road melted, at night the sultriness made it impossible to sleep.

I looked at Fido, then outside the window, and then at Fido again. "Would you like to know what's in my head?" I felt the urge to share myself with it, but I knew I wouldn't be able to erase the recording once the words came out of my mouth. "I'll go out for a run."

A few minutes later, I was outside, sweating away my uneasiness one step at a time. The waters of the Tiber River reflected a full moon, and I stopped in midstride to take a look at it from the balustrade on the Saint Angel Bridge, not far from my apartment. I remembered when the towering cylindrical building had been under construction and Rome had looked so different. If I closed my eyes, I could still see the former Mausoleum of Hadrian, now known as Castel Sant'Angelo. I had still been in Rome around the first century after the beginning of what humans called the Common Era. Then, the waters from the Tiber had looked and smelled different. I came back in the fourteenth century only to find the tomb transformed into a fortress and the city morphing into its modern look. The distant echo of live music, transported by a most welcome breeze, brought me back to the present. I had a change of heart and strode back to the studio where I sent a mental call for

Areel, who immediately accepted my invitation without giving me the time to prepare a place for our meeting.

"Hi." He smiled at me and looked around at the place. "Where are we?"

I shrugged. "Just a place."

His eyes darted from one corner to the other of the courtyard I had just walked past on my way to my apartment. "Is this on Earth?"

"I didn't expect you to be free." I waved my hand in the air. "This is the last space I saw before I called you."

"Do you live there?" He looked up and saw the night sky.

"No, this is outside—" An idea came to my mind. "Would you like to see where I live?" The proposition was unorthodox, and I didn't know why I had voiced it out loud. As a fail-safe mechanism, Observers always maintained detachment from the worlds they were studying.

Areel seemed startled by my question but nodded after an unnervingly long pause. "I admit I'm curious to see your place."

"I'll call you back." I exited the Astral World, steadied my breathing, gave a good look at my one room, closed my eyes, and visualized it. Then I called Areel again.

"Well, there isn't a lot to look at, is there?" He laughed and turned on his heels to take in the bare walls, the solitary clock, the one chair, and the unmade bed—I hadn't bothered to doctor the astral projection of my studio. He then lowered his eyes to the tiled floor. "I like the pattern."

I summoned a second chair for Areel.

"Thanks." He walked to it and sat. "How are you?"

"I needed a friend." I turned the back of the vacant chair to face him and sat on it astride. "I wanted to talk to a friend."

"Is Kam coming?"

I averted his probing eyes. "I didn't call him."

"I see." He smiled and adjusted his long legs to fit the chair. He was still incarnated in his last body—Cromians had looked humanoid enough that he could be confused for an extremely tall one. "What do you want to talk about?"

"I've felt lonely."

"We always call on you."

"I know."

"And you normally are either too busy to answer or barely answering at all."

"I know." I looked for the right words to say. "It's not that I don't want to meet with you, but…"

"I see."

I shivered at the idea my friend could really see what was happening to me. Anger slowly built up inside me. I wanted to tell Areel about *my girl*, and despite the fact that I couldn't confess how troubled I was, my mouth opened before I managed to shut it off. "I have feelings."

He smiled again. "It's normal."

"What is normal?"

"Having those kind of feelings." He gestured toward the window opening onto the Roman night. "Earth is a beautiful planet, and I'm sure I would be fascinated by it."

"Were you… fascinated by Crome?" I had almost asked if he had been interested in the Cromians. I held my breath.

"I was. I still mourn Crome's demise." He raised his hands before his eyes. "I can't get rid of this body."

In the past, I had meant to ask why he hadn't gone back to the incorporeal state Observers enjoyed between missions. At the end of my first mission, I had spent several cycles in a Commune, finally free to Share without the limitations a body forced on my mind. "Why?"

"I loved the Cromians."

I gasped and regretted my outburst. "I'm sorry. I didn't mean to offend you."

"I understand your reaction. I failed my mission."

His downcast look made me feel terrible. "You didn't fail them. They, as a race, failed themselves. It's not your fault they weren't worthy of saving."

"That's not what I was saying."

"No, you're right. It's not." I stood up and went to the kitchen where I opened and closed the tap twice before asking him if he wanted to drink some water.

"Yes, please." He stood too and stretched his legs.

When he was standing, his height was impressive, and I had to look up when I gave him his glass.

"My Ancestor Guide is helping me a great deal with refocusing my inadequacy feelings toward a more useful frame of mind. He said it isn't uncommon for Observers to go native." His eyes, bigger than human eyes and a deep violet shade, stared at mine.

"I heard that too. And I don't think you went native." I was going native.

Areel sighed. "I went too far in my affection for Crome."

Listening to his confession made me feel worse about my closeted feelings. "You were poorly matched."

"And yet, I should've done a better job." He blinked and then went back to the chair. "But enough about me. You needed a friend to talk. I'm here."

I didn't move from the sink. "You already helped." A lie. I never lied. "Thank you."

A few words later, I managed to dismiss him, and I was back in my studio apartment in Rome, wondering once more why I had invited Areel to the Astral World's representation of that place. Fido approached me to check on my vitals, and I pressed a hand on my speeding heart to slow the heartbeats down. A moment later, the purple light turned blue again. "I wish I could talk to you." I patted the metal box and felt lonelier. The first light of dawn entered the room and painted a pattern on the tiles. I was drained, but after a look at the uninviting bed, I decided to go for a long drive.

I let my mind wander and ended up driving through the Roman ruins on the Appia Road, where, two thousand years before, I used to walk on leather sandals. When I had lived in Rome, at the height of the Roman Empire, I enjoyed long strolls from the forums to my house, a small tufa building I bought just outside the city proper. So many things had changed on Earth since then, but the smell from the Roman pine trees was the same. A momentary ache shot through my heart, and the thought that those smells, those trees wouldn't be there in the future pained me. I would be there to witness the change, and I didn't want to.

I drove away from the ruins of a city that was still called "eternal" and focused on the road. Finally, the stores and bars were opening for business all around, and I stopped my car before her building. Quartiere Trieste had been my ultimate aim, and I was tired of wandering. I missed sensing her aura. After parking a block from her place, I walked toward it. The humidity in the air was rising and, with it, the heat. I knew I should go back to the car and drive to my studio soon, but I lingered a moment before the building. I didn't walk any closer, standing on the other side of the sidewalk, but I felt her presence. She was back in Rome, and she was happy.

Later, when I finally lowered my heartbeat and left the sidewalk on shaky legs, I was smiling.

"Are you okay?" Kam asked.

He had called while I was driving back to my studio, and I told him I would call him as soon as I was in my room.

"You sound cheerful." Areel had joined us at Kam's invitation.

We were at our dorm. For the first time in a long time, I was relieved to be there. "I feel great." I summoned my favorite rugs and pillows and sat on the floor as was my custom. My friends preferred the couch.

"What happened?" Kam was sipping one of his drinks.

"Nothing." I was surprised at how lying had become so easy. I knew it would only take a Share to unveil my deceit, yet I couldn't stop myself. "How are you?"

"Still waiting to be assigned to a new race." Kam finished his drink and then went to the dispenser for more. "Do you want some?"

Areel thanked him and said no. I accepted the offer, glad for the familiar gestures. We had been meeting in this astral representation of our dorm since we had left the Academy, but for the first time I recognized how much I needed it. More than anything, I needed the reassuring familiarity of it. This astral room had been created in our minds long before there was life on Earth. We would still summon it long after life on Earth was gone. I would go on other missions. One day, millions, trillions of years in the future, I would finally relinquish consciousness and drift away. Lex, my Ancestor Guide, had told me he was looking forward to being one with the universe again. Right there and then, I was glad to be with my friends.

"At least you can spend some time in the Commune." I brought the cup to my lips and sipped the drink.

"Yes, that is always nice." Kam was in a new body, an asymmetrical reptilian structure I didn't recognize as belonging to any race I knew. He still had limbs that let him act as Areel and I did. "I can never get enough of mind sharing."

"Incarnation can be pleasant—" Areel started.

I inwardly smiled. I missed the bickering between the two. The rest of our time in the Astral World passed as pleasantly as it started, and when I left and opened my eyes in my studio, I felt regenerated.

The sensation stayed with me for a while. In the next days, I went through my routine, and while checking on my girl, I managed to record some data for my mission. Her aura left excited shadows all over Quartiere Trieste. I followed her, never coming close, but content with what I had accomplished in sticking to Observers' rules. Then, her activities became clear, and I forgot all my good intentions. At first, her comings and goings were erratic, but then I noticed a pattern forming. I saw traces of her aura at a bookstore, and from the large window, I saw her mental prints pulsing strongly around the travel section. Her next step, a few days later, was a small store that sold travel items, her mental fingers on two wheeled suitcases. Then came the travel agency's turn. A week later, her aura shone with renewed energy, and she was back at the bookstore. I entered the place and went straight to the place where her aura's presence was the strongest. It was the travel section once again. Her aural fingerprints were localized on a specific group of books. I took one of them and read the title, *Seattle and the Great Northwest*. I followed her mental breadcrumbs and flipped over two other books she had left on the shelf: *Living in the Northwest* and *One Hundred Things to Do when in Seattle*. I noticed a hole on the bookshelf, and the book next to it was titled *What to Expect when Living Abroad*.

I let the book fall on the closest coffee table and then ran outside, retracing my steps to all the places I knew she had been. At the end of the day, when I felt her aura near a clothes store called All About Rain, which aptly specialized in rain gear from umbrellas to raincoats, I wasn't surprised. I had missed her by a matter of minutes, no more.

That same night, I asked for an official meeting with Lex.

"My pupil." He looked calm as usual. No matter which shape he decided to appear in, Lex was always serene. Lately, he had opted for an elf-like body. In Solean fashion, he showed his age by sporting long, white hair, cerulean eyes, and thin limbs. When standing, he was as tall as I, his aura exuding power usually kept under strict control. Despite the lengths he went to to hide his strength and rank, I could never forget who he was.

We were in his place, a whale-like animal swimming lazily over our heads. He had once explained that he often came to this portion of the Astral World to relax. Although the violet hues and liquid sounds were conducive to mental and physical relaxation, I was too distraught.

"I wanted to inform you I'm done with collecting data in Europe and I'm moving to the United States." I had given the idea some thought and had rehearsed my speech.

His ancient eyes stared into mine. For a moment, I thought he would see through me. "Very well. Do you expect a change there?"

I repressed a sigh and nodded instead. "Yes, I do. The political situation is about to explode. Malcontent has been brewing in the population."

"And you are done with Italy."

"I might return to Europe later." For an Observer, it was common practice to travel every two or three decades between places. What I was doing, staying in a country for only two years, wasn't common. I mentally held my breath. Lex could always ask for a Share, and I would be obliged to comply. I would stand before him and let him touch my forehead, my whole existence laid out for him to peruse at will.

His eyes never breaking contact with mine, he relaxed and said, "You are one of the most brilliant Observers I have ever had the pleasure to tutor. I trust you."

We weren't many. Lex had only chosen a few Soleans to be his pupils. A pang of guilt tore at me, and I automatically pressed my hand to my chest.

He raised one eyebrow. "You look better than the last time I saw you."

I wasn't sure if he meant it as a statement or a question.

"Are you better?" He walked closer to me.

The distance was still considered polite on Solo yet was too close for my rattled nerves. It took all my strength not to lower my head. "I am."

"I'll check on you when you're settled in your new residence."

3

Seattle. My new home.

I left Rome a week after my conversation with Lex and found *my girl* almost right away. This time, the hunt for her multicolored aura was easier. I knew the chances she was going to rent a place close to the University of Washington were high. Out of the airport, after two flights, and with no sleep in eighteen hours—I hadn't slept for longer than three days prior to the trip—I hired a taxi and went straight to UW. My senses on full alert, I smelled the air and looked for her distinctive color palette. Fifty-six hours later, I found her. Soon afterward, I allowed my body to crash on a bench in a park near the place she was staying.

I woke some time later, aching and covered in dew but eager to establish a new routine. First, I looked for a rental close to her apartment and found that the building in front of hers had several vacancies. Slow economy and a rise in the college tuition made my job easier than anticipated.

"What do you think of this one?" asked the landlord, a small Asian woman in her fifties I had tracked down by calling a number scribbled on a torn piece of paper hung by the entry door. We had visited four apartments before this one, and she was growing impatient with me.

An overwhelming sense of contentment radiated through me as I entered the small place, and I felt the girl's aura calling to me from the other side of the kitchen window. "It's perfect. I'll sign for one year."

The landlord asked me for a down payment, and I reached for my backpack where somewhere on the bottom was my wallet. I hastily grabbed a few hundreds and gave them to the woman. At the beginning of every mission, Observers were taught to accumulate wealth by bartering goods. Anything ordinary today would become vintage, antique, and then ancient tomorrow. At the rate I was spending the money I had earned several hundred years ago—money I constantly exchanged for the newest currency—I wouldn't have to be worried about working for another two or three millennia. I still liked to work once in a while to be in touch with humanity. It grounded me.

She looked at the money and raised an eyebrow. "Thanks. I'll come back at the end of each month."

"I'd rather set up automatic payment." Something I had come to appreciate about modern times was how the Internet had simplified life for someone like me.

She gave me her bank's routing and account number then looked around and warned me about not trashing the place.

"You don't have anything to worry about with me." I accompanied her to the door, forgetting all about the woman once I locked her out. In two steps, I was by the window. I placed a chair by it and sat, my eyes on the apartment in front of me, basking in the residual rainbow of the girl's aura. I must have slept at some point because I found myself leaning on the windowsill, my forehead resting against its hard edge. Disoriented, I looked outside, not knowing if it was night or day. The sun still shone outside, but one look at the clock on the wall told me it was evening. Then I remembered Seattle's latitude and went to lie on the bed in the small bedroom my landlord had showed me in her hasty tour of my new home.

"What am I doing?" I looked at the ceiling and then at the barren corner where my Fido should have been. I sent a call to Areel and Kam to meet at our dorm. I sat cross-legged on the bed, regulated my breathing, centered my focus on a spot beyond the wall before me, slid into a trance-like state, and prepared the place for them. It took me a few moments to arrange the furniture—usually one of my two friends took care of that.

A door appeared on the wall I had just erected, and Kam strolled in. He gave the place a glance, his eyes lingering on the beverage dispenser I had added as soon as I saw him. The corners of his mouth twitched as if he was suppressing a smile. "Feeling domestic?"

"I miss my health-bot." I gestured for him to join me at the window. Outside, the fiery purple and pink of a Solean sunset bathed the luscious green of the valley surrounding the Academy. "And I miss that." I closed my eyes and felt the warmth of the sunbeams on my face. A few years ago, I would have gladly withdrawn into the Astral World. Observers were allowed to retreat there when their missions were on a hiatus. While following the lifespan of a planet from beginning to end, civilization after civilization, dead time was a welcomed recurrence.

"I was there a few cycles ago." Kam's voice was close, but he kept a courteous distance. Sharing was initiated by touch, and, at the time of the first incarnation, Soleans learned to mind their movements when around people of their species.

"It will be the first thing I do when I'm done with Earth." I repeated what I had been thinking for a century or so and discovered it didn't sound as satisfactory as it had sounded before. Being done with her planet was a thought that opened a tunnel in my chest and sucked out all the air in my lungs. I opened my eyes and gave one last look at the sunset. "Let's sit while we wait for Areel to join." Kam followed me to my rugs.

"Never understood your fascination for sitting on floors." His long body was stiff, and his joints cracked when he lowered himself onto the rugs. "Where is your bot anyway?"

"I didn't know where I was going to stay when I left Rome. I'll call the moving company I left my Fido with and I'll tell them my new address as soon as I'm back on Earth." I had already consented to pay more to have it delivered in three days.

"I wouldn't do without my health-bot." Kam rearranged his double-jointed legs and finally found a position he liked. "I should try your body. It seems easier to work with."

"I like it. I prefer it to the huge Radeskian forms." I stretched my legs in front of me to show Kam their versatility. "I wonder where Areel is, anyway. He said he was coming."

Areel didn't come; he sent a brief message halfway through our session: another last-minute session with his guide. My heart went out to him.

As promised, once I closed the communication channel with Kam, I called the Italian moving company—it was morning on the other side of the hemisphere—and gave them my new address.

When, five days later—there had been a strike at the Italian airport—the metal box greeted me from the crate with a chirp, I laughed. I had missed an appliance as if it were a friend. When it headed for a corner of my bedroom, after I let it check my vitals, I felt I was home.

Meanwhile, I hadn't left the apartment once. I had everything delivered to my doorstep, Fido included. Soon after my health-bot arrived, I almost ran out to meet my girl. It was a rainy morning with gray clouds looming over the skyline. Looking outside my kitchen's window, I saw her aura shining brightly, so close to me and yet unreachable. I was at the door already when my code of conduct kicked in and I felt ashamed of myself. "I am an Observer," I repeated under my breath, my hand tight on the doorknob, my forehead on the wooden door, my whole being out of balance. "What am I doing? What is happening to me? I don't understand." I dragged my feet to the other side of the room and sat on a chair. I looked at Fido, which had followed me back and forth. "Do you know what am I doing?" It chirped its response, and I dutifully lowered my index finger to the purple blinking light.

Later, I realized I had freely spoken before my health-bot. I didn't care, but I made a mental note to be more careful in the future.

The next time I spotted her aura, I stood at the window, my right hand splayed on the glass panel. The girl came into view with her back to the window, but I would have recognized her even if she was wearing a different body. She was sad; her colors were off. I lost my inner balance. Outside, the trees shook, and the small objects that until a moment ago had lain on the ground, flew higher and higher, caught in a vortex I was unwillingly causing. Energy filled my hand and reached my fingertips, asking to be released. The glass surface molded around my hand like a glove.

She started to turn when another girl entered the room. I moved out of their line of sight before they could catch me, and I flattened against the wall and then slid down. I pressed my hand on the floor and let the energy flow out of me. The hardwood warped with a dry crack and then went back to normal. I gasped. I had just scared myself. I never scared myself. "I am an Observer. I am in control." Reciting the mantra sounded good. "Damage control time." I looked at Fido, its lights all flickering at once, knowing what was coming next.

What's happening to you? Lex's summoning resonated too loudly inside my mind.

I was already in his presence before I could make an attempt to compose my thoughts. I trembled and stuttered. "I..." The waters above our heads were darker than usual. No animals were swimming. The silence all around was eerie.

"Talk to me." His words were gentle, but I was terrified he would finally raise that hand and start the Share I had been dreading all along.

"I need help." Admitting it didn't feel as good as I hoped would feel. On the contrary...

"I am here to help." Lex sat on the shore.

Only then did I realize we had been standing. He patted the stretch of sand by his right side, and I squatted there but didn't sit. "I don't know what's happening to me."

Lex patted the ground again. "Are you developing feelings for the subjects of your mission?"

Subject. I nodded.

"You must sit and relax."

I did as ordered and sat by him. Relaxing was another matter, but I had to try. I crossed my legs and breathed in and out, lowering my heartbeats and filling my mind with calming thoughts. I went back to that window open to the Solean sunset. I found my center and let the purple light in; then I let it out and, with it, my fear of the inevitable. "Do you want me to Share?"

Lex's right hand was hovering close to my head. He gave me a penetrating look and then shook his head. "No. Not today."

"What, then?" I steadied my breathing once more. The relief of not having to share my innermost thoughts with him would throw me into an agitated state if I didn't promptly intervene. "What can I do?"

"Would you be willing to achieve the Dark Void?" Lex asked at once.

The true meaning of what he was giving me almost left me speechless.

"You honor me." I bowed my head. The Dark Void was a technique so advanced it was rarely taught to young Observers. It was called dark because its origins were unknown, and the path to achieve it required a selfless soul, a soul strong enough not to succumb to its lure, a soul that could come out of it without being tainted by the darkness. Every Ancestor Guide was bound to pass the technique once in their lives, but not everybody did. "I know you have never taught it to anybody else."

"You are different." Lex smiled. "It will be my honor to teach *you* how to reach total focus." His eyes softened and became liquid. "My pupil, you are my Chosen. You will bear my legacy."

"Lex, you still have a long journey ahead of you—"

He stopped me. "It's decided."

"Then I'm ready."

"Be aware: it is going to be a long process."

I nodded, and he started teaching me.

We met several times during the next two months. At first, our sessions together were more pain than joy. But I guessed that was his plan all along, to keep me busy enough to forget that a reality outside of our astral world existed. The Dark Void required a commitment that no other technique did, and a busy mind was never prone to wandering incessantly.

I still thought of her, and I still spent the majority of my waking time with my nose against the window, hoping to bathe in her colors. She was still sad, apathetic. The other girl was there with her most of the time, especially at night, and I reckoned she was her roommate. The idea she had someone to share her sadness with comforted me. At least she wasn't alone.

I didn't have another episode, and I was able to fight my urge to contact her by sending positive vibes her way. The more I worked on mastering the Dark Void, the easier it became to manipulate the natural elements. I used my newfound mental dexterity any time I felt she needed help regaining balance. When, in the middle of the night, her aura broadcasted that she was utterly distressed—humans experienced nightmares quite often—I created a soothing environment for her. Her aura quieted down in a matter of minutes, and I could relax and resume the training her anguish had interrupted.

Finally, one afternoon, Lex walked me through a whole routine and smiled at the end when I emerged from the deep trance.

"Now, I want you to do it again, by yourself."

I blinked.

"Try."

In earth time, several hours had passed since the beginning of the session, and I was mentally tired. Almost certainly, my physical body—lying on the bed—was aching as well.

"You must trust me."

"Of course." I summoned my key image, of when I had gone deep diving in one of the seawater pools near the Academy. Lex had asked me to find a memory that symbolized my reaching for the innermost part of my soul, and that image had stood out. I shed my clothes as I had done that day and dove into the bright turquoise waters. I had wanted my human eyes to have turquoise flickers in them to remind me of those waters. I kept diving, and the colors all around me darkened. Soon, I was surrounded by black waters, but I wasn't scared. I felt at peace, cocooned in a warm, safe liquid. I was ready for the next step and surprised it had taken so little effort. I switched my point of view and, as I had done in the previous sessions guided by Lex, opened my eyes to a different scenario. I was in Seattle, but I wasn't. I levitated over the vast expanse of the city, myself as big as the sky, levitating over the roads and the buildings. I expanded my consciousness. I stretched my ego until I was no more. I looked down and saw reality as a constant stream of mathematical possibilities. Every single action taken by the individuals living down there could be explained and predicted with great accuracy. I lingered to analyze one of the possible futures this city would live through in ten years. I fast forwarded to one century. Then, I came back to five minutes from the present. A second later, I was in the now. "Amazing."

Lex chuckled, and when I looked at him, his eyes sparkled. "You, my pupil, are the youngest Observer to ever achieve the Dark Void with barely a mission in."

"I wouldn't be the Observer I am without your guidance."

Full of energy, I left the Astral World with the knowledge that I was able to withstand any temptation.

Early the following afternoon, I went for a walk outside. I had called Kam and Areel, but they were both busy. For once, the vibes from the girl's aura were positive. I myself was still thrumming with positive energy. I looked at the scenery from my bathroom window; the sun was shining between bouts of light rain, and the foliage had turned a vivid shade of orange-red. "Some fresh air will do me some good." Fido, by my side even when I wanted a private moment, welcomed my words with a blue light. "I'm glad you approve." I splashed some water on my face, went to my bedroom, and changed into a heavier t-shirt and shorts.

I liked Seattle. An Observer like me could live in that city for a long time. I appreciated the easygoing lifestyle its inhabitants had mastered. I could have shown up in the middle of the street in my previous body and barely raised an eyebrow. Also, I didn't have to watch constantly for other people, as Seattleites maintained a safe distance when interacting with others. In Seattle, the American concept of "private space" was taken to the next level. A large Asian presence in the area made my life much easier. I shared their dislike for proximity. Not that touching a human would automatically translate into a Share—it required a mental connection to work— still, it made me nervous.

I walked aimlessly for several hours, my first official outing. I went up and down Seattle's many hills and savored the colors and the vibrations each different neighborhood emanated. Three hours deep in my wandering, I reached Pike Place Market. For a moment, I considered going in, but despite the late hour, too many people were still milling around, and I moved on after buying something to eat at one of the restaurants facing the market. I chose the venue for the number of people—just a boy behind the counter—rather than the food served. The flaky pastry of the pirogi melted in my mouth, and I was happy the eatery had been temporarily deserted. Daylight still illuminated the sky, but the night would soon find me stranded several hours away from my apartment. I left the market and decided to walk back home. On my way, I strolled by a car dealer and remembered I needed a car if I wanted to work on my mission. I saw the kind of cars the place sold and, on an impulse, walked in.

"Looking for an Italian beauty?"

I smiled at the well-groomed man who approached me. "Yes, I am." I had never cared for anything material, but one of the dark cars displayed on the floor called to me. "I'd like to buy that one."

The salesman arched his brow for the briefest moment but immediately composed his features in a smiling face. Seattle was known as a place where millionaires wore thrift-store clothes with holes. "Of course. The Alfa Brera is one exquisite car, a driving experience only a few can appreciate. Excellent choice." He then asked me if I wanted to take her out for a ride.

It wasn't dark, and I had nothing better to do. "I'd love to." I would rather have gone alone, but I understood the guy couldn't let me leave with a brand-new car. I entered the Alfa and lowered my body onto the leather seat.

"May I suggest a scenic route?" he asked while I was adjusting the seat to my length.

I nodded, my hands on the wheel. I decided I liked the smell of leather; it had an organic quality. "Where to?"

"What about Queen Anne's lookout?"

"Okay."

We left the store without further words, and the salesman didn't attempt small chat, only giving me directions. I enjoyed my ride and the silence. For a moment, sliding through the evening traffic—the sun had already set, leaving behind that pink glow that fades into the darkening sky—my mind projected an image of the girl sitting at my side and I would have run a red light if it weren't for a car merging from the left and honking loudly at me.

"Sorry." From then, I focused on the road until we reached our destination.

"I love Seattle." The salesman's eyes were on the view from Queen Anne's lookout.

We had parked a block away. The place was teeming with couples taking shots of themselves with the skyline in the background. Among the crowd were two newlyweds and their families patiently waiting for their time to be immortalized. I liked people-watching.

"I'm sorry, but we should head back. I must close shop—"

The idea of stopping to take a moment to enjoy the view had been mine. "You can leave me here." I wasn't ready to return to my apartment yet.

"But—"

"I'll come back to the dealer tomorrow morning to finalize the sale."

The man opened his mouth to say something.

I smiled at him. "I'll be there."

"Well, then, if it's okay with you, I'll leave now."

He offered his hand to me, and I accepted the parting gesture before giving him the car keys. The act was meaningless to me, but it was an established routine for humans. Plus, this man and I didn't have any spiritual connection; I wasn't in any danger of starting a Share with him. I had never been in such a danger with anybody in all my time on Earth.

I waited for the tourists and the newlyweds to finish their photo shoot and then walked to the parapet overlooking the Space Needle and the Seattle Center; the Experience Music Project shone brightly under the tall structure, and the dome of Mount Rainier was semi-hidden by menacing clouds. I basked in the evening breeze and colors. Humans knew how to build their cities.

The first stars appeared in the night sky. The air turned chillier, and I was still there, sitting on the parapet. I massaged my bare arms—the shirt I had hastily donned before leaving was made of heavy cotton, but it couldn't keep the cold at bay anymore. It was time to find my way back to the apartment and my Fido. Before I turned, I felt her. The view before my eyes disappeared behind dark spots. I forced my breath in and out, visualizing its path from my lungs to my mouth, until I could see again. Then, I turned and almost lost consciousness.

The girl was sitting inside an abstract metal structure gracing the lookout. She was inside the lower hollow cube, her eyes closed, her head nodding in time with the music she was listening to. I should have left, but I couldn't control the urge to let myself be known to her. I channeled my feelings, and they smelled of wet wood and wildflowers on a sunny morning. My overloaded senses picked up the music she was so enthralled by and amplified the melody. Soon, her hair and clothes were moved by a scented breeze while she stood at the center of an open-air concert. The girl opened her eyes and gasped.

Still rooted on the spot, I watched as she stood up and blinked several times. I fought the urge to run to her because I wanted to touch her, to feel her in my arms. Then, her eyes filled with tears, and I couldn't control myself anymore. I jumped down the parapet and covered half the distance to the metallic monument while mouthing, *Please, don't cry.* I was at a safe distance, the place I had planned to reach before doing anything I would regret later. *Just one step more.* And then it was another. And another. And I was too close to her.

"Hi." The word was out of my mouth before I knew what I was doing. Her aura erupted in a display of fireworks. If a moment earlier I had thought I could control my reaction, now I had the certainty I couldn't. "I missed you." I'd had eons of training as an Observer, and here I was breaking several rules at once. Her aura changed colors and became pure orange and red. I wanted to breathe her in. "I missed you so much."

She shivered, and my right arm moved toward her of its own volition. It took all my will to stay my fingers from touching her face. Instead, I traced its contour in the heated air between us, and it was my turn to shiver. She closed her eyes again while I followed the line between her left ear and her jaw. My fingers itched to close the gap. I wanted to feel the softness of her skin under my fingertips and inched closer. The warmth emanating from her body brought the physical scent of her to my nostrils. I was drawn by her lips. She opened her eyes. Her expression was serene, and I kept drawing her profile in the air. *One step more.*

I couldn't see anything else. I couldn't feel anything that wasn't her. My legs moved toward her. *No!* Every muscle in my body commanding me to go forward, I slowly stepped back. My limbs were made of rocks, anchoring me to the spot. I summoned the last of my strength and kept stepping back.

"Wait!"

Her voice reached me in a haze. I stopped.

"Wait, please, don't go."

Thankfully, she didn't move, or I would have been lost.

"Tell me your name."

I wanted to stay and listen to her voice. Her eyes widened, and my pulse quickened. I had to leave before it was too late. "Give me one." I whispered the words in one single breath and then turned and walked away before I ended my career as an Observer with one single gesture.

4

My name.

I already had a name, of course. I never cared to be called by it because I had never cared to be *one*.

Noticing the dark sky had lightened to a shade of pink, I kept walking with the intention of reaching home. I was a few blocks away from Queen Anne when I found myself changing plans and aiming toward the car dealer instead. I reached the shop in time to catch *my* guy intent on opening the glass door and turning the sign around from closed to open.

"You are an early bird." He showed me inside and walked me to his office.

Several hours later, I exited the place, driving my new car. The guy had tried to sell me another vehicle, but I wanted the one I had driven the night before. I didn't care that there were better options. He told me all about engines and the quality of the Italian leather and asked me if I preferred automatic transmission over manual. "I want that one," I'd had to repeat three times before the salesman understood I wouldn't change my mind.

"You'll love your new Italian car. The Alfa Romeo Brera is a jewel," he had finally said while seeing me out of the store.

I drove for hours, too keyed up to think about getting some rest. I headed out of Seattle toward the Canadian border, and I was lucky to find almost no line at customs. A tired-looking officer asked for my documents and the reason for my staying in Canada. I told him I had a business transaction to attend to and then showed my Italian passport—one of many I had—and the visa I had obtained as a private consultant for a research group I had founded a few years back for such occasions. While in recent times traveling between continents had become increasingly easier thanks to the new means of transportation, entering countries had become harder. Past the border without problems, I reached Vancouver in time to catch the sunset from one of the benches in Stanley Park. A few minutes later, I was back in the car driving in the opposite direction. Once home, much later that night, I sat on the bed, not knowing whether my human body or my Solean mind was going to give up first. I was exhausted and full of energy at the same time.

"I am happy." The sentiment surprised me, and before Fido could catch on and send a report about my mental health to Lex, I left the apartment and headed to the communal landing where I waited until I could make sense of my state. "I am happy," I repeated to the walls covered in graffiti. "What am I going to do now?" When my heart slowed down, I went back inside, but I felt too restless and wanted to share my newfound joy with my two friends. I thought about seeing them but initiated and stopped the mental summoning several times before I let the call through.

"What's wrong with you?" Kam was the first to ask after he and Areel stared at me for several seconds. They had both come right away.

"Nothing is wrong with me. To the contrary, I've never felt so good." I arranged our astral place as I spoke. In my haste to see them, I hadn't thought things through. Three couches and several chairs lined the place a moment later. I laughed.

"You look different." Areel sat on one of the couches, but his eyes never left my face.

"Do I?" I felt different.

"What did you do?" Kam preferred one of the chairs.

I couldn't keep still and paced the room as I added details to the dorms. "I went for a long walk."

"That sounds—" Areel started.

"Uneventful," Kam finished.

My friends exchanged a long stare, and then Kam raised one hand. "May I?"

I should have known that would happen, but I couldn't help shouting, "No!"

Areel gasped.

"No?" Kam asked.

"No, you don't have my permission." I saw the shock on their faces, but I would not allow a Share and let them find about *my girl*. After such a breach of etiquette, I couldn't remedy the situation, and I dismissed them mere minutes after I had asked them to join me.

My unbalanced state of mind kept me in a haze. I was torn. Soon, I was a prisoner of my feelings, and if it weren't for my Fido, my ill-conceived happiness would have ended my life on Earth. Eating, sleeping, and keeping myself hydrated weren't my biggest concerns. Lex routinely checked on me, but my friends had not sought him on my behalf because he never requested a Share, and I lied most reassuringly that I was fine. Once or twice during that time, I made a mental note to thank them later. "I'll also ask them to forgive me—don't look so disappointed in me," I once said to Fido, which wouldn't stop blinking at me. "I wish I were a metal box. Human emotions aren't easy to deal with. You are lucky."

* * *

When I regained control of my mind, I realized that time on Earth had passed—in fact, almost three weeks, the last seven or ten days spent in deep relaxation. I came out of my haze and accepted that I would look for her again and again, but I had to find a way to act upon my desire without breaking my code.

"It's beautiful out there," I told Fido, looking at the world outside the window where a wet gray morning had replaced the quiet darkness of dawn. I had woken from a fitful night a few hours earlier and stayed inside my apartment without knowing what to do, fighting again the impulse to run to hers. "I'll go for a walk through the campus." I let Fido take my health reading for the day and, satisfied with my decision, exited the apartment feeling light. Following the traces of her aura like breadcrumbs, I strolled down Greek Row and then paused a moment to look at the UW entry and reorient myself via the many paths she had already taken countless times. I waited for the pedestrian green at the intersection and passed the big metallic sculpture representing a *W* at the entrance of the campus proper, and five minutes later I was walking on Red Square, dodging students hurrying to their classes. A misty rain covered the English-looking buildings bordering the place, the girl's comings and goings etched on the red bricks of the square. I wished for one of the hot cups of coffee so many students held between their hands. The Suzzallo Library was on my right, and I saw people coming out of it with steaming foam mugs. I climbed the stairs in a hurry to find where they had bought the beverages. My stomach rumbled, and white dots danced before my eyes. I knew Fido reminded me to eat and drink at regular intervals, but the health-bot was calibrated to keep my body alive, not necessarily functional. When I saw the small cafeteria just inside the library, I went straight to the counter to order a cup of Americano and the first edible item that caught my attention. The girl's presence was all over this place, her mental fingerprints on tables, chairs, and even the walls, but the need to replenish my body obfuscated any other thought. After tearing apart several small brown packets and pouring the equivalent of five or six teaspoons of sugar into my coffee, I grabbed the white paper bag containing the slice of lemon Bundt cake I had hastily ordered and went to sit at one of the tables facing the windowed wall. I drank the first gulp of coffee and let the hot liquid enter my system, my eyes closed. A moan escaped my lips when I bit into the soft slice of Bundt cake. Had I ever cared about food? I decided I should care from now on if I didn't want to faint for lack of sustenance in my body. Having eaten the last crumb of the cake, I finished the coffee and thought a refill was in order. On my way to the counter, I saw a small crowd of girls standing by a bulletin board.

"Did you read this?" one of the girls asked. "It sounds so romantic."

A second girl nodded. "Just yesterday, someone was talking about it in class."

One of the men working at the cafeteria walked closer to the group. "Those Post-its are everywhere, even inside the library rooms upstairs."

"I saw one of them on the student board outside English lit. Who knows who posted them?" another girl asked.

The first girl sighed. "It would be nice, I think, to know what's the story behind those words, no?"

The whole group agreed.

I went for my refill, ordered another slice of cake, and waited until the girls left to glance at the crinkly paper on the board. Despite all the sugar and caffeine I had just ingested, I felt lightheaded again. I steadied myself against the wall on which the board was affixed and took a second look at the pink Post-it.

"I have your name, please come get it," the note said in a bold font. Then in a much smaller typeface, it added, "I'll wait for you at the anthropology department."

I caressed the paper with my fingertips, tracing what remained of her aura, after other hands had touched her message. I gulped down the coffee and ate the cake as I went, and I was out of the building and running before I could rationalize what I was doing. "Where is the anthropology department?" I yelled at the first person I encountered on the Red Square. I heard the directions and saw the clear path her aura had recently left at the same time.

I entered the anthropology building with my heart lodged in my throat. She was everywhere. The essence of her pulsated in the air. I was intoxicated. I walked through the hallway and then up a flight of stairs until I was almost blinded by an explosion of colors coming from around the corner. I slowed my pace and reached for an open door. If possible, my racing heart increased its beating to a frantic gallop as I approached the door.

I peeked inside the room—a kitchenette—and froze at the doorframe, breathless. She was alone, her back to me and facing the opposite wall, but she had sensed my presence. Her aura had changed color when I had rounded the corner. I walked to the center of the room, drawn to her the same way magnetized objects can't escape each other's pull. I moved around her, feeling the air near our bodies saturating with electricity, until I was facing her. I smiled and made an effort to stick to the human code of conduct. "Hi."

Holding a mug, she stared at me with her hazel eyes and whispered back, "Hi."

For a moment, frustration had me. I wanted to communicate freely, without physical barriers. For someone like me, who had all the time in the universe, I was being irrationally impatient. "My name?"

She seemed to think for a few seconds and then looked at me with a satisfied expression. "Elios." She paused and then, when I didn't say anything, added, "Your name is Elios."

Elios. I loved how the name—my name now—sounded on her mouth.

"Where are you? I thought I was the one late. The presentation's starting," a muffled voice said from one of the pockets on her lab coat, and she was startled. The mug she was holding fell and broke. I knelt to pick up the pieces, careful not to come too close to her. I wasn't prepared to experience overwhelming pleasure simply at touching what she had just touched.

She reached inside the pocket and retrieved a cell phone. "I'm so sorry. I have to go, but I'm coming back as soon as I can," she said when I looked at her.

"I'll wait for you here."

Her aura screaming relief at my words, she left running.

Left alone in the room, I had time to think about the question that had been disrupting my existence for the better part of the last two years. *What was I doing?* I had already considered all the reasons why it was better for everybody if I put an end to this. *It isn't rational. Or ethical.* I had no reason to be there, waiting for her to come back. *But it's going to be fine as long as I don't touch her. I'll be careful.* I couldn't help but laugh. The model student, the purist Observer, the most disciplined cadet of the whole Academy, was falling from his pedestal so easily. The recent memory of her expression upon seeing me erased all my doubts. *Falling down feels too good to be wrong.*

I moved to the big window facing the street. Outside, the rain poured in earnest, and it looked chilly, but I couldn't stand to be inside that room any longer. I needed fresh air. Those four walls were too small to contain her energy, and I couldn't trust myself to control my actions. I wanted more of her, much more. *I must build a tolerance.* I was lost in my struggle when I heard her approaching. I sensed her stopping where I had stopped before, and I felt her eyes on me. I turned and smiled at her. "Love my name. It's the best I've ever had."

It was the first time I had been named by someone else. I had inherited my Solean name from my family and simply confirmed it when I had become corporeal, but her naming me felt much more intimate. A thrill ran through my spine at the idea. "Thanks for giving it to me." I wanted to say so much more. Instead, I moved closer, but not so close that resisting the urge to touch her skin would be impossible. "And your name is?"

"My name is Gaia."

Gaia. I liked her name, but it took me a few seconds to understand its meaning. Then, I remembered and realized our names meant something together.

She was Gaia, and I was Elios.

Earth and Sun.

"Thank you. Our names are perfect together." Her aura spiked at my words, and I felt mine responding accordingly. I fought the urge to close the gap between us. "In ancient Greek, Gaia is the Mother Earth, while Elios is the Sun. You couldn't have chosen better." I even liked she had chosen the Italian spelling without the *H*.

"What's your real name?"

"The only name I have is the one you gave me." I didn't even remember the other name anymore. "My name is Elios. A pleasure to finally meet you." I knew she was waiting for me to take her hand in mine. *It's just a handshake. No, with her, it's not.* I stood before her, thinking of all the times I had touched a human and felt nothing. "Do you want to go outside for a walk?" I had reached the point where I couldn't think straight anymore.

She immediately answered, "Yes, I'd love that."

As soon as we were out in the chilly rain, I played a little with the elements. I summoned a warmer current from the south, adding lilac scent and a shower of flower petals to it. I led her for a few steps and then stopped on the sidewalk. "May I ask you something?"

Gaia's eyes widened. "Sure."

"Have you ever thought about me?" I never wanted to initiate a Share so much in my life. Her lips called to me. All I had to do was to lean and brush those lips with mine, and we would be *one*. Before my body would act on my whim, I redirected my energies into channeling the elements reacting to my mood. A wayward eddy of petals was already forming behind her back. I made it stop before she would notice.

"I think of you all the time," she said very softly. Then just slightly more loudly she added, "I've been waiting for you." Her aura became a deep orange.

I stood before her, my hands firmly hidden in my pockets, calling on all my training, to behave as expected of an Observer. *I can't touch her, but I can still talk to her.* "I've been looking for you for so long. I tried to... but I couldn't wait anymore."

The orange in her aura changed to a deep red. "You have been looking for me?"

I felt her heartbeat elevate. *With a Share, it would be so much simpler. Did I just scare her?* "Would you say my name again, please?"

Gaia relaxed. "Elios."

Her voice evoked an image of cold silk on hot skin on a summer night. A barrage of colors and scents hit me. The rain drenching my clothes and my hair and falling down in rivulets on my face added to the sensory overload. I barely managed to keep myself in check that time. "I love the way you make it sound like a song."

Then, she stepped toward me and moved too close. At this distance, I could have touched her by mistake. No. Not by mistake. I would have touched her because I wanted to. I stepped back. "I can't come any closer to you. I'm sorry."

"I don't understand." She was shivering, her aura a cold shade of blue now.

I had lost control of the weather around us, and her lips were starting to match her aura in color. "I'm sorry about this." I had never lost control of something so simple like the natural elements in such a restricted area.

She didn't say anything.

"I'll come to your place tonight. I'd like to see you again." A sudden doubt. "If you want to see me."

"I'm free now. I don't have to go back to the lab."

For a moment, I hesitated. I wanted to please her more than anything else, but the situation was getting out of hand. I made a rational decision, the first one of the day. "I must go." It didn't feel good leaving, but I really didn't have any option at that point. I was already around the corner while she was giving me her address.

"What am I going to do with the rest of my day?"

A passerby heard my question and answered what I could do with it. I was surprised someone had noticed me, and I laughed at the crude remark. *I shouldn't let my guard down.*

Once back at the apartment, after a fast walk through the icy rain, I didn't bother with a hot shower. Instead, I sat by the kitchen window and waited for Gaia to come home. I wanted to know she was okay. For a moment, while in her presence, I thought of telling her we were neighbors then thought better of it. "I don't want to scare her," I confessed to Fido, which didn't approve of my elevated heart rate.

Her apartment came to life. Gaia and the other girl who lived with her walked past the window several times. Finally, I sensed she was alone and only half awake. Her aura sent shimmers in pale hues. I helped her relax and reach a deep sleep. I imagined lying with her and cradling her in my arms. I waited until she went into REM and then let her sleep the day away.

I couldn't sleep. I was too nervous and excited to lie on a bed and relax. "There's something I can do to pass time." Fido chirped, and I went to sit on my bed, legs crossed and back against the wall. For the first time in several weeks, I worked. While I had been too self-centered to notice the planet was still spinning on its axis, the president of the United States had been elected, and the political climate seemed positive, overall. I dictated a few notes to Fido about the possible outcomes of this president's foreign affairs agenda, and then I tried to meditate. I needed to shed some of the humanity from my mind because it was obfuscating my rational thinking.

I needed to talk with someone. Swallowing my pride and knowing apologies were in order, I tried to contact Areel and Kam, but I found it difficult to reach the level of meditation I needed to enter the astral world and it took me several tries. In our virtual cafeteria—I had decided at the last moment for a different venue, the liveliest part of our dorm's compound—I found Kam waiting for me. He was already approaching the buffet cabinets. I found myself liking his alien incarnation less and less.

"Areel?" I asked after greeting him. I would have preferred to confront both of them at the same time.

Kam gave me a long stare. "He's at his Ancestor Guide's—"

"Again?" Absorbed in my problems, even before my latest unacceptable behavior, I hadn't sought Areel as I should have and felt guilty for not being an attentive friend. "Is he in any trouble?"

Kam shook his head. "No, no trouble. He's just updating his mental signature. Which reminds me that it's almost time for mine as well. I also should take time to complete the psychic gun course." He grimaced. "I keep postponing it."

I instinctively shuddered. "I don't envy you. That thing scares me. Just the idea that you can so easily erase someone else's memories—" I couldn't finish the sentence. That kind of power was just revolting.

"It makes updating our mental signatures even scarier." He went to the food counter to load a few delicacies on the tray he had just materialized in his hands.

I chose something to eat as well and made a mental note to remember to eat once back in my body as well. Astral sustenance helped the mind, but I needed to take better care of my corporeal entity. Just surviving wasn't enough anymore.

"I don't want to know what passed through the mind of whoever built this weapon with the caveat that you must use one person's mental signature to load the gun you're going to use against him."

We both shuddered again at Kam's words.

"Not that I have a choice not to go through this class." Kam was in the scout division of our army; knowing how to use a psychic gun was a requirement.

"Remember that the sooner you finish the class, the sooner you are done with it. You'll never use it anyway." I didn't understand why we still maintained that course at the Academy since I had never heard of the psychic gun ever being used—at least not during my lifetime. I was ready to change the subject and start with my apology when I noticed Kam eyeing me with a puzzled look.

"Oh, I see. You have another name. I couldn't understand what was different about you when you called." He chuckled. "And may I ask why did you do it?"

"I didn't decide the name."

"And who did?"

"I have something to tell you." I added two of the couches from the dorms to the cafeteria's furniture and sat on the edge of the closest one to me.

Kam stood by the food counter, ready for seconds. "I'm listening."

I tried to keep my eyes on his face. "I'm sorry for what I did last time."

He turned toward me, his right hand in mid-air, palm up. "Well, I would be lying if I told you it didn't affect me."

Sweat formed on my forehead. "I know, and I'm truly sorry."

He was back at the counter. "Why would you refuse a Share?"

I lowered my head and then forced myself to face him. "It's a long story."

Kam slowly looked around. "We have all the time in the universe here."

Right. I opened my mouth to talk, but nothing came out. I cleared my throat twice before I was able to whisper, "I didn't want to share with you that I have feelings for a human."

Kam's loaded tray disappeared from his hands. "What did you say?"

I cleared my voice a third time and then repeated, "I have feelings for a human."

"You're serious." After a moment of hesitation, he went to sit on the couch opposite mine.

I waited a moment to confess the rest. I was feeling dizzy.

Kam's expression changed. "Are you okay?"

"Why—?"

His eyes followed my body from feet to head and then back.

I looked at my hands and gasped. My astral projection was unfocused. It was more a ghost of my Earthly image than a proper solid projection.

"What kind of trouble are you in?"

I tried to straighten up my astral self, and after a few attempts I was content with the result, even though it wasn't my usual solid projection.

Kam said, "You should call Lex."

"No!" My hands became transparent. I breathed in and out and forced my body back to a more solid image. "Lex can't be involved in this." I paused a moment. "Please, do not contact him."

His raised eyebrow spoke volumes. "I can't—"

I held my head in my hands. "Please." I raised my chin to look at my friend.

Kam passed his long fingers through his spiked hair, his reptilian face an unreadable mask. "At least talk to me."

"I'm trying to." My body quivered between stages, one moment solid, the next transparent. "It isn't easy."

He waited until I stabilized my form. "Start from the beginning."

I lost control again.

"Unless…" He raised one hand but didn't move from the couch.

The idea of a Share sent me into a paroxysm of shaking.

"Okay. I won't ask again. Just calm down, and let's talk if that's what you want."

A cup with a steaming beverage appeared on a coffee table next to my couch. "Something to steady your nerves." He gestured for me to take the cup.

I did as suggested. "Okay." I gingerly held the beverage to my lips. It smelled minty, but it tasted more like a hot, diluted mango juice. "Thank you."

He nodded. "One word at a time."

I drank from the cup and did feel calmer after a few sips. "Everything started two years ago in Athens." I took my time to tell Kam the whole story of how I met Gaia and what had happened after that first chance encounter.

He listened to me without interrupting me once and at the end of my tale said, "You must stop this at once."

I shook my head. "I can't."

"You are her planet's designated Observer. You have to."

His words hurt. "Don't you think I know? But, just *observing* her is not enough anymore. I need much more than that."

"You wouldn't attempt a Share, would you?" He sounded shocked.

I avoided his eyes for a moment. "No, of course not." He didn't comment, and I felt the need to add, "I would never betray my oath."

After a long pause, Kam relaxed his stance and nodded. "I believe you."

I released the breath I was holding. "Thank you."

He smiled a thin smile. "Then what's your plan?"

"I'm going to see her tonight, at her apartment." My legs were starting to shake again, and I didn't dare look at the state of my corporeal image.

"You shouldn't."

I sighed and couldn't help a smile. "I agree."

"I see." Kam was silent for a while.

I didn't say anything. I was waiting for him to be ready to talk.

"So, your name is Elios now."

"Yes, my name from now on is Elios." I moved on the couch and leaned against its cushions.

It was his turn to sigh. "I don't know why this is happening to you. You were always the most dedicated of all of us—or maybe *there* lies the answer."

I raised my eyebrow, waiting for him to explain.

"Maybe your integrity, your superior level of commitment, created this situation."

"I don't understand."

"Actually, it's really simple after all. You have always been the best element of our class. Your first assignment was an example for everybody. Your achievements are the ones everybody else has to measure up to. You obtained purity of mind in denying matter, in whichever form you were. In doing so, you missed something crucial to your growth. Probably in this human, this Gaia, you found a sympathetic soul. The problem is that you found her while incarnated in a human body. You inherited the matter that comes with it. Gaia is not only a shiny soul; she comes with a body, and you know that for humans the two things can't be divided."

His in-depth analysis of my predicament left me wordless for a moment. There was some truth in what he had just said, but I wasn't ready to discuss his theory. "I'm terrified I will fail this mission."

He snorted but immediately checked himself. "You can't leave Earth now. It's too late, and nobody else can continue your job. We are stretched enough as it is, and if you leave, humanity will be damned to oblivion."

"I couldn't survive the regret. I gave my word to protect Earth when I took the job."

"Then I know you'll find a way."

I was taken aback for the second time by his words. "Thank you, Kam."

"Although it's clear you thought otherwise, you are not alone. You should have confided in us before you reached this state of agitation. Even if we can't grasp what's changing you, we can still be here for you."

"I don't know what to say."

"Say that you'll ask for help next time."

"I will."

Before leaving, Kam paused at the door and turned. "And Elios—"

"Yes?"

"I won't say anything to Lex."

I heard the unsaid "for now." "I'll keep it together. I promise."

A moment later, I was back on Earth, disoriented and tired. As soon as I opened my eyes, I walked to the kitchen windows and looked outside. Right in front of me, the light pouring out from the opposite apartment's windows gave me a clear view of the object of my desire. Gaia was awake, slow dancing and looking radiant. I wanted to be part of that happiness. I wanted to be the cause of her happiness. A mere moment later, I had left my place and was outside her apartment, knocking on her door before I could think twice about what I was doing.

5

She opened the door, and a rainbow of colors welcomed me, along with a loud cat.

"Hi."

"Hi. I am glad you came. I wasn't sure you got my address."

"Sorry I had to leave that way, but I couldn't stay. May I come in?"

"Please." She gestured for me to enter the apartment. The cat demanded to be acknowledged and she sighed. "I'm sorry. I don't know what's gotten into him."

"No worries. I love animals." I leaned down and gently caressed the cat's back. "What's his name?"

"He's called Pallino. Do you have pets?"

I was going to say I had Fido but then thought better of it. "No, I don't."

Pallino attached to my heels, I silently followed her through a narrow hallway, and we ended up in a small but sunny kitchen, which I knew all too well since my kitchen window faced it.

"Would you like something to drink? I brought my moka from Italy. I could brew some real espresso for you." Gaia looked at me with her hazel eyes. "Or a cup of tea if you prefer. San Pellegrino water, maybe?"

"I'd love to try your espresso. It's been a while since the last one I had in Rome." I reached for one of the two chairs pushed under the table and sat, extending my legs. Pallino followed me and curled up by my right leg.

A smile escaped her lips. "You lived in Rome?"

"Si, per quasi due anni." *For almost two years.* At the moment, I felt like showing off a little. Kam was right. Humanity was infiltrating my mind. I was acting like a primate trying to impress a female prospect. I watched her as she reached for the last shelf on the cupboard. I wondered if I had to offer my services, but the kitchen was too small, and I wanted nothing more than an excuse to touch her. She rummaged through the shelf, moving items out and putting them back.

"Oh, really. Wow, I'm impressed. You don't have any accent." She gave me a smile. "What did you do in Italy? And do you mind if we keep talking in Italian?" She reached for a coffee can then opened a drawer and retrieved a spoon she used to scoop the coffee beans, and poured them in the coffee grinder on the countertop.

"Not at all. Italian is one of the languages I like the most. And to answer your question, I worked on a personal project. I also collected some data about the political situation in Europe. I've been working on it for a while." I switched to her language in mid-sentence without thinking.

"This is what you were doing in Greece as well?" She hastily mopped up the coffee powder she had just spilled all over the counter.

My heart grew two sizes at the mention of Greece. "Yes, and before that, I was in France and in England. I'm part of a worldwide organization that collects statistics about the growth of and equilibrium between societies." I paused for a second to collect my thoughts and saw she had put the moka on the stove, had grabbed other teaspoons from the drawer, and was now sitting opposite me at the table. "I travel a lot and take up different jobs in every place, to be fully immersed in the culture I'm studying at the moment."

"What a coincidence that my field of study is the same but related to ancient civilizations. Well, I don't travel that much—" She paused a moment. "It takes time to study a culture, and you seem very young to have traveled so much already."

"I look much younger than I am." I wished I could have told her about all the things I had seen during the French Revolution and the Victorian Era in England.

She kept staring at me with an enigmatic smile on her face.

"You don't like the idea that I am older than you?" She moved her legs under the table, and I immediately brought mine closer to my chair. "I never thought that age was going to be a problem."

"I don't mind if you're older than me. I like you."

I felt an enormous pleasure in seeing the way her aura reacted to her words, a wave of orange and red.

"I like you too."

With a start, Gaia stood up and went to the stove. Burnt coffee scent filled my nostrils. I couldn't resist following her like a shadow.

"I like you. More than you think." I was mere inches from her and saw the way her hands stilled in the act of cleaning the dark liquid from the stove and how she trembled slightly at my closeness.

"I…" Without finishing her sentence, Gaia walked out of the kitchen.

I followed her back to the entry, which was also the living room. Pallino moved at once with me. "I'd like to find a way to tell you more about me."

"I'd like that."

"I can't now. Maybe one of the next times." I looked at the room and noticed a stereo system and the stacks of CDs lying around. "Do you mind if we just listen to some music?" I hoped music would help me focus on keeping my wits together.

"Sure. What kind of music do you want to listen to?"

"The kind you like." I sat on the couch, and while Gaia chose the first track, Pallino jumped on my lap. When she came to sit by my side, I stood still and limited myself to stroking the cat's fur. I was glad for Pallino, because he gave me something to do with my hands. The music poured out of the speakers, and I recognized the Italian singer she had chosen. I remembered attending one of his concerts. He had a rough voice, and I liked his style. I knew that song by heart and sang along.

I loved singing for her, especially that song. I played with the atmosphere in the room: some basic mood enhancement, her favorite perfume. I imagined Gaia waiting for me in a bedroom, her body draped in ivory silk, kissed by the orange of flames coming from a fireplace. I saw myself driving, impatient to reach her. I was picturing the situation described in the song. I couldn't move an inch with my body, but I found an outlet in my fantasy.

Gaia was breathing irregularly, still looking at me, listening to my voice.

"I'd give anything to be that man."

Her eyes were wide, her mouth so delicately red and soft. "Elios…"

"Yes, my Gaia." *I can't share you with anybody else.* The possessive before her name sounded so right in my mouth.

"You make me feel things I can't put into words."

"You make me feel emotions I shouldn't have." *I really should leave now, when no damage has been done yet.* I adjusted my body on the couch, painfully aware of how close to me she was. "Would you rather do something else?"

"I just want to stay here with you, listening to some more music and talking, if you want to." She left the couch and reached for the stack of CDs.

I was momentarily relieved she had vacated the couch; my hands were growing restless. "I can do that."

"What about Lions and Lambs?"

"I like them." She had decided on a local band, and I sang the first notes of one of their songs. "'Caterpillars' is my favorite."

"Mine too." She skipped tracks until she found that song. "Are you from here, from Washington State?"

"I'm not from here. Actually, I'm not American."

"And you aren't Greek."

"No, I'm not. I've been living in so many places, I feel that I am from everywhere. And nowhere."

"A true citizen of the world." She smiled.

"Worlds," I automatically said and immediately changed the subject. "Do you like it here? Seattle is so different from Rome."

"Oh—she blushed—I like it way better now."

"I agree." I felt dizzy and laughed to release some of the tension bubbling up inside of me. "I love everywhere *you are.*"

"Since I ruined the coffee, do you want some water?"

"Yes, please."

Gaia disappeared down the hallway and I went to the stereo system. Pallino complained when I gently put him down on the floor, but then he decided he had had enough of me and scampered after Gaia. I looked among the discarded CDs for anything soothing. I found a CD of a string quartet recently famous for rearranging modern songs in classic versions. The first song was playing when she came back with a tray holding two tall glasses and a San Pellegrino bottle.

"Please." She gestured toward the glasses she had already filled with water. I took one of them and savored the coolness of the sparkling liquid against my lips. She sipped from hers, and a few drops of water fell on her shirt. I stared at the wetting fabric for a moment and then managed to look away.

She finally sat back on the couch. "You don't talk a lot."

"I'm not used to interacting a lot with people." *A Share would be good now.*

"I can hardly believe that."

"Am I boring you? I am not sure how to talk to you."

"You're definitely not boring me. I just wish you were less cryptic." Gaia looked at me from under her hair, her face slightly tilted at an angle, and laughed.

"We wish for the same thing." I smiled. "I love when you laugh like that, such innocence in your face."

At those words, Gaia moved slowly on the couch, dangerously reaching for my body.

My first reaction was to move toward her mouth. Her lips had become the center of my gravity, and I moved as slowly as I could to feel them without touching the skin. And then, just a fraction of an inch from her lips, I stopped and stood up, putting enough space between our bodies. Tears clouded my vision. Anger coiled inside my stomach and burned through my lungs, looking for my heart.

"I don't understand. I was sure—" She was crying.

I owed her an explanation, an apology. "I shouldn't have contacted you. I didn't stop myself even though I knew better."

She didn't say anything, but the look in her eyes made me pause.

"I want to explain to you."

"So do it."

Her voice startled me. I had to say it. "I'm not allowed to interact with you, physically." I looked at her, waiting for her reaction to my words and hoping I would have the strength to finish what I had started.

"What. Are. You. Talking. About?" Gaia had raised her voice to match the fury in her eyes. "I know you like me. You can't deny that."

"I'm not going to deny the truth, and for what it is worth, I'm going to try to be honest with you." Her aura was sending wave after wave of pain, and I could barely breathe. "I've been following you around since Athens. I've been in Rome because of you. I'm in Seattle for you. I'll be wherever you want me to be. Away from you if you so decide." I shook my head and whispered, "Although I hope not." I moved away from her some more. "I can't do any harm to you, and neither would I."

Her eyes were big, and she was staring at me in a way that I instantly regretted my sudden spurt of honesty. "Don't worry. I am not dangerous. Just stupid."

"Okay." Gaia seemed to agree on that.

I rearranged my legs in front of me. "I need to tell you something about myself that might be easier to understand."

"I'm listening."

I wanted to stop the tears from falling but couldn't control my body's reactions. I was so engaged in keeping my mind safe, I couldn't add another task to the routine. "I was born to a society that doesn't utilize touch as a form of social behavior the same way you are used to." I had no idea of what kind of reaction she would have to my words. "We do touch each other mentally, and some of us will experience the act of physically touching others in our lives, but it is reserved for special unions." I fought the urge to clean her tears away. "Remember what I was saying, about my job?"

She nodded imperceptibly, and I kept going. "I am part of an elite guard, and I made a vow of physical abstinence."

She flinched, and I felt a fist squeezing my heart. "I'm what you probably can define as a... monk." I didn't have better words to explain it.

"You are a *monk*?" Her aura was showing me much more than her words.

It pained me in a way I would have not thought possible.

"What kind of monk are you?" she shouted.

"A soldier monk, who is forbidden to even hold hands with you."

61

I could see the different emotions painting a mask on her face, and her anger scared me.

"This is a cruel joke, and it's time you leave. Now." Her voice broke down.

"Gaia—"

"Get out."

"I'm sorry."

"I can't understand what kind of kick you get from hurting me, but there you have it; that's the door." Gaia stopped looking at me, and she turned her head away with a resolution that made me gasp.

I left the room as ordered. Even with the door closed behind me I did hear her last words.

"Never come back."

A dagger perforated my body and my mind. I knelt down with one arm on the wall. I felt empty and ashamed of who I was for the first time.

"Please. Never come back." That was all she said.

I dragged myself out of her building and didn't find the way to my apartment until much later. I wandered through Seattle the whole night and part of the next morning. For the first time of my living on Earth, I finally understood why humans abused substances to take the edge off of reality. I didn't seek that kind of help though. I was still an Observer.

* * *

A week passed. Then another. Then a month. I spent the majority of days looking at the windows in front of mine, and the nights helping Gaia sleep. More than once, I found myself reconsidering my loyalty to the Observers Army. Shame of what was becoming of me followed. I had moments when the ache in my heart was so unbearable I wished for dullness. I wished for my consciousness to disappear.

Kam and Areel came to my rescue as soon as they realized that my aura—without me being the wiser—was sending loud distress calls. At first, I was able to ignore their summons.

Around mid-December, one rainy afternoon—Gaia had disappeared a few days earlier and hadn't come back to the apartment yet —I ventured outside my lair for some fresh air. Fido had been annoying me to no end with its constantly blinking purple lights. Cold rain hit my face once I exited my building, and I lingered out there for a few minutes, enduring the weather and looking up at her window. Gaia's aura had stopped signaling her presence all at once, which led me to believe she had left Seattle. I tried to convince myself it was just for Christmas time, fearing she had gone back to Italy for good. I tried to reason with myself that it was probably for the best. I failed. Hair plastered to my face, cold seeping through my bones, instead of climbing back the stairs to my apartment, I sprang into a run, heading anywhere my legs would take me. Eventually, a few hours later, I went back home, only to collapse on the floor, my back against the door I had just closed with my falling body.

I stood there, breathing slowly, hoping to sense her aura and feeling bereft without her mental presence to soothe my pain. Without warning, a familiar but unpleasant feeling possessed me. Darkness embraced my mind, and I was sucked up into the tunnel before I could react. I was enraged but not surprised to see both Areel and Kam at the other end waiting for me. "What did you do?"

Kam tilted his head to the side and blinked, his eyelids closing against each other vertically. "You didn't give us a choice."

"And you thought forcing me here would be for the best?" I had never come to feel so close to wanting to punch anyone. Physical energy built in me and needed to be released. "You thought involving Lex to give you my mental signature would be a good idea?"

"We didn't know what to do—" Areel stepped forward, and I stepped back. "I'm not going to force a Share on you!"

"Wouldn't you, now?" I looked at them, and they flinched. "What did you tell Lex?"

"Nothing." Kam lowered his eyes to the ground.

I shook, fists at my side. "Lex wouldn't have given you access to my mental signature so you could summon me here against my will for nothing. What did you tell him?"

"That you needed a vacation but you were too busy with your mission to be bothered to take a break." Areel gestured for me to look around.

Only then, I finally took in where we were, and it wasn't our usual spot. "What are we doing on Karillion?" It was a place we used to go on vacation, a tropical island close to our Academy. Ancient pink sand beaches with perfumed seawater and warm temperatures made the place the perfect destination for the Academy's cadets. I looked down at my feet, already buried in the shore. Fine pebbles mixed with the sand and moved at once with the water, rolling back and forth and creating a melodic sound, almost music. I had always thought it was the most relaxing place in the universe—but not at that moment. "I am still doing my job. This, what you did, is uncalled for."

Areel kept his gaze on me. "We only wanted to help."

I felt angrier. I didn't like to feel vulnerable, and right then I was devastated. "I wouldn't stop working on a mission for anything, and you know it."

"That wasn't our concern." Kam discarded the cloth around his waist and waded into the water. "Come."

"We couldn't leave you suffering so much; you know that." Areel attempted a smile and then reached Kam, who was waiting almost entirely submerged by the rising and falling of the waves.

I couldn't have either, had I been in their position.

"Your distress was tearing at us as well," Areel added.

Kam nodded. "We couldn't ignore your pain. And you know it."

"I only want to be touched." The words spilled out of my mouth, and I was the first one to be shocked at revealing my secret out loud. "And to touch."

Kam and Areel stood still in the water for a long moment, staring at me, Kam in his reptilian form, which didn't give away his feelings, and Areel who had not yet shed his last incarnation and showed his shock plenty on his humanoid face.

"You mean touching... her?" Kam finally asked.

"Gaia. Her name is Gaia. My Gaia," I said. "And yes, I want to caress her skin. I want her to caress mine."

"I don't think I understand." Areel's already big eyes became even wider.

"What I just said." I leaned to pick up a small, flat pebble and threw it far away. The stone hit a wave on the first bounce and sank.

Kam emerged from the water and walked toward me. "How can you forget everything you have been taught?"

Areel stepped forward as well, and the two of them towered over me.

I raised my chin defiantly to answer Kam's question. "I haven't forgotten I am an Observer. But I had two years to think things through and—"

Areel raised one hand and stopped me. "Two years on Earth are nothing compared to your real age. It isn't enough time to change the way you think."

"I haven't just changed." I put my arms around my chest, feeling cold despite the warm breeze blowing from the sea. "I'm different." I shrugged. "I've evolved." I looked straight at Areel and then turned to face Kam. "I'm better. Can't you see it?"

Areel commanded my attention. "I can only see your suffering."

Some of my rage came back. "Don't you see it in me at all?" I asked them. "I can understand humans now."

Areel was the first to talk. "You think you are better because you can understand humans in a more compassionate way. Is that what you think?"

Kam shook his head. "You know you can't become one of them."

I ignored Kam and nodded at Areel. "The suffering is changing me. I can understand things I couldn't before." I sighed. "Lately, I've been thinking about the way we do things." I paused.

After a few seconds, Kam cleared his throat. "And?"

"I am not sure you want to hear it."

"Don't worry, everybody passes through similar phases. You had it on your second mission. It doesn't have to ruin your career and your life." Kam was repeating what both Areel and Lex had already told me.

"My case is different."

"Of course it is," Areel conceded. "But it's nothing you can't work out. You are still the best cadet out of our class."

His words left me deflated, and I felt alone. I shook my head. "The first time we met, we established a spiritual connection." I was angry I had to explain myself when everything was so clear in my mind. Yet the idea of sharing myself with them to let them understand repulsed me. "I'm terrified to admit it, but Gaia and I... we belong to each other. We have a bond that is going to last even if I leave Earth."

Two astonished faces stared back at me.

I smiled sadly. "Don't worry. I wouldn't be able to fail her race. Especially not for this reason. It would be the end of me." I closed my eyes for a moment and let the rhythmic ebb and flow of the water lapping at my feet center my thoughts. "She has a part of my soul I didn't know I was missing."

"So your new name isn't just a whim?" Areel asked.

"Elios is the essence of who I am." I met his eyes. "I hope you understand I have to go back to Gaia."

Kam waded a step closer to Areel. "You have decided then?"

"Yes, I have."

Kam nodded. "Then don't do anything you'll regret, please."

This time, my smile was heartfelt. "The only thing I'd regret is doing nothing."

As soon as they released the hold on my mind, I left the Astral World to go back to my body, only to find that several months had passed on Earth. If worries about Gaia hadn't filled my mind, I would have applauded my friends' cunning. Thanks to the help of my Ancestor Guide, who had not only given them my mental signature but also instructed them on how to put me in a trance so deep I didn't need food or water, they had kept me out of trouble long enough. One glance out my kitchen window told me everything I cared to know. Gaia was in her apartment, and it was past time I paid her a visit.

6

I passed my hand over my face and found it smooth enough not to need a shave—a perk of the deep trance I had been forced into. Not that I would have taken the time to go through the motion. I couldn't bear to be separated from her any longer. The night was dark outside, probably not the best time for an explanation, yet I ran to her apartment. I knocked at her door several times before I heard movements through the walls.

I knew it wasn't Gaia.

Her roommate asked who I was without opening the door. My friend Pallino had come to greet me as well. Even if I couldn't have seen his aura, his purring would have warned me of his presence behind the door.

"I'm Elios."

"You are kidding, right? You sure have some nerve," the girl hissed but opened the door nonetheless. Pallino almost jumped on me, but she got hold of him and held him tightly to her chest. "What do you want now? Didn't you have enough already?" Her tone was bitter, and the posture of her body protective.

She stood before me, hiding from sight the rest of the room behind her. Gaia's aura was sending loud signals of distress, and when her roommate moved slightly, I looked over her shoulders. Gaia was peeking around the corner, looking back at me with red-rimmed eyes.

"Do you want to talk to him?" she asked Gaia.

"Yes, please." Gaia nodded slowly.

"I don't think it's a good idea."

"It's okay, Sara," she said to her friend, her eyes still locked on mine.

Sara finally walked away and went straight to Gaia. "Are you completely sure you want to spend any time with him?"

"I'll be fine. Don't worry."

"I don't think you're in your right mind." She raised one hand and added before leaving us, "I'll be in my room if you need me."

Gaia put a hand on Sara's shoulder and thanked her then waited until her friend left the room and sat on the couch. She remained silent and didn't invite me to sit.

I couldn't sit by her and knelt on the floor instead. "Gaia, I know you told me to leave you alone, but I can't."

Silence. Gaia sat there, a difficult expression to read on her face.

I found it hard to confront her and lowered my eyes. "I want you to know why I said what I said."

She nodded this time.

"Last time we spoke, I didn't lie, but I wasn't completely honest either. I edited bits and pieces. I did it mostly for me; it would've made my life much easier, and for that I apologize. It caused more pain than good to the two of us. But I'm not sure you're going to like the truth—"

Her eyes told me to keep going. Gaia slowly shifted her body, maintaining a regal stance, reminding me how unreachable she really was.

"I can't stay away from you."

Something changed in her aura, and for a brief moment, she seemed more present.

"I know you feel something for me. Maybe not exactly the same, but I can read you better than you think. I want to find a way to make it work for us. I *need* to find a way to be together, but I still don't know how. I can't become something I'm not, but I'm not who I was before meeting you in Athens."

"You are still a monk then?" Her words were razor sharp.

"In certain aspects, I am what you would define as a monk, yes. I made vows to keep my mind pure and to treat the body I wear with the utmost respect." I wanted to give her as much information as I could, but doing so was getting increasingly harder. "I'm studying your society, and as an Observer, I can't interact with the object of my research. I must maintain scientific neutrality."

She grabbed one of the pillows lying on the couch and held it tightly. "Stop now. This scientist-monk nonsense is making me sick. You're talking like I'm part of a guinea pigs' colony." Gaia's aura was fierce now, and her words matched the cold colors she was emanating. A strand of beads broke off the pillow she was holding, and the small round beads fell on the floor. "Give me a single reason why I shouldn't kick you out right now. Why should I listen to all the crazy things you're saying? I don't understand why you even bothered coming back here, and in the middle of the night."

I wished for the one hundredth time I could act against my oath and share myself completely with her. And once again, I forced myself to steer away from the blasphemous thought. "How much do you think you want to know?"

"What kind of question is that?" Gaia answered, her liquid eyes a darker shade of brown under the soft, ambient lights of the room.

One of the beads rolled toward me, and I absentmindedly reached for it. At the last moment, the bead changed trajectory on the uneven hardwood floor and landed closer to her ankle. I stilled my hand just in time before brushing her skin. "I'm going to ask you again. Please listen to what I'm asking and then decide. I'm begging you to consider your answer carefully."

"What could be worse than not knowing?"

I almost sighed out loud at her question. She didn't have a clue of what could be worse. "Please, Gaia, I need to be sure you understand what I'm asking you."

"I want to know." Her mouth was a trembling white line on her strained face, yet she maintained the same elegant posture without moving one muscle of her lithe body, but I could see the strain on her arms, pressing the pillow against her stomach.

"As you wish." Changing position on the floor, I breathed in and out to stabilize my mind. "But before I start, I want you to remember I care for you in a way I wouldn't have thought possible. Even if you're going to reject me, to reject *who* I am, I'll still have your memory. And it will be enough for me."

Gaia stared down at me, and I shivered.

"Our encounter in Athens wasn't meant to be. I shouldn't have felt anything for you. It happened though, and you can't imagine how glad I am that you're in my life even if you don't want me in yours. I've lived for so long as a well-trained soldier. I've spent my life in the most absolutely ascetic way. I never longed for anything material. I never longed for a companion. The mental communion I had with my close friends was enough." I badly stammered the sentences and concepts without being able to say clearly what I really wanted because I needed more time to explain and I was worried that Gaia wouldn't let me. But she had changed expressions. "Stop me if you want to ask me something. Anything at all."

She shook her head. "Keep going."

"You can't imagine what it means to me, having the opportunity to explain my situation." It would have been so easy to just cave in and let Gaia see for herself what I meant, but too much was at stake.

"Again, please, keep going because it's getting late."

"When I met you, something changed in me. For the first time in my life, I had feelings I didn't know existed. I even forgot I had a human body to care for after I saw you again here in Seattle. I think I can't survive, at least not in this form, if you decide not to be with me. But I can't leave. I have responsibilities toward your… my research."

"I don't understand." Gaia moved on the couch and released her hold on the pillow.

"I want to be with you, but I can't stay without ruining the objectivity of my research. The consequences of my negligence could be disastrous, and my conscience could not bear the result should I fail." I mentally debated if it was wise to keep talking, and then I followed my heart. "I need you to understand I'm looking for a way to make it right. But I'm torn. If I stay with you, I'll compromise my research by letting you know things you shouldn't be aware of. If I don't tell the truth tonight, I'll lose you forever, and the pain will impair my capabilities and cloud my judgment. In this second scenario, I'll be removed from the mission and demoted immediately."

Gaia cut me off, and her tone was both angry and surprised. "So, what you are saying is that you are worried about losing the job over me?" She hugged the pillow once again.

"Losing the job over you is not what worries me."

"And so what is it?"

"If I am with you, I'll want to save the object of my research, no matter what. If I'm not with you, I won't be sure if I can trust myself with the best decision. I thought I was stronger, that I could manage this situation, and that I could remain objective. At least, I thought so at the very beginning, two years ago." I paused. "After I left you, I realized I wasn't that strong anymore. I'm still trying to obey my commandments the best I can. But it isn't easy anymore. I don't regret it, though."

"I want to believe you, Elios, or whatever your name is." Gaia abruptly stood up. "I need something to drink."

I followed her through the hallway. "Please, stop."

Rage came off her in waves, yet she stopped and turned to face me.

"I told you, my only name is the one you gave me."

"I want to believe you because it'd be easier on me, but..." She walked back to the couch and laid a hand on the backrest. "But I'd be delusional."

"What we share is real. It's different from any other human relationship. But it's real, and I want to prove it to you." I had to make her understand what I was trying painstakingly to explain. I had said enough already. It was time I showed her what I meant when I said I was different.

I expanded my conscience to cover her body with a mental veil, and then I manipulated the colors in the room. I wasn't subtle this time and unleashed my consciousness to please her with music and perfumes. The last time I was at her place, I remembered seeing the CD of an Italian string quartet group she must have particularly liked because the traces from her aural fingertips were stronger on that one. I played it on the stereo system and created an open air vignette with wild rose petals swirling around. A rainbow of colors and sounds danced around her body. I left my aura to express itself and look for hers. If these were the last moments we had together, I wanted them to be memorable.

I closed my eyes to open all my senses. She gasped, waking me from my trance. Her face was expressing many emotions I couldn't read, and her aura was a vortex of contrasting colors.

She then spoke. "Who are you?"

Finally.

"I'm not human."

* * *

I never thought in all my life that I would be so pleased to expose myself. I couldn't help but feel good, even while contemplating the certainty of my demise as an Observer. Millennia of work would be all for nothing soon, and I smiled as I resumed my position on the floor. "Questions?"

Gaia sat on the couch, inches from me, "Yes, definitely." She frowned briefly and then quickly added, "How long can you stay?"

"I have all the time in the world for you." *And some more if we need it.* I relaxed my muscles and adjusted my legs on the hardwood floor.

"Where are you from?"

"I'm from Solo, a planet geologically similar to Earth. My species is older than the human race. We also developed in a different way. Humans rely on their physical senses and live physically separated. We rely on mental senses, and we used to share our souls with no separations between individuals. Eons ago, after an unknown cataclysm, we lost that ability and got separated. The separation caused the loss of our inner equilibrium as a race. We simply forgot what we were. The population was decimated because they lost the willpower to keep on living. A few individuals, our strongest ancestors, worked hard to rebuild our society or at least tried to keep together what was left of it. After several millennia, when the situation had been stable for a while and the suicide rates had slowed to the point of disappearing altogether, the council of the Wise Ancestors decided that our pain and sorrow could be put to work to help other civilizations so they wouldn't have to suffer our agony."

"That's a lot to digest."

I waved my hands in the air. "You asked me for the truth."

She smiled. "I want to know more, please."

Gaia's eagerness was such a gift to me. I still could barely accept the idea that she was here listening to me and that she had not run away from my incredible tale.

"And you'll definitely have more." I carefully looked for the next words and then sighed in frustration. "It isn't easy—"

"It's okay. I can take it."

I wished I could share her certainty. "From now on, my story gets difficult to tell because it involves us. It's about if we should stay together after all is explained or if we should try to look at the bigger picture."

"What about us?" Gaia had this habit of going right to the point, but I could see from the slight trembling of her fingers resting on the cushion that she was nervous about my answer.

It made my task harder. I couldn't stray from the absolute truth, but I was also worried about it. "Let me explain again who I am and what I do. It will help you understand what I meant." I had to collect all my thoughts and organize them to give her an idea that was succinct but clear. "As I told you before, I'm part of an elite guard called the Army of the Observers. Our only task is to protect other civilizations from falling victim to our fate. If a world proves its worthiness, we are bound by our credo to protect its memory. In doing so, we give them the gift of living in another state of existence, a metaphysical one, but only when their physical existence is at the very end. In several human religions, there is a similar concept; you would loosely call it *heaven*. The main difference is that our version is meant for the race as a whole, not just for single individuals. To establish if a civilization is meant to reach the metaphysical state, we have to collect as much data as we can. To collect data, we physically descend on the inhabited planet we are studying and live through the life span of the planet itself. We also have to incarnate in a body to better comprehend their way of life. Every intimate social contact is strictly prohibited. In order to maintain absolute objectivity, we can't fraternize. It's a matter of salvation or damnation for the species we are observing. We can't interfere in any way. We can't sympathize or hate because, one way or the other, we might misjudge."

Gaia was staring at me. Was she finally scared of me? Had she already understood the implications of what I was trying to say? I had probably used the wrong words. Gaia seemed to shrink on the couch, hugging herself as if she wanted to shield her body from something. Me?

Then she raised an eyebrow and shot me a perplexed glance. "Wait a second. Did you just say that you follow the entire life of a race?"

"Yes, from beginning to end."

Her curiosity was natural and was both good and bad: good if my words were going to please her somehow, bad if my longevity was going to scare her.

"Are you saying that you're older than Earth?"

Talking to her was heaven and hell combined. It felt right to be honest, but it also utterly scared me. After a pause, I started talking again. "Actually, I'm way older than that. Earth is my second mission, and before my first mission, I spent quite some time at the Academy studying."

Gaia was more focused now, as though she finally had started to form some sort of opinion about me.

"How long can you live?" She seemed quite reluctant to ask, and that was exactly what I had been dreading the most the moment I had decided to tell my story. Sooner or later, one of my answers would be the last one she wanted to hear from my mouth. Which one was it going to be?

"I'm not immortal. I was born, and I have parents, siblings, and friends. My life has a span like yours. It's just longer."

"It doesn't sound like mine at all."

"It's just a matter of perspective."

I wanted to paint myself as human as possible, and I realized that, at the moment, I didn't want to be who I was. While I was immersed in my thoughts, Gaia was shivering. As she covered herself with a blanket, I noticed the drop in temperature in the room. At least that I could easily fix.

She moved slowly on the couch. "Last time... you didn't want to come closer to me."

I didn't have a clue why her aura was giving off so many different colors. Was she remembering something? Was she just mad at me? One thing was sure: the memory Gaia had just evoked was painful for me. Because of what had happened that night, I had not seen her all these months.

Gaia didn't give me time to answer. "Is there something about me that prevents you from…?"

Her question left me speechless for a moment, and she hastily added, "We are from… different cultures after all."

"I wanted to touch you." I kept my hands from acting on my desire. "I want to touch you."

"But?"

"There isn't a single thing about *you* that could prevent me from getting closer."

"Then, why not?"

"What I want and what I can do are unfortunately two different things."

The idea of keeping myself away from her was becoming impossible to accept. It had been easier at the beginning. In Athens, I was too confused to understand what was happening to me. In Rome, chasing her through the city had been a full-time job. Once I found her though, something had started to change in the way I wanted her.

I remembered how I had suffered when she was in the company of her male friend. To make her suffer for my actions was the last thing I wanted, but on certain subjects, I didn't have a choice. I had to make myself clear. My desire for her was the strongest feeling I had endured in my life. Not being allowed to hold her while I was saying this made my aura scream in agony.

"I'm going to say it again; I've been raised in a way different from what you're used to. The human race depends on physical contact more than mine. Humans normally convey emotional messages with touch. A newborn needs his parents' touch to grow mentally stable. A lover needs his or her companion's touch to be reassured of their mutual affection. Lust is conveyed by touch, and so is hate. My species expresses something more than emotional messages with physical contact. We share our selves completely. My whole entity is transferred with a simple touch. All my memories, all my experiences are shared with the other being I establish a physical connection with. Before the Dark, we lived in total communion. We were single entities living in harmony with no possibility of miscommunication.

"We lost that, and we almost ceased to exist in the aftershock, but we managed to retain at least a spark of that precious gift. We partially regained this ability, but we also learned that in order to accomplish our task as Observers, we could not use it at our whim. I was trained to refrain from any physical contact if I wanted to remain impartial. As part of the Observers Army, we can still share our lives, but we have to ask permission because it's the most intimate thing you can ask of another being. Once you do it, you are linked forever to that being, altering his or her life."

I was exhausted. I knew there still were things to say, questions to answer, but I was not used to communicating this way; talking wasn't easy for me. I lacked the experience and the practice, and mostly I wasn't sure that my words were right. I could lose her over this.

She brought my attention back to the room with the sound of her voice. "It sounds intense." She seemed to think about it for a moment. "You don't want me to know you... in that way?"

"Oh, no, no." The feeling of inadequacy returned, and I shook my head. "No, it's not like that. It's beyond me and you actually." Restlessness possessed my limbs, and I mentally quieted down my desire. "I want more than anything else to share all of myself with you. It's the most beautiful experience you can imagine."

Gaia stopped me in a way that was becoming strangely familiar.

"Is it harmful for my species? Could I be damaged by this experience?" She grabbed the pillow behind her back.

"No, no damage of any kind could be done to you or to any other species. At least, not that I know."

Her hands tightened their grip on the pillow. "Then why can't we...?"

In moments like that, I honestly wanted to forget the reason I had to restrain myself from unconsciously reaching for her. "Because a great deal of damage can be done to your race."

"By us touching?" Still cradling the pillow to her chest, she left the couch and went to look out the window.

76

Outside, the sun was already rising; we had spent the whole night talking. Faint noises coming from somewhere else in the apartment alerted me her roommate was awake. I wanted to be able to finish what I started and followed her to the window.

She slowly turned and looked at me. "Elios—"

I was lost in her hazel eyes. I raised my hand and held it up close to her lips. In the morning light, I could see glowing dust dancing around her skin, like golden pollen on a silky rose petal. A small eddy danced around her body, where I would have liked to caress her, and her mane rose above her shoulders, as if carried by waves. The pillow she had been clutching fell on the floor.

"We're already attuned in a way that isn't normal, not even for me." Reluctantly, I lowered my hand, letting the moment pass. "I have never experienced this range of emotions and physical reactions before, with anybody of my race or with someone from another race. There's something in your soul that reacts to mine. This could be the reason why we found each other. But it's also the reason why it complicates our staying together. I can have casual physical contact with almost anybody, but since we are not just acquaintances, I can't stop the process with you. If I touch you, we will be one, and we'll share everything we are completely because of the feelings I have for you." I had to avert my gaze for a moment. "If I touch you, even once, my already insane dependence on you will become so strong I'll lose the ability to analyze data the way I should. My objectivity will be compromised, and I'll feel the need to save your planet because I'll want to be sure that you personally are going to reach the next phase even if Earth shouldn't be saved."

She shivered. "I don't like what you're saying."

I agreed with her wholeheartedly. "We don't have a choice in the matter. No contact with you can be casual. We're on the same spiritual channel. Even the slightest touch of your skin would initiate the process."

"I don't have to like it."

"I hate the fact I can't touch you." I couldn't help but raise my hand, open it before her heart, and wish I could be human just once.

Gaia's aura spiked in a burst of orange mixed with the red and the pink.

I brought my raised hand to my heart and held it in place there with the other. "It's taking all my discipline not to."

"Would it be so wrong?"

No, it would be perfect. "I've been trained to follow my ethical code of conduct to the full extent of my possibilities. I told you already that you could think of me as the equivalent of a monk."

"I hate when you say that." Gaia's eyes were staring at mine. "How can you live this way?"

I am not so sure anymore. "My morality is what has kept me going all these years. The certainty I was doing something right, even when I couldn't interfere in the human struggle, was the only way I could manage to collect data impartially. Can you imagine having the power to change a wrong and making it right but being denied that freedom in the name of a bigger picture? What would you do if you were able to save someone but your hands were bound by an oath to just observe him dying?"

I let Gaia consider my words. I'd had eons to get used to the responsibility I had embraced. I remembered several students at the academy who had decided to leave after a while. Time and experience made it slightly better to endure, but sometimes not intervening was hard. I had been lucky with my first mission. The planet I had examined had turned out to be worth saving.

"I can't imagine having to bear that kind of responsibility." She looked outside. Noises from the outer world intruded upon our haven. "I'd go crazy. I couldn't just let kids die."

I nodded. "There are moments I must repeat to myself that what I do is right. I can't let doubt into my heart. I have watched the horror of war and famine and let it be because I knew I could bring a different kind of solace to the dead and dying. The preserved memory of a race is more important than its individuals."

"But what if you save a race that doesn't deserve it?" She faced me again.

"It's a possibility. When I became an Observer, I accepted the responsibility to decide another race's fate. It was a decision I made out of love."

Gaia was shivering again.

I gently summoned a warm breeze to caress her face. I lingered a moment on the effect her reaction had on me. I couldn't keep my eyes from hers. "And love is what is giving me ethical problems now."

We both heard sounds in the kitchen.

"Sara?" Gaia called.

"Yes?" the roommate answered from the door, grinning. "Oh, you're here. Good morning to you." She then looked at me and nodded. "Did we have a party?" Her smile became wider. "I could hear some Rondò Veneziano last night. Very romantic."

"Good morning to you too. And it's not what you think. At all." The color on Gaia's face became a shade of deep pink.

Time for me to leave. "I'll come back later; I think we need to sleep after last night."

"See you later." If possible, her friend's smile widened even more.

Conscious of my lack of social skills when it came to interacting with humans, I left before I could say or do anything improper. As soon as I was outside the door, I let my aura express my feelings. I hadn't known I was capable of producing such a spectrum of colors.

7

I ran down the stairs two and three steps at a time and reached ground level in a haze. Outside the entrance, the crisp morning air laced with the wet scent of fir resin welcomed me but didn't chase the fog from my mind. The entirety of my thoughts fiercely focused on Gaia, I walked back to my apartment. Although I should have tried to sleep, I spent several hours uttering half sentences to Fido. Later in the morning, when the chirping of the health-bot had grown to a loud, worried pitch, I went for a hot shower and at least managed to soften my muscles. Only then did I realize how tired I was. "I'll have a nap. Happy?" The last thing I saw before falling asleep was Fido's blinking light turning off.

For the first time on Earth, I dreamed. I knew I was capable of dreaming, but I had never let my mind relax enough to enter REM. I didn't need it and had never felt the need to experience it. I dreamed of Gaia with such intensity I could almost feel her presence in the room. In my dream, I touched her. My fingers were on her soft lips. Her skin was warm and soft under my touch. Then darkness came, and I woke. My training had kicked in even in my dreams.

Nevertheless, after only one hour worth of sleep, I was rested and in a great mood. I remembered to drink some water. Lately, my body had suffered enough for my negligence. I let the water run for a few seconds and then filled a glass with the cold liquid. I drank the contents in one gulp and refilled the glass several times before feeling satisfied. Finally, I went to the kitchen window. Outside, the midday sun was shining, and I felt reinvigorated by the light filtering in the room. I was looking directly into Gaia's apartment and decided I had to tell her where I lived before she freaked out.

My heartbeats quickened when I saw her busy in her kitchen. I had another quick shower, just to calm myself again. Lately, I had noticed that just thinking of her raised my heartbeat consistently. I wasn't used to having to care for my body so much. I put on fresh clothes and ran to her building. Sara was leaving the apartment when I arrived. I could hear Pallino making a scene behind the door already.

"Hi, there. Did you rest well?" She smiled at me.

I nodded a greeting, and although not used to chit-chatting, I forced a smile onto my face in response to hers. "I slept profoundly. Thanks for asking."

For some reason I couldn't fathom, she laughed at my words and disappeared inside the elevator. I reached for the door, which was still open, and I found Gaia looking at me. This time, I automatically matched her happy expression with one of mine. Pallino launched himself against my leg.

"Hi, Elios." Her face was illuminated by sunlight from the landing window behind my back, and her hair changed color— darker and lighter blond—as she moved.

"Hi, Gaia. You look radiant." I leaned down and picked up Pallino.

"Would you like some pasta? I don't like eating alone, and I'm hungry." She walked toward the kitchen and then stopped and turned to face me. "Do you eat?"

I had stepped back at the very last moment. "Yes, I do." I loved the idea of doing normal human things with her, sharing this aspect of her life, and my stomach was sending my brain clear signals about needing food.

"Good." She smiled and almost imperceptibly leaned forward while cradling her arms to her chest.

I moved back when I wanted more than anything to move forward and take her in my arms.

Her smile faltered for the briefest of moments. "Let's eat, then, while the spaghetti is still good."

"I'm embarrassed to confess I'm hungry too." The smell of cooked food wafted to my nose, and my body responded to it. "I forget to eat sometimes." We laughed at the noise my stomach was making.

I followed her to the kitchen and let Pallino down. He complained only long enough for Gaia to serve him food as well. Then he disappeared around the corner. We ate silently while I kept looking at her, studying her delicate features, her warm colors, the way she elegantly moved her hands, and the way she nodded her head slightly when she was thoughtful. I loved how the natural light from the side window painted shadows on her face. When she looked back at me, I saw that her eyes changed colors from deep hazel to dark green to golden brown, depending on the light.

Soon, the room felt too small.

"What?" she asked.

"Nothing." It took me a few seconds to regroup my thoughts. "It's a beautiful day."

"It is."

I laid the fork on my empty plate then tilted my head to the side and pointed at the window. "If you don't mind, I'd like to go out today."

"No, I don't mind at all. Let me grab my jacket." Gaia left the table with one graceful movement and walked toward the door.

It occurred to me that I wanted to play with her a little bit. I summoned a gentle breeze and waited for her to turn, then I closed my eyes and raised my hand to caress the air in front of her face. I wanted to recreate the vivid dream I'd had only a few hours earlier. But reality was better than my imagination. Inexplicably, I felt her touch on my skin. I gasped and opened my eyes. Gaia was there, with her hand raised in front of my face. I stopped the breeze. "What did you do?"

"Just what you were doing. Why?"

"What you did… you touched me in way that was different. Not something I expected."

"But I didn't touch you at all."

"You reached something deeper than my skin."

"Do you feel the same way I do?"

"Never thought about it before. I guess so, since I have a human body."

"But we aren't going to find out…?"

I groaned inwardly. The room was saturated with the smell of her hair, and I couldn't regain full control of my body. I led her outside, walking slowly to give me time to come back to my senses.

The scented spring air did me some good; my mind cleared a bit. I moved closer to the vehicle I had bought on a whim and almost forgotten I had, hoping we could have countless rides together. "That's my car."

Her glowing skin and hazel eyes made a nice contrast against the dark shape of the Alfa. Gaia turned her head for a second, and I sighed and then remembered what I wanted to tell her about my quarters in Seattle. I reached for the keypad and unlocked the car. "So…" I hesitated. "As I was saying, this is my car, and that's the building where I'm living." I waved my hand upward, gesturing at the building facing hers.

Gaia made a face, her eyes huge. "You've been living here the whole time?"

"Well, I've been looking for you for so long, once I found you, I couldn't stand to live away from you. I wasn't sure I was ever going to contact you. I knew I shouldn't have, but I wanted to, so I looked for a vacant apartment facing yours. I was happy catching glimpses of you from the window." My mouth felt dry. "I have to admit I did it any time I felt I was going crazy."

She looked up and then at me. "I felt your presence."

"I know." I opened the passenger door for her, and at that moment the sunlight played another trick with the color of her eyes. They were almost golden with little green dots. "I know your face so well. I could draw your features anytime. Even with my eyes closed." I raised my hand to air-trace the line of her nose, then I lowered it to trace her lips and then her chin.

Gaia mirrored my act, and as before, I felt her touch on my skin. Shivers ran through my spine. "Thanks… thanks for this unexpected gift." I commanded my legs to walk away from her then around the car to the driver side. I opened the door, sat, and positioned my hands firmly on the steering wheel. "Do you like Alki Beach?"

"I love Alki Beach."

I turned on the engine and drove away from the University District. I had so many questions I wanted to ask her, but I didn't know where to start. The mere fact that we were together was momentous, and I didn't want to ruin the atmosphere.

"Do you mind if we talk about you today?" I asked after a while.

"Not at all."

"Tired of listening to me?"

"You gave me lots to think about, but I'll never tire of listening to you." She turned away from me for a moment. "I love Seattle."

I followed her gaze outside and had to agree with her. The city shone under the sun.

She tilted her head toward me. "So, what would you like to know about me?"

"You're still a mystery to me. There're so many things I want to hear from you: what you like, what you hate, any little thing that makes you, *you*." I couldn't help but smile.

She relaxed by my side, and despite my previous request we spent the rest of the time talking about little or nothing. By the time I turned into Alki Beach, I had settled into a pleasant rhythm of small talk and smiles.

"By the way, nice ride," she said after one long silence. "My dad would be begging you to let him drive this car. Love the color."

I was surprised. "Do you know a lot about cars?"

"Not about cars in general, but my dad is an Alfa aficionado and, strangely enough, never cared for soccer. My sister and I grew up watching more car shows than we ever cared for."

I wasn't sure what had possessed me to buy that car, but I was now happy I had done it. Alki Beach was packed, the drive an obstacle course, but I was more interested in stealing glances at her than watching the road. Once, there had been a luscious forest where the whole city of Seattle was. I wished Gaia and I were living back then, riding horses, alone. I wished I could have shown her how quaint the city had been at its inception. I had passed through the Americas for a brief period of time, no longer than three decades, and I had stopped for a few months in Seattle when it had been nothing more than the last frontier. I would have liked to chaperone her around. Although I had hated the unrefined garments that passed for clothes then, I knew Gaia would have looked fine in calico cotton. Or maybe we could have abandoned society altogether in favor of the plains and a more natural way of life.

I had stepped on the brakes one time too many when she said, "Maybe you should look ahead."

I couldn't help but keeping my eyes on her a moment longer. "I certainly should."

Her eyes shone brightly, then she looked ahead and pointed to the right side. "There. There's enough space to park between those two cars."

I nodded and pulled the car to the side to start the maneuver. The spot she had suggested was tight, but after years of parking, first in Athens and then in Rome, parallel parking was as easy to me as breathing. I eased the Alfa between two SUVs, turned off the engine, and went to open the door for Gaia.

She exited and, after taking a good look at the parking spot, gave me a big smile. "My dad would be proud."

My chest inflated at her words. We walked for a while in silence. Gaia seemed interested in watching the unique variety of people walking alongside us. I was more interested in looking at her. I bought some coffee at a little coffee place by the seaside. We sat outside at one of the tables facing the sea, where we could admire the skyline.

"I'd like to know something more about your studies. You seem to enjoy that a lot." I sat on the plastic chair and arranged my body at an angle. The table dividing us was small, too small.

"How do you know so many things about me?"

"Not human. Remember?" I found the conversation amusing. "And lots of time on my hands." The contents of my cup were still too hot to the touch. I removed the lid and sipped the coffee. "So, about your studies?"

She brought her cup to her lips, grimaced, and set it back. "I'm studying the artifacts from an archeological dig in Bremerton where, just recently, an ancient Native American village was found. The climatic conditions, the composition of the soil, and a series of fortunate accidents actually helped preserve the site way longer than usual, like the Ark of the Patriarchs on Mount Rainier. My job is to define what kind of social structure they had and find affinities with other cultures if there are any."

"Our jobs are similar; we both study societies."

She played with her cup for a bit. "My team discovered that we could have a match between two different pieces of pottery. The first one is a Native American piece that was found in Bremerton. The second comes from Italy, and it's Etruscan. We also have a third one with a similar picture coming from India, but we need better pictures, so we sent someone there. Sara and I took care of the Italian piece when we went for Christmas…"

Her aura shivered in blue tones, and it pained me. "I felt lost when you left. I worried you weren't coming back."

"I couldn't stay here any longer." She took a few sips of her coffee.

I traced the air by her jaw. "I'm sorry. I should've handled things better."

She arched her neck slightly. "Something good came out of my Christmas vacation. At least we could take good pictures of the Etruscan piece." After draining her cup of coffee, she threw it in the trash bin beside her. "The fragments are really small, so we are hoping that the archeologists will discover something bigger and possibly with the same painting on it."

"That's interesting." The coffee, scalding only minutes ago, was now cold and bitter. I drank what was left of it and crushed the Styrofoam cup. The only trash bin in sight was the one by her side. Instead of throwing the cup, I reached for the bin and found myself staring at her eyes. A moment later, I was staring at her mouth. I barely escaped the pull. "If they do, what would it prove?" She sat still, unblinking. Then, she absentmindedly bit her lower lip, and I couldn't help but wonder at how soft it looked. "If the pieces are similar…"

"Depending on how similar the pieces are, a correlation between cultures separated by oceans and time could confirm the theory that different civilizations grow in predictable ways." She turned to look at the crowd gathered to catch the last rays of sun, and then her attention was on me again. A strand of her hair fell before her face, and I almost reached out to brush it away. That time, my self-control showed up later than usual. Every single time, it was kicking in later and later. How long before I couldn't control myself anymore?

Gaia moved. "I like this."

"What?"

"Just this. You and me. Silly, little things."

"I like them too." The breeze from the sea brought her scent to me in waves, and I had to excuse myself for a moment. "I'll buy some water," I explained. I entered the coffee place and let out a sigh of relief. I leaned against the fridge and then squatted.

"Hey? Are you okay?" the waiter, a young man, asked from the other side of the room.

I breathed in and out and pushed on my legs to stand up. "I'm fine. Thanks."

"Are you sure? You're as white—"

"I'm okay." Despite my words, my head was spinning. I concentrated on my actions, turned, opened the fridge, and grabbed two bottles of water. "These two." In three steps, I was at the counter where I laid them before the man.

"Sure. I'll ring them up for you." He scanned the barcode of one of the bottles. "Nothing better than a cold San Pellegrino when it's hot outside."

It wasn't hot outside, but I didn't comment on that. I thanked the man and walked out of the shop. At the doorstep, I lingered a moment to look at Gaia waiting for me. She couldn't see me from where she was sitting, yet she turned and located me as soon as I took my first step toward her. I watched as her eyes widened and her lips turned up in a smile at my sight.

"Thanks." She took one of the bottles and then clinked it with mine. "Cheers."

"Would it be possible to take a look at the pictures of the pottery pieces?" I set myself on the chair, arranging my body as far away from hers as possible. I found it as painful as being close to her.

"Right away. I have one of the Etruscan pieces on my cell phone. I usually take backup pictures of anything important." She busied herself with her cell phone, found what she was looking for, and then angled it toward me. "Look, isn't it curious that they draw a human hand with six fingers? Etruscans were highly skilled when it came to—"

Her words raised the hair on my skin. "A six-fingered hand?"

She nodded. "For being a cell phone camera, the resolution isn't half bad, don't you think?"

"May I?" I reached for her cell phone, already regretting having asked her to show me the image. When I finally took a look at the picture she wanted to show me, I had the proof I was right to be fearful. *It can't be.* The image went out of focus for a moment. When I blinked, it was still there. "It can't be."

"What did you just say?'

"I have seen this drawing somewhere else."

I had an excellent photographic memory and I didn't have a doubt about the similarities between the picture of the human artifact and the one I knew was carefully conserved on my planet. We had only a few findings from the ancient times before the Dark. From the quality of the pieces left behind, our archeologists had been able to determine that our ancestors lived in a very sophisticated and highly technological society. Unfortunately, almost everything of their civilization had been destroyed, leaving us wondering about their terrible fate. The scarcity of the artifacts found made each one of them of extraordinary importance.

And that is why I couldn't be mistaking what I saw.

As citizens of the planet Solo, from an early age, we were encouraged to visit the archeological museum to commit to our memories what little was left of our history. After eons, we still felt like orphans looking desperately for their parents. The only things that remained from their time were a few shattered pieces of daily life. We clung to these little broken objects with almost religious reverence, hoping they could talk to us and reveal the truth of what had happened. What I had just discovered was of such magnitude that at first I didn't even fully realize its complexity.

Darkness was engulfing the sky, and Gaia was staring at me, perplexed.

"Something wrong?" Gaia was biting her lips, her face half covered by a shadow.

A cold shiver went through my arms and legs. "Something I can't explain."

"So, I'm curious, where did you see that painting before?"

"I have looked at this figure so many times I've lost count."

"Where? Do you know of other places with similar pieces? I thought we contacted pretty much everybody working on similar archeological excavation sites."

"I didn't see them here." *I'll have to leave.*

"Was it in China? We're still waiting for Beijing's anthropological museum to get back to us."

"It wasn't here on Earth."

"Where did you say you saw it?"

"On Solo."

Gaia's eyes widened as she closed her mouth.

"I saw the same figure on an ancient fragment conserved on my planet, guarded in our equivalent of an archeological museum." My head was pounding. I didn't need the coming headache. "I need to ask you a favor."

"Anything."

"I need to see the pictures of the other pieces you have in your department. Is it possible?" I understood that kind of research was maintained under some sort of secrecy until discoveries were announced and books were published. I was already thinking of alternative ways to obtain the information I needed.

Gaia had kept biting her lips, but then she nodded and smiled. "Sure. It's not like you're going to disclose secret information to anybody—"

Despite the seriousness of the situation, I couldn't help but reciprocate the smile. "Nobody on Earth."

With a resolute expression, Gaia stood up. "If you want, we can go to the lab now. The Native American artifact is still there. We got permission to study it and take as many pictures as we wanted before returning it to the tribe who's claiming it for the proper burial."

Deep inside me, I had hoped she couldn't be of help. I would have reoriented my efforts somewhere else, and it would have taken time. "Perfect. Thanks. It means a lot to me."

She casually waved her hand in the air. "It's nothing."

As we walked back to the car, the crowd was slowly thinning out, and the skyline was bright with city lights. I opened the passenger door for Gaia and wished I had more time to enjoy the view. At the moment, I wanted to do nothing more than sit relaxed, with her by my side, talking about something silly and passing time together. What I saw in that picture had changed everything in a single moment.

We drove back to Gaia's apartment because she needed her badge to access the lab. I wanted to keep up some pretense of communication, but my mind was racing somewhere else. Hoping against hope, I wanted to find a solution. Any outcome that would leave me on Earth was welcome.

The ride from her apartment to the university campus was as silent as the previous drive; fortunately, it was much shorter. The anthropology department was deserted, for which I was grateful, so she didn't have to make up reasons for my presence.

We entered the lab in almost religious silence, our steps softened by the strikingly clean linoleum floor. My mind was numb, but I still realized that the lab where the Native American findings were guarded was kept at a set temperature, with the humidity level constantly adjusted. Our mere presence would alter that ecosystem. I didn't want to cause any damage to the small pieces of pottery resting on white cloths under the carefully placed cold lights, and I changed the temperature and the humidity around us. Gaia went to look for the Native American piece, and I followed her like a drone.

She stopped before one of the tables and leaned over a small piece of pottery. "Here it is."

Unwillingly, I took a look at the little piece resting on the white linen. Before my eyes was the second proof that my lost ancestors had somehow mingled with the humans. Unfortunately, time had ravaged the colors, and the quality of the material the Native Americans had used wasn't very durable. Nevertheless, even incomplete and mutilated, this little fragment had undoubtably striking similarities with the Etruscan piece and therefore with the Solean one. But I still needed more proof, as if I didn't know enough already.

"Is there any chance you also have a picture of the Indian artifact?"

She pointed at the door on the opposite wall. "Yes, in there."

I walked beside her, delaying the inevitable.

"I'm the one in charge of the archives, and I file everything carefully. I know exactly what it's under." She went to the file cabinet on the left wall and opened one of its drawers. Her fingers expertly leafed through a row of folders until she extracted a yellow one. With a satisfied nod, she selected an image from the folder. "It's not a great picture. But it's clear enough to see the details."

The vibrant color of the folder reminded me of a sunflower field I had once seen in Italy. I imagined being there, with her. I forced myself back to the present. One look at the picture confirmed that it was the third proven documentation of a connection between the Dark on Solo and Earth and my sentence to exile.

"What is it?" She had been smiling not a moment ago.

Raw awareness reached my stomach, and I felt sick. "I'll tell you everything. I promise. But if you don't mind, I need to drive."

I silently sailed through Seattle. Gaia didn't even try to start a conversation, and after a while she contented herself to sing along with the radio. Her voice was just a soft whisper in the cold night but was enough to warm my frozen heart. I wanted to tell her how much I liked listening to her singing, but a lump in my throat didn't let me. I grabbed the wheel until my knuckles turned icy white while my vision blurred in a sea of sadness. I turned toward my window to hide my angry tears.

I kept driving in circles through neighborhoods I didn't recognize, but by the time I saw the sign for Magnolia's Lookout, I'd had enough time to compose myself. I swiftly wiped my eyes before opening her door and leading her outside. Maintaining the Solean distance now felt wrong and unnatural. We sat on a bench facing the sea and the starry sky.

She stared ahead, her eyes focused on a dark spot. I looked at her. Her delicate profile was bathed in the white light of the quarter moon. Her hair had become a dark curtain on her fair skin. Gaia felt my eyes on her, and she turned. When she spoke, her voice was warm and liquid, all *r*'s and *l*'s dancing around the vowels. "Can you explain to me why your mood has changed so much?"

I was in such pain, I couldn't talk.

"I'm getting worried, and your silence is not helping. I don't know what to think."

"You won't like it." *I don't. I hate what I am going to say to you.* I had to start from somewhere. "That little piece of pottery you showed me is connected to my lost progenitors' history." I was counting every word I was saying because they were going to be the last.

"That's great news."

I felt like screaming, but I didn't. "It could help us uncover the truth behind our long-lost civilization. I don't know what kind of link exists between the human race and ours, but there's something."

"This is great. Isn't it?"

For Solo, yes.

"Elios, please tell me; what's going on?"

"Not sure." I lied and had to look away. "I'm sorry—"

"For what?"

I had my eyes open, but I didn't see anything while I recited the explanation I had been rehearsing in my mind for the last three or four hours. "I have to report it personally. This is an extraordinary finding, and it's mandatory for me to present the proof in front of a council of Superior Observers. We have never before found links to our past on another planet. After I've talked to my superiors, a court of Wise Ancestors is going to study my memories to analyze the details of what I have seen."

"Who are those people you're talking about?"

"The Superior Observers are my direct superiors."

"And the others?"

"The Wise Ancestors are a group of elders—" I paused for a moment. "They're the depository of our knowledge. They're our fathers."

"You have to go to report to them, right?"

"Yes."

"Well, I understand why you have to. But then you're coming back."

I stilled my heart and said, "No, I won't."

"But you told me how important your mission is here on Earth. You said it. It's against your moral code of conduct to fail… us."

I turned to look at her. "The moment my memories are shared with the Wise Ancestors, they'll also know about us. I'll be demoted. I won't be allowed to come back to my mission… to you."

"Why?"

"Because I've broken my vows—"

"But you haven't touched me. Not once."

I wish I had. But I was glad I hadn't. Otherwise, I would have put her in danger of having her memories erased: Observers' standard procedure when it came to dealing with botched-up missions. "It doesn't matter anymore. I developed feelings I shouldn't have. It's beyond you and me."

"There must be a way."

"It's the only thing I've been thinking since you showed me the figure. I've tried to find a way, but there's none."

"Maybe those people will understand you haven't done anything wrong."

"But I have, under the Wise Ancestors' laws."

"Then they can't be that wise if they're ready to punish you for doing the right thing."

"I'll be punished for falling in love with you."

Her aura bristled at my words. "What kind of monsters are they?"

"Don't say that. You don't know them. The head of the Wise Ancestors, Lex, is like a father to me."

"What father would be so cruel?"

I wanted to explain how our society worked, but I didn't know where to start, and I didn't want to waste time.

She spoke before I could say anything. "Stay with me."

Something inside me broke at her request. "I can't. I must go back to Solo. I can't betray my race."

"I don't want to lose you."

"I can't bear to lose you, and yet I must." I was numb, from head to toe. The pain, the terrible ache tearing through my heart, paralyzed me. I could talk, but I couldn't feel my lips moving.

She was shaking. "Take me back to my apartment."

Her angry request pushed the dagger further inside and pierced my aura. I bled pain and sorrow and regret. "Please, not now. Not like this."

Her aura changed color at once, and I knew she would stay.

We passed the night on that bench, waiting for Seattle to wake up. I never unlocked my eyes from hers. I brought the distant sound of a violin concert for just the two us. We slowly caressed the air around our faces. Our auras danced around each other. I wept.

8

Lex, we must talk at your earliest convenience. I'll be waiting outside your office. I sent the call first thing the next morning, once I left Gaia at her apartment. I didn't give Fido time to read my vitals.

"What's bothering you, my pupil?" Lex looked at me from his chair behind the slab of dark, polished rock he used as a desk in his office at the Ancestor Guide's quarters. The astral version of that place was lifelike, and not a single detail was missing.

He had answered in less than an hour, but in the meantime I had driven myself insane with worry, checking on Gaia's aura every minute. Her distress was hard to ignore and fueled mine. I succinctly told Lex what I had discovered.

"Are you sure of what you saw?"

I found his question unnerving, considering all I was willing to give up for my race. I had to remind myself he couldn't know. He would soon. "I know what I saw. Etruscans, Indians, and Native Americans had contacts with the Solean cultures. I don't know how or why."

He thought about it for a moment and then raised a finger. "Stay where you are. I'll summon your Superior Observers right away."

I had dreaded my voyage back home would be delayed. If I had to leave Gaia, let it be now. "I'll wait for my orders." I arranged my body on the chair facing a now-empty desk and went through several breathing exercises. When I had reached the end of my patience, Lex came back, and he wasn't alone. Two high-ranking Observers had accompanied him, and they were excited. The three of them asked me questions for a while and then talked among themselves. The atmosphere in the room was joyous—exalted, even. I felt nauseous.

"We've already sent for you," Lex finally said before dismissing me back to my corporeal body. "I see that your level of anxiety is high. I'll help you with the wait."

He used my mental signature to send me into a deep trance without asking my permission, for the second time in less than six months. I couldn't fight against his push, and while embracing the dark quiet of unconsciousness, I thought it was better this way. Gaia needed time to process what had happened, and so did I.

Despite my good intentions, when I finally woke—or rather when Lex let me wake—I ran to her apartment. Without thinking, I was out of my room and then outside her door. I might have blinked once on the way over.

I had to see her one last time.

"Yes? What can I do for you?" a young man answered the door. His hair was disheveled, and he wasn't wearing any shirt over his pajama pants. A hushed feminine voice laughed somewhere inside the apartment.

For a moment, blind fury colored my vision.

"Hey, man? What you want?"

Taking a big breath, I willed my rage away and looked behind his shoulders, but the apartment colors were all wrong. The scents clinging to the walls were different. "Is Gaia home?"

The young man shook his head. "Gaia? There's no Gaia here."

I already knew. Gaia had left the apartment, and she and her friend had been gone for a while. The traces from her aura were old and dry. Had I waited a moment longer after waking from the trance, I would have discovered it sooner. The residual anger changed to an ache. The ache became longing in the span of a breath. I was massaging my midsection as if the act would ease my suffering when I received a mental call from Lex.

My pupil, I have news for you.

I'll be with you in a moment. I was outside Gaia's ex-apartment. I reached the end of the hallway and faced the window. It was midmorning and rainy. I looked down at my bare feet and noticed the hem of my pants was wet. From the colors outside and the warm temperature in the hallway, I deduced it was a typical summer day in Seattle. More than two months, possibly four, had passed since last time I saw Gaia. Where was she? What had become of her? A mental nudge reminded me of my impending conversation with Lex. I closed my eyes and let him guide me through the tunnel and into his astral office.

"Your ship has arrived. The pickup point is on Mount Rainier. You must depart tonight. It is expected to be cloudy, and a meteorological balloon will hover over the same area for several hours and will cover the ship's maneuvers." He gave me the exact coordinates of the rendezvous.

"I'll leave at once." I bowed and returned to my body in the hallway, where I leaned against the cool glass pane of the window and stood there, still and unthinking, for a while.

A door opened, and steps echoed in the hallway. "Yo, dude!" the young man called.

I turned. The man wasn't alone; a brunette was at his side.

"Are you looking for the Italian girls?" she stepped out and asked me.

I nodded.

"I sub-rented from them. They left a few days ago and went back to Italy. Some university project."

I thanked them and dragged my feet all the way to my place. Only a few days. I had missed Gaia by only a few days. I hated Lex and his timing.

Around noon, depleted of any energy, I started making preparations to leave Earth. For such a task, my exodus was rather anticlimactic. It took me less than an hour and one phone call to my landlord to close my rental contract. In even less time, I gathered my earthly belongings. Once Fido was safely boxed in the crate in which it had travelled from Italy, I left a final check on the kitchen counter for the landlord as she had requested per any damage she would find, and closed the door behind me. If asked, I wouldn't have known the color of the ceramic tiles in my bathroom, so little had I lived in that place I had called mine for a few months.

I filled the Alfa's tank, bought a camping backpack and a pair of hiking shoes at the closest store specializing in outdoors gear, and set off toward Mount Rainier. Traffic and road blocks slowed the driving and gave me time to think. I was glad Fido was in the trunk and it couldn't detect the changes of heart I had on the road.

Near the Skagit Valley, during a longer wait—workers were paving a strip of highway ahead, lanes were closed, and cars were taking turns for the right of way—I turned around and headed toward the airport. I drove for full ten minutes before I slammed on the brakes and screamed. A car barely avoided hitting me at the last moment. Angry words and loud honking followed. I waved my hand in apology, turned off the road, parked by a field, and cried. When the air inside the Alfa was saturated with my despair, I opened the door and stumbled outside. I went to sit on the edge of the road, facing the vast expanse of land, which was being prepared to host tulips the next spring. I closed my eyes and saw Gaia. I opened them, but her image was still there. The wound in my chest felt raw and bloody, yet my eyes had dried up after so much crying. Before me, towering over the valley, sat Mount Rainier. I almost smiled when Areel nudged at my mind. Not even a minute later, Kam called too.

We heard you're coming home, Kam said.

Lex told us, Areel added.

Did he tell you to make sure I would board my flight? The echo of their blushing reached me loud and clear. *Don't worry. I'm on my way.*

See you soon, they both told me.

See you soon. I blinked and willed Gaia's image away. *Addio, amore mio.* Goodbye, my love.

By the time I changed direction again and was on the right course toward Mount Rainier, the traffic had cleared up, and the workers had gone home. It was late in the afternoon when I reached Mount Rainier National Park. Before approaching the main entrance to the park, I left the Alfa in one dusty driveway, where I removed Fido from the crate and hid it inside the camping backpack I had just bought. Then I pulled off the light shoes I was wearing and slipped into the new hiking pair. I moved away from my car, and another piece of my heart broke. Abandoning the Brera made me weep. Gaia's aura and scent were all over it. With Fido safely ensconced and only lightly weighing on my back—despite its size, the health-bot wasn't heavy, thanks to its materials—I forced myself to walk toward the park. At the entrance gate, I waited until the ranger was busy with a few cars checking in for the night at one of the hotels, and then I strolled undetected inside the park proper. It wouldn't do to unleash a search party for a missing climber.

On my way to the Wonderland Trail's entrance, I hitched a ride from two teenagers driving toward the Sunrise Visitor Center, where the hike started. At the cafeteria inside the visitor center, I consumed a hot meal consisting of a generous slice of soggy pizza and a cup of vegetable soup that was too salty. On my way out, I bought two bottles of water, some energy bars, and a small flashlight. Thanks to the Washington State latitude, I knew I could count on several hours of light, but the hike to my rendezvous point would take at least five hours. Two hours of unrelenting hiking later, I was looking down at the valley from Skyscraper Pass. From there, I descended to Granite Creek Camp, carefully passed the moraine of the Winthrop Glacier, and continued toward Mystic Camp. Finally, I emerged from the small forest bordering the camp and found Mystic Lake, my final destination on Earth. It was near midnight. It had taken me almost seven hours to reach the lake. I should have kept a better pace, but after ten at night, the light had disappeared, and I had to use the small flashlight to guide my steps.

I'm here. I sent Lex the message and looked for a spot where I could unwind. Ahead of me was a solitary rock shaped like a cushion with a flat top. I walked the few steps to the natural seat, grimacing in pain. My feet had blistered during the long walk with the new shoes, and I couldn't stand anymore. I sat heavily on the rock and carefully removed my shoes and peeled away the socks. I entered the frigid water of the lake with a sigh of relief and waited for my ride to pick me up.

Lex's call came a few minutes later. *Get ready. I'm imprinting the ship with your mental signature.*

A shadow against the dark night, the sleek, pitch-black shuttle was descending silently toward the placid waters of the lake. I easily guided the pen-shaped vessel, now officially *my* ride, toward me and landed it flat on the meadow just south of me. It took me forever to slip socks and shoes back on, but the moon was coming out behind the clouds, and I tried to rush.

The cargo door opened with a *whoosh*, a retractable step rolled down, and I hopped inside. After so long since my last ride, I had forgotten what a Solean passenger shuttle looked like inside. Instead of making me feel at home, the sleek design, the sharp lines, and the metallic colors made me feel out of place, neither human nor Solean. Built for one passenger, the ship's main cabin had space only for the sleeping capsule, which I entered with great relief. I would be unconscious for the entirety of the voyage while Lex used my mental signature as a beacon to bring me back to Solo. I desired nothing more than to be unconscious and not have to think.

However, sleep didn't come soon enough, and my mind filled with what-if questions about Gaia. Unable to bear the agony, I sought my friends for a final mental session before I went into deep sleep. I didn't have the energy to summon any place, and I left the astral meeting space bare, foggy gray and nothing more. Areel answered the call immediately and had the tact not to comment upon the bleakness surrounding us.

"Kam can't join us. He's taking the psychic gun test he has postponed for so long."

"His Ancestor Guide finally cornered him?"

Areel laughed. "Yes, he did." He paused a moment and lowered his head. "Soon, we'll be reunited."

"Yes, very soon."

"You'll see; you'll feel better once you're home."

I absentmindedly nodded. "Areel…"

"Yes?"

"I can't help but wonder about the softness of her skin and the pleasure we would have experienced with the briefest sharing of our thoughts."

Areel gasped, and for a moment, his image faltered. "But you haven't attempted a Share with her? You told me you hadn't—"

"I'm the epitome of the perfect Observer." I looked at him and shrugged. "Never touched her. Never kissed her."

"Good. That's good. Because you know what would have happened to her if you had."

I raised one hand to stop him from spelling it out for me. Every Observer knew the rules, and I didn't want to talk about scraping her mind clean of my memories.

But Areel keep talking. "She could lose her mind through the process."

"I know." The procedure was the equivalent of a sophisticated lobotomy.

"You know the exposure to us changes the subject's DNA—"

"I remember." *The subject transfers Solean DNA in their genes and passes the memories of us to the next generation, and then the next, changing both their history and ours.* Back at the Academy, the ethic instructor had drilled that lesson into our minds until we could have recited the passage by heart. *There are too many implications in having a superior knowledge way far ahead of time, especially for a violent society like the humans,* the same instructor had warned me before I left for my second mission. "I did not touch her."

"I trust you." Then he whispered, "It makes everything easier."

The pull of the deep sleep finally dragged me down, and I had just enough time to say goodbye to him and close the channel before darkness claimed me.

The vessel jumped through several wormholes, navigated through star systems, covered a big portion of the known universe, and reached the Solean atmosphere without me being the wiser. While I was still asleep, Lex took control of my ship, superimposing his mental signature over mine, and escorted me down to Solo.

"I hope you had a regenerating time." Lex came to greet me personally once I woke from the deep sleep.

I blinked a few times before my eyes focused on the person who had spoken. "Lex…"

"My pupil, don't fret. I bought you some time before your hearing starts."

The room I was in was slowly revealed to me, one detail at a time. I couldn't remember if it was normal to feel that disoriented. "Where am I?" White and silver surrounded me.

"You are in your temporary quarters in the Ancestor Guides' compound."

"At your place?" I focused on Lex in his corporeal form and was about to ask him why he was wearing a body, but my mind drifted away when he spoke next.

"Yes, I convinced your Superior Observers that it was for the best to have you close to my quarters."

It was highly irregular. Between missions, Observers were expected to live at the Academy where they could join a commune or just bond with their friends. I was glad for the opportunity to be alone before confronting Areel and Kam. "Thanks."

"The only important thing now is that you feel better."

I heard the distinct sound of water dripping over a hard surface coming from my right. I tilted my head and saw a fountain beyond the arched opening in the wall. My nose caught the scent of a burning meditation stick. "Thank you," I repeated.

"Now, rest." Lex patted my leg and rose from the edge of the bed. "As soon as you feel better, I'll send you over to the body-lab, so you can incarnate into anything you want."

"Wait—" I hesitated before voicing my request.

"Is there anything you need?"

"Yes, there is."

"What is it?"

"I'd like to maintain this body."

"But I thought…" Lex raised one eyebrow then, before leaving, said, "You can keep this body, of course." Before closing the door behind himself, he turned one last time. "I'm sending a keeper. He'll take care of you."

I didn't want a keeper. "Fido?"

"Your health-bot is being examined as we speak. Anything else?"

"No, thanks."

And he was gone.

Once alone, I swung my legs out of the bed, placed my feet on the heated surface of the dark silver flooring made of smooth slabs, and gingerly took a few steps in the octagonal room. I swooned, and steadied myself against one of the two columns framing the entry to the bath. The smaller room was equipped with all the amenities needed to take care of my current bodily needs. What I had at first thought was a fountain, was a steaming, ever-flowing shower carved into the rock wall. I discarded my clothes and entered the basin one foot at a time, testing the warmth of the water pooling on its floor. It was hot, and I had to wait a moment to get used to it, but once I did, I was glad for the heat. I sat on the polished seat protruding from the wall and bathed. Tears mingled with the stream of water, and I flattened my palms over my heart. Finally, I sobbed.

While I was showering, the keeper Lex had mentioned had come and left new clothes for me. I found them carefully folded in a neat pile of weightless fabric, sitting on my bed. Lex or the keeper had chosen for me garments resembling the ones I came in with, and I realized with a pang of guilt that they had gone the extra mile to make me feel at ease. I donned what at a first glance looked like a graphite, silvery-black Japanese kimono, and almost laughed at the reflection in the mirror when I wondered if Gaia would have liked it. My hair had grown during the voyage, and my long curls were dripping water onto the floor. I looked among the toiletries for something I could use to tie my hair and found a black leather ribbon. I looked at myself in the mirror once again and smiled sadly. Only a katana was missing from my costume.

A soft voice—coming seemingly from nowhere—intruded on my thoughts. "Please exit the room and follow me."

Outside, a young humanoid waited for me. He bowed as soon as I opened the door. "I hope the garments are to your satisfaction." Much smaller than me, the keeper had big, child-like eyes staring at me in awe.

I didn't know what to make of that. "They are perfect. Thank you."

The humanoid smiled. "It's an honor to be your keeper, sir."

His words made me uncomfortable. "Where to?" I looked at the long hallway stretching endlessly both ways. Lights shone at regular intervals on the white walls, amplifying the luminosity of the place. I passed my palms over a wall and found it cool and abrasive. I instinctively cleaned my hands on my pants.

"To the Council Room. The Wise Ancestors have gathered for your hearing." The keeper gestured for me to follow him down the hallway to the right.

I raised one eyebrow. "Already? I thought I would have talked with the Observer Council first."

"The Head of the Wise Ancestors believes it is not necessary for you to have two hearings." The awe I saw in his face a moment earlier was now reflected in his tone. My being Lex's pupil had that effect on people.

Not for long. Soon, Lex and the rest of the Wise Ancestors would discover my sin.

I fearfully followed my keeper, whose name I hadn't thought to ask. At first, I focused on every step I took in an environment I had failed to recognize. Once we progressed farther, the walls of the hallway changed from white to iridescent purple, their surface as smooth as a mirror. I looked at my reflection, and it came back distorted.

"We are almost there. We must pass the pink gardens and the azure alcoves." My escort gestured ahead and smiled reassuringly.

"So many things have changed since last time I was here." The architecture and fashion of the building was new to me. To my right, a section of the wall moved and revealed another hallway that opened to the outside. A glass fence was the only barrier between the few people strolling by and a long fall. The Wise Ancestors' compound towered over the plane of Tanis and its purple sea. In the distance, I could see the spirals of Kartena, one of Solo's megalopolises, where the Observers Academy shone as a beacon, catching the first light of the day and illuminating the buildings nearby. Despite the early hour, the aerial highways were already crowded. For a moment, the longing to be floating weightless in the sky brought me back to my cadet years and all the flights Kam, Areel, and I had taken. Many times, we had launched from the observatory balcony on the last floor of the Academy, spending hours riding the thermals with our monoflyers instead of spending time in the low-gravity gym. The first time I was caught, I argued with my superior that flying was a better way to exercise my new body than squatting for one hundred repetitions.

"Maybe later there will be time to visit." The keeper gently tugged at my left sleeve.

I heard his words but didn't move. A beam of pink light had caught my attention. It hit the transparent wall and came out on the other side in a rainbow of colors. I had missed the Solean dawns. People walked through the opening in the wall, then it closed behind them, hiding the other hallway from sight.

"We must go."

This time, I heeded his gentle order. Hastily walking toward the Council Room, I glanced in passing at the pink gardens and the azure alcoves, and my heart throbbed with renewed longing. I wished Gaia was with me. I wished I could share the beauty of my home with her. She would have liked the succulents hanging from balconies and the pools of swirling waters. I would have taken her flying over Kartena. I would have rented an alcove for us—

"We have arrived." The keeper stopped before a portal.

My eyes couldn't contain the whole sight of it. The imposing doorway was made of rock. An intricate design was carved into a white slab veined with pastel shades of red and orange. Circles ran through the whole surface, overlapping in places and creating a hypnotic sight. I blinked twice.

"You're expected." The keeper looked at the portal and tilted his head, motioning for me to enter.

The surface in front of me looked forbidding in its massive height and width. Feeling dwarfed by it, I hesitated.

"Your mental signature will open it." The keeper sounded envious. "Touch one of the circles."

I wanted the whole ordeal to be past already, but I was scared, and my hand shook when I raised it.

"I know. It's such an honor to be admitted into the Council Room."

I smiled at his misunderstanding. My palm pressed against the surface, and I stopped breathing. The circle I had chosen—the closest to my eyes—rotated around its center, spiraling into nothing. I found myself somewhere else. One moment I was in the hallway with a child-like keeper, and the next I was inside a room as grand as the portal had hinted it would be.

Once I adjusted to the bright light bathing the enormous chamber, I was surprised to find corporeals among the spectators sitting in the three-tiered dais ahead of me. At a second glance, I discovered they were all corporeal. I wasn't expecting that. If the protocol was still the same as it used to be, before being formally addressed, I should have a few moments to look around. Listening to the low hum coming from the audience, I slowly walked toward the center of the room, and there I stood, silently waiting for orders. I sensed the majestic weight of the Wise Ancestors' presence filling the place. I knew they were already testing me, and I maintained my stance without moving, letting only my eyes wander. From what I could see without moving my head, the Council Room apparently had no ceiling and merged with the outside floating garden in complete harmony. A bubbling spring emerged from the distant wall on my left. Its water formed a narrow stream and ran through the room, only to stop at the center of the mosaic flooring. The stream pooled in a shallow basin excavated from the rock beneath the mosaic tiles. For a brief moment, I wondered about the large presence of rock throughout a building that was higher than any skyscraper on Earth. Solo wasn't the planet I had left so many millennia ago. What else would be different?

Walk toward the Sharing Pool.

I was hit by the mental power of the united council and reeled back. The command was repeated, but this time, only Lex spoke, undoubtedly for my benefit. I reached the pool and looked into its water. Slim creatures resembling mermaids from Earth folklore swam in it. With the touch of their long fingers, they moved the surface in radiating rainbow-colored circles. Their long hair waving around them, their hands elegantly cutting the water, they appeared to be plucking the strings of harps. I was staring at the dazzling scene in the pool when I heard in my mind the creatures' thoughts. The rainbows amplified their mental reach like speakers. Every time one of the creatures reached for the outer edges of the rainbows, forming patterns in their languid dance, a new thought formed in my mind.

One of the circles—the biggest and most colorful—rippled twice. *My pupil, there is nothing to fear. Relax.*

I looked away from the pool and searched the audience for Lex. He sat at the center of the first row on the dais and was openly smiling at me.

I promise it will be painless. His voice came from my right. I turned in time to catch the last ripple of the big circle.

Other voices joined Lex's, and the circles, one by one, danced at the sound of their words.

Those are our auras.

My guide's statement confirmed what I had just understood. Still, I gasped.

This is a new ceremony. I didn't immediately recognize the voice.

I felt a stranger in my own home. After that exchange, silence ensued. The room was cold and white. The absence of sound enhanced my fear instead of assuaging it. My eyes went to the corporeal audience, which was mostly composed, from what I could see, of ethereals. Thinly elegant, the ethereal form had been the Ancestors' favorite incarnation choice before I left for Earth. They all looked like Lex. Something hadn't changed, at least.

I felt the Ancestors' light probing inside my mind. They were studying me, and the silence had a presence of its own. I shivered. After what seemed an eternity—judging from the painful stiffness in my legs—music filled the room. One of the mermaids—a beautiful, big-eyed, slim-bodied incarnation—floated out of the pool to hover before me. The creature raised one long arm and reached for my forehead while humming a lullaby in time with the music. The melody sent me into a trance. Unable to move a muscle in my body, I was conscious when I saw my aura leaving my body. The creature spun my aura like a thread around her index finger. I was terrified.

"It will be over soon." Lex spoke through the mermaid, who carefully deposited my aura in the pool. Once in the water, it uncoiled and became one of the circles. Paralyzed, I watched as all the creatures swam to the edge of the pool, and a merging activity ensued among the circles.

Beautiful patterns formed, colors aligning within the range of the same palette, reds with oranges and pinks, and blues with greens and violets. The result was an abstract painting that shifted every few seconds, like oil colors on water. I felt I should have been mesmerized by the experience, but I wasn't. In my trance, I couldn't estimate how long had passed, but I blinked, and the creature wasn't at my side anymore. I was whole again. After a moment of disorientation, I remembered the protocol and knelt down. Then I lowered my head, waiting for instructions.

A warm breeze brought Lex's whisper to my ears. "Your Ancestor Guide wishes for you to stand up and have a talk."

I obeyed and raised my head to face the ancient being who was like a father to me. "I am at *your* orders." I stressed the formal plural *you*, and I lowered my head again. Something had shifted in our dynamic. I wished he would call me "my pupil" again. His physical presence emanated greatness, and I was dwarfed by his company.

He proceeded slowly, signaling me to follow him. We stepped outside onto a floating garden and strolled toward an outdoor studio, where he sat on a carved stone bench. Before us flowed a stream full of purple fishes, flanked by luscious vegetation that gave us some privacy. Above us, the sun was already high in the sky. The session had lasted longer than I'd thought. He made a come-hither gesture with his finger, and I knelt on the ground at his feet, on the soft green grass, the dew from the stems wetting the fabric of my pants.

"Come, sit with me."

Despite his reassuring smile, something was out of place in the way he was dealing with me. I raised myself from the ground and gingerly sat on the edge of the bench. We were face to face, but I couldn't bear his gaze.

"We will be forever grateful to you. You can't imagine the extent of what your discovery means for Solo, but we can."

I didn't dare to say anything. The other members of the Council had reached us and were standing in a semi-circle around the bench, waiting for their elder to voice their resolution.

"Shortly, we will share the news about your findings with the population." He paused, his eyes unfocused for a moment. "Your fate has been decided." He hesitated before adding, "You've put us in an unprecedented situation."

Some of the Ancestors nodded sadly.

"You deserve great honor and fame. Thanks to you, we finally have a lead on how to solve the puzzle of our lost history."

A mild wind moved the foliage of the trees in the garden. Leaves fell on the ground like dry rain. White flowers followed the green-yellow leaves on the meadow. Fleshy white petals disintegrated in my fingers as one little perfumed flower hit my hand by accident.

Tears rolled down my face.

Lex gave me a moment and then spoke again. "Your service will never be forgotten. Your name will be written in our history books as the one that gave hope back to his people." He stared at me, and his eyes were full of love and regret. "You are a hero." Another sad smile stretched his pale lips. "And as a hero, your name will be celebrated because your people deserve it."

I knew he would then deliver my judgment, and my limbs went numb.

"What we found in your memories, unfortunately, we can't forgive."

My vision was a blur of clouded images already.

"You will not be allowed to return to Earth to finish your mission."

I had expected as much, but the pain flared anew.

"Considering the great amount of distress the idea of leaving Earth unprotected is causing you, we found your replacement already."

A sob escaped my mouth. At least I hadn't damned the human race.

"As for your fate, you have left us no choice. You are no longer part of the Observer Army. You will spend the rest of your life in exile on the planet Silenzio. The planet's magnetic field will make it impossible for you to communicate with anybody." He stood up, and silently moved away.

When I didn't react, another Ancestor came close to me. "The sentence starts immediately."

I had been dismissed.

At the end of the path, Lex turned and looked at me one last time. I felt his presence inside my mind, and then he talked to me using our private channel. *I'll miss you dearly, my pupil.* On his diaphanous skin shone a single silvery tear.

A few minutes later, I was outside the Council Room, my back to the portal, facing my keeper. He escorted me to my room, and I was glad for his silence. I felt drained, not able to think coherently. I went to the bathroom, took off my clothes, and entered the steaming water, hoping to dissolve. I sat on the floor hugging my knees and let the hot water soak my body until I lost contact with reality. My mind drifted for some time like a lonely kite at the mercy of a capricious wind, without purpose or knowledge, just existing. The keeper came at regular intervals to bring meals and drinks. I thanked him, waited for him to go away, and then flushed the food down the toilet. Soon, I blissfully lost consciousness.

9

The keeper found me with a smile on my face.

He frowned but didn't ask why I was smiling. Instead, he took my wrist between his thumb and index finger then rushed away. I heard the door open and close.

A few minutes later, the same sounds were followed by hurried steps. "Here, drink." A tall glass was pushed into my hands, but I stared at it in confusion. "You need to hydrate yourself." The rim of the glass was pressed against my lips, and fresh liquid wet them. The keeper coaxed the drink into my mouth and patiently waited until I drank the entire contents of the glass. "I should have checked on you more closely," he murmured while checking my vitals again. Reassured I wasn't going to die on his watch, he helped me walk to the bathroom. "You need a bath."

"I can bathe myself. Thanks." I swatted his hands away when he reached for my clothes and raised the hem of my shirt. "I'd like some privacy."

He gave me a worried look but then bowed slightly and exited the room. I was in and out of the shower in a matter of minutes and found something clean to wear, another kimono-style tunic, on my freshly made bed. Once fully clothed, with my helper firmly at my heels, I headed for the bathroom again, where I teetered before the mirror. I almost couldn't recognize the haunted face and the lifeless eyes staring back at me. The keeper tied my hair with the black leather ribbon I had around my wrist. I didn't remember when I had put it there.

"Now what?" I asked the mirror.

The keeper thought I was asking him. "I was asked to escort you to meet your replacement."

I nodded and silently followed the guy outside. He headed to the opposite side of the hallway we had taken last time and then took several left turns. We stopped before a large landing enclosed in a transparent dome. It was crowded, people aligning and hurrying at dizzying velocity, seemingly riding fluorescent lines on the floor. On the far wall, I could see the entrances to several tunnels, each one a different color. The tunnels continued outside as sky bridges and stretched for a considerable distance. I couldn't see where they ended.

"We must ride the lines. Your appointment is three buildings over." He raised his chin toward a faraway point behind the transparent dome, but I couldn't see anything.

I shrugged. "Okay."

He then lowered his eyes to the floor and showed me the ivory strips dotting the colored rails at regular intervals. "You must latch your shoes on them." He proceeded to step onto the rail, and I heard a *click*. "Like this."

I followed his instructions.

He looked pleased and then pointed at the crossroad ahead. "We'll take the magenta line." We shuffled toward the chosen line. "Ready?"

I wasn't, but I didn't mention it. After the first acceleration, I found the experience pleasant. It felt as if the rest of the building was moving and we were just standing by. Had I not been so utterly beside myself, I would have appreciated all the marvels my society had created while I was gone. We were soon inside the magenta tunnel, suspended miles high above the shores. The only thing I could think of was that Gaia would have loved the ride.

At the end of the tunnel, we stopped in a naturally lit plaza of immense proportions. The place was full of greenery and flowers. At its center lay a pool of dark-blue water, this one also excavated from the rocky surface beneath the flooring. It seemed that Soleans had grown fond of water since I had left. The place was full of people busy in their daily activities, running, walking, and riding lines in groups of two or more but seldom alone. The illumination in the plaza came from a glass ceiling. I looked up and felt the warmth of sun rays on my face. A few clouds played in the sky. The way the light played with the shadows reminded me, with a sudden ache, of my last afternoon in Seattle.

A buzz of excitement traveled around the place. Like a swelling wave, every head in the plaza turned around at the same time. I turned as well, incapable of sharing the crowd's feelings but puzzled nonetheless. I blinked my watery eyes several times when I realized what the exhilaration was all about.

My face and my Solean name were being projected on an immense screen dominating the farther wall from where we were standing. A sad smile appeared on my ashen image. It probably mirrored the expression I had on my face at the moment. Lex had promised that my name and my discovery would have been celebrated. However, it wasn't the name I wanted to be remembered by.

My keeper discreetly turned the other way, giving me some privacy to wipe my tears. Then he led me through a smaller hallway while the crowd started applauding and everybody looked for someone else to hug, tears of joy all around.

A day to celebrate, a day to remember.

The Day.

I was the only one not crying for joy.

I walked beside my keeper, unseeing, for several minutes. We stopped before a plain door, and he pressed his hand on the white material wrapping the frame. He waited a moment and then sang a series of notes. The door disappeared before my eyes without a sound.

"You can go inside. I'll wait here until you're done."

I thanked him and entered the room without knowing what to expect, whom to expect. Once inside, I was surprised to find a familiar aura in a human body. "Areel."

Relief possessed my mind, and I felt hope for the first time since I had left Earth. Wanting to say so many things at once, and not finding adequate words to convey my sentiments, I strode through the space dividing us and fell at his feet. "Not everything is lost." Even kneeling on the floor, I felt dizzy. "My Gaia is going to have a chance."

With dark, straight hair, black almond-shaped eyes, my friend resembled an Asian knight with tan skin. He looked at me and winced at my appearance. "Elios—"

Elios.

A knot in my throat didn't allow me to talk.

"I'm so sorry for you. I was contacted before you left Earth, and I was told I would take your place leading the mission on Earth."

I shook my head and then smiled at him. "I'm happy they chose you."

"I'm sorry," he repeated and then hesitated before adding anything else.

His eyes went to my temples, and I understood. "I'm not ready." I knew I had to brief him on his new mission. "I can tell you."

It was Areel's time to smile at me, but his attempt was thin. "I don't have a choice but to ask you for a Share."

I knew he was telling the truth, but the memories of Gaia were so pure, so intimately mine, I could barely stand the idea of someone else experiencing them. "Elios is not just my name; it has become my true essence. I am not completely Solean anymore." The next thing I was going to say was pure blasphemy. "I don't want to share my whole essence with you." I slowly and deliberately enunciated my words, which sounded like a slap.

Areel's face, the unfortunate recipient of that slap, went blank.

"I am ashamed of myself, but there are parts of me… images so dear to me that I don't want even you to see."

He blinked. "You refused to share with me and Kam before, but I thought—" He looked at me with hurt in his eyes. "We thought it was a moment. Maybe you weren't feeling well. You were exhausted. I didn't realize the extent of the… problem."

I reeled at that last word. I didn't have a problem. "I have memories so beautiful I want to save and preserve them like a treasure. They are etched inside my very heart, and the only person I want to share them with is Gaia." The picture of a delicate white lily withering before my eyes formed in my mind.

Areel was looking at me with a different expression, and for a moment I saw pity on his face.

"I am not fallen." I stood up slowly because my head was spinning, and I went to sit on the little red couch in the corner. Areel, who had maintained an unsettling silence through my emotional blathering, went to the sink in the corner and brought me back an intricately decorated blown-glass cup. I accepted the offering with a nod of my head and drank the red juice. The beverage was sweet and sour and perfectly summed up my feelings at the moment. "I'm going to pay for my sins. I broke a sacred oath. I left Gaia. I knew from the beginning I wouldn't find a way out of my misery." I raised my chin to look at Areel. This battle was already lost, and he and I both knew it.

He moved his hand toward my forehead but stopped halfway. "Elios, my brother, may I have your permission to touch you? Please."

I couldn't have denied it anyway. It was noble of him to ask. Forestalling wasn't going to impede the inevitable. I raised my head to meet his hand.

The Share lasted longer than I thought bearable. I kept my eyes shut, enduring the process with the last shred of dignity I had, while biting my lips. Meanwhile, I was transferring all my experiences, my thoughts, in the same exact way I had felt them. Sharing worked like having a realistic and detailed first-person dream. Areel was looking at Gaia with my eyes, feeling the same shivers that had assailed my body when she had mirrored my actions the first time.

Areel experienced my unbearable longing for Gaia while he was looking at her hazel eyes with my intensity. My good friend was unknowingly invading my privacy in a way I hadn't even thought possible, making me feel angry and powerless. I felt a sharp sting of resentment toward him and my own society, which were putting me through such an ordeal, while physical pain burnt mercilessly through a hole in my stomach. The knuckles of my fisted hands became white. I started feeling violently nauseated. The sensation worsened until I saw a white curtain covering my vision while my skin felt unnaturally cold. When he finally removed his hand from my skin, I fell on the floor and passed out.

Elios—

You, come here. I need help!

Elios, wake up!

What's happening to you? What's happening to him?

"Elios?"

"Hmm…" I opened my eyes and found Areel looking at me worriedly. To his right, the keeper held the cup I had drunk from.

They both sighed in relief when I tried to stand up.

"Easy. Let me help you." Areel put his arm under my right armpit and gently pulled me up.

My face and the tunic front were wet.

"You wouldn't come out of it." Areel pointed his chin at the cup the keeper was still holding. "I think he needs something to drink."

The keeper nodded and went to the sink where Areel had filled the cup earlier and came back with more for me.

I thanked him and brought the cup to my lips, but my head was still swaying. After a moment, I managed to drink a few sips of the concoction. "Would you please wait outside for a moment?" I asked my keeper. "I need to talk to my friend alone."

"Sure. Take your time." He turned and exited the room.

This time, Areel started the conversation. "I hope you feel better. Don't be worried about your… my mission. I will be as scrupulous as you would have. I promise."

I smiled at him. "I know." I closed my eyes and willed the tears away. "After me, you are probably the best one for the job."

"Elios, what I saw…" He paused a long moment. "I don't have a name for what you feel, but it is something so strong and so holy in its own way, I can't find in my heart the courage to judge you." He looked at me then with nothing but compassion in his eyes. "I hope you'll find some peace where they are sending you."

The corner of my mouth automatically rose in a glimmer of a smile; at least something good had come from my torture: a bit of comprehension that words alone couldn't have achieved.

"Elios, I am so sorry for you. You deserved a better fate."

"Thank you." I felt depleted of any energy. Leaning my body against the wall, I pushed myself up and slowly walked toward the hallway. The door was already open, and my keeper was waiting for me. I looked back to Areel for the last time and again thanked him silently. Areel raised his hand to bid me farewell. A sad moment for both of us. I knew I would never see Areel or speak to him again, and I realized how much our chats in the Astral World had meant to me.

I automatically followed the keeper, and we reached the Ancestors' compound and my room in what could have been the blink of an eye to me. Outside my room, I found two Superior Observers waiting for me.

"It's time," one of the two, the older looking, said to me.

The keeper stepped in front of me. "Can't the voyage be delayed a few clicks? He doesn't feel well."

The second officer shook his head. "We are here to escort him to the dock."

"But I'm sure that if you ask his Ancestor Guide, he would tell you—"

"His Ancestor Guide gave the order." The older officer gave me a sad smile.

I looked at my keeper. "Thank for your kindness, but I'm well enough and eager to leave as soon as possible."

In less than one hour, I was already inside the sleek silver shuttle that would take me to Silenzio—my final destination.

"Welcome aboard *Her Lady of Solo*," the captain of my ride said after we were officially presented. "For the next seven weeks, you will be our guest." He made a grand gesture encompassing the whole of the small passenger ship. "It's two weeks to reach the first wormhole, three to reach the second, and it will take another two weeks to enter Silenzio's atmosphere. You can either sleep the whole time or be awake, but you won't be allowed to contact anybody in the astral world."

I eyed the space that would be the antechamber of my more permanent prison and found it soothing. *Her Lady of Solo* was small but luxurious, all sinuous lines and relaxing colors.

The captain gave me an appraising look. "Of course, we are both aware I can't enforce the ban. It's entirely up to you to obey."

"I prefer to remain awake, and I give my word I won't contact anybody."

The captain nodded, relieved. "I hoped you would say that." He pointed at a row of seats facing the cockpit and the big window behind it. "You'll have a nice view from there."

I chose one of the seats and strapped in, waiting for takeoff.

"You are free to do what you like on the ship. We'll try our best to make your ride comfortable." He gave me another look and added, "Your punishment is rather severe. I'm sorry."

The captain and crew of the shuttle were the last people who were ever going to ever talk to me, and they knew it.

* * *

The flight went as smoothly as expected, and seven weeks later, Her Lady of Solo landed on Silenzio. I was disembarked with enough food and supplies to live for eons to come—and my Fido. When the captain opened the health-bot crate and revealed its contents to me, I wept. The crew looked elsewhere when I hugged the piece of metal. The captain commanded the crew to build a shelter for me and kept asking for changes on its layout. Eventually, my future abode was finished and he ran out of excuses to hover and had to leave.

"I wish I could have done more for you." He waved his hand before disappearing behind the closing ship's gate.

I watched as *Her Lady of Solo* gracefully took off and disappeared behind the purple clouds of Silenzio. "We are alone." I looked down at Fido. "I am alone."

Completely alone for the first time in my life.

10

Severed first from Gaia and then from my own species, any reason to live eluded me. I just lay on the ground outside my shelter and didn't bother to go inside.

I slept for great lengths of time. Fido—which in the meantime had been altered with the addition of several arms—had been programmed to administer sedatives to keep me calm. I should have been outraged, but it didn't matter to me because I didn't care about anything anymore. When for the first time Fido approached me with a syringe, I let it do to me whatever it had been programmed for. At my lowest point, I never felt truly awake, and I probably didn't even have the physical strength to rebel against the health-bot. My mind was a blank slate that never got filled with fully constructed ideas or feelings, but just with vague remembrances of things that once had meant something to me. My body was but a shell, nothing more than an empty vessel, kept functioning without my knowing why exactly, daily enduring the offense of being alive.

Time passed.

One day, I opened my eyes and took a look at my surroundings. I couldn't say whether I liked it or disliked it. I didn't have enough strength to make that kind of mental decision. Then, something caught my interest, and that by itself would have been something worth celebrating... had I remembered how.

I touched my face and found it wet. My hand slowly went to my hair; it was wet as well. While I was checking the rest of my body, I felt my skin being caressed by a warm embrace, and I raised my head. The simple act proved to be too much for me. I lost my focus and had to lie back again. I forced myself to remain conscious, and after a few seconds I opened my eyes for a second time. From the green sky above, silver drops of water fell to the ground and on me. It took me several minutes to process the information and realize it was raining. I didn't take shelter. Instead, I lay on the grass with my weak arms painfully raised to the heavens and my dry mouth open. I welcomed the replenishing warm water on my skin. I loved the rain.

Once, a million years before, I had played with the water and the elements to make someone happy. It had been the most beautiful time of my life. The water had woken both my body and my mind. Soon exhausted by the act of articulating thoughts, I lowered my eyes to the ground and found myself facing a pool of water. My reflection was terrifying.

I was skeletal. My hair hung lifeless and almost colorless, my eyes were dark and sunken, and my clothes were the only thing in order because Fido had taken care of them and compelled me to change every other day. I was clean and shaved for the same reason. I stupidly tried to stand up and couldn't. I pushed myself to a more manageable sitting position. My achievement lasted the whole of five minutes, then my head started spinning. But at that point, some kind of survival instinct had finally kicked in, and I decided I couldn't keep destroying myself passively. Maybe the idea of feeling something again stirred me from my catatonic state. Or maybe I had just reached the bottom of my desperation. Either way, I decided to keep on living.

Getting better proved to be, all in all, a long and strenuous process. Several days passed before I could stand upright for more than a few minutes at a time. Meditation helped me to focus on positive ideas, while my robotic companion took care of the physical aspects of my convalescence. Little by little, I regained some tone in my muscles by taking advantage of the healing power of the sun. I went for little walks around the shelter. Even though on those first attempts, I didn't succeed in going very far, my strolls made me aware of the landscape surrounding me.

The planet where I had been dumped was magnificent. In the distance, I could see rivers, pools of crystalline water, terraced green hills, and beautiful dawns and sunsets, without the darkness of the night on Earth.

"Such beauty, and we are the only ones enjoying it." Meanwhile, I had resumed my one-way conversations with Fido. "Can you believe I haven't seen a single bug flying?" The only sounds I could hear were natural: the distant river slowly following the serene terrain, the raindrops caressing my skin, solitary leaves playing with the gentle wind.

And in this maddening beauty I slowly spent my sentence to life in solitude.

Once my physical condition had sufficiently improved, and I was able to spend most of the diurnal hours awake, I started practicing a few mantras I had learned at the beginning of my training at the Academy. Those mantras were repetitions of mental exercises meant to overcome psychological limits. As freshmen, we used them to strengthen our communication skills. It was useless on Silenzio, but I had always liked the sensation I was left with after that kind of deep meditation.

One morning, maybe inspired by the soft rain, I idly started thinking of Gaia. I visualized her, not a mere memory of what I remembered, but her whole essence. I played for a while with the representation of her, and it took a few hours to reach some resemblance. At the end of that first attempt, her image looked like a picture in sepia. "Isn't she the most beautiful thing you have ever seen?" The image vanished before Fido could answer me, but the exercise left me with a sense of peace I hadn't experienced in a long time.

After that first attempt, I exercised my mind to create better images. I alternated the mental drawing with the mantras, and I realized two things after a while: first, Gaia's images were becoming more and more realistic, and second, my mind felt sharper. Every day, I pushed the exercises and the mantras a little bit further than the day before, in a constant process of betterment, which proved to be beneficial for my health, both physical and mental. Days, weeks, and probably months passed while I was busy with my hobby, and then one day I realized in a daze that the image staring back at me was not only extremely detailed but almost lifelike. I had created a tridimensional representation of Gaia. The image lasted longer than the previous times and left me wanting for much more.

I immediately made another attempt, but I was stopped by an odd tingle at the base of my neck. At first, it was just an unimpressive nudge. I focused on a mantra, sure that the feeling would go away. Instead, the nudge grew in intensity until I could no longer ignore it. When my neck tingled as if connected to an electric outlet, I was forced to give the phenomenon my undivided attention. My immediate reaction was to try a slightly different mantra, a variation of the ones I had been practicing. I thought the new exercise would help me reach the deeper relaxation I needed to untangle that physiological and emotional knot. For all my good intentions, the nudge didn't vanish, and I redoubled my efforts. When the electricity started radiating from the base of my neck to the rest of my skull, I wondered if I should let Fido know something was wrong with me. I decided to make a last attempt and combined the mantras for awareness with the mental exercises I used to create Gaia's images, which I already knew had a calming effect on my psyche. After several minutes, the sharp needles in my head vanished, and I was left with the most realistic image of Gaia I had ever created. Without thinking, I reached out my hand to touch the 3-D rendition, and the image moved.

"It's impossible."

Gaia—her image—looked at me, her mouth opening and closing as if she was talking to me. No sound escaped from her lips, but I knew she was mouthing my name. The Gaia looking back at me wasn't as joyous as I remembered. Her eyes were still ever-changing hazel, but her hair was longer, and she looked tired. "This is not my doing." I would have never imagined her that way. I blinked, and the image was gone, but for a moment, it had been like seeing Gaia again.

Part of me knew I had lost my grip on reality, but when you are faced with eons to live the way I was meant to—alone and in exile— you don't disdain help... even when help is a figment of your imagination. I wasn't the first person gone crazy trying to create a companion to ease his solitude. I just had a more trained mind.

More time passed.

I focused on being upbeat, but sometimes sadness prevailed, and I practiced the mantras to balance the dark urges to let myself go again. After a few times, I noticed there was a pattern to my ups and downs, and I was summoning my fictitious Gaia at regular intervals. But I was more interested in the instant gratification her imaginary presence gave me rather than elaborating on why it happened when it happened. Session after session, Gaia's image changed. Soon, she was smiling more and looked different. She didn't always wear the same outfit. It shouldn't have been possible, but I blissfully accepted the anomaly without asking too many questions.

One time, Gaia wore a pink shirt I thought I had seen on her. Other times, Gaia wore clothes I didn't remember. All her clothes had something in common I could not pinpoint at the beginning, then I realized that everything Gaia wore could be used to sleep in. I was imagining her in pajamas. I had an explanation for this. In my loneliness, the longing for intimacy was getting harder to ignore. I wanted to be close to Gaia, closer than I had ever dared before, and my subconscious was acting out.

Satisfied by the explanation I had concocted, I let myself fully enjoy the experience. With every session, she became more real. Every time, I futilely talked to her. I talked to her as much as I talked to Fido. I normally greeted her, and then I usually told her about my day. Once, I described to her my hike to the nearest terraced hill. "It has been so long since I exercised in earnest. It felt wonderful to be tired at the end of the day. And the lake at the top of the hill—you would've loved it. The water was so cold I thought I would freeze. But then I dove in and felt like never before. The water was a shade between green and blue. I wish you were here with me."

After a while, I realized I could finally sleep at night, and that came as a nice surprise. I had been sedated for so long that I didn't think I would ever be able to sleep without chemical help from my robotic companion. I proceeded to divide my time in day and night slots. I needed rules and schedules: when I could eat, when I could meditate, when I could see Gaia. I couldn't afford to lose more weight and sleep. I had to take care of my body. The next session, I told Gaia all about it, and she smiled.

When my body was finally able to walk for longer distances, I left the shelter to draw a map of the territory. It was a sunny morning. I felt ready to give my life a new spin, and I wanted to start by getting to know my new home better. From the little I had seen and the curvature of its horizon, Silenzio was a smaller planet than Earth. It didn't have a clear night and day division or seasons, which led me to think that its rotation and revolution times were long, which was incongruent with the apparently small size of the planet. I found Silenzio full of mystery and poetic beauty. In truth, I wrote something about it I later recited to Gaia. Her face illuminated at my rhymes, and she even mouthed a smiling *Thank you.*

Meanwhile, I had covered lots of ground and filled several pages with drawings of Silenzio's landscape. I found that, several walking days north of the shelter, the distant peaks of a mountain range came into view. A few days later, still keeping north, I came across a system of rivers. Taking advantage of Fido's new appendages, I build a rudimentary raft using the wood I cut from a nearby copse. The trees were small, and their trunks were barely bigger than my arms. I bundled them with the softer branches to create a platform big enough for Fido and me, hoping the bindings wouldn't come apart at the first taste of water.

It took me from dawn to dusk to put the raft together, but when I contemplated my handiwork lying on the ground, I was proud. "What do you know? I'm not completely useless after all." Fido blinked in agreement and then warned me I was low on sugar. I offered it my right arm, and dinner was injected into my bloodstream—as breakfasts and lunches had been administered to me since I had landed on Silenzio. "Never cared for solid food, but all this physical activity must have triggered something in my human brain, because I'd give anything for a piece of warm bread right now." I sighed at the thought of freshly baked bread straight from the oven to my mouth. Then a different type of hunger made me sigh. "Time to visit Gaia."

Over the past few days, I had entered the deep concentration I needed to recall Gaia's image with increasing ease. Almost as simple as breathing in and out. I closed my eyes, tuned out Silenzio, and concentrated on the object of my desires. One moment I was alone, the next Gaia was looking at me, a big smile on her face. The resolution of the image had improved to such a level that I could have sworn I smelled the fragrance of the shampoo she had used to wash her long hair: vanilla and grapefruit.

Her mouth opened and closed, her eyes lit with excitement, and I wished I could hear what she was saying. When she paused, I started talking. It took me longer than usual to narrate my latest adventure, but her image stayed long enough to let me finish. When I finally went to sleep, I was satisfied with my day.

The next day, I woke energized and in a good mood. After getting my dose of nutrients, I tested my new means of transportation. When I saw that the fruit of my labor was sound enough to withstand the river waters, I carefully placed Fido in the middle of the raft and then joined it. Several hours—and scares—later, I found navigating peaceful.

Several months passed.

We—Fido, Gaia, and I—traveled by water until we reached a different geological landscape. The climate was warmer. The trees and the vegetation were typical of a tropical region. Big, colorful flowers dotted the luscious bushes, and a sweet scent permeated the stillness of the nights. Another month of lazy navigation passed by. The days became hot, and I had to stop to build an awning for the raft. Soon after, the river ended its journey—and ours—at a pinkish-purple sea.

The sun was low on the horizon. The gentle white waves broke the sea's surface in a hypnotic pattern. I brought the raft to the shore, secured Fido on a high dune of fine, golden sand and ran toward the sea again. Ignoring my health-bot's blinking warnings, I removed my clothes and dove into the warm water. For hours, I floated like a leaf, enjoying the sun on my skin, letting the water cover my eyes and cleanse away a tiredness that wasn't only physical. Once tired of swimming, I relaxed on the hot sand and let my mind fly away.

And then I saw Gaia, without having summoned her image.

She was there, beside me on the sand, resting, the salt drying on her skin, leaving white stripes on her body and on her face. Her hair was lighter than the last time I had imagined her, the color of her skin darker, the muscles on her body more defined. When she opened her eyes, I could see that the sun was filling them with pure gold. Her lips were dry and a darker shade of pink.

Gaia moved one hand toward me, and I heard her calling my name aloud. "Elios?"

My name was the first sound I heard on Silenzio.

I moved closer to her. "Gaia?"

Her image disappeared the same way it had materialized.

That night, I went to sleep deeply confounded. But I didn't sleep for long. Not even an hour later, I saw her again. She looked happier than usual, and I could almost hear her talking to me. I thought I even understood a word or two. Then she smiled one more time, said, "See you later," and disappeared once again.

That time, I knew it wasn't a dream. I could have sworn that I had done nothing to start the process. I had been trained to keep my mind in a dormant state when I slept. I could dream if I wanted, but I couldn't activate any mental process that needed any form of deep meditation.

Maybe there was something about Silenzio that triggered my delusions without me being the wiser. Solitude could defeat even the strongest person. "Yes, that must be it." Then I had another, completely different thought. *What if—*

I couldn't even dare to say it to myself. But what if I was right? Yes, solitude could have been the cause of my insanity. But when in extreme situations, one's mind can stretch to uncharted limits and overcome the biggest obstacles. Desperation, when properly channeled, can break boundaries nobody thought possible to break. My sentiments for Gaia were strong enough. *What if I have found a way to reach her through time and space?* "You think it is not possible."

Fido didn't react to my statement.

"You have never heard of it. But there is always a first time for everything. Isn't there?"

A faint hope that I was right slowly crept into my heart… until I was certain of it.

11

"I have found a way to communicate with Gaia," I proclaimed to all and sundry two days later. It didn't matter that only Fido was there to witness my joy. I didn't have a doubt about the certainty of my words anymore. Gaia had contacted me again, without me prompting the communication.

When I realized she could see me, I became self-conscious of my appearance, but thanks to the physical activity I had been engaging in since my departure from the shelter, my muscles had gained back their definition, and my skin had a healthier color. I didn't have a mirror, but I was sure my eyes weren't sunken and lifeless anymore. My hair had grown long and was constantly in the way. The salt in the air made combing impossible, so I started braiding it.

After discovering I wasn't alone in the universe, my routine changed. I left my nomadic life and built a new shelter. I even tried to differentiate my diet and used Fido to test whether the berries and fruits I picked up were compatible with my system. I exercised my mind by meditating three times a day, and I reached for Gaia every evening after dinner. Sometimes, it was Gaia who activated the process. She always looked excited to see me and eager to share her day through a few audible words and signals of her hands. She showed me her new outfits or a new hairstyle. Once, she gestured for me to turn around so she could see my braided hair.

With time, verbal communication improved and yet remained erratic. Sometimes, we could talk for several minutes; other times, we just had to nod at each other. But I didn't complain. We had achieved the impossible.

One afternoon, she called me earlier than usual. I was fresh from my last meditation, and my mind was particularly sharp.

"I'm working on rescuing you." Gaia's words were but a whisper, but by now I had learned how to read her lips.

I thought I had understood as much in one of our previous conversations. I didn't have the heart to tell her that rescuing me wasn't a possibility. I smiled. "How?"

"I found another link between Earth and Solo."

Despite everything, I was curious. "What is it?"

She talked for a few minutes, but in her excitement, she moved, her lips blurred, and I couldn't decipher what she said. A fragment of a longer sentence reached me. "Areel is helping me."

I was taken aback by that last statement. "Areel is there? With you?"

She nodded. "He came to meet me a few months ago." She smiled, said something else I didn't hear, and then added, "You'll be free soon." She blew a kiss with her hand. "I love you." Her image faded, became transparent, and then disappeared altogether. Although the quality of our meetings had constantly improved, their length was still beyond our decisional power.

Some days later, during one of our encounters, she wasn't alone. Areel and her friend Sara were in the room with her. At the sight of Areel, I was overwhelmed with joy. I had never thought being so happy was possible, but for a moment, I had everything I needed. Areel and I tried to talk to each other, but the audio was off, and soon enough their images disappeared.

Later, Gaia contacted me again, by herself, and we talked about their latest discovery, an Etruscan bronze spear with a Solean inscription. I was intrigued by that detail and I wished I could talk to Areel about it, but the occasion never presented itself. I tried to call him several times, in fact, but I was never able to summon him as I could Gaia.

Life passed, and for a blessed, long while, I was content with what I had made of it. But one day, Gaia's image materialized, and I knew something was wrong with her. She was visibly distressed, and her eyes were red with tears.

"I love you…" she whispered and then disappeared. This time, her leaving was different, as if she had been swallowed by a vacuum into a state of non-existence. I contacted Gaia right away, but she didn't answer. At first, I tried to keep my worries at bay and called her every two or three hours. Then I called her the whole night without results. I went for a swim, came back, and tried again. And again… and again… and again…

Over the next four days, I tried nonstop, mornings, evenings, and nights to no avail. I went through my relaxing mantras multiple times a day but failed to achieve the desired result. I had too much time to think. All kinds of scenarios ran through my worried mind, none of them comforting. I went from one hypothesis to another and then back again to "Lex discovered what I did, and he's punishing me." My head hurt so much I had to accept chemical help from Fido.

On the fifth day, I had worked myself into a state of worried frenzy. I had spent the whole previous night slumbering only a few minutes at a time. I had just closed my eyes again when a loud sound startled me. I jumped up, scared, looking right and left, then saw a comet was falling toward the mountain range I had left behind so many months ago. I could see its tail on fire; first it was bright orange, and then it became blue and green, reacting with the atmosphere. At the last moment, the comet changed course before crashing on Silenzio, as though it was trying to avoid a collision.

"Have you ever heard of an astral body changing direction like that?" Fido didn't even blink its annoying lights. "Thought so myself." The comet slowed down almost imperceptibly, but it was still too fast and hit the ground with a blast.

At the same moment, a sudden feeling of anguish broke into my thoughts. Fear of darkness as I had never experienced in my life left me breathless. As suddenly as it had manifested itself, the phenomenon ceased, leaving me with the certainty that I had felt Gaia's fear. For a fleeting moment, she had been within me, and I now felt her absence like a physical blow to my chest. She was gone, and I knew she wasn't coming back. Something had happened to her. The pain in my heart intensified, and I knelt on the sand. Fido was immediately by my side, its arms reaching for my right forearm. I was beside myself and didn't feel the needle, but in a matter of a few heartbeats, the sedative worked. Later, when the opiate's effects vanished and a new form of anxiety replaced the stupor I had felt, I looked at the sea for help.

I jumped from a low cliff and dove into the deepest blue under the superficial purple. I stayed there as long as I could without losing consciousness. Beautiful, multicolored corals and sea plants welcomed me on the bottom. A rainbow of purples, reds, yellows, and oranges helped me regain some clarity of mind. When my lungs screamed for air, I swam back to the surface, went to the beach, collected the few things I needed, and I walked toward the mountains, followed by Fido.

* * *

It took me a month to find the "meteor."

When I finally reached the source of the pyrotechnical show I had seen from the beach, I was relieved I had been right all along. Before my tired eyes was a spaceship that had excavated a big hole in the lowland just a few kilometers south of the mountain range.

The black spaceship was covered in an opaque alloy that seemed to absorb light. The vessel, tubular in shape with two cylinders attached under its belly, looked somehow antiquated, but it had also taken a big hit in the landing. I approached it carefully. The hatch was already open. It had probably opened at the moment of the collision. Or its crew had done it. The opening was at my chest level, and I had to hoist myself up, using Fido as a step. Barely breathing for fear of warning anybody, I tiptoed inside. The antechamber was dark. I waited for my eyes to get used to the dim light, and then I saw the place was deserted, its floor covered in dust. I followed the narrow hallway from stern to bow.

The ship wasn't big and didn't have a cargo bay. From what I could see in my hasty perusal, it looked like a recreational, possibly privately owned vessel. I entered each room I found, but the four cabins were as deserted as the antechamber. Nobody was in the storage room; nobody in the gym; nobody in the hydroponic pod. Finally, I reached the command center and couldn't help but gasp. Sitting in the two chairs facing the cockpit were two mechanical servants hovering over two still bodies. The ship owners were larger than average humans, their facial features thin but very much humanoid.

They were holding hands.

I walked around the chairs to take a look at them. A lump formed in my throat, and a strange discomfort assailed my stomach as I approached them. Their united hands told a sad tale. I had been ready to fight for my life, to beg if necessary, but I hadn't expected a love story tragically ended. When I finally faced them, tears swelled in my eyes. The one with feminine traits was pregnant.

They belonged to one of the most beautiful races I had ever seen, with elongated fairy-like features, mother-of-pearl-colored skin, and gentle expressions on their faces. They both had long hair. The woman had a mane of blond curls intricately decorated with flowers and ribbons while the man had darker hair, straight and tied in a ponytail. They wore simply cut dresses in pale hues of sand and green.

I couldn't help myself and touched the woman's belly. Despite her stillness, she was unnaturally warm and soft. A small thud resonated under my fingers. In my mind, I saw the image of a small being, almost fully formed, a baby girl. Without notice, the woman opened her eyes, startling me. She looked at me and said something in a language I had never heard before. She kept chirping sentences in a melodic tone, which almost sounded like singing, then she finally decided to talk to me in signs. She indicated the male first then looked at me. She repeated the signal twice then pointed her hand toward me and her companion.

"You want me to touch him? Is that it?" I went to him and waited for her consent. Meanwhile, the two mechanical servants, probably health-bots like my Fido, had begun a frenzy of activity around the woman.

She touched one of the two bots, and they both quieted down, then she looked at me and chirped something that sounded like, "Ka—ii to'a, Rah," and lowered her head.

"I take that as a yes." I touched the male's forehead. A mere blink later, he opened his eyes.

He stared at me in surprise and then looked for the woman. As their eyes met, a smile appeared on his mouth, and he chirped a long sequence of notes. At her short answer, he pushed himself up, trying to reach her, but fell on the ground.

"Easy, big fellow." I hooked my right arm under his and helped him to his feet.

Given his size, he was surprisingly light. He gave me a thankful smile then knelt by the woman and rested his head on her belly, and while gently caressing it, he sang to the baby.

Feeling I was intruding in their private moment, I looked away and made to leave.

The man grabbed my hand and stopped me. "Tankiu." He looked at the woman and then back at me. "Tankiuforsevingrea."

"I'm sorry. I don't understand."

"Tankiuforsevingas." He smiled. "Tankiu."

I repeated what he had just said in my mind and I finally understood. His accent had tricked me, but he had actually spoken in Standard, a common travelers' language.

"Thank you," he said one more time when I smiled. "Your soul healed us back to conscious life."

I shrugged and stepped back to take a better look at him. "I've done nothing."

He frowned and then leaned forward and outstretched his hand toward me. Before I could stop him, he triggered a Share. His recent memories invaded me like a flood of images.

His words echoed in my mind. *This is what you did.*

When I had reached for him a few minutes earlier, as had happened when I had touched the woman, an empathic connection had been activated. I had imagined their story like mine. I had felt their love and their pain in losing each other. With my touch, I had jumpstarted their consciousnesses back to life, as he had just said.

I shivered. *You looked dead.*

We were in non-life.

I don't understand.

Our bodies had shut down. We waited for help. Your love saved us. He removed his hand and closed the sharing.

I couldn't reply. I was too overwhelmed.

"Thanks; we owe you everything." The man shifted his position and knelt before me with his head low.

"No, please, stand up." I reached out for him.

He accepted my help. "My loved ones are alive because of you." He then gently lay my hand on his woman's belly.

I heard a soft chirp and then a laugh. My mind was filled with the baby's emotions. The mother had done an excellent job of protecting her during the last moments of the unsafe landing. I saw the girl's aura, and she was the most innocent soul I had ever seen.

The mother smiled at me then, lowering her chin toward her belly, sang, "Kiri'a. Katita lei, Kiri'a."

The baby girl's aura reacted to her mother's voice and became pink. She cooed, and a small bump appeared on the mother's belly. I removed my hand to disconnect myself and give them some privacy.

"Kiri'a—" The man lowered his head and brushed the bump with his lips. "Kiri'a, katita lei."

I stepped back. "Thank you for sharing this with me. What you have... it is precious."

"I hope you will experience it yourself one day." He slowly rose from kneeling but stayed by the woman's side, one hand on her shoulder. "Let me follow etiquette and introduce us properly. My given name is Rah, and my beloved wife's name is Reah." His eyes went to her belly. "And she is Kiri'a."

"My name is Elios." I bowed my head then waited for Rah to continue talking.

"I apologize for my earlier action. Although distressed and confused, I should have asked your permission before invading your mind, but if you will allow it one more time, I'd like to share our story with you." He tilted his head toward me.

I hesitated. Recently, I had had nothing but time on my hands, and more than once I reflected on the whole Solean soul-sharing process. I couldn't help but think it was flawed. It couldn't be just all or nothing. I wanted the option of deciding what I wanted to share. The human concept of privacy was finally clear to me. But it was Rah who had requested it, and I didn't want to offend him with a refusal. I could put to test a theory of mine, though.

I bowed to both of them then reached for him. "I'd be honored." I placed my splayed hand on his right temple. Slowly breathing in and out, I stretched my mind and concentrated on filtering his thoughts, something I had never thought I would be able to experiment with. I relaxed and tentatively tiptoed through his mind, trying to avoid sections with the mental equivalent of closed doors. The first try was a success, and I became more confident. I carefully ignored memories that were too intimate for my prodding. Rah's mind was quite different from mine, which made skipping sections easier for me. I traveled inside his mind as if traveling by train. I visited the main cities on the route without stopping at every station. I relived their story, and even with my surgical approach, I was blown away by the intensity of the man's memories.

Rah and Reah were from a planet called Karcum. The child she was bearing was the fruit of forbidden love. Rah and Reah's union was interracial and prohibited by their religion because of the chemical differences in their physiology. When they had discovered that Reah was expecting, they had feared for their baby's life and flew away looking for sanctuary. Silenzio had been their choice. A planet that forbade any type of communication was the perfect hiding spot. Furthermore, Silenzio's natural beauty, mild weather, and apparent lack of predators made it fit to raise a child.

I interrupted the Share and looked at their peaceful faces and their intertwined hands.

One of Rah's memories resonated strongly with me. He had returned from a business trip and found that Reah had been sick in his absence. He had worried over her and felt guilty. She had taken his head in her hands, caressed the contour of his face, and whispered to him, "Nothing matters if we are together."

Rah smiled at me, gracefully moving closer to Reah. "Thanks. I appreciate the respect you showed me and Reah. Privacy is important to us. We don't share everything."

His mind was more sophisticated than I had realized. "You can open and close the communication channel as you wish?"

"Yes, we can."

His statement took me by surprise. "And yet you granted me full access to your mind."

"I thought it was your way and followed custom."

That was how, I then realized, the first time he had touched my hand nothing had happened. Had I had any time to think about that,

I would have thought we hadn't initiated a Share because we weren't acquainted. I never would have guessed he was intentionally stopping the process. Something clicked in me then. "I'd like for you to know my story."

He slightly lowered his head. "I'd be honored as well."

With my new insight on the process, I wanted to Share myself with him, as if I needed to unburden my soul. When it was done and I had let Rah relive part of my last two years, I knew we had bonded on a deeper level.

"Thank you." He smiled at me.

Then Reah made a sound, and he was immediately concerned with her.

"It's nothing. Baby just kicked." She massaged her belly and then gasped and chuckled. "See? She is in a playful mood."

Rah bent to caress her belly as well then gave me a glance and helped Reah on her feet. "If you don't mind, she needs to be examined."

"Sure." I walked back to the hallway, saw them enter one of the smaller bedrooms, the one that contained a medical bed, and nodded at Rah. "I'll be outside." I exited the ship and went to check the damages it had sustained in the collision. Outside, I didn't see anything out of place beside the expected aftermath of the crash. I went back inside. The couple was still in the medical bay. I passed the closed door and told them I would check the cockpit. I waited for their consent and then proceeded to the other side of the ship. Its command system was simple to decode and based on individuals' mental signatures, resembling Solean technology. I was pleasantly surprised it wouldn't take lots of skill to navigate the little vessel. I sat on one of the chairs and studied the intact control panel. Everything seemed in good condition, and I couldn't understand what had caused the ship to lose control.

The couple came back, and I immediately vacated the seat for Reah to rest on it. "Rah?"

He looked at me.

"What is wrong with the ship?"

"With the ship itself, absolutely nothing—" Rah squeezed Reah's hand, lifted it to his lips, and kissed it.

"With our own world's intolerance, everything," Reah finished for him. "Someone we trusted sabotaged our ship."

Rah brought Reah closer to him. "But it doesn't matter anymore. We are here, and Kiri'a is fine."

"I'd still like to find what the problem is." I nervously moved my weight from one leg to the other.

Rah waved his hand. "Please. We are tired and in need of rest."

I jumped out of the ship once again and found Fido waiting for me, lights blinking already. "I'm fine." I gave it my right arm and was rewarded with several pinches. "Happy now?" I leaned to pat the health-bot when something under the ship caught my attention.

I hadn't noticed it on my first perusal because the metal was deformed by the collision with the ground and the ship was half buried in vegetation, but something small and shiny protruded from one of the two black cylindrical capsules positioned underneath. I made a mental note to ask what exactly the two cylinders were, and I crouched to take a better look at the shiny anomaly in the middle of the pitch-black alloy of the rest of the ship. Up close, the thing was something so alien that I couldn't even imagine its use. It looked out of place and clearly not made from the same material as the ship. I didn't even try to remove it from where it was safely anchored. I suspected that its body went deep inside; otherwise, at the moment of impact, it would have disengaged itself from the hull.

A few hours later, Rah and Reah emerged from the ship holding hands.

"Hungry?" he asked.

"I've been fed." After tilting my head toward Fido, I raised my arm to show them the needle's punctures.

"Then keep us company by the fire."

"I can do that." I longed for some conversation rather than a monologue with a robot.

Rah accompanied Reah to a flat rock, helped her sit, and gestured for me to accompany him. "Let's gather some wood."

"Sure." I helped him with the task, and we came back to start the fire. Rah climbed up and down the ship several times, carrying what he needed to cook a meal.

"Thankfully, the cryonic pad wasn't damaged in the landing." He cut and sliced what I thought were vegetables and then added them to the pan on the fire pit. Any time Reah attempted to help, he gently told her to rest.

We conversed lightly during the meal, about their planet, my planet, Earth, Silenzio. Despite what I'd said about being fed, I partook of the warm food and found that conversation with an intelligent being wasn't the only social interaction I had missed.

Illuminated by the warm glow of the campfire, Reah kept shifting her body to balance her weight, and Rah rhythmically massaged her back to ease her discomfort. On more than one occasion, I had to avert my eyes from them. Rah seemed to exist just to take care of her. He seemed to wait for her to breathe. Even when he wasn't looking in her direction, I had the feeling he knew exactly what she was doing.

I caught Rah looking at me once, and I blushed. Then, I remembered my mental note and asked him if he knew what the gleaming object attached to the cylindrical capsule was.

Rah immediately rose. "Show it to me."

"This way." I led him around the ship and crouched under the capsule. Meanwhile, the sun had set, and the place was covered in shadow, but the shiny protuberance stood out. "Here." I prodded the object with a finger but didn't apply any pressure to it. "Do you know what this is?"

He leaned closer, sighed, opened his mouth to say something, then breathed in and out. "It is what I feared it was." He paused, stepped out from under the ship's dark shadow, and looked up. "We had hoped until the end that some good was left in our people—" He crouched on the ground and held his head in his hands. "This is the proof of our naiveté."

We hadn't noticed Reah approaching from the other side. "No!" She covered her coral mouth with her thin fingers.

In two steps, Rah was at her side, holding her trembling body, soothing her with a few melodic words. When Reah was calm enough, he focused his attention back on me. "We already knew who had sabotaged our ship, but we still hoped we were wrong.

Unfortunately, the way our vessel has been sabotaged is a signed autograph of the member of the family who did it."

At his words, Reah sobbed anew. Rah stopped talking, raised her body in his arms, and started rocking her gently as if she was a child. "Give me a moment," he said to me while carrying his companion inside the ship. A few minutes later, he was back outside, carrying a long stick ending in a metal disk.

I eyed the object with curiosity. "What is it?"

He went to the capsule without breaking his stride. "It reads the level of the radiation coming from the bomb."

I heard the instrument ticking when he touched the shiny shard with it and held my breath. So much depended on the ship being functional.

The instrument abruptly emitted a louder sound and then stopped. Rah nodded and then said, "Good news. We don't have to immediately look for a shelter. There is no residual radiation left to harm Reah and the baby."

I sighed in relief.

"There's nothing else we can do for tonight. I say we rest. You can use one of the bedrooms."

I thanked him and chose the first room on the right. I sat on the soft mattress and wondered when I had last rested on a bed. As usual, before going to sleep, I attempted to contact Gaia, but I didn't have any luck.

When I woke from my fitful slumber, Rah and Reah were cooking breakfast in the ship's kitchen. Seeing them working together, chirping to each other in their melodic language, was a pleasure.

They both smiled at me in unison, and Rah poured some hot liquid beverage into a cup for me. "You look like you need some of this."

"Should I ask what is it?" Despite my words, I accepted the amber beverage.

"Something… invigorating." Rah gestured for me to drink it. "You look like you didn't rest at all."

I sipped at it. "Well, it's definitely invigorating. And sweet. Thank you." I gulped down the rest of the drink. It was exactly what I needed to start what I hoped was my last day on Silenzio.

Reah had already prepared a plate for me, and I sat at the kitchen table with them. We ate a dish that resembled a cake, white and fluffy and soft but savory and spicy, with a hint of meaty flavor.

After chewing silently for a few minutes, I put the food down on my plate. "Rah…" Words choked in my mouth before I could say what I had started to. I felt bad taking advantage of them, but I had to go back to Gaia.

Rah raised one hand and interrupted me. "Reah and I would like to lend you our ship."

"Oh…"

Reah caressed her belly before saying, "We owe you our lives. Please, accept our help."

Rah added, "Reah and I have decided that we will honor our original plan and have our baby on Silenzio. We can't go back, and Reah is due soon."

She made a face and then laughed. "I feel it could be even sooner."

"I can't wait." Rah gave her a peck on her cheek. "You can leave today if you want; we just need a hand with disembarking what we need, and then you will be free to leave." He tenderly placed his hands over hers on her belly and smiled.

I kept thanking them the whole time we were hauling equipment and boxes to the ground. The day was almost done when we disembarked the last box. I spent a few hours telling them what I knew about the planet, and I left them the incomplete map I had been drawing for a while.

Finally, I had to part ways with Fido. I couldn't have my health-bot signaling my presence as soon as we were out of Silenzio's atmosphere. Leaving my robotic companion proved to be an emotional moment for me. It had been part of my adult life for longer than I could remember. "You be a good boy." I patted the metal box one last time and then jumped onto the ship.

"You'll see, you won't have any problem." Rah had explained how the navigation panel worked. "Just program the first jump and

Earth's coordinates. The ship is programmed to fly solo while you are in deep sleep." He had released control of the ship to me by superimposing my mental signature over his.

"Have a wonderful life." I waved at the couple one last time from the tailgate then mentally commanded the ship to initiate takeoff. The vessel was immediately airborne.

After a few days of getting used to the control room, I finally programmed the route to reach Earth in the fastest time possible. My borrowed taxi wasn't as fast as the shuttle that had brought me back to Solo, but it was fast enough to cover the distance between the four wormholes between Silenzio and Earth in just six months. Waiting and worrying for half a year wasn't an option I wanted to consider. I tried one last time to contact her with no results, and then I lay down on the deep-sleep cot.

I closed my eyes, thinking of her.

12

As soon as I entered deep sleep, the dream started, which by the intrinsic nature of deep sleeping, shouldn't have happened.

Also, I was aware my dream was different from any other dream. Still perfectly conscious, although I shouldn't have maintained presence of mind while asleep, I thought the ship's technology was alien and it might have interacted with my human physiology and Solean mind. My *dream* was an oneiric experience composed mostly of sounds. It started with a stream of incoherent vocal expressions, which slowly took some intelligible form. At first, what I heard was just a voice, and then I recognized that voice, even if it was distorted by other noises.

Pain. Fear. Alone. Dark. Alone. Pain. Alone. Cold. The words repeated in my mind over and over. It was Gaia's voice, and the dream soon morphed into a bleak nightmare. I was immobilized in the dark, and I was hearing Gaia's voice.

I shouldn't have been able to think about anything at all. The whole point of sleeping through the entire length of an interstellar voyage is to give the mind time to de-stress completely, a sort of mental cleansing, while the body regenerates. Instead, I was wide awake, stuck in a dormant body for the rest of the trip.

Gaia's voice was in my head almost the whole time. When she spoke, her words were frantic, with an insane edge; the terror in her voice made me recoil in pain. When she didn't speak, absolute fear froze my heart.

During the whole voyage, I didn't have a single moment of peace. Any time I heard her voice, I was afraid of what she would say the next time, and I would count how many seconds and minutes passed between her words. The worst part was that we weren't communicating. It was a one-way channel. I could hear Gaia talking, but she didn't seem to hear me. She never answered my questions. I never saw her face.

After some time, Gaia's thoughts became more rational, an improvement compared with the nonsensical blathering I'd gotten used to.

I'm naked, lying on a hard surface.

Her words were more painful to listen to.

After a while, I tried to rest my mind when she wasn't talking. I needed my brain fresh enough to be able to process some of the information she was feeding me. Maybe I could find a way to help her whenever I woke up, while orbiting Earth already, I hoped. My only consolation was that my body would be in perfect form, thanks to the machines I was attached to.

One day, she finally became fully aware of herself.

I am Gaia. My name is Gaia.

My name is important.

My name means something else too.

My name is gaiagaiagaia.

Gaia is the name of something else other than me.

I was relieved her mental processes weren't damaged. It had taken her so long to remember her name that I had feared the worst. After that first time, Gaia's progress was steady, and she kept talking to me every time she was awake.

Earth?

My name is Gaia. Mother Earth.

To exist, I need something. Someone.

Life on Earth can't survive without it.

My life has no meaning without him.

Some time later, she said my name, and I wept.

Light. Warm. Life. Sun.

Sun...

Elios?

Elios, Elios, Elios. Gaia's sun. My sun.

I got so used to her voice inside my mind, when I didn't hear it, I craved it like a drug addict waiting for the next dose that never comes soon enough.

Unfortunately, her senses must have been somehow impaired, or she was kept in confinement, because she didn't seem able to describe where she was or why. She sounded constantly terrified.

Cold fingers. Naked. Flat surface. Pain. Touch. Cold. Bright light. Dark. Cold. Tied. Bed. Surface. Can't move.

She found solace only when thinking of me, of my body radiating warmth and covering her trembling face with my kisses.

The idea that Gaia was naked, strapped to a bed, and helpless ripped at the seams of my soul. I wondered more than once if I could bear more of this emotional rollercoaster. Sometimes, she seemed to suffer through terrible headaches, and I wished I could take her place. I heard her when she summoned my memories to lessen the physical ache. She was desperate and didn't think she would survive. Yet she spent all the energy she had left thinking of me.

I heard her when she recalled in detail the color of my eyes or the way I smiled.

Once, her physical pain reached a new level. Gaia repeated my name like a mantra until she was calm enough to think more articulate thoughts. Another time, she screamed about a bright light piercing her eyes. Her voice was so frightened, so full of physical pain, so loud in my head, that when she abruptly stopped, I feared I wouldn't hear her again. She didn't talk to me for a while. My fear blossomed into certainty that something had happened to her. Time passed, and she didn't come back. The idea she was dead took residence in my heart, and I couldn't chase it away. Unable to move a muscle in my body, I lost my desire to keep on living.

Free to move, I would have altered the ship's course and made it plummet into the closest star. My training reminded me of how unholy the act of suicide was considered in my culture, but I was past that kind of compulsion. Angrily, I thought that my loyalty was the reason I had been too late to save Gaia. I had followed all the rules; as a dutiful Observer, I had sacrificed us, our love, for the greater good of my species.

I didn't owe anything to anyone anymore.

The only person I owed everything was dead and I with her. I couldn't see anything past that terrible reality. Gaia was somewhere, cold, alone, her body unprotected.

I had never touched her skin, never kissed her full lips. I wasn't there when she had needed me the most; my body had never comforted her, I had never hugged her. She would have been so small in my arms, so soft; she would have curled up and hugged me back. She would have reached for my lips.

I hoped I was finally at the end of the trip. I needed to wake up and end my misery. The ache in my heart had become excruciating. Attached to a machine, I felt beyond repair. I hoped for the pain to increase so even the machine couldn't keep me alive anymore.

Then I went catatonic. Without her voice in my head, I existed in a place where I couldn't feel emotions, where I wasn't able to think of her fragile body, broken and cold, lifeless. I wished I had the strength Gaia had shown me. She had tried to survive the horror, but I couldn't. Thinking of her was too painful.

Death would have been a gift.

Time passed with no thoughts, no feelings. A hopeless darkness. Nothing.

Then, *Elios*.

Her voice. She was alive.

It was impossible to describe the magnitude and complexity of the feelings that assailed me. I went insane with joy.

Cold. Elios.

Something on her end had changed. Her thoughts were less erratic. Gaia was still desperate and missed human contact, but she was mentally stronger.

A young man, dark skinned, almond-shaped eyes.

A young woman, fair skin and golden-red hair, beautiful smile.

Friends.

My friends.

Sara and Areel.

They're my friends and were there with me when something happened. But what?

Soon after, she sent me a sketched image of her new location.

I am in a different place. What is this place? It's big. Darker. No one other than me here. No jailers. No needles. No pain. No bright lights.

For the first time, Gaia was able to think further than the immediate sensorial stimuli.

I need to remember what happened to me, Sara, and Areel.

At first, any time she tried to retrieve her lost memories, piercing headaches didn't let her continue. Then, without knowing she was doing so, she applied one of the many mantras used to overcome physical pain and achieve clarity of mind. She imagined, in detail, an outing with me. Once calm enough, Gaia tried to remember.

An onslaught of sounds and images invaded my mind. The colors were so vivid and the sounds so sharp, I felt like drowning. It was the first time she broadcasted visual images; until that moment we had shared an entire universe of pure thoughts. Following the chaos she was broadcasting wasn't easy, but after a moment, her ideas became clearer, and I was inside of her mind.

"That's it." Finally the idea that had been nagging at the back of my mind since we had come back to the apartment took proper form. *"The stolen boxes contain clues about what happened to your planet. Once the Etruscan exhibit was open to the public, you would've known for sure and consequentially reported. I bet the missing link we're looking for is inside one of the boxes."*

"It does sound... plausible." Sara walked to the table to see if any coffee was left in the moka.

I had drunk the last cold cup a few minutes ago. "Your kind has lived eons without knowing anything about your lost past. Doesn't it seem strange to you?"

Areel shrugged. *"We have good reasons to keep the past in the past."*

"Or maybe someone is trying to keep it that way." Sara settled for what I had left of the orange soda.

I felt a strange euphoria possessing me. "Finding the bronze spear must've triggered an alarm and forced them—whoever they are—into the open. It can't be a coincidence that it happened just after I found it." A chill went down my spine. The police catching us seemed almost trivial in comparison. Someone was out there, knowing about us, interested in keeping us in the dark. *"Why would anybody want to erase your history? Can you think of any reason?"*

Areel's eyes widened as if I had just committed blasphemy. "None. Our history was wiped out by a natural catastrophe."

"But what if there is something else?"

"Like what?" Sara asked.

"Like, I don't know, a reason why Solean people shouldn't know what happened to them." Thoughts were crowding my mind, and coherently expressing them wasn't easy.

"It would make sense only if the Dark on Solo was deliberately caused." Areel made a face indicating how improbable the mere idea was.

I opened another soda can and gulped two long sips of sugar and bubbles. "But what if?"

"If what almost annihilated the Solean culture wasn't a natural catastrophe—" Areel's voice got low, and then he looked first at Sara and then at me. "If someone did this to us, it would be..."

"You are talking about—" Sara couldn't say it either.

"Genocide," I said, and everything clicked into place.

Areel turned around to stare at the clouds illuminated by the first lights of the morning. A freezing breeze extinguished the flames of the candles spread both on the table and on the terrace floor. Only when the empty soda cans started dancing around, hitting the coffee cups and the moka, did Areel seem to hear the eerie noise, and the blizzard subsided.

When he finally turned, I saw his face and felt even colder than before. "I'm sorry," I said to him.

"Areel—" Sara reached out for him, the instinct of giving comfort by touch so ingrained in our human brain. She stopped at the last moment, but he didn't realize what had almost happened. Areel was lost in his thoughts, far away from us.

Suddenly, something made him shiver from head to toe. I felt something too, like electricity in the air, and for a moment, the lights inside the apartment dimmed.

"What is it?" Sara was looking at the kitchen.

Areel covered his mouth with one hand and ran inside. I saw him heading toward the bathroom. Sara ran after him. I followed her to the bathroom. I saw them. I screamed in anguish, and then my thoughts went to Elios. "I love you..."

There was a loud and colorful blast, and then everything went black inside of her mind and mine at the same time. I was overwhelmed by the experience so similar to a Share. After I recovered from the initial shock, I set out to understand what had happened to Gaia, Areel, and Sara by studying Gaia's memories.

Meanwhile, she kept sharing her thoughts with me, and there were moments when her words broke my heart anew—over and over again.

I'm at the hospital. Why isn't my family here to hug me, to tell me everything's going to be okay? Why has nobody talked to me? Why am I naked?

Elios. Please help me... hug me... cover my body. I feel so miserable without you. Please hurry. I don't have much time.

Remaining calm was hard when she said things like that, but for both our sakes I tried. Mantras came to my aid, and even though it took me longer to recover after hearing such pleas, I forced myself to analyze what she was sending my way.

Several things stood out in her memories.

The more I thought about it, the more I was convinced she wasn't in a hospital but being kept somewhere against her will. Gaia had involuntarily shared with me her last moments of freedom, and even though in her memory the blast was an explosion, I was quite sure it was something else altogether. Had I not seen Areel and Sara kissing, I would have made the same guess. Never before I had witnessed such a display of emotions, but without a doubt the explosion of colors in Gaia's apartment had been caused by Areel and Sara's auras combined. The range of so many overpowering feelings had triggered some sort of reaction I didn't know was even possible. Normally, only trained people, Observers, were able to see someone's aura, and Gaia wasn't one of them.

From what I saw in Gaia's mind, Areel seemed to have forgotten his training, his responsibilities. He had accepted, even reciprocated, Sara's physical proximity without thinking of the consequences of hugging her, kissing her.

The word "genocide" was drilling a hole in my already tired mind. Areel believed the Dark on our planet had been the result of some systematic act of genocide. The idea by itself was maddening.

147

I understood why Areel had reacted that way. He had clung to Sara as if she was the last sanctuary.

In any other circumstance, that kind of knowledge would have driven me crazy as well. Not anymore. Not after I had been helplessly forced to endure Gaia's torture. Not after having believed she was dead. My mind wasn't whole anymore, and there was a distinct possibility I was already crazy. My heart was divided into hundreds of pieces, and the only force keeping it together was the hope of saving Gaia. Physical pain, one can eventually overcome, but the kind of pain I had endured… it changes you forever.

My changing had probably already started on Earth. Accepting my name had triggered a response in my psyche that had altered my existence. While I was on Solo waiting for my trial, I had thought I knew the extent of my evolution, but I had no idea the change would reach such an extremity. If once I had thought I was something more than just Solean and also human, then I could see I had gone through a deeper transformation. Recent events had shaped my soul, and inside of me was a darker side.

I felt free to follow my personal moral code. I had my own laws now.

I had now the luxury of being able to rationalize about the genocide of my ancestors and maybe find the truth behind their senseless demise. Gaia's abduction was part of a bigger picture. Now my only purpose in life was to save her, and to achieve that, I had to solve at least part of the mystery surrounding my own origins.

My voyage continued. I was somewhere in space, resting, not at peace.

Given that I was heading toward Earth, I hoped Gaia was still there. Once, during an earlier contact, she had mentioned a cycle of warm yellow light followed by a silvery one. If she wasn't on Earth—and I didn't even want to start analyzing that kind of possibility—then all my hopes were gone.

So Gaia must have been on Earth.

That became my personal mantra. It kept me company every day, several times a day. I could finally understand the need humans have to pray. Praying keeps one's mind anchored in place when everything else in your life is falling to pieces.

Time passed.

As a diversion from the mantras and the constant worrying, I started to fantasize about the moment I would finally see her. I created a whole scenario where everything was perfectly normal and safe for her. She was still working on her research, and nothing had happened to disrupt her life. In my happy-ending dream, I was human. We would have met again after some trip or some other very ordinary activity that had kept us apart. It would have been perfect, romantic, and breathtaking. We would have hugged each other for hours. We would have whispered in each other's ears how unbearable not being together had been. A simple life. I had enough time to perfect my fantasy. I named our two kids and planned on seeing them married and having kids as well.

Gaia was talking less lately.

Chunks of time passed between Gaia's sporadic appearances inside my mangled mind. She was tired. Her spirit was like a candle almost consumed. She had still some flame in her, but I could hear the little flickering at the end, just before the wick drowns in the melted wax.

I imagined our impossible, perfect life with a new intensity, almost a maniacal impulse. I had so much free time now that I had to do something with it. Finally, I grew tired of inventing fairy tales I wasn't going to experience, maybe because, in my anxiety to create a whole parallel universe, I had gone too far.

Or maybe because the game had been acceptable when Gaia was still talking. Since she was mostly absent from my mind, I had to accept the reason behind it. I couldn't delude myself anymore. Then I started thinking about what we had, what I would have done differently, and I prayed for the miracle of finding her alive, having time to do something differently.

My only thought became my biggest desire: find her alive and hug her, warming her body. My mind was sustained for the rest of the voyage by this hope. Time passed in silence. Fewer and fewer times I heard from her. Then I didn't hear anything at all for a good while.

I knew I was going to slip into the same destructive routine I had experienced before, and I was waiting for it gratefully. I was sure that this time I wouldn't make it through, and I was counting on that.

13

What I wasn't counting on was finally reaching the end of my journey.

A low hum was followed by a pattern of blinking lights. After a while, I realized my eyes were wide open and I was staring at one of the ship's health-bots. I let the machine do its job until it declared my clean bill of health by floating away. I lingered a while on my bed, lazily moving my arms and legs, just to be sure I wasn't dreaming anymore. I pushed myself up and slowly sat on the bed. I waited a moment, breathed in and out and put my feet on the floor. I pressed down with my legs and bent my knees. Everything worked just fine. I tried a few steps and exited my room, heading toward the kitchen. I used doorframes and furniture on the way as aids in my quest to reach the sink. I turned on the faucet and filled a glass with water. I drank until satisfied and walked to the control panel just a few steps away. It took me a moment to remember how to read the controls and make sense of them. Relief washed over me when I saw I was exactly where I had programmed the ship to take me. Earth's blues, greens, and whites loomed below me.

I changed the coordinates for my landing destination. Gaia had provided me with enough information to safely assume she wasn't in Seattle anymore. I didn't know where she was, but she had shown me exactly where she had been before the abduction. When Gaia had shared her last vivid memory, she had also indicated involuntarily where her apartment was. While she was following Sara and Areel, she had briefly looked at a calendar on the wall. It was nothing more than a local retailer advertisement, but it listed the address in clear letters. I already knew Gaia was back in Italy. Our meeting on the beach had told me so; the color of the sand and the landscape were unmistakable parts of the Roman charm. Back in Seattle, Gaia had showed me the picture of the artifact found in the seaside city of Tarquinia, which hosted several Etruscan archeological sites. It wasn't just a coincidence the address on the calendar belonged to the same city. I would start my quest in Tarquinia, hoping to find clues that would bring me closer to Gaia.

I spent several hours looking for a place that was driving distance from that city. The main problem was that I needed some geographical privacy to land, and Tarquinia didn't provide secluded spots to do so. Fortunately for me, Italy is a small country, very rich in geological diversity, which is the point when one needs to hide a landing ship and still be close to where one wants to be. I circled a big area radiating from Tarquinia and encompassing the closest mountainous peaks in the Lazio region. It was full summer in Italy, and Terminillo was most likely crowded with tourists escaping the Roman heat. I zoomed out of Lazio and included other regions in my search. In Tuscany, Mount Amiata and the Abetone would be equally populated. Then I noticed the geography of the park of Monte Peglia in Umbria and found it perfect. A lesser-known tourist destination, Mount Peglia was only a three-hour drive from Tarquinia. I double-checked the meteorological conditions for the next night, and when I was sure it would be cloudy and moonless in Umbria, I punched the coordinates for the landing and went to have a shower. What I would do while waiting to land was a detail I didn't want to contemplate at the moment.

After sitting under the jets of warm water for a while, I had enough and exited the shower stall to dry myself. A mirror hung over the sink, and I passed by it on my way out of the bathroom. Inadvertently, I got a glimpse of myself and didn't recognize the face staring back at me.

I blinked several times, but the image of someone who wasn't me was still there. I looked older, which I should have expected. But it wasn't just that. My hair was considerably longer. And completely white. A mane of silvery snow framed my ghostly face. I was right after all: one can't live through the kind of mental strain I experienced without one's body being involved. I would wear it like a battle scar.

I looked at my reflection one more time and then I braided my unruly halo into a simple plait, with a perverse sense of satisfaction.

My communion with Gaia was tangible; what happened to her mind reflected on mine, and what happened to her body had consequences on mine as well.

I had changed in more than one way, and it was more visible than I'd thought.

I went looking for clothes to wear instead of the Solean kimono. I hoped Reah, who had looked my size, had left something behind in her bedroom. I didn't find anything in the recess in the wall where their clothes must have been, just linens and pillows with tubes attached to them. I remembered having seen a small utility closet in the hallway just outside the kitchen. I was in luck and found two pieces that resembled a white shirt and some tan shorts. The fabric, more than the cut, didn't look like anything made on Earth, but I wasn't planning on wearing the ensemble for long.

The clothes fit, so I went back to the control room and started planning how to reach Tarquinia from the remote place I was landing in Umbria. Land transportation was a minor hitch to take into consideration since I didn't have a car or current currency. I didn't let those concerns discourage me. I was in too much of a hurry to stop and think about all the little things that could go wrong. My only worry was finding Gaia, and unfortunately, I didn't know how. Her life, and consequentially mine, depended on it, and I only had time to focus on that; everything else was relative. Any little holdup was easily fixable.

I synchronized my orbit over Europe and then resigned myself to wait until the right moment. Though on any other occasion, meditating would have helped me, this time I knew it would be futile. I exercised instead. I went through repetition after repetition of sit-ups and squats. I lifted weights. I even ran around the ship. I hit the shower several times before I felt tired enough to close my eyes and rest. The whole time, I thought, and despite my resolution not to waste time worrying, I did worry I was too late.

On Earth, a day passed. A moonless night welcomed me back to Italy when I slowly descended toward the peninsula. Helped by the ship's dark opaque exterior, I let my ride glide over the rolling hills bordering the ancient city of Orvieto then headed toward Mount Peglia Park. From above, I looked for a remote spot. I scouted for more than an hour before finding a small but dark canyon in the midst of several recesses. It was big enough for my lightweight ship to land and then take off, hiding the byproducts of the combustion. My chosen spot was also close to a big arterial road. I figured I just had to hike for a few hours and then I would hitch a ride to Tarquinia.

Despite my worries about the ship being seen from below, landing was easier than I thought. The night was completely dark, and nobody was camping nearby—I had checked for human presence by scanning the area twice with the infrareds. Once the ship was safely on the ground, I programmed it to take off and remain in orbit over Umbria, waiting for my commands. I secured the ship's remote—a sleek oval resembling a car key fob—inside a hidden pocket in a backpack-looking satchel I had found while scouting for anything useful, and then I left the ship.

After a first moment of dizziness, I let oxygen into my lungs and regulated my breathing. By the time my eyes adjusted to the darkness, my ship had already taken off. I was alone and without a sound plan. Doubts assailed me, and before I knew what I was doing, I let out a mental cry to give my distress an outlet. I crouched and swore under my breath. "No more mistakes." I sat on the ground crosslegged and ran a set of meditative exercises to focus my thoughts on the success of my mission. When I was satisfied by the state of mind I had achieved, I stood and searched the glade, looking for the safest trail.

I put one foot after the other, testing the terrain that soon became treacherous. Several hours later, I reached the main road and followed it, descending toward a hamlet I hadn't seen on the map. I double-checked my appearance. I looked strange but not threatening. Backpacking foreign pilgrims were a common sight in Umbria, as they often visited Assisi—Saint Francis's city. Umbrians were accustomed to helping stranded souls in the middle of the road. I definitely looked the part.

The first lights of morning shone in the sky when I finally reached the town of Castel Viscardo. After hiking up and down the canyon then walking on asphalt the whole night, I was exhausted, and my legs were starting to cramp. I sat at the edge of the road, my empty stomach rumbling, and I remembered that I didn't have money.

I was also thirsty. Fortunately for me, thanks to their Roman heritage, Italian cities had fountains everywhere. Sure enough, after entering the city limits, I found a small but elegantly decorated iron fountain. I slowly drank the cold liquid and felt sharper right away. With my stomach sloshing with water at every step, the hunger pangs became difficult to ignore. I had to eat something before heading toward Tarquinia. Begging for money wasn't out of the question; the only problem was that nobody was out so early in the morning. After a brief perusal of the main square, I saw on the other corner a store with its roller shutter half open. My nose caught the characteristic aroma of freshly baked bread, and my stomach growled. I headed for the bakery either to beg or to offer some service in exchange for some bread.

I knocked on the roller shutter. "May I come in?"

"Walk around. Can't leave the oven," a male voice answered from somewhere inside the bakery.

I followed the contour of the building and found the back entrance opening on the lateral alley. "Hi, there." As soon as I entered the small room, I was assailed by unbearable heat and the smell of baked goods.

"Hi back to you. What can I do for you?" The young guy sweating in front of the industrial oven smiled at me.

"I was wondering if I can do something to earn a meal."

"Are you hungry?" Without waiting for my answer—probably my emaciated face was answer enough—he took a loaf of bread resting on one of the shelves by the wall and broke it in half. "Tell me if it's any good."

"Thank you." I accepted the bread and proceeded to finish it in a few bites. "I'm Elios." Manners came back to me when the hole in my stomach was partially filled.

"Marcello. What about some breakfast?" He walked to the next room. "Come. I'll brew you a cup of cappuccino, and you can have fresh croissants and rosemary focaccia."

I followed him to the bakery proper, and at his suggestion, I sat at one of the three small, round tables. "I can do anything." I looked around the room to see if there was anything I could help with.

Marcello dismissed me, waving his hand in the air. "I know what it means to be hungry and penniless." He loaded a tray with two cups of cappuccino, pastries, and focaccia, then walked to the table. "Eat, and you'll feel better." He sat heavily on the chair opposite mine and smiled. "I'm glad for the interruption. I started the dough at three thirty this morning, and I'm ready to crash."

I brought the cappuccino to my mouth and tilted my head to him. "Thank you again."

Marcello bowed his head in response. "Four years ago, I travelled through Africa and got lost between villages in the Kenyan desert. I didn't speak Bantu, and I had been robbed blind the day before. If it weren't for two strangers who took pity on me, I would be dead. They even paid for my ticket back to Italy. Since then, there hasn't been a time I've refused help to someone in need. Karma, you know?"

Three cappuccinos later—Marcello insisted I needed the energy booster—I thanked him again, and with a plastic bag full of bread and cookies, I left the city of Castel Viscardo. Marcello, true to his commitment to paying it forward, gave me a spare change of clothes—which I immediately wore—and even money for the bus ride to Tarquinia.

I was waiting for the bus to arrive when I experienced a sudden and brief intrusion into my head.

Someone was contacting me. Actually, the correct definition was that someone was looking for me. My brainwaves had been scanned. Somebody was trying to verify my identity. Whoever had done it knew exactly what he was doing and preferred to remain anonymous. Another Observer was looking for me.

How could Solo know about my escape from Silenzio? It was inconceivable. Communication was impossible in and out of Silenzio... unless Fido had been altered in more ways than I had discovered and had signaled my departure.

I sprinted toward the woods at the edge of the road even though I knew the attempt was futile. If Solo was after me, I had no place to hide in the universe. In the stillness of the morning, the yellow sun barely touched the highest branches of the trees, giving me temporary shelter.

I heard the engine of a motorcycle. The driver sped around the corner of the curvy road that ended at the Monte Peglia Park, in the direction opposite where I was heading. The motorcycle drove past my hiding spot and raised a menacing breeze in its passage. My heart skipped a few beats.

When I didn't hear anything else, I decided it was safe to go back to the road and catch the bus to Tarquinia. Soon after, I saw it coming down from Monte Peglia. I made myself visible and signaled for the bus to stop. The orange-and-blue vehicle appeared and disappeared behind the curves of the winding road and finally came to a halt before me. The bus driver, a tired-looking man in his fifties, opened the door and was about to let me inside when I heard someone calling my name from the outside.

"Elios!"

I turned toward the direction the voice had come from, but I couldn't see anyone at the back of the bus.

"Elios let's go; I don't have time."

I was frozen on the second step when the bus driver said, "In or out. You are letting the cold in, and I must get going." I apologized and climbed another step.

Then, from the rear of the bus, a dark shadow moved, and the bike I had seen earlier came into sight. A ray of light was reflected by the black helmet when the motorcycle driver cocked his head to the side to look at me. "I really don't have time. Get out." He removed his helmet and at the same time, a familiar voice commanded in my head, *Now!*

I stared speechlessly at Kam's human face.

"We don't have the whole morning for you to decide what you want to do." The bus driver showed me the way out of the bus. "Tourists…" Several people inside the bus added their own comments to the unfinished sentence.

I had barely backed off the bus when the bus driver closed the door in my face. The motorcycle took the place of the bus a moment later. A man in his mid-twenties was looking back at me. He had pale-blue eyes and brown hair and was definitely irritated.

Elios! Snap out of it! Kam's thought exploded in my mind.

I was still so surprised, it took me a long moment before I said anything. "What are you doing here?" He was the last person I had expected to meet on Earth.

"What are *you* doing here?"

"It's a long story." I still couldn't get over the shock of seeing him. "Let's go somewhere else first."

"Okay." He reached behind the bike to retrieve a second black helmet, which he promptly pushed toward me. "Jump on."

I fastened the helmet and mounted the bike at the same time. The motorcycle purred to life violently and almost tossed me onto the road. I grabbed Kam's waist and closed my eyes. He drove the whole time as if an enemy was on our tail. Fortunately, very few cars were on the road so early in the day. The landscape was a blur of yellow fields, blue and green pools of water, terracotta roofs, and finally brown sand and dark-blue sea. Kam left the main road and turned toward one of the deserted beaches dotting the coast. He drove until the sand disallowed it then parked close to the shore. When I dismounted, my legs felt like gelatin, and my neck was sore from my unnatural position during the ride. Every time Kam had leaned over to ride the curves lining the whole road from Monte Peglia to Tarquinia, I had craned my neck to avoid hitting the asphalt.

Kam walked around the bike and then halted a few steps from me, his body language betraying his restlessness. "What did you do?"

I laughed. "It's hard to get used to you as a human, but I'm glad to see you too."

Kam was about to say something back but gave me a onceover, and his expression changed. "What happened to you?" His eyes lingered on my white hair.

I automatically combed a stray lock behind my ear. "As I said, it's a long story."

"You look like you went through a lot." He gave my mane another glance before looking away.

"You have no idea." I looked for a place we could sit and talk. Closer to the shore was a pattino, a typical Italian lifeboat, parked on the sand, and it had a seat large enough for two. I gestured for Kam to follow me there. "Where do you want to start from?" I watched as the pink dawn slowly morphed into the morning sunlight.

"I heard your distress call and couldn't believe it was really you."

I shook my head. "That was stupid on my part."

"I wouldn't have found you otherwise." Kam rubbed his hands together and murmured something under his breath about being corporeal and having to regulate body temperature. "How did you leave Silenzio?" he asked when he stopped shaking.

The salty breeze from the sea tickled my nose. "It is probably better if you don't know the details."

He sighed. "Don't worry. I won't report you." He found a small pebble on the lifeboat and threw it toward the incoming waves.

"You came all the way from Solo to bring me back, and you won't report me? Why?"

"I am not here for you." He jumped off the pattino and collected a few pebbles.

"You are not?" I tried to stop his hand before he could throw the pebble. "Then why are you here?"

He managed to finish the throw. The pebble skipped over the crests of four waves. "Areel went missing six months ago."

"What do you know about it?"

He turned toward me. "Not much. I lost contact with him several months ago, and when he disappeared, I was sent here to rescue him. I've been living between Tarquinia and Marina Velca since then." He frowned. "You already knew, didn't you?"

I nodded. "I am here because six months ago, something happened to Gaia. She was working with Areel, looking for a way to rescue me from my fate, and they found something."

"And how do you know all of this, being that you were stranded on Silenzio?"

"Gaia and I found a way to communicate."

"You did what?" The pebble he was about to throw fell to the sand.

"I know it sounds incredible, but it's the truth."

He smiled at me. "Well, if anybody could pull such a stunt, that would be you for sure."

"What were you doing on Mount Peglia?"

"Last night, I detected your aura broadcasting from there. Imagine my surprise."

"Well, you surprised me too. May I ask you why you aren't going to report me?"

Kam sighed heavily before answering, his eyes focused on the faraway horizon. "Because before disappearing, Areel confessed to me that he was in love with Sara." He waited for me say something. "But of course, you know all of that." He waved one hand in the air. "Is there anything you don't know?"

"Where are they now? I don't know that."

He sighed. "I've been looking for them for the last six months with no success." He turned toward the sea once again. "Anyway, to answer your question, I wouldn't have reported Areel, and I won't report you."

"But why?"

"Because I didn't want him to be sent into exile like you had been. And now, I don't want to send you back there. I thought your punishment was exceedingly severe. I even told Lex so." Kam crossed his legs and sat on the lower part of the pattino, his fingers trailing over the sand. "Areel showed me the last time he saw you, what had become of you after they forced you to be separated from Gaia." He winced. "It is enough to watch one friend suffer the way you did. I am not going to betray Areel. I only want to save him."

"I'm so glad to hear that." I sighed in relief. "So what did you find so far?"

"A few days before disappearing, Areel reported to his Superior Observer he had found an Etruscan bronze spear with an inscription in Solean language on the blade."

I remembered Gaia mentioning the bronze spear when she had shared her memories with me. "What did the inscription say?"

"'I bring you peace.'" Kam shivered. "Soon after the discovery of the bronze spear, the camp where they were working got robbed, and the spear was among the stolen artifacts. The bronze spear was part of an incoming Etruscan exposition, and only the boxes with the exposition seal had been stolen."

"Did you ask around about them?"

"Of course. It was the first thing I did. I tracked down where Areel was renting, but I didn't find anything there. The place was barren, as if Areel had never lived there."

"What about Gaia and Sara's apartment?"

"It was my next move. I went to the archeological camp where they had been working and asked around. A kid named Danilo told me the girls had moved back to the States for their research and left Tarquinia in a hurry."

"It isn't the truth."

"I figured that already. When I called their apartment's caretaker and asked if I could rent their apartment, he told me it was still rented by two girls who were out of town. "

I felt restless. "I need to contact Gaia's family." I stood up, shook the fine sand off my pants, and walked toward the bike. I was physically and mentally exhausted, but I had to keep going.

Kam reached me at the bike and before handing me back the helmet, he tilted his head toward the road. "We can ask that guy Danilo I have been talking to. Maybe he knows their numbers. The camp is ten minutes away from here. I know he works the early morning shift. After the robbery, several things have changed for the people working there. They are very strict about who can enter the site."

I didn't even realize we were on the road. My mind was elsewhere. We reached the camp in no time, and Kam went to the front gate and asked the policeman for his *friend*. Danilo, a young man, tall, with a shaved head and dark eyes, came to greet Kam a few minutes later. Kam made the presentations and I took the man's proffered hand.

Danilo looked over his shoulder at the policeman and then at us. "I'm sorry, I can't let you in today."

Kam stepped out of the gate's shadow. "It's fine. I only need to ask you if you know Gaia's family's phone number."

Danilo frowned, and his eyes turned imperceptibly my way, his body tensing. "What do you need it for?"

I felt Kam bristle beside me. I gave Danilo a straight look and then lied through my teeth. "Gaia lent me some books, and I want to return them to her."

Danilo's stance relaxed. "Okay. I can look for it. Give me a moment."

I smiled. "Sure."

Danilo walked back to the camp and disappeared inside a tent. Kam and I stayed behind the gate, holding the officer's gaze. I was losing my nerve when Danilo reappeared, waving a small piece of paper in his hand. He and Kam exchanged a few words, and we thanked him and said our goodbyes.

"Do you have a cell phone?" I snatched the piece of paper from Kam's hand.

"Here." He reached into his jeans' back pocket and took out a small phone.

I grabbed it and punched the numbers Danilo had written for us. My hand was shaking, and I had to repeat the process several times.

"Let me do it for you." Kam gently removed the phone from my hand, made the call, and when it started ringing, gave it back to me.

Gaia's mother answered on the third ring.

"Hi, I am Elios, a friend of Gaia's. Is she home?"

"Hi, Elios. No, I'm sorry, but Gaia is back in Seattle. She has been there for a while now."

"I didn't know. I was overseas myself. I just came back and was hoping to catch up with her. Is there a number I can reach her at?"

"Sure, I'll give you her cell phone number. But don't bother trying to call her right now. She's hiking on Mount Rainier with Sara, and the reception is terrible."

I thanked her and ended the call.

"What's wrong?"

"Gaia's mother told me she and Sara are in the United States." A part of me wanted to believe that Gaia was safe and sound, hiking with Sara. I wanted to believe that alien technology was the reason for the nightmare I had lived through the last six months and that I had had suicidal thoughts over nothing. I wanted to believe there was an explanation for Areel's disappearance and that he was somewhere, maybe with them.

I wanted more than anything else to call her cell phone and hear her voice, tired from a long hike. I couldn't bear to call. I gave Kam the phone. "Please, call this number for me."

Kam punched the numbers, and we both waited for the call to connect. When not even the answering machine answered, he shook his head and closed the phone. "Whoever kidnapped them has gone a long way to cover any trace."

I choked back a cry.

Kam patted my shoulder. "Areel would have followed Sara anywhere, and even if he had gone rogue and tried to hide from Solo, I would have found his aura by now."

Only one plausible explanation emerged. "They aren't humans."

"What?" Kam raised an eyebrow, his hands on the bike, ready to mount.

I secured the helmet under my chin and signaled for him to get going. "Their kidnappers are not humans."

"How can you be sure?"

"Because. Gaia, Sara, and Areel disappeared without a trace. Nobody is looking for them. Their families are sure about their whereabouts. Anyone who has the means to create a cover so plausible is using a non-human technology." I marked every item by raising a finger from my fisted hand. "Let's go to Gaia and Sara's apartment. Areel was there before they were kidnapped. Maybe we can find something."

Kam drove us to the apartment, where we were told by the caretaker's wife we could find him at the bar on the corner. When we entered the small bar, traces of Gaia's aura were everywhere, and I had to exit and breathe some fresh air. Kam inquired after the caretaker, and once the man finished his coffee, they both came out and joined me.

The caretaker, an older man with bright eyes, looked at us as though he were weighing our worth and then, after I expressed my desire to enter Gaia's place, he shook his head most vehemently. "I can't let you snoop around someone else's apartment."

"I understand, but Gaia called me from Seattle asking me if I could retrieve a book for her." I raised a hand. "You can ask her mother. She knows me."

The man squinted at me. "I never saw the two of you visiting the girls; how do I know that you won't steal anything?"

I could see that convincing the man to let us in would take some finesse. "We don't need to enter the apartment. I can tell you where the books I am looking for are. Gaia told me where I could find them."

"I don't know..."

"No, it's okay. I'll tell you the titles and where they are, and you can pick them up for us. We wait here." I felt Kam's stare on me and hoped I hadn't gone too far with my charade.

Finally, the man relented. "Tell me those titles."

On the spot, I invented half a dozen different titles in English, hoping he didn't know the language and waiting for him to feel overwhelmed at having to remember all of them. Luck was on my side.

While I was reciting for the second time a list of books that had never existed, the caretaker's cell phone rang. "I apologize. I have to take this."

I nodded and held my breath.

"I'm sorry, guys, but there's a broken dishwasher in 2B." He gave us a look, waved his free hand, and while still on the phone, mouthed to follow him upstairs. He opened Gaia and Sara's apartment door and followed us inside. "You have five minutes. Okay?"

Both Kam and I answered at the same time, "Okay." We hurried inside, and my heart stopped beating.

I could see Gaia in every corner, reading a book, drinking tea, listening to music, sleeping, eating, and talking to Sara. Her presence was still strong, as though she had just left for some errands. Six months had passed, but in her apartment, time had simply stopped moving. I found her room immediately. I remembered it by heart even though I had never put a foot inside it.

My conversations with Gaia had mostly taken place in that room. I opened her closet and found lots of clothes I remembered as well. I hugged some of them and filled my nostrils with her scent. I fell on the floor, dragging with me a bunch of Gaia-perfumed dresses, and covered my face with them. All her belongings were there. Wherever she was, and I knew too well that wasn't Seattle, she didn't have anything with her. All her books were there, supporting my lies at least, and everything else as well. In the bathroom, I found all the personal hygiene items, things they would have taken with them if they had really left voluntarily. Brushes and combs, necklaces, soft bathrobes, pink slippers. Touching her things was painful.

Every time my hand stopped on an object that was Gaia's, my lungs had trouble breathing, my heart skipped beats, and my mind filled with memories I couldn't have. I saw Gaia smiling, preparing herself to go out, talking to the mirror.

I *saw* her, and that shouldn't have happened. I heard the caretaker, remembered our five-minutes deal, and went back to Gaia's room to grab a handful of books to keep the charade alive when I suddenly noticed an almost-imperceptible smell that didn't belong to Gaia or Sara or Areel. Or to any human.

The caretaker rushed us to the door, and I only had time to shoot a sideways glance at Kam, who looked back at me with a knowing look on his face. He had sensed it too. With the books under my arm, I thanked the guy, and we walked out of the building and toward the bike without speaking.

Only when we reached his motorcycle did Kam ask me, "Did you sense it too? It was so faint, I almost missed it. But the scent was different from anything else inside the apartment." He took the books from me and put them inside the small carrier on the back of the bike.

I raised my eyes to where Gaia's apartment was. "The smell was more similar to ours. But it wasn't Areel's. We have to go back inside."

"Okay."

"We are going back tonight when the caretaker is sleeping. I think that right now we should return to the archeological site. We

165

have enough time to take a look at the place where the boxes with the Solean artifact were stolen and to see for ourselves if we can find something that human senses may have not detected." I hesitated and then asked, "Let me drive, please."

"Just don't kill us." Kam threw the keys at me.

"I don't have time for that now." I mounted the bike and waited for him to sit behind me. I had memorized the road to and from the camp, and driving occupied my mind and gave my body something to be busy with. Kam's investigation was saving me precious time and the need to ask too many questions, but I still thought that wasn't enough. I felt I was drowning in a sea of uncertainty. I had bits and pieces of the puzzle, but I was still missing too much.

"Think of a good excuse to visit the camp again." I raised my voice to be heard over the bike.

"We can't enter from the front gate. The policemen already saw us today, and I can't ask Danilo to chaperone us through the camp. Maybe we can enter from the beach side." Kam led me to a dirty road that ran parallel to the camp and made me stop before the dirt gave way to brown sand. I looked around as I dismounted the bike.

"There." I indicated a semihidden trail covered by sand dunes and high weeds. "I think we can enter from there."

Kam nodded, and we walked toward the trail. The beach was crowded with young couples more interested in themselves than the rest of the universe. It turned out to be just perfect because nobody looked at us twice. I walked on the soft sand, sinking at every step, but I managed to keep a natural pace. Kam was just behind me, being careful as well. At the end of the trail, we had a welcome surprise; ahead of us was the beginning of the camp. It had a fence with signs saying to keep off the premises, but that didn't bother me. I could also see a policeman guarding the perimeter, but we only had to wait for the right moment to slip in unnoticed.

The key part of my plan was *waiting*. I would rather have jumped before bullets if that would speed up the process. I was probably at the end of my physical strength, and slowing down was actually a good idea, but I didn't want to be left alone with my thoughts. The necessity for silence forced my mind to go where I didn't want to. My fear for Gaia was growing. We were dealing with intelligent beings who had taken time to manufacture evidence that she was somewhere else and keeping in regular contact with her family. The thought of her mother talking to someone impersonating Gaia was sickening. I had heard her voice and knew the horror she was living through while her family thought she was safe. I had to hurry. I had to find her. Gaia's voice, telling me that her time was almost up, was playing inside my head like a broken record over and over again.

It made me feel ill at ease, and I needed to concentrate on what I was trying to do. Kam pulled my arm softly and made me look to my right where the policeman had just gone to stretch his legs. The guy turned his head toward the camp and away from us. Someone was calling him, and he kept talking back and forth; then he just turned and started walking briskly toward the person that was vehemently calling him. We slithered under the fence. We walked crouched low to the ground, hidden by the bushes, until we reached a big dune just behind a tomb. We just had time to enter inside the tomb when the policeman came back, still shouting back at his interlocutor. I wasn't comfortable inside the dark, humid chamber. I didn't like the idea of desecrating a resting place, but I couldn't do otherwise given the situation.

I leaned on the wall to support my back and touched the floor. I was immediately swept away by a vivid memory of Gaia sitting in the same spot, her heart racing, trying to keep her breathing under control but being too scared to achieve it. Then I saw that she hadn't been alone; Sara and Areel had been with her. I couldn't make any sense of what I was seeing, but I knew I was reliving one of her memories. She had been there; my ability to sense her presence through the objects she had touched had reached levels I didn't know I could achieve. Though before I had to fill in to understand what she had been doing or where she had been going, I could then see Gaia as though I was there with her. Had I had this kind of power before, I would have found her right away in Athens and then in Rome and in Seattle. We could have stayed together longer; maybe I would have found a way to make things really work. Maybe...

I had to concentrate on the present, but it wasn't easy when her presence was so intoxicating. Finally, Kam brought me back to reality by pinching my arm. He showed me the way out, indicating that the man had left his spot. We ran outside, trying to make no sound at all, and I mentally thanked nature for the presence of the sand. We moved toward another dune and crouched again before the policeman had time to come back. Kam and I turned our heads at the same time when we caught a familiar scent in the air, coming from a darkened patch of soil—possibly a fire pit—on our left. Even after all these months, the residual burnt smell of a lightweight space shuttle engine was still strong enough for us to sense it.

14

"Well, we did expect extraterrestrial technology." The smell had saturated my nostrils and left an unpleasant aftertaste in the back of my throat.

"Yes, but I wasn't expecting a technology so close to ours." Kam cleared his throat.

I followed suit, but I couldn't get rid of the bitterness in my mouth. "No, definitely not."

"What does it mean?"

"I am not sure. Let's get a closer look." We left the safety of the dune and stealthily moved closer to the burnt circle, barren of vegetation, in the middle of the sandy meadow. I had grabbed a handful of soil when the distinct sound of a cocking gun got my attention. I turned to face the policeman we had been hiding from, taking aim at us. Kam and I slowly stood up and raised our hands.

"You two! What do you think you are doing?" The guy was young, and his hands weren't steady.

"Sorry, Officer... we just curious." I faked a Swedish accent. I guessed I could pass for northern European with the color of my hair.

He looked at us as though we were idiots. "You cannot stay here; can't you read?"

"Sorry... we very sorry," Kam said, imitating my accent.

The policeman sighed and then waved his gun away from us and toward the beach. "Okay, disappear and don't come back." He enunciated the last sentence one word at a time.

I nodded. "Yes, we go. Thank... Officer." We thanked him one more time on our way back, and I made sure to say something in Swedish to Kam so that he could hear us. While we were almost out of his sight, we heard him muttering on his radio, "No, no trouble. Just the usual UFO maniacs." The irony wasn't lost on me.

The beach was almost deserted now, just two or three couples left, minding their business under the moon, and we silently walked to our parking spot. "Back to Gaia's." I reached out my hand, silently asking for the bike's keys. Kam granted my wish once again.

On our way to Tarquinia, I reflected on everything that had happened so far, and the emerging picture was looking more and more frightening. "It's going to be a long night."

We had just arrived at Gaia's building, and judging by the lit windows in the apartments facing the square, most of the tenants, included the caretaker and his wife, were awake. I drove around and parked the bike by a nearby alley. Then we walked toward the marble fountain dominating the center of the square. People milled about it, and our presence would go unnoticed. I sat on the smooth edge of the fountain and patted the space next to me. "We better make ourselves comfortable."

Kam hesitated and then sat. "May I ask you something?"

"Sure."

"You look different—" Kam lowered his eyes. "Not just your body. You. What happened to my old friend?"

I sighed. "I feel different. More in control of my mind."

"How?" He shuffled his feet on the cobblestones.

I weighed the pros and cons of showing him what I meant and decided I needed a subject to test whether I could stop a Share. I raised one hand and outstretched it toward him, palm open.

He looked at me, puzzled. "Are you asking me to touch you?"

I nodded.

Kam's confusion deepened. "Are you sure?"

"Yes. I'm sure." I tilted my head. "Please?" He hesitated before raising his hand, and I waited for him to make contact. When he was about to lay his palm against mine, the memory of my last share with Areel came back to me, and I fought the urge to step back and stop the process. I steadied my resolve and closed the gap between our hands. At the same time, I summoned the image of a metal gate and closed my mind to Kam. I heard him gasp a curse in Solean.

"What just happened?" Kam had retracted his hand and was looking at it.

I exhaled. "It works."

He locked eyes with mine. "I didn't think it was possible to stop a Share."

"Me neither, until I started questioning lots of things we take for granted." Several lights were turned off in the apartments facing the square, but I could see the caretakers and several other people still up and about. "When I went back to Solo to report my findings, I felt I didn't belong to my race."

Kam gasped at my words.

"I don't know how to explain this, but I felt guilty about it, and at the same time I couldn't deny my feelings. I started doubting the rightness of certain assumptions." I paused for a moment when the illumination in the other three apartments went off. The caretaker was still busy in his kitchen. I turned to face Kam.

He looked back at me, attempted a smile, and then averted his eyes. "What you just did, what you're saying is hard to swallow."

"I should start from the beginning." I chuckled softly and shook my head. "Believe me, until a few months ago, I could barely even acknowledge my own ideas. I tried to conceal them from myself. I couldn't bear the thought that I was questioning the way of our culture." I saw Kam relax by my side, and that gave me the strength to keep talking. "When Areel saw me on Solo, I was already changed, but the process didn't stop then." As it was, I had barely had time to analyze my unusual condition, but it could wait. "During the last six months, while I was traveling, I was forced to witness Gaia's agony. I don't know how it has been possible, but I have a connection with her that has kept us united in spite of every obstacle. We have been communicating. I don't have an explanation for any of the things I am going to tell you, but the truth probably lies there. While I was on Silenzio, we started *seeing* each other. Sometimes, we could even have brief telepathic conversations. That is how I found out about Areel and Sara. I would have never thought of disobeying direct orders; I was content knowing she was fine. I was selfish, of course; I can see this now. I just wanted to have Gaia in my life even if it meant sacrificing her freedom as well, because as I told you, I didn't think to escape. I had changed, but I was still an Observer, and deep inside I thought I deserved to pay for my sin.

The more I wanted Gaia, the more I desired her, the more I felt I had betrayed everything I had been raised to believe. At the same time, I couldn't understand how something so beautiful, so holy, like the love we felt, was so wrong. How could it be wrong? I know that what I am saying doesn't mean anything to you, but Areel saw in my mind how important Gaia was to me—what I was willing to do to keep her safe. All the time I spent on Silenzio, the only reason to keep on living was Gaia. She was fine; I was fine. She was happy; I was happy. My peace ended the day we lost contact. I knew something had happened to her. At that point, my only thought was how to reach Earth again."

I paused to drink water from one of the many faucets sprouting from the main body of the fountain. Kam took his turn after I was done. When he faced me again, I resumed my tale. "I was lucky two generous souls, Rah and Reah, became stranded on Silenzio. I was able to help them, and they lent me their ship. During the six months it took the ship to reach Earth, I had the most radical transformation. Gaia's thoughts were inside my mind the whole time. My body was sleeping, but my brain never rested. Gaia's mind reached for mine while she was living through a nightmare. She needed my support to survive, and I couldn't do anything. Just listening to her incoherent thoughts, her heartbreaking fear, made me crazy. Gaia was constantly cold, and sometimes she screamed in pain—" I couldn't talk about it, not now that I didn't know how she was.

"I can feel your anguish, but it's so raw, so—"

"Alien? Is this the word you are looking for?"

His eyes widened, and some color darkened his cheeks. "Yes."

I leaned over the faucet and filled my hand with cold water then splashed it on my face. "I am alienated from my culture. It is true, and I didn't look for it. I have become something different, but I didn't ask for it. Can you understand the difference? I hope you do. I don't know if what has happened to me, to fall in love outside my race, to betray my oath, could happen to every other Observer or to any other Solean, but it happened to me. It did happen to *me,* and do you want to know what is really scary? I don't regret any of it. What I feel for Gaia justifies everything, the punishment, the pain, whatever horror is in store for me."

Kam raised one hand to stop me. "You're scaring me." He looked about to bolt.

I gave him a pleading look. "What is happening to Gaia is so frightening that I am constantly terrified for her. At some point during my deep sleep, while I was immobilized inside my own body, Gaia stopped thinking. You can't imagine how painful it is just remembering it. I was sure she was dead. My mind died with her; my only hope was that, once awake, I would kill myself."

Kam's gasp was loud enough to turn several heads our way. He lowered his voice to a whisper, but his eyes were bright and his body tense. "You can't talk about suicide! You make it sound possible. It is too wrong. It is obscene!"

I nodded. "Yes, it is wrong. But I did contemplate ending my life because living without Gaia is not possible." I paused for a moment. We both needed time to absorb my words. Talking out loud about what I had been so close to doing had drained my energy. Kam looked too shocked to reply. When I started again, my voice was fatigued as well. "I physically survived that mental pain, but I paid a price." I pointed at my white hair. "I feel alone. I'm apart from my own race. I am not human. I am not Solean anymore. I can decide if I want to share myself. I am separated from the culture I embraced all my life. I'll never be able to go back to my planet because I am a danger to my own society. I could be the end of it. Can you understand how much I suffer?" I mentally braced myself for Kam to get up and leave me there by the fountain.

Instead, Kam looked at me with watery eyes, quietly shaking his head. "Elios, you are not alone. I am here. I am not sure I can help you, but I am here for you."

His words warmed my heart when I needed it the most. "Thank you."

After that exchange, we waited silently until the last window on Gaia's building went finally dark then walked to the main entrance. Kam looked right and left and forced the lock with a piece of thin metal he retrieved from his rear pocket. "I picked up several useful skills in the last six months."

"I can see that."

In less than a minute, we were inside the ground-floor hallway. We climbed the stairs with soft steps and reached Gaia's apartment's door in no time. Kam produced two flashlights from the same pocket he had reached into for the thief-kit, and he handed me one. He opened that door as well, and we entered, careful not to make any noise when closing it behind us. As soon as I was wrapped in the warm darkness inside the apartment, I gasped for air. I tried to shield myself from the deluge of Gaia's memories assailing my senses with every step. We couldn't stay the whole night, and I should have focused on looking for clues. It wasn't easy because the pleasure I felt was overpowering, and lately the only sentiments I'd had were centered on negative feelings: fear more than anything else, but also desperation. Experiencing joy again was such a treat.

And here every memory was happy. Even without my new, magnified ability, I could have seen that Gaia had had a good time in that place. She had painted all the red landscapes on the white walls. A symphony of vibrant shades of reds gave life to the monochromatic palette of the apartment. The paintings chased each other, depicting one single story, a beautiful summer day in the country, the sun shining on the freshly opened poppies here, the sunflowers lazily turning their heads there, people cooling down in the fresh waters of a lake.

The good vibe was marred soon enough by the bite constantly devouring my stomach. I couldn't even breathe for a few seconds without remembering I had to hurry. My mind already far gone from the happy place I had visited, I removed a small canvas from its spot on the wall, a painting that Gaia had finished just before disappearing, judging by the date she had signed it. It depicted a sea of indistinct red geraniums in the background, pink hydrangeas, and a blue sky with big white clouds creating a stark contrast with the flowers. I knew the moment I looked at the painting how much Gaia loved hydrangeas. Hydrangeas were her favorite flowers. We deserved to live our story. We needed more time to learn about the little things.

Meanwhile, Kam was efficiently searching for the origin of the smell that had caught our attention earlier in the afternoon. The apartment had two bathrooms and three bedrooms. Since I already knew which one was Gaia's, we went looking for the room where Areel had slept while he was living there. In every room, everything had been left as if they were just gone for the day. We gave another look at the kitchen. We didn't go outside to the terrace; we just looked from the windows, worried that someone would see us. The view outside was serene, the caretaker had clearly been watering the plants, and the furniture had been covered. We went to the second bathroom, most likely the guest bathroom that Areel had used.

I reached for the brass door handle, and suddenly I was in the room with them. Once again. Gaia was looking worried. Sara was on the floor with Areel. I had already seen that scene when Gaia had thought of it, but now I was physically in it. I could see details Gaia couldn't remember.

Like the shape reflected in the mirror that didn't belong to Gaia.

She was looking down at her friends, her face showing compassion. I moved inside the room, changing point of view, until I was at the same level as Areel and Sara. Areel was hugging Sara, and his eyes were full of despair. Sara turned slightly to find his mouth. They kissed. Gaia raised her hands to cover her lips, astonished. Then it happened.

Every color in the room got amplified and then exploded. A sound like a blast invaded the peace of the night. I changed point of view again, and I was standing next to Gaia. I could smell her warm body. I could hear her irregular breathing. She was scared.

The mirror was by her left side and she never moved her head in that direction, otherwise she would have seen someone moving behind them, hidden by the poorly illuminated hallway and the fake explosion. I tried to look directly behind Gaia, but my vision was limited by her memories. The image in the mirror had been impressed on her eyes even if she had not realized it. The last thing her eyes had seen in the mirror was a white light that had touched her shoulder and then nothing more, just pitch black.

I found myself on the bathroom floor covered in sweat, struggling for breath and unable to talk. Kam gave me a glass of water and sponged my forehead with a wet cloth. I was starting to react when we heard the door opening. My legs weren't cooperating, but with Kam's help, we reached the kitchen and used the unlocked window that opened onto the terrace, located to the right of the door, to go out. We heard the steps coming closer and tried to find a place to hide in the dark.

We stepped carefully to the next attached terrace. I hoped nobody from that apartment would venture out for fresh air. We crouched on the floor and waited. After a few seconds, we heard someone opening the door to the terrace. At first, I couldn't understand what was happening because the steps went back and forth, then I heard the sound of a sloshing liquid. I cautiously peeked over the low partition wall and saw the caretaker watering the plants.

I immediately crouched down when the man walked in our direction. I held my breath. Even if he couldn't see us through the wall dividing the two balconies, the only thing he had to do was simply to lean out and look down at us. I froze while I waited for the man to find us. He reached the separating wall, and I could hear his regular breathing when something soft and warm brushed my back with a low sound. At the same time I heard the man calling with a gentle voice, whispering toward us.

"Pallino? Pallino? Come here, kitten; here is your chow. Come here, little kitten."

Pallino kept brushing my back for a few seconds and then, bless his soul, decided he was hungry. The cat gracefully jumped the wall and landed on the other side with a satisfied meow. The caretaker waited until the cat had finished eating and then left, carefully closing the door behind him, but leaving the window open for the cat. We moved back inside and then left the apartment the same way we had come in.

Once outside the building, I had to squat down and breathe through my mouth because my legs were trembling so much I couldn't stand up.

I still had the painting with me, and Pallino was waiting for us by the bike. The sun was rising. I grabbed Pallino in my arms and gave the keys back to Kam.

"I'm crashing." I wasn't even sure I had the strength to hold onto Kam. Pallino purred against my chest.

* * *

The sun was shining, and a few clouds were scattered in the light-blue sky outside the open window when I woke. I blinked. "Where am I? What time is it?" I heard steps outside the room I didn't recognize and then the noise of keys inserted into the lock of one of the four doors opening into the room—the door on the opposite wall. "Kam, is that you?" I was lying on a sofa bed in what looked like a studio apartment. On my right was a small kitchen, on my left a big window that framed a portion of a sandy beach and the sea.

The door opened, and Kam greeted me with a smile, then he turned, disappeared for a moment, and came back carrying two bags full of groceries. "You are up. How do you feel?"

I had to think about my answer. "Fine." The sunlight made me squint, and I remembered it was already dawn when we had reached Kam's apartment. "How long did I sleep?"

"The whole day and the whole night." Kam laid the bags on the kitchen counter.

"Really?" I stretched first my legs then my arms.

"Like the dead." Kam opened the bags and proceeded to sort the items that went into the small fridge and the ones that belonged to the pantry, a cubicle left of the fridge.

"It's probably the first time I've slept in six months." I was rested, but it felt wrong. I didn't want to feel better if Gaia was still suffering. But I couldn't help her if I wasn't one-hundred-percent functional. I had to be strong. I had to push all the anxiety away and use that fear to propel myself to action.

A sudden movement from my left made us turn at the same time. A furry creature entered the room by jumping over the sill of the open window and landing on four paws by my sofa bed. I scooped up Pallino, and he curled by my arm. "Where were you?"

In response, the cat licked his mouth where something feathery and white had stuck out a moment earlier. I stroked his head, feeling the low hum from his throat growing louder.

"For the most part, Pallino has been lying on your chest, cozily rolled up like a doughnut. You both snore, by the way."

"No wonder I slept so well." I regulated my breathing with Pallino's. "Must tell you something."

Kam *hmm*ed in assent while pushing a bag of frozen vegetables into the freezer compartment.

"Someone else was inside Gaia's apartment the night they all disappeared."

"How do you know?" Kam closed the fridge's door and turned to face me.

"I saw the person who kidnapped them. At the apartment, when I touched the door Gaia had been leaning on before she disappeared, I saw what happened. I was there with them. Literally. I could move in the room and around them. Areel was on the floor on the verge of losing control, and Sara was kneeling next to him. Gaia was looking at them. Sara reached for Areel. She cuddled him like a child, and then they kissed. Their auras exploded. The bright light engulfed their bodies, even Gaia's. She thought she heard an explosion and then everything went black. But I saw who created the explosion. I saw him shooting at Gaia's shoulder."

"*He* shot her. Who is *he*?"

"The image in the mirror was familiar." I brought Pallino closer to my chest, his regular breathing helping me concentrate on recalling the memory.

"Okay, familiar how?" Kam walked to the sofa and crouched at my level.

"*He* is more like us than human."

"Someone from Solo? Are you insane?" Kam threw his hands in the air.

"He used our technology and had a mental signature close to ours."

"This person can't be one of us. What he did… it just can't be. It goes against our morals." He stood and walked to the window.

I lowered Pallino onto the sofa and joined Kam at the window. The salty breeze from the sea hit my nostrils, and I inhaled it in a long breath. "I said the person I saw has a mental signature *similar* to ours." I hesitated before adding, "You should open your mind to the possibility that the world you think you know is more complicated than what we have been raised to believe."

Kam looked at me, and he didn't say it, but his censure of my words was clear.

"I know what I revealed to you is a lot to digest, but I could really use a friend now."

His expression softened. "You know you can count on me."

"I needed to hear that. Thank you."

We stood in amiable silence for several minutes, then an idea took shape in my mind and I had to act on it.

"Regarding my newfound capabilities…" Seagulls flew close to the window. Their flattering wings resembled my erratic heartbeats.

"Another surprise?" Kam's voice had a resigned edge.

I stretched my hand toward him, hoping I hadn't abused his patience already. "I know it's a lot to ask, but I'd like to test something else. If you don't mind."

Kam gave the marine life one last look before facing me. "May I ask what is it about, at least?"

I nodded. "I want to try to shield my memories during a Share. I know I am capable of skirting through someone else's memories." I saw his puzzled frown and added, "I tried it once already on Rah, and it worked. Now I want to know if I can do the same for myself."

"Okay. Let's do it." His hand was already raised to meet mine.

Reassured, I placed my right palm on his. The warmth emanating from him felt comforting. I could now understand humans' fixation with physical contact. I released my consciousness at the touch and tried to select the amount of sharing. I didn't edit my darker side, but at the same time, I pushed my mind and shielded all my memories of Gaia I didn't want him to see. I also allowed him to know that. When I was done, I simply dropped my hand to my side and stepped back.

"You have complete power over your mind." He blinked several times then stared at me for a long moment. "Thanks for letting me know you were putting up walls to hide your memories. I wouldn't have known on my own, and you didn't have to."

"I was as surprised as you are when I met Rah and Reah and discovered it was possible and that it was their custom to do that. Their race has developed a different approach to mind sharing. Anyway, this was the first time I attempted to fully shield thoughts. I'm actually surprised it worked out so well."

"It opens a whole new world of possibilities." Kam brought a hand to his chin and stroked it.

"I know. I could have used it on Solo."

Kam moved to the kitchen and opened the bread box. "Hungry?"

"Last time I ate was two… three days ago?" Time-wise, my memories were blurred.

"How about a sandwich?"

"Sounds great." I sat in one of the chairs tucked under the island table protruding from the wall and waited for Kam to fix our meal.

We ate in silence, only Pallino's purring interrupting my thoughts. When I was done, I realized I was still wearing the clothes Marcello had given me. "May I take a shower?"

"Of course." Kam pointed at the door on the left by the window.

The bathroom had the same view of the sea as the main room of the studio.

Looking at my reflection in the mirror, I had the feeling that I hadn't showered in a century. I couldn't look so worn out after only two or three days. "I look like crap," I said out loud.

Kam answered from outside, "Yes, you do."

I had a hot steaming shower while contemplating the view from the open window. Seagulls were flying on circular raids above the calm blue expanse of the sea. The salty breeze mixed with the warm water and the scent of the shampoo. I borrowed a spare razor from Kam's supplies on the edge of the sink, and I shaved my face. My hair formed a white halo around my thin face. I had lost more weight.

Kam knocked on the door. "I put a change of clothes on the wooden bench for you."

I turned and saw the neat pile by the tub. "Thanks." Once clothed with the white shirt and a pair of jeans that was one or two sizes too large for me, I went back to the mirror and braided my hair, closing the plait with the black ribbon I had kept with me the whole time. After one last look, I decided I'd had enough of myself already and left the bathroom.

Kam was sitting at the table, drinking from a ceramic mug. Another cup, a teapot, and a plate loaded with cookies were on the table. "You look like you're from another planet."

I raised one eyebrow. "I borrowed one of your spare razors."

He gave me another look. "You should shave your head. Your white mane is too exotic for Italian standards."

"I've thought about that, but..." A sheepish look crossed my face and I half smiled. "Gaia likes my hair longer."

Kam snorted but didn't comment on my statement, instead reaching for the teapot and filling the other cup for me. "Let's go to the terrace." Carrying the cookie plate, he left the table and reached for the French door opening onto a small patio.

I followed him outside, thankful for the jute overhang protecting us from the sun's rays.

"I find this to be my favorite place here on Earth." Kam lowered himself onto the rocking chair facing the beach. "At first, my priority was to rent the first available place I found near the archeological site in Marina Velca. In winter, I found plenty of vacancies, and I chose this apartment because of the view. It reminded me of the sandy shores of Xiann. I miss it."

Xiann was one of the capital cities on Ura, Kam's first mission's planet. I never knew he had formed an attachment so profound with that place, until now. I sat on the deck chair, relaxing my legs on a matching stool.

Kam took a bite from a cookie and then put it down on the small coffee table between us. "So you think Areel was taken by another Observer."

"The person who kidnapped them has an aura *similar* to ours," I repeated.

"Yes, but nobody else has the knowledge and the resources to track him down on Earth. Areel found something he shouldn't have, and he was clearly losing control of his relationship with Sara. An Observer was sent to retrieve him." He kept his eyes trained on the seagulls dancing with the wind. "I'd like to think otherwise."

"The only way to know for sure would be to ask Areel's superior, but as soon as you contact him, my location would be discovered. I'm sorry, but I can't let you do that."

"There must be something—"

I thought about what we had put together, and an idea sprang to my mind. "There might be something we can attempt. Kam, you are going to discover a new Solean artifact, and we'll wait until someone shows up and tries to silence you as they did to Areel, Gaia, and Sara."

Kam took a sip from his cup and seemed to think about it for a moment. "Do you really think it is going to work?"

I shivered despite the growing heat under the canopy, the distant shrill of a seagull unnerving me more than it should have. "It's not like we have lots of options." I brought my cup to my mouth and let the warm tea chase away the sudden chill I was experiencing. "You'll talk to the people who supervised the cataloguing process for the exhibition and try to discover if there were any more artifacts displaying the Solean language. You'll poke around a bit, asking questions, and then we'll wait for someone to take the bait."

"I don't think it is as easy as you make it sound." Kam reached for the cookie he had discarded and dropped it again on the coffee table.

I finished my tea. "You're probably right, but I'll be there for you the whole time."

"Okay."

"You are okay with my plan?"

"No, I'm far from being okay with what you call a plan, but I can't come up with a better solution, so I'll give it a try." He took my empty cup and his and walked back inside. He filled the cups with fresh tea and brought them to the coffee table. "Wait a moment." He left again.

"Sure." I closed my eyes and focused on the sounds coming from the beach.

"I guess we better get started on this plan." Kam sat again and opened the laptop he was carrying.

I watched his fingers flying on the keyboard. "What are you looking for?"

"The names of the people from the excavation site involved in the Etruscan exhibit." After a moment, his eyes lit in recognition. "Here they are, in alphabetical order."

It took us several hours to sift through the list of possible contacts. We eliminated two professors and their close assistants, plus the whole American team, who had left two months ago. We ended up with two guys who were still working in Tarquinia but temporarily relocated on another project. One of them was Danilo, and we couldn't use him. The other one, a guy named Saverio, received a phone call from me, acting as a Swedish journalist interested in writing a piece about the lost exhibit.

"Is it okay to meet tonight? I have a few questions for you."

"Tonight works for me. Since the mess with the robbery, we have been relegated to clerical work, and it's so boring. A change of scenery would do me good. Where to?"

We had decided beforehand on a place that wasn't close to the excavation site where someone could recognize Kam but was full of people where Saverio could be seen talking to strangers.

"What about the Covo della Sirena in Civitavecchia?" The city was a mere half-hour drive from Tarquinia.

"The one on the restored pier by the old harbor?"

"That one."

"Cool. At what time?"

"After dinner. Let's say around ten p.m.?"

"Perfect. See you later."

We arrived earlier and had dinner at one of the many restaurants lining the pier. The night was mild and the place crowded. Lots of people walked back and forth along the length of the promenade at night. After dinner, we moved to the bar we had picked for our meeting. The place was open to the sea and the street and was full of young people. A local band played live on the opposite side of the promenade. We sat, ordered drinks, and waited for Saverio to arrive. I would lead the interview while Kam would play the photographer. Saverio arrived on time, accompanied by a girl he introduced as Ilaria, his girlfriend. We resorted to speaking in English while Kam and I faked the Swedish accent once again. The young man wanted to impress Ilaria and was forthcoming with all kinds of information. It worked just fine for us that he wanted her to think he had a promising career in the archeology field because it led him to talk about things he wasn't supposed to divulge. I let the conversation idle for a while, and then I finally threw the bait. "So, I assume the pictures for the exhibit catalogue had been already taken when the boxes were stolen."

Saverio drank the third refill of a pink concoction he had ordered and then enthusiastically put the tall glass down on the table. "Oh, yes, of course! Unfortunately, the catalogues disappeared the same night along with the boxes." He tilted his head toward his girlfriend. "Very few people know about that." He was rewarded with a beaming smile from Ilaria. "New catalogues are being printed, of course. At least, the three-year commitment to the Etruscan project will have public recognition after all." He looked at the girl once more. "I know the graphic designer who is putting together the new art for the books."

I sipped from my glass—I had ordered white wine—and casually asked, "Would it be possible to take a look at the new catalogues?"

Saverio shook his head. "The art and the content are kept secret, even from us. There were unexpected leaks during the first months of the case, and the police had taken special measures to prevent that from happening again. Only the curator and some of the senior archeologists know exactly how many pieces were going to be shown at the exhibit. If you are not one of the archeologists that worked on the project, you simply shouldn't know anything about them. If you do, you are a suspect. My colleagues and I had been grilled for a while soon after the robbery."

Soon after that exchange, Ilaria commented on the hour being too late for her and having to go back home. I thanked Saverio for his help, and we all stood to leave the bar.

"Could you wait for me? I want to show you something," Saverio whispered to me, his back to Ilaria, who was talking to her cell phone.

"Sure." I made a sign to Kam to sit again. "The night is still young, the music is good, and the ginseng orzo espresso sounds promising," I said out loud for Ilaria's sake.

Saverio left with his girl and came back one hour later alone. "Thanks for waiting; there is something I wanted to show you, but Ilaria is not supposed to see it yet. It's a surprise for her." He ordered the caffeine cocktail spiced with ginger I had mentioned earlier, and after tasting it from the lip of the milky-white blown glass, he finally decided to talk again. "Ilaria and I have been together for a while, and two months from now is going to be her birthday, but she's leaving soon after to study in London, and I wanted to give her something special." He sipped silently for several interminable minutes and then started again, "Her family is quite rich, and she has everything she wants. I wanted to be original. A month ago, the graphic designer came to our camp to talk about details concerning a particular picture that wasn't clear enough, asking my professor if he had a sharper image he could use for the catalogue. They left the room I was working in, and while they were on their way out, one copy of the images they were carrying inside a folder fell on the floor. I went to pick up the picture to give it back to them, but I couldn't help but give a look. I didn't remember that particular piece because it wasn't one I had personally worked on, but it was so beautiful that I couldn't resist shooting a picture with my cell phone before giving the image back to them. I'm very good at drawing, so I could recreate the details that weren't clear." Saverio reached into a jacket pocket and procured a small black velvet box. "I asked a jeweler I know to recreate the exact same design from the object in the picture." He opened the little box and showed us a piece of jewelry. Gently resting on a little cushion was a golden ring with a geometrical design depicting a never-ending loop, like one of the Escher drawings I had seen once in a book. The central part of the ring was a flat oval with an incision that created another infinity design. The incision was in an archaic Solean dialect.

15

"What do you think, isn't it the most original idea? I can't wait for Ilaria to wear it!" Saverio beamed.

We were speechless.

"So, anyway, I came back to show you the only image available at the moment. Of course I had to erase the picture I made with my cell phone as soon as I sketched it on paper, and I asked the jeweler to destroy the drawing." He gave the ring one last look and then closed the box.

"From the picture, could you tell what kind of object had this design?" I asked.

"The picture wasn't clear, but I think it was a bronze spear, one of the decorative items found in the Hunters' Tomb." At my puzzled reaction, Saverio promptly explained, "The whole exhibit was about recreating a hunter's themed tomb. It is called the Hunters' Tomb because it only contained hunting gear and hunt-themed paintings on the walls. No feminine jewelry whatsoever, reason why it didn't get looted and was found in relatively pristine condition."

"Do you know when the catalogue books will be in the museum bookstore?"

Saverio bit his lower lip. "The graphic designer is working hard on it, but the curator has decided to hold the release."

"Why would the curator do that?"

Saverio called the waiter passing by and ordered another coffee. "He still hopes the police will find the contents of the boxes in someone's house. I know he asked the graphic designer to be ready to add a whole chapter with the Hunters' Tomb pictures. In any case, he'll have to open the exhibit to the public within the year."

I inwardly groaned. "May I take another look at the ring?"

"Sure." Saverio reopened the box and let me hold it.

Kam was suddenly busy with a phone call.

"It is beautiful. Your girlfriend will love it."

Saverio beamed, pleased by my words. "To think we can barely grasp the Etruscan language, and something like this is discovered. What a challenge for an archeologist! Who knows what the inscription means."

"Forever yours." I couldn't help answering and immediately realized my slip. "Would be nice to think that was what it meant, given the never-ending design."

Saverio smiled. "I like it." He took the box from me, finished his coffee, and stood, ready to leave. "I have to ask you to keep *this* between us." He tapped the lid to close the box.

I nodded. "No problem. Thanks for your help."

I waited until the man was out of earshot before asking, "Did you get a good look at it?"

"Yes, I did." Kam smiled. "Time to go home."

Thirty minutes later, we were back at his apartment. I was tired and ready to go to sleep, but I needed to talk with Kam, who had gone to the bathroom for a quick shower. I sat on the sofa bed and waited for him, staring at the open window. A combination of the calming sound of the waves crashing against the shore coming from outside and Pallino's soft, low purring reverberating against my leg relaxed me, and I soon fell into a trance.

"Elios." Gaia's voice echoed inside my mind.

"Elios?" Kam's voice intruded on my trance. "Elios, are you okay?"

I felt Kam's hand on my arm, pushing me gently to consciousness. "I'm fine. I think." I stood too quickly and fell again on the couch.

Kam sat next to me. "What happened? I heard you talking from the bathroom."

I frowned at his words. "I don't remember having said anything. Gaia just reached for me. There was a note of fear in her voice." My heart was beating quickly, and I couldn't breathe. Pallino jumped on my lap with a graceful little leap, and his purrs calmed my nerves. "We must hurry. I don't think she has long left."

Kam went to the kitchen and tinkered with the teapot. "I think we've made big progress today. I didn't expect to find anything useful so soon. Our next move would be for me to report the discovery, but that would betray your presence on Earth." The teapot hissed, boiling. He opened one of the two cabinets over the stove and selected a tin can. "Some chamomile is what we need." He poured the hot water into two ceramic mugs, added the teabags to each, let them steep for a minute, and then brought the cups back to the sofa.

"About what you just said—"

"Yes?" He offered one of the cups to me, and I put it on the floor by the sofa.

"I think there's a way for you to report our finding without having me discovered."

He tried a sip of the chamomile and made a face. "How?"

"I'm not sure it's going to work, and I must have access to your mind again."

He sat on the chair next to the sofa and put his cup on the floor as well. "Is it dangerous?"

"Don't think so, but you must be willing."

He leaned to retrieve the cup and took another sip. "You make it sound scary."

I stretched my legs and crossed my arms over my chest. "You have seen what kind of control I have on my sharing process. I was thinking that maybe if we are mentally linked, I can shield part of your thoughts and memories as well." I now knew I had the power. The realization had come, without understanding the importance of it, when I had successfully attempted my guided Share with him. When Soleans shared their souls, they automatically became one single mental entity. It had occurred to me that my control could have several applications.

Kam, who had been drinking his tea, choked at my words.

I raised one hand. "Forget it. You don't have to do it. It was just a suggestion to speed up the process. We'll think of something else."

"You want me to—" Kam looked at me with wide eyes.

"Yes, I was suggesting helping you to build up walls during your sharing." I picked my cup from the floor and tested if it was still too hot. It wasn't.

Kam waved his hand, and as result, some of his chamomile spilled on Pallino, who hissed. "No, what you are suggesting is more than that. You'll have to take control of my mind to do that. You'll have absolute power over me. You could make me do things against my will." He petted the cat, who regarded him with a dissatisfied noise. "It sounds awfully similar to using a psychic gun—"

I recoiled at his suggestion. "How can you draw a parallel between what I suggested and a psychic gun? I would never do anything against your consent. And you would know it anyway."

On Solo, violating someone's soul was considered an atrocity, at the same level as homicide and suicide. The three of them had occurred so seldom in our history that they were considered horrifying and inexplicable deviations. Every possible precaution had been taken to prevent outbursts of any kind, and that was why we weren't explicitly taught how to take control of someone else's mind, and only few were allowed to use the psychic gun. "Just in theory, for the sake of talking..." Kam hesitantly started.

I nodded. "Only for the sake of talking."

"How does it work?" The line between Kam's eyes deepened.

"I have never done it, and I think it should be tried before—"

Kam stopped. "Remember, I have only agreed to talk about it."

"Right..." I shifted through several positions before settling into a comfortable one. "Right. It is actually really simple. Since I can override the fail-safe and I can protect myself against any unwanted probing, it is only logical to assume that if I am mentally linked to you, I can also protect you. It is going to be a passive process, I would just build a wall from where I can hide myself and my memories. The person I would be sharing the link with would be fully capable of thinking and making decisions, completely aware of everything. I would never take control." I felt restless and reached for Pallino to pet him.

Kam lowered his eyes to the floor. "I am sorry I said that."

With my free hand, I took the cup and drank the contents in one gulp. The chamomile was now lukewarm. "Anyway, still for the sake of talking, you would be the one to decide what to say ultimately. I would be the one hiding behind you, so to speak. You could kick me out at any moment and therefore leave me in the open. I wouldn't do anything to make you change your decision. I would be the one in your hands. It is I who has to trust you, not the other way around."

He raised his face, and our eyes met. "I didn't realize that."

"So, what do you think now?" My head felt heavy, and I longed for a night of dreamless sleep.

"I don't know what to say." He looked outside, then at Pallino, then at me again. "Aren't you worried I could betray you?" His voice was but a whisper.

"No. I trust you." Pallino snuggled closer to my heart. "Do you want to give it a try?"

"Yes." Kam leaned closer to me and then bent for me to touch his forehead.

"Okay. Let's start." I closed my eyes, concentrated on Pallino's purring, and spiraled down Kam's consciousness. *Try to kick me out.* I was fully immersed in his memories.

Okay.

I felt his push, and I was out of his mind. I severed our physical connection. "See?"

"You were right." He looked at me, relieved. "Let's try again."

We resumed working on his memories, but the long day was taking its toll on me. *I think we've practiced enough for today.*

Wait. I would report now if you trust me.

You know I do. I exited his mind and went for a glass of water then sat on the floor, where Kam joined me.

"Now, please," he said.

I crossed my legs and waited for him to find a relaxing stance. When he gave me the okay, I linked myself to his mind once again. I built several walls that would look like uninteresting memories, daily little things of no consequences. *Think of the conversation we just had with Saverio.* He promptly obeyed, and I removed my presence from his memories as he recalled them. When I had the reasonable certainty we were in control of the situation, I told him to contact his officer.

Kam didn't hesitate and invited his officer for a meeting in the Astral World. Kam was the first to arrive and sat down in one of two small couches, the only pieces of furniture in the room where his officer received him. The room was austere and dim. I looked around and got the feeling the guy didn't like to spend time in the Astral World. But he did like to play mind tricks, judging from the time it was taking for him to arrive. Kam was starting to get nervous—and I with him—when the officer appeared at the door at the end of the big gray room. I noticed he didn't excuse himself and entered the room exuding an unsettling aura. When he came closer to Kam and I saw his face under the only light illuminating the space, I almost lost my calm. I manage to regain control of both my mind and Kam's before he could gasp and betray me.

Kam's assigned officer was the same person who had kidnapped Gaia, Areel, and Sara. I relaxed immediately and let Kam know everything was fine on my end. Fortunately for us, my brief moment of shock had happened before the Share was initiated. Kam started with the usual pleasantries, but the officer cut him off abruptly, asking the reason for the report. He was in a hurry to get rid of Kam. I was glad the process would be short because I was starting to feel fatigue.

Kam smiled and let the guy touch his forehead. When the Officer saw the memory of the ring, his thought patterns displayed fear, but he regained control immediately. My mind raced through several conjectures while Kam stiffened on the unwelcoming little gray couch and let the officer scan his memories at his leisure, which was exactly what he was supposed to do without asking for reciprocation, something that was only appropriate between friends. The Share went as expected, but the strain on my tired mind was wearing me out, and keeping the walls up inside Kam's mind was getting harder.

The officer kept visiting the memory of the ring, studying it with a strange curiosity. Once again, he displayed the strange anxious-worried-surprised feeling. This time, he lingered on that thought slightly longer than the first time, and he knew Kam had sensed something. After that, he interrupted the sharing and almost didn't bother to salute Kam.

The officer left the room as I lost control of Kam's mind. We both gasped at the same moment and exited the Astral World to get back to the physical plane. I removed my hand from Kam's forehead, and I just lay on the cold floor. My head was swinging, as if I was sitting on a boat. I was feeling sick, and my stomach was heaving. I reached the bathroom just in time.

Kam followed me. "It worked."

"Better than we could've thought." I rested on the floor by the toilet and managed a feeble smile. Pallino came to my rescue and rubbed his soft body against my outstretched legs. "Your officer is the person I saw in Areel's bathroom, reflected in the mirror."

"Crap. Oh crap. You are sure?"

"Without a doubt. Expect a visit soon." I pushed myself up, and my ears rang. I was on the floor before I realized I had fallen.

"You need to rest." Kam helped me to my feet and then accompanied me to the sofa bed.

I slipped into a dreamless sleep almost immediately.

The next morning, I woke to the smell of freshly brewed espresso. I looked around and found Kam outside on the terrace, having breakfast, his cell phone on the coffee table. "Saverio just called. He has something new to show us. We have an appointment at the Santa Severa Castle."

"We don't have time for this." I sat on the deck chair and poured some espresso from the still-fuming moka.

"I think we should go."

Kam's tone made me look at him. "Why?"

"Saverio just mentioned he has information regarding a new *finding* at the excavation camp." He tapped the glass surface of the table with his index finger.

I shrugged.

"It's not an archeological artifact. It is rather modern."

"What is it? Did he tell you?"

"He said something along the lines of a 'futuristic-looking knife.'"

"Still."

"I'll go. You can stay here. It is just a short drive to Santa Severa, and I need to get out of here."

"I'll come with you, but we'll make it a short visit."

The drive, as Kam had promised, was short, and although I would have enjoyed the sightseeing at any other time, my current mood prevented me from even giving a second glance to the Roman ruins spread through the Maremmana country. Once we reached the medieval castle, a sense of malaise possessed me.

"Let's make it brief." I walked through the main gate and entered a large square from which opened several alleys leading to other squares. "Where to?"

Kam pointed at a pole sporting several wrought-iron signs indicating the various locations inside the castle. "He told me we would meet at the Lovers' Arch." He found the name he was looking for among the signs. "That way." He stepped over the cobblestone road on our right, the clicking of his shoes echoing in the deserted place.

The sun was obscured by a passing cloud, and I couldn't help but shiver. "It is the middle of the morning, but nobody is here." I entered the alley, feeling the smoothness of the cobblestones under my shoes. "Why did he give you an appointment here of all places?"

"He told me he's working part-time here at the castle." Kam doubled his pace. "Come. I can see the arch."

Gushes of salty air mixed with water sprays hit my face. Ahead of us, the castle walls bordered the beach, and I could see a stormy sea through the louvers.

Kam turned into a smaller and darker alley on the left and stepped up to an arch.

"Where is Saverio?" I asked.

"Maybe we are early." Kam opened his cell phone, looked at its screen, then snapped it shut.

"Maybe he's late." I walked under the arch to take a better look at the graffiti that covered almost every inch of its stones. The inscriptions—some of them a century old—were declarations of perennial love and devotion. "We'll wait ten minutes, and then we'll leave." I wondered if Maria and Luca were still together after committing to eternal love in the long-lost summer of 1968 with a pocketknife. For a brief moment, I thought it would be nice to come back with Gaia and stroll around the castle. I snapped out of my reverie when I saw Kam disappearing around the corner. "Where are you going?"

"I can see Saverio at the fountain," he called.

"Coming." I left the graffiti lovers to their memories and passed under the arch and the whole length of an even dimmer alley, at the end of which I could see a large courtyard with a big marble fountain at its center. Kam had his back to me and was talking to Saverio, who acted as if drunk. As I hurried toward them, my friend moved to the right and a third person came into view, a man whose face was hidden by Saverio standing close. From my limited point of view, I saw Kam receding toward the fountain, and I heard him saying, "You can't!"

A knot of fear seized my lungs, and I started running. Saverio staggered to his left, and the third person revealed his face to me. It was Kam's officer and he was saying something to Saverio I couldn't hear, but Kam reacted loudly. "Release your hold on him!"

I was halfway through the square and had almost reached them when Saverio raised his shaking hand, and I saw he was armed and aiming at Kam.

"Don't!" I lunged at Saverio, but it was too late. The shot of the gun resonated loudly in the square, and doves that had been standing on the edge of the fountain flew away. Kam fell backward into the fountain, and a stream of his blood stained the clear water. I screamed and unleashed my rage on Saverio. I hit his hand, and the gun skated away on the cobblestones. I kept hitting him in blind fury, but he didn't attempt to hit me back. A flicker of a doubt assailed me.

When I felt the coldness of metal on my temple, I realized my mistake.

"You should have minded your business, Observer," the officer said.

The thought of Gaia, lying somewhere, alone and scared, gave me strength, and I acted on survival instinct. Before the officer could shoot me, I was on his body and forcing his wrist to the ground. A sharp metallic sound accompanied the man's cries when I pummeled his face and chest with my fists. He reached for my eyes, but I moved my head slightly up at the last moment, and he carved my right cheekbone with his fingers. I didn't budge when he tried to roll me over on my back and kept him under me, but he still managed to find a way to kick me in the groin. Sharp throbbing invaded my senses. I involuntarily let go of him and curled into a ball on the floor, angry tears wetting my face. The officer scuttled to retrieve the weapon he had lost a moment earlier. It was a sleek gun and had slid under the edge of the fountain. Still unable to breathe for the pain, I saw him looking at Saverio, who was now keeping a struggling Kam down in the water. I pushed myself from the ground and then threw myself against Saverio, managing to break his hold on Kam, who arose from the water coughing and spluttering.

The officer reemerged from the other side of the fountain, aiming the gun at me. "This ends now." He stepped closer to me and pointed the silver cylinder at my forehead.

In a daze, I heard Kam scream, "Move out of the way!" and then I saw him jumping from the fountain.

The officer yelled, "No!" and a cloud passed over me. The gun fired a single shot that pierced my ears. I closed my eyes. At the same time, a hard body collided with mine. A wet, warm liquid wetted my face, but I was alive. I opened my eyes and found myself staring at Kam's bloodied face. His eyes were glassy, and I feared the worst.

"What did you do?" I rolled out from under him and checked his pulse. When I found one, I cried in relief. "Kam, wake up."

He blinked and opened his mouth to speak, but his voice was barely audible. "He didn't shoot me..."

My eyes went to the blood on his face and saw it was gushing from a deep cut. "But he fired a shot."

He shivered. "It's a psychic gun. It was trained on you."

"What—" I shook in disbelief. The small cylinder *was* a psychic gun. The realization paralyzed me.

Saverio screamed, his hands pressed against his temples, his eyes crazed. He convulsed and then threw up.

The officer walked toward him, his hand reaching out for Saverio's forehead.

He shook the officer's hand away. "Don't touch me!" His eyes locked with mine, then he saw Kam, looked at his own hands, and screamed once again. "No!"

The officer managed to touch Saverio's right shoulder, and the young man's eyes went blank for a moment. The next, he was running away.

It's a psychic gun. It was trained on you. I rose from the ground, seething rage shocking my body. The officer teetered and stepped back, and I hurled myself at him. My fist slammed the psychic gun he was still holding. Not that it mattered anymore. The weapon had already discharged its only lethal bullet.

Trying to strike each other with kicks and punches, we lost our balance, and our bodies flew through the air, on a collision course with the fountain's marble edge. Before crashing against the hard rim, I moved my body out of his reach, and threw a last-effort roundhouse kick, hoping to hit him. I did. The officer screamed and landed facedown a few inches from the edge. I cursed at his luck, but I was on him before he could turn around. I pinned him on the ground with his arms under my knees. He jerked, visibly in pain, and I knocked him out with several punches.

I felt dirty. My knuckles bled, and I wanted to keep punching him until I felt satisfied. The psychic gun charged with my mental signature glistened in the afternoon sun. A pain impossible to describe seared my heart, and my fist went down one more time. I reached for his forehead, knowing the truth already. I wanted to be wrong with all my being. I took the psychic gun with one unsteady hand, hating what it represented. I pressed my free hand to his temple, shivering uncontrollably. I needed to know the sordid details of how my mentor, my guide, the man who had become everything to me had imprinted my mental signature into the weapon built to erase my memories. Lex, the Wise Ancestor who had seen me growing, who had been my counselor, who was the only keeper of my mental signature, had betrayed me.

Tears obfuscating reality, I pushed my mind inside the officer's. I knew he was only a pawn obeying higher orders, but I didn't care. He was there, and that was enough for me. Memories washed over me like a viscous black tide. I almost interrupted the contact when

I saw Lex ordering him to look for me. The officer's mission was to eliminate Kam, to wipe my mind clean, and to take me back to Silenzio. The coldness he showed in sharing something as sacred as my private mental signature with a virtual stranger made me recoil. I gasped for air and kept going despite the throbbing pain in my head. When I thought I couldn't take it anymore, I finally found what I was looking for—what I had thought I was looking for. The shock of the revelation made me interrupt the contact. A truth surpassing any possible imagination unfolded in crude details. Lex wasn't Solean. He belonged to a race called the Pures.

I moved away from the body, nauseated. I threw up for several minutes. Then I finally cried for joy.

16

That night, I was flying over the Sardinian region of the Sarrabus-Gerrei. Kam was resting on the cot where I had spent six long months. The officer—who really wasn't one, who wasn't even Solean—an unwelcomed guest forced on us by the events, was locked in one of the cabins.

* * *

After the first moment of shock at discovering the truth, and once I could think straight again, the whole day fast-forwarded before my eyes. I acted in automatic mode. I soon would be reunited with Gaia, and that was all that mattered. I made a list of what I needed to do to and followed it to the letter. Every action crossed off my list brought me closer to her.

I wasn't proud I had stolen a car to leave Santa Severa and take Kam and the unconscious officer to Mount Peglia. I hoped the owner, one of the tourists who had parked his vehicle at the castle's parking lot and went to the beach for a day of relaxing, would find his beaten but spacious Volkswagen in good condition if not nearby. After a frantic detour to Kam's apartment to pick up Pallino and grab anything we would need later—changes of clothes, shoes, dry foods, and anything else I managed to stuff into three heavy-duty plastic bags—I drove my stolen ride up to Mount Peglia Park. There, I reached the trailhead leading to the crevice where I would land my ship. I left Kam guarding the officer while I went to park the car a few kilometers south for the police to spot it.

"What now?" Kam asked me once I came back after my late-afternoon hike. He had been in and out of consciousness the whole four-hour ride with Pallino nested on his lap. The officer had ridden inside the trunk where I wouldn't have to look at him.

After such a day, the brisk walk had exhausted me. I trained my eyes on the spot in the sky where I knew my ship was waiting for me, and I wished I was flying away already. "Now, we wait until it's dark."

Kam moaned.

"How do you feel?"

"Like I've been shot twice." Pallino, who had refused to be parted from Kam, burrowed his head deeper in his embrace and purred.

"Soon, you'll be fine." I checked the makeshift bandage I'd made for him by tearing a piece of my shirt. The bandage was now covered in blood flowing from his right arm and shoulder. The cut on his forehead had closed although his face looked like a battlefield.

"What about you? Will you be fine?" He gave me a penetrating glance.

"I will. In time. Now, it hurts too much." I pressed my hand over my chest.

"How did Lex know you were on Earth?"

"Same way you did. One single mistake on my side, and I warned you and him of my presence here…"

Kam nodded. "He expected you to get in contact with me, and Saverio must have confirmed your presence."

"Most probably." I shrugged. "But at least I finally know where Gaia is. Where everybody is."

"Sardinia. Who would have ever thought of looking for them there?"

"Without the exact coordinates, we would've never found them." During the ride from Santa Severa to Mount Peglia, I told Kam I had discovered our friends' location in the officer's memories. The isolated and scarcely populated region of the Sarrabus-Gerrei on the island of Sardinia was the perfect place to hide an alien facility.

"I still can't believe they have been kept in an underground building in the middle of Mount Arbu this whole time." He breathed in and out, his face paler than a moment ago. "And I can't believe his race—" his eyes lowered to the still shape of the officer I had deposited on the ground "—was behind our Dark. I didn't even know the Pures existed, and now I can't wrap my head around the idea of them."

"I know." I had found out the whole story about the Pures during the same forced Share with his officer, and I briefly told Kam, but I couldn't talk about it yet. I couldn't talk about Lex. I focused my thoughts on something productive instead. "When we reach the facility, we'll have to split up at some point. Gaia, Areel, and Sara are kept separate in three different sectors." My eyes went to his bandages.

"Don't worry about this." Despite his words, he touched his wounded arm and winced but then relaxed his frown and even attempted a smile. "You can count on me. I won't be a burden. I promise."

"Thanks."

Finally, the long-awaited darkness surrounded us, and I called my ship. Two hours later, we were flying over the stretch of sea separating Lazio and Sardinia. Unable to deal with the Pure's presence, I had put him in deep sleep. I commanded the ship to land, and I went to check on Kam, whom I had sent to rest. I found him already on his feet although disoriented after the brief nap.

"How do you feel?" I offered him a glass of water.

"I think I experienced a nightmare. Damned human physiology." He accepted the glass and drank the entire contents at once. "I was sent here to find Areel, and I can't believe my mission was just meant as a decoy."

"We don't have time to dwell on that."

"Is *he* well guarded?" Anger flashed in Kam's eyes. Pallino rubbed his body against his legs in a figure eight.

"Yes, he is. And no, I don't think it is a good idea for you to visit his cabin." I had seen him looking toward the hallway. "I need you focused."

"Tell me the plan."

While we were silently landing on a small plateau framed by hills on three sides, the fourth one facing a plain and, far away, the Sardinian Sea, I explained to him how I intended to enter and exit the place and rescue the three prisoners.

At the end of my speech, he nodded. "Okay. Let's find a spot for him." He pointed at Pallino, who was trying to climb the leg of his pants.

With Pallino safely dozing off on Kam's bed, we walked back to the control room and prepared to put my hastily hatched plan into action.

"Wear this." While Kam was sleeping, I remembered the utility closet where I had found some clothes and went looking for something else we could wear. I had been rewarded with two black, tight-fitting body armors resembling scuba wetsuits. Before leaving the ship, I secured the psychic gun I had confiscated from the traitor inside a pocket on my left sleeve. During the flight, I had changed the charge to neutral, and then I had gone the extra step to alter its functions. The silver cylinder was now ready to be used as a blade. The dark desire to use it on the Pure had kept me company the whole time. Wiping his mind of all his memories and emotions until he was an empty shell seemed to me an appropriate punishment for his involvement. I had decided to neutralize the gun to be sure I wouldn't change my mind and use it on him. My rage was misplaced anyway. The man I thought was my putative father had requested I be obliterated—not killed—something much worse than death for a Solean. The mere idea made me sick again. After my stomach settled down and before I left the ship, I went to visit the sleeping Pure.

"I pity you. You didn't have a choice. But I do." It made me feel slightly better.

Outside, the night was moonless and cloudy, and I thanked our luck for it. Dressed in black, we blended with the darkness and moved silently across the rugged terrain. The distant sound of waves crashing against the rocky coast kept us company while we proceeded to the opening of the alien facility concealed by a big rock. Surrounded by the dark, walking on treacherous terrain in a place I had never seen before, I didn't need any light; my gloved hands knew exactly where to touch and what to move, thanks to the traitor's pristine memories. The heavy metallic door moved on its rail without any resistance. We left it slightly open by jamming the rail with a pebble and then took a staircase that spiraled down with a large stairwell at its center. The building had ten floors excavated in the dark rock, the perfect bunker with no sound escaping from it. The traitor's memories had revealed something that had made me move even faster than I would have anyway. The Pures were moving out as their mission on Earth had been already compromised. They were anxious to regroup in a safer place. Gaia was the only subject they were still working on, and her floor was the only one guarded. Areel and Sara had been spared from the Pures' painful tests because he was from a race they were well acquainted with and Sara had proved to be not mentally strong enough. Sara and Areel were on two different floors, cared for by robotic nurses, and isolated. While he was lucid and locked in a cabin, Sara had been sedated at the beginning of her captivity.

There were few blind spots in my plan, but playing it safe wasn't really an option at the moment. I would fix problems as they presented themselves. I breathed deeply, in and out. I exhaled with a faint sigh and then entered the claustrophobic darkness of the alien facility. Kam was right behind me. I could hear his breathing, slow and controlled.

Inside, it was as dark as outside but also uncomfortably warm. At the first plunge into the unknown, my lungs stopped working, but I forced myself to overcome the feeling and started descending the stairwell.

We descended until we reached a landing opening on the first floor and came to a halt before a transparent door. To keep walking down the stairs, we had to pass that door. Kam gave me a worried look.

"There should be only three cleaning-bots on this level." I flattened myself against the dark, metallic doorframe and tilted my head toward the transparent surface of the door. A long hallway stretched from the entry to a cavernous and dimly lit space. No living being was there, just the few droning machines I expected. The robots resembled my Fido, short, black boxes on wheels. "As soon as it's clear, we proceed to the next floor down." We waited until the closest machine turned its back to us, then we headed for the stairwell and slowly descended to the second floor, where we found the same layout as the previous level. Behind the second

transparent door—this one framed by a rusty-green metallic arch—
seven robots moved around in a smaller space, which I recognized
from the stolen memories as the pharmacy.

"Watch out. This floor is better guarded, and there could be
Pures." I gestured for Kam to move swiftly to the other side of the
doorframe while I had to wait several minutes until the machines
moved out of the way all at once for enough time to let me pass the
door. I found myself starting to shake, and when it was finally safe
and I made my move, I had to remember to breathe.

"Areel is kept in a locked room at the end of the hallway on the
third floor." I looked down at the next flight of stairs we had to
conquer, my legs growing heavier at every step. Once on the landing
of the third level, I saw a pale-green screen covering the entry door
and hiding what lay behind it. I hadn't seen that screen in the Pure's
memories. "It doesn't look solid." When I tentatively reached out
my hand toward the surface, it flickered, and I stopped before
making contact with it. I saw Kam studying the screen. "Do you
know how does it work?"

"I do. When I had to take the psychic gun course, I also had to
study psychic locks. Give me a moment, and I'll take care of it." He
walked past me to the left side of the doorframe, which was green
like the rest of the door, and stood before a lock jutting from the
frame and emanating a series of colors in a pulsing pattern. Kam
focused on the task, not moving a single muscle for several long
minutes, apparently studying the pattern of colors dancing before
his eyes.

More than ten minutes passed with Kam staring at the moving
colors. I tried to remember how many robots were on the third floor,
but fear and anxiety were getting the best of me. I finally saw
comprehension flashing through Kam's engrossed face, and almost
at the same time, his fingers touched the colors on the lock as if he
were playing piano, quickly and with dexterity. For the longest
moment, nothing happened.

I was on the verge of striking the lock when the green screen
vanished. One moment it was there, and the next it wasn't.

Kam turned to face me and smiled. "I'm glad I took those
wretched courses."

"So am I." I didn't have time to rejoice at my friend's achievement because four machines appeared at the end of the long and narrow stark-white hallway the screen had hidden from us. "Areel's room is at the end of this hallway." I anxiously waited for the robots to sweep the floor and then head back. When they rounded the corner at the end of the hallway, I ran inside, followed by Kam. We passed several doorless and empty rooms. The Pures' moving was well underway. Almost at the end of the hallway, just before the corner where the machines had disappeared, I saw a translucent screen preventing entry to a room. "It's Areel's."

Kam nodded and stepped closer to me. "The bots outside are coming back any moment now. We must hurry to find a way in."

We positioned ourselves at either side of the door. I took a glance inside. Areel was lying on a bed, guarded by two machines silently moving from one side of the room to the other, crossing paths every few seconds. The bots were white but similar in shape to the others we had encountered.

"Working on it." Even though my nerves urged me to jump into action, I waited patiently while I counted the seconds it took the two machines inside the room to reach a blind spot, then I ran in front of the screen. I was but a blur, but I hoped Areel had seen me. I knew he was conscious and probably awake, and I needed him to cooperate in my plan to rescue him. I was frustrated that I couldn't reveal my aura to him. He would have recognized me immediately, but so would have the Pures who were tormenting Gaia, floors below.

A sudden sound of softly moving wheels made Kam and I turn our heads in unison. The sound was moving closer to us, and it came from around the dark corner where the hallway continued. We ran back toward the exit, silently thanking the fabric of our black suits that covered the soles of our shoes and softened the sounds of our panicked steps on the hard concrete floor. Kam made it just in time to call back the screen and lock us out of the third floor.

I gasped when the green screen appeared, and almost at the same moment, one of the machines scanned it with a continuous ray of blue light. Kam looked at me with a smug expression, called my attention to the lock, and focused on the luminous pad. "Tell me when they are gone."

It seemed an eternity, but eventually the robots exited our side of the hallway, and Kam opened the lock. The second time around, it took him only a handful of seconds to unlock the door. A moment later, we were before Areel's room once again.

"You got seven minutes." Kam's eyes went to the directions the bots had gone around the corner.

"Okay." I waited for the machines inside the room to hit the blind spot and then I stepped out, hoping to make contact with Areel. I stood there a few seconds more than I should have.

"Move!" Kam turned toward the corner.

I jumped out of the way too quickly, and I almost twisted my ankle.

I fell on the floor with a yelp. Rage at my clumsiness almost made me lose control.

"Run!"

I half jumped and half hopped but managed to find my way back. I had a few minutes to steady my heart while Kam closed and then reopened the lock, then for the third time we were outside Areel's room.

"We must enter his room. There's no time to wait for the machines to reach the blind spot." Kam immediately began tinkering with the lock jutting out of the doorframe.

When the screen disappeared, we braced ourselves to duck the robotic guards inside, and I almost punched Areel in the chest as he appeared in a midair somersault right before me. He landed softly by my side, giving Kam enough space to close the screen. I didn't have time to ask what had just happened because our allotted seven minutes were almost expired, and I could hear the wheels coming back again. We sprinted for the staircase with Areel at our heels. Areel and I were already running down the stairs while Kam closed the screen behind us for good this time. We passed the fourth floor without a single hitch. The fifth, sixth, and seventh called for a little bit of caution, but with the help of Areel, the three of us could manage the machines just fine. The surveillance was really minimal, and between one floor and the next, Areel and I had time for a very succinct conversation.

"How are you?" I turned toward him. The piercing pain of my swollen ankle helped focus us on the task ahead.

Areel shrugged. "Alive."

Even in the dark, I could see how thin and pale my friend looked, but I knew he was the one in good condition. "I'm sorry it took me so long to come rescue you." Every sentence a floor.

"Considering you shouldn't be here at all—" Areel stopped walking. "Thanks."

"I couldn't have done it without Kam." I moved the weight of my body from the injured ankle to the other. "We can't rest now. We must keep going."

"Sara?" Areel resumed descending the stairs.

"Here, eighth floor." I stopped before another screen—this one pale yellow and semitransparent—guarding the level. I was waiting for Kam to unlock the energy screen for us to enter the hallway and rescue Sara when someone let out a scream. I stepped out of my spot, and if it weren't for Kam shoving me down with some force and keeping my head out of view when one of the machines abruptly turned around, I would have been discovered. The screaming grew louder until it pierced my ears painfully. Kam looked down at me, worried. I covered my ears with my hands, but the shrieking agony didn't go away and didn't become any softer. Then the scream ended as abruptly as it had started. I was on the floor, my stomach sick, and my abdominal muscles aching. Areel and Kam both were looking at me with concern in their eyes.

"That voice screaming—" I retched on the floor before finishing the sentence.

"What voice?" Kam looked first at Areel, who shook his head, and then at me again.

"It was Gaia's."

They shook their heads, first Areel and then Kam.

"It's too late." I ran away from them and flew down the stairwell, gliding like a heavy leaf, landing with a soft thump on my good ankle and compromising that one as well. But I couldn't feel anything, thanks to the powerful combination of adrenaline and fear, a blessed occurrence in an otherwise awful situation.

I reached for the pocket where I had put the silver cylinder, to draw some strength and reassurance from the cold metal, and then I took a good look at the arch that opened to the hallway of the tenth floor. There was no screen here, and that detail gave me pause.

No, I had to believe that Gaia was still alive. I waited a few seconds to hear the now-familiar sound of the wheeled machines. Absolute silence greeted me, adding anxiety to the already existing sense of doom crushing my tight chest.

A sudden burst of pain exploded where my heart was. Mechanically, I put my hand on my chest, trying to ease the ache while gasping for air. I didn't want to think about the way the screaming had ended abruptly, cut off in the middle of what had sounded like excruciating pain. I couldn't bear the thought of being too late after having chased her through galaxies, and at the same time I knew that I had to find a way to force myself into a more controlled state of mind. Conscious that I could only go forward with my plan, since it didn't matter what I feared the most, a sudden and completely unexpected memory popped into my confused mind.

Once, eons ago, at some point in what now seemed the distant past, Lex had seen fit to teach me a daring technique. It was clear now that he had meant the lesson to keep me sedated and at peace with myself when I was losing my mind over Gaia. But how perfect to use it against him and his race to regain my peace *and* Gaia.

A grim satisfaction tinged my thoughts before I started emptying my mind to reach the Dark Void. Soon, the crouching position I had maintained since my landing started to be painful. The throbbing in my ankles radiated to the rest of my legs, spreading physical awareness that made me feel more than alive. In a rare moment of revelation, I blessed the pain because right there and then, I decided that even if everything was lost, I would still avenge her, possibly with my life. Nothing else mattered anymore. Then an overpowering clarity took control.

I sat down on the floor, covered by the shadow of the staircase, and started to slow my breathing. I forced myself to reach the meditative state that would allow me to react to any situation in a logical way. The Black Void would help me disregard my emotions regarding Gaia and privilege mathematical equations instead. At least I could thank Lex for something. Then again, I hated him with all my guts.

I pushed the sentiment out of the way and exhaled his tainted memory at the same time I pushed the air from my lungs. A bitter scent lingered a few seconds in my mouth, and then it dissipated as I progressed in my exercises.

Soon, sweat and tears were matting my face. My body went rigid, like a slab of solid rock, while my mind loosened to receive the awareness I so much needed. I lost track of time, but when I woke up, I was conscious that exactly fifty-seven seconds had passed from the beginning of my trance, although my mind had roamed for the equivalent of a lifetime. Without pausing to think, I stood up in one fluent movement and ran through the hallway, noting each point of light, each door, each noise, and each different smell coming from the rooms opening behind the doors.

I didn't look sideways, but I still saw everything with my peripheral vision, as if I had other sets of eyes pointing in all directions simultaneously. Three rooms had people inside, eight of them busy with various tasks, closing boxes, moving oddly shaped objects, spraying a pungent liquid on the walls, and talking to each other.

They were moving so slowly compared to me that they didn't see me using the pipes on the ceiling to vault my way from one to the next. I landed behind a door silently, like a cat. It took me less than a fraction of a second to assess that I had to enter there. The sharp smell of a freshly used medicament was still lingering in the air, mixed with the aroma of fear and despair. Blood had been spilled. Not Gaia's.

I could see on the floor the traces of a wheeled bed recently taken somewhere else. The smell of the rubber wheels being hurriedly pushed on the linoleum floor was still strong. I closed my eyes and calculated which door of the four opening into that room was the most plausible. I opened my eyes again and, without a moment of hesitation, ran to kick open the one at the far end of the room.

Everything was in slow motion again. Ten eyes rose from the table they had been facing, startled at my sudden entrance. While everything started moving, my face was turned in only one direction, straight ahead, focused on only one thing: Gaia's body, white and motionless on a table.

Metallic instruments had been cutting her skin; her blood was dripping down on the floor.

The scream that I unleashed gave me a charge of adrenaline. I was utterly insane and entirely rational at the same time. My fury powered my body. My logical trance powered the synapses in my brain.

Without unlocking my eyes from the body on the table, I saw a blazing white light reaching for my forehead. It was too slow and never had a chance to harm me. A simple equation told me the right angle where I had to slash the air with the silver cylinder, which had found its way into my right hand. Someone screamed; blood splattered on the floor, creating an expanding flower. Another silver cylinder was safely in my left hand. Stupid of them to think to use any weapon against me. I could disarm them and use their weapons to inflict pain any way I wanted. And I wanted to make them suffer.

With the two cylinders, I reached over my head while crouched on the floor, and more blood gushed onto the tiles. Two people were now in front of me, standing on either side of the table. One of the two was reaching for Gaia's forehead. A sudden realization. Time lost any meaning. Everything froze in the room. The scalpel that had been at Gaia's forehead was now at the guy's head. The woman that had been inserting a needle in Gaia's arm was unconscious on the floor. I noticed with pleasure that her arms were badly scratched and still bleeding.

I found a large blanket sitting on a chair and wrapped Gaia in it. I scooped her up in my arms. Her body was so fragile, a weightless feather against mine. I carried her like a newborn baby, careful to hold her head safely tucked inside the blanket. The cold fabric and my gloves were the only barriers separating us. We had never been so close, and still we didn't touch.

On my way out, I barely noticed other people coming at us. They were disposed of, the same way I disposed of the machines they were trying to use to stop me from leaving that horrifying place. My mind took care of every action that my body faithfully executed. Limbs scattered on the floor, and I was not curious enough to care whether they were mechanical or not.

Red stains covered the walls while I was passing through. People screamed. Then all activities ceased. I didn't stop to contemplate why. I was already sprinting toward my final destination: out.

17

I regained consciousness inside the ship.

I found myself lying naked on the medical bed of my ship with a health-bot hovering quietly over my body. "Enough. I'm fine." I gently swatted it away and raised my head just for a moment. Everything in the room moved in circles, and the machine was at my side at once. Recent memories filled my mind, and I frantically searched the room for Gaia. My heart stilled when I saw her.

She was lying on the other medical bed. She was beautiful, her face relaxed, her brown hair with honey blond strands falling toward the floor, curls and waves like a waterfall. Her hair was darker, her skin paler. Her mouth was still full but almost with no color at all. All her freckles were gone. Her body was covered by a blanket. I was grateful for that merciful thought. I couldn't stand the idea of letting her body suffer more coldness. One arm was gently curved on her stomach, her long fingers resting gracefully.

I tried to extend my arm to reach her, but my fingers just grazed the blanket. I didn't wait for the health-bot to finish my examination, and I jumped out of the bed. I passed out.

When I reopened my eyes, I found I was on the floor and closer to her bed. I stood up and put my hands on either side of her shoulders, then I sat on the edge of the bed to look at her. I inhaled the faint mimosa scent of her skin and slowly leaned over her. My arms started trembling, and my head got light. Her closeness was overwhelming. My mouth reached for hers. When our lips touched, the world exploded.

No words exist to describe the colors that danced around our bodies. No music can compare with the celestial sounds that played in the room. No fragrance is as sweet and refreshing as the perfume that our auras emanated. My heart experienced absolute happiness when my lungs stopped pumping air because I was breathing through her.

Gaia's lips were soft, warm. I gently cupped her head with my hand and brought her closer to me while, with the other hand, I held her back. Gaia's arms rose, seeking my neck, and I felt shivers running through my body. Our lips moved slowly. I caressed the bare skin of her shoulders. Gaia found the ribbon still tying my hair and undid it while tenderly brushing my neck.

At her touch, my mouth searched deeper for hers, and I gave myself to her as a gift. All I was, all I had ever been was hers. My whole being, my memories, my hopes, all my knowledge was hers. Forever. She absorbed my memories, and I felt her reactions as she discovered me.

We are on a ship? Were you injured? What are we going to do? Her thoughts were loud and clear in my head, and I loved it.

We are together. Nothing else matters.

She nudged my nose. "You're right. Nothing else matters."

I cried. She cried.

"Elios."

"I'm here. I won't ever let you go. Never again."

"Elios," she repeated, and then my mind was invaded by hers. Gaia was reciprocating my gift.

I felt whole and loved beyond human comprehension. I lived through her memories, experiencing all the highs and lows of her short and precious life. I had a special thrill when she showed me the first time she saw me in Athens. It gave me incredible sadness when I saw how she lived through my absence the first time we got separated. My chest swelled with pride when I saw how Gaia managed to get back on her feet when I had to leave Earth to go into exile. She had never given up on me. She never doubted we were meant to be together. Gaia never lost faith. She was stronger than me. She had survived only on the idea that I was coming back to her.

During the long months of her captivity, whenever she had lost consciousness, I was the lighthouse she came back to. Her pain, her suffering reverberated in my heart, in a much more concentrated form than the one I had experienced during my sleeping-wake on the ship. Gaia felt my distress and slowly caressed my head and led my thoughts to a happier memory: the memory of how she knew I was coming to save her, how she had fought to give me time to reach the tenth floor, how she had sensed my body in the room, even with her eyes closed.

Our auras were embraced and swirling, sounds and colors still dancing together. Orange and pink were mixing gracefully with deep red and sun yellow. A quartet of violins was joyously accepting a duo of angelical voices. Bouquets of fresh tangerine scents and sweet freesias lingered around us. A fresh marine breeze moved our hair, blending my white locks with her honey-brown curls. A tangible and physical manifestation of something profound, divine—our love. We now shared everything. We were one single mind living in two separate bodies. I opened my eyes to look at Gaia again, and she was there looking at me. We didn't need to talk, but I loved her voice so much.

"I love you."

Gaia smiled at me, her lips finally full of color. "This is the happiest moment of my life."

"Our life." I brushed the contour of her jaw. I loved the way my touch painted her skin pinker. I loved the way her breathing followed my same erratic pattern whenever I brushed her. I did my best to stabilize the temperature in the immediate proximity of our blazing bodies. Gaia's body was finally warm.

"Thanks." She smiled again, blushing this time at her thoughts, which were mine as well.

The room was burning. I thought of a cold misty waterfall I once saw during my visit to Hana. Gaia supplied another memory of refreshing and cleansing waters, a picture she had taken during a hike on Mount Rainier. The instant communication was a treat. With a sudden realization, I understood what my ancestors had lost, what had doomed them to a blissful insanity. They had lost what I had just found, a permanent mental link with loved ones.

Gaia was looking at me, love and joy pouring out from her smart hazel eyes. I wondered briefly if the sensation was the same for her.

"It's the most romantic gift I could hope for," she reassured me.

It was a treat to listen to her melodious Italian voice.

"I hope you'll never tire of my simple thoughts." She smiled.

"You are anything but simple. You changed the core of my existence. I'm more worried that one day you'll want to escape from *this*." I pulled her head closer to mine and rested my forehead on hers while stroking her arm.

"Never." Gaia laughed, and her aura exploded in delight, colors like fireworks casting light on her hair.

"Only you." I was already kissing her mouth, my aura playing with hers, the fireworks growing in intensity.

"Forever you." Gaia showed me other images of relaxing places where she would have loved to be with me.

"Soon." I was only aware of her body. The rest of the universe was lost to me. I could have spent all my life just looking at her beauty. I thought of us as a self-contained microcosm.

"I like that." Her lips were moving with mine, soft and warmer than a few minutes before, and then she softly bit my bottom lip. "We are a mini solar system." *I am your planet, you are my sun,* she thought.

"I'm everything you'll ever need." I rested my head on her chest, listening to her heartbeat through the thin layer of the linen sheet, to get mine in sync with hers.

"I know." Her hands were tracing patterns on my back, her mouth kissing my hair with the same tenderness parents use to touch their children. She suddenly changed her train of thought when she looked for one particular memory in my mind. Tears wet my hair, and I looked up to meet her eyes.

"Don't. Don't be sorry for me." I sent her waves of peaceful and calming feelings.

"Look what I did to you." Gaia was staring at my white mane with a pained expression on her face. She hadn't noticed before, so taken by the whole experience and seeing mostly through my eyes.

"No, please. It wasn't your fault. I don't mind it at all." I raised her chin with one hand, and with the other I held her head. I kissed Gaia while reassuring her mind about what I had just said.

"I really did change you."

"I actually like it," I whispered in her ear while kissing the little spot between her earlobe and the jaw.

She shivered. "I see you do."

"It is like a war wound, like a scar. It's my tattoo."

"You are proud of *this*?" She played with a strand of my hair.

"Immensely so." I pushed her body to rest on the bed, and I lay gently to her side, balancing myself on the edge of the narrow cot. Gaia saw my precarious act and pulled me to rest on her. The fireworks engulfed the room, the music grew louder, and the perfumes released in the air by our crazed auras obfuscated our minds. Breathing became impossible. I was aware of my clothes, of the linen sheet, of the blanket, of every single molecule standing between us. I saw only her eyes, deep pools of hazel water staring at mine. I bathed my soul in them.

"I want to hear what your tattoo says." Gaia's voice sounded like the waves crashing on the wet sand at night, refreshing, mysterious, and comforting in their eternal loop.

"I'm yours. You made me. You named me. I was born for you." I still couldn't breathe by myself. I needed her air.

"My whole body is a tattoo that says the same to you." She reciprocated the kiss, matching my eagerness.

I extended my arm against hers, comparing the different shades of our skins, contemplating the way our arms curved gracefully, mine cradling hers, like pieces of a puzzle. "We are perfect together."

"I can only be with you." Gaia took my hand and kissed it and then put it to rest over her heart.

"I know." I already saw all the memories she had about other men. I couldn't even think of their names. A sharp pain cut through my thoughts, and I found my hand closing on the linen, twisting the fabric with anger. One memory among the others was especially upsetting. Someone's hand, I knew his name, but I wouldn't think of him, sliding on Gaia's bare skin, lingering on the small of her back.

Gaia didn't let me continue and showed me how that night had ended. "I broke Marco's heart by refusing him."

"You left Rome because of what happened that night."

She nodded. "I was kissing you while I was with him. Your face was the one I saw. Your voice was the one I was calling."

I couldn't help but feel better already.

"I felt your hands on my body that night, not Marco's." She kissed me. "Your presence was so real, so intoxicating."

"I know. I'm sorry." Jealousy was a furious emotion, so intense, so primeval—strong enough to make me forget what I had already seen in her mind. I had been blinded by a single thought. Even the idea that other guys could have feelings for her was upsetting.

"Doesn't matter," Gaia reminded me. "You're my first and my only love." She put her hand on mine, caressing my hand to relax my fingers clenched around the linen. "I'm thankful you never had any human physical experiences."

I smiled. "I don't think it could've ever happened. You're one of a kind. Before seeing you for the first time, my life was on a different path. I was on Earth to observe humanity, not to mingle." I laughed at the mere idea.

"Nevertheless, I can't stand the mere thought of you *mingling* with anybody else but me." She tugged at my hair. "There was nobody before you." She brushed my lips.

"It took me too long to find you."

The room was now illuminated by relaxing colors slowly dancing across our bodies. We were tired, and our auras were reflecting our state. I kept caressing her arms while our minds exchanged memories. We had so many desires, so many things we wanted to do, so many places we wanted to visit together. Our eyes were already closed, our heads touching. We had waited so long to be together that the mere idea of sleeping seemed inappropriate.

"I love you, Elios."

"To the end of time, Gaia."

* * *

We woke up embracing, Gaia's head resting on my chest, our hands united on hers. We had dreamed together and imagined a universe where nothing bad had happened to us, a perfect place where we never had to spend a single moment without the other. It was our way to heal our wounded subconscious.

Colors and music still lingered in the room, but they were subdued. I shifted onto my side to better look at her. "I love you." I hid my face in her hair. I breathed for several minutes through her

216

curls and then kissed the top of her head. "Hi." I still couldn't believe that Gaia was there with me.

"Hi," she whispered in her sleep.

She was recovering well, judging from the reading on the health-bot's panel. She was strong, but she had gone through a lot and needed time to heal.

I was still shaky but otherwise able to function. Without waking her, I carefully adjusted her body and then moved out of the bed. I knew someone was anxious to talk to me. I had seen shadows passing behind the opaque glass door, but neither Kam nor Areel had dared to intrude. It was time to meet them. I found a change of clothes neatly folded on the chair by the bed, donned the white shirt and dark pants, and looked at Gaia one more time. She looked peaceful and happy, and I fought the urge to lock the door and forget about the rest of the world. I sighed and walked out.

Before confronting my friends, though, I had to take care of finding a better sleeping solution for Gaia and me. I already knew what I had to do, and it didn't take lot of time. An hour later, I was on my way to finally talk to my friends. I found them together in the common room. Kam nodded at me from the chair behind the control panel while Areel was at the kitchen nook, drinking from a fuming mug.

Areel poured a red concoction for me from a transparent carafe. "Have some."

"Thanks." I leaned beside him by the kitchen counter. The hot, steaming liquid was good and had a distinct lemony flavor. "I needed this." I raised the cup to him. "And thanks for everything you did while I was out." I had tried to recollect my memories of the time I had spent in the Dark Void, but I couldn't remember a few things regarding the events leading to our escape.

Areel shrugged. "Not a lot, actually." He and Kam exchanged glances.

I drank the beverage and then handed the cup to Areel for a refill. "You rescued me. That counts as a lot to me, so thank you."

"What I meant is that we didn't rescue you because you didn't need any help from us." Areel shook the carafe and then served me more of the beverage. "In less than ten minutes, you were in and out of the tenth floor, we were behind you—"

Kam continued, "We had just freed Sara and were running down the stairs to help when you sprinted out of nowhere. Without seeing anything or anybody, you led our way out, destroying anything on your way." He left his seat and joined us at the kitchen counter where he accepted a cup from Areel. "You managed to get Gaia on the ship, and then you collapsed on the floor of the medical room. We only directed the health-bot your way."

At their words, bits and pieces came back, but I didn't want to go there at the moment. "Sara?"

Areel's face changed expression at her mention. "Sara is fine; she is recovering in the room we are sharing." While talking, Areel made me a sign to follow him, and we went to their room at the end of the hallway.

He opened the door and let me in. Sara was sleeping, her head resting on a pillow from which two probes came out and latched to her temples. I wasn't surprised to see Pallino curled at the end of the bed.

Areel approached the cat with a smile and petted him. "He came running as soon as we entered the ship and hasn't left her side since I lowered her onto this bed."

"How is she?"

"She suffered severe psychological trauma when we were abducted."

I saw how her eyes slowly moved under her eyelids as if watching a tennis match at half the speed. "I didn't even know the ship had this kind of technology."

"Kam and I explored the place and discovered that in every room were health-bots and those strangely equipped pillows stowed in the closets. Their usage was self-explanatory." Areel sat on the edge of her bed and took one of her hands in his. He reverently kissed it and pressed it against his heart.

A memory came to mind. "I saw them, but at the time I was too distraught to think about what they were for."

"Fortunately for us, Karcum's medical technology is advanced in the psychology department; even compared to the Soleans', it is decades ahead."

I leaned against the wall by the door. "How do you know?"

"I tried said technology on myself. I wasn't going to implicitly trust the ship's medical equipment without testing it first." Areel leaned over Sara, brushed her forehead, and then released her hand and laid it by her side. He gestured toward a heap of clothes lying on the nightstand. "We found a bag full of women's garments in one of the empty rooms by Sara's. Who knows how many of them the Pures experimented on?" He shivered. "Let's go back to Kam."

Before leaving the room, he whispered something to Sara, and I stepped into the hallway to give him some privacy and closed the door behind me.

Areel came out a moment later, a worried line over his eyebrows. "Physically, she is in perfect condition, which is more than I expected..." His eyes went to the door, and the line deepened.

"But?"

"But she's human, and I'm Solean. I can't help but think that Karcum's medicine worked on me, but it might not work on her." He closed his eyes and squeezed the bridge of his nose with two fingers.

"You are in a human body, and the way your mind works is affected by that."

"But what if she rejects me as a side effect of the therapy?"

"Why would that happen?"

"I don't know. I'm going crazy." He relaxed his stance slightly. "You might be right." He gave me a tentative smile. "I reached the same conclusion myself when I had to decide what to do with her."

"What happened when you tried the psychological therapy?" I gestured toward their room.

"It helped me sort out my feelings. Anxiety and fear have been polarizing my thoughts lately. I was worried that these emotions were too strong to be erased and that they could cripple me later in life, but after one session, I feel much better already. The way it works it is quite clever because it makes you interact with your feelings. It forces you to confront your deep anxiety and transform it into a creative source of power, sending you suggestions of what you have to do to overcome the obstacles stopping you from achieving your potential." He walked into the hallway and headed back to Kam.

I matched his pace, and a moment later we were in the main room again. "When I interacted with them, I did reckon Rah and Reah were from a sophisticated race." I sat by Kam's side at the control console. Areel took a chair from the kitchen island and placed it before us. "You did the right thing. Sara wouldn't have a better chance at healing anywhere else. Human psychotherapy hasn't reached that level of finesse."

Areel nodded. "That's what I thought as well."

"And the process is completely painless. It resembles a visit to our astral world." Kam nervously swiveled in his seat.

Areel's eyebrows shot up in surprise. "Did you use it too?"

Kam lowered his eyes for the briefest moment before facing us again. "Yes, I did. After giving you the tour of the ship, and while you were taking care of Sara, I went and had a therapy session. I had some loyalty issues I had to deal with." He opened and closed his hands. "In less than a week, I have become a renegade, a traitor to our sacred customs, and I have strong feelings about our sleeping prisoner. I found myself outside his room with instincts I'm too ashamed to talk about. But I feel calmer and in control now."

A long silence followed Kam's confession, but I knew we weren't done with the business of dealing with unpleasant topics. The sooner we had the talk out of our systems, the sooner I could go back to Gaia. "You must have questions for me."

Areel hesitated before saying, "We know, at least in part, what you did. One of the machines we had to pass to free Sara had a monitor connected to the other floors. When you started the mayhem on the tenth floor, the machines automatically started streaming the images to call for help. We had a good glimpse of what was happening before we had to destroy the bot."

"Ask me." I left my seat, went to the kitchen counter, and when I saw the carafe with the red beverage was empty, I filled a glass with water from the faucet.

"I have never seen anybody reach that kind of mental control under stress." Areel followed me to the kitchen counter and opened one of the overhead cabinets. He then reached for a container and extracted a red powder from it, which he poured into the carafe and mixed with water. A moment later, the carafe was filled with more of the beverage he had offered me earlier.

I wondered how much I still didn't know about the ship I had spent six months of my life in.

Areel interrupted my musing. "It was the very first time I've seen someone using the Dark Void, and not even in a controlled environment. It was something—"

Kam looked straight at me. "We saw you killing." He shivered. "You didn't even stop to wipe the blood off your face."

"We had to incinerate your clothes; we couldn't handle them." Areel placed the carafe on the countertop then braced himself. "I'm sure you were merciful to those lives."

I shook my head. I briefly wondered if I should lie to them but decided to tell the whole truth and let them decide for themselves about me. "I wasn't merciful, for I didn't kill anybody." I saw the misplaced relief on their faces. I took the carafe and poured some of the beverage in my glass, but I didn't drink it. Instead, I played with it by pushing the glass from hand to hand and watching the way the red liquid reached the rim and then fell back inside. "Mercy wasn't on my mind when I calculated the maximum amount of pain I could inflict without killing them."

With a harder push, the contents of the glass spilled on the countertop and on my hands, staining my fingers red. I looked at my friends, and they looked back at me in shock.

"Why?" Areel was faster than Kam.

I opened and closed the cabinets in front of me, looking for something to wipe my hands of the viscous beverage covering my fingers, but I didn't find anything and washed them under the faucet then dried them on my pants.

"Why did you do what you did?" Kam stepped closer to me.

I automatically stepped back. "Because they had been torturing Gaia for months, and they were going to kill the three of them very soon."

Kam rocked his body, moving his weight from one foot to the other. "Even though… I don't know if I could have—"

Anger flared inside me, images of Gaia flashing through my mind, but I knew Kam couldn't understand what I had gone through. "You weren't in my place." I turned toward Areel and addressed him. "How much did Kam tell you about our prisoner?"

"There wasn't time to go over a detailed report. You were… unavailable, and he had to deal with Sara first." Kam reached for a mug in one of the cabinets and then served himself some of the red beverage. He sipped at it and then looked at me. "I was waiting for you to talk to him together."

I nodded at him and then turned to face Areel once again. "From his aspect, our prisoner might appear human, but he is not. He has lived among Soleans, even worked as an Observer, and he was Kam's contact. He is a spy and belongs to a race called the Pures. They have numerous similarities to our kind because we were among their first victims. Earth was supposed to be one of the newest outposts; they were still debating if humans were worth the trouble. That is the nature of the research they were conducting on Gaia." I paused for a moment and drank what was left in my cup. Areel promptly refilled it for me. I waited for his questions, but he kept silent. "This race, the Pures, have a very peculiar and sick addiction: they need to absorb someone else's emotions to function. It wasn't always in their nature, though. They were a rational race when they arrived on Solo. Their existence then was regulated uniquely by the mathematical rules they had developed over millions of years. They were content with what they had. They had already reached the stars and were peacefully exploring other galaxies when they found us. Our way of life was particularly interesting for them. We lived in perpetual mental communion with our loved ones. Soleans had never experienced loneliness. We didn't have such a word in our vocabulary. The Pures lived as separated beings; they didn't have sentimental attachments. Everyone lived by a mathematical code, their way of communicating resembled a binary code more than a form of speaking. In their language were no words expressing sentiments because they had never felt any. Solo was the first planet they reached that was so utterly different from theirs." I was tired of talking already. I went to sit on the couch by the kitchen area. Kam and Areel stood at the kitchen counter. I refreshed my mouth with the tangy liquid and reorganized my thoughts. "Our ancestors welcomed them as brothers long gone. The Pures didn't know what to do with us. We were completely different in every aspect of our lives. They were organic robots. We lived regulated by our sentiments. Their planet had a monochromatic landscape while Solo was full of colors. The two cultures were both fascinated with each other. The Pures asked our ancestors' permission to live among them and have time to study our culture. They accepted the proposition with genuine enthusiasm, and the cohabitation started. After a while, the Pures living on Solo started changing, but at the beginning, nobody recognized that. The Pures only realized the importance of the alteration when it was already too late. One delegation of Pures went back to their planet to report their studies, and while they were flying, the crew started experiencing a strange malady. The more they moved away from Solo, the more they got anxious, to the point of not being able to command the ship. The ship went on autopilot, and they reached their planet nevertheless, but only a few survived the journey." I looked at my friends, who were transfixed by my tale. Once again, I gave them time to ask me anything, but they both made signs for me to continue.

"The nine that survived went crazy. They kept repeating words that didn't make any sense in their language, as if they had invented a new one during the journey. They craved each other's company, and when they got separated, two of the remaining ones committed suicide. Nobody on their planet knew how to help the seven who survived. The Pures sensed that our planet could have been the source of that madness, and they decided to retire their contingent on Solo. Nobody answered their request. When officially asked, the Solean Government responded that the Pures on Solo had requested asylum. The Pures accepted the situation but sent another contingent to check on the ones gone native. An army of hyperlogical soldiers reached Solo with the intent of studying the phenomenon. They were treated with kindness, all of them free to roam on our planet. When the last Pures arrived, they started to experience some differences in their mental structures; the change was so subtle but radical that they managed to go back and report, but they also infected their kind with the virus that was our way of life. The result was horrible for everybody involved. In their lucid madness, they thought that our essence could be mathematically extrapolated. It didn't work, but they kept trying and redefining the process until they found a way that did the trick." It was painful to have to talk about it. It had been horrifying the first time I had seen it, but elaborating on the concept again was nauseating. I could see in their faces that Kam and Areel were already sick, and they barely knew what was coming. I wanted to tell the story and get over it more than anything else, but I was shaking.

"Go ahead, please. We need to know." Kam spoke at last.

"The Pures literally fed from our emotions. They found a way to extract our feelings, but it cost us our sanity. Our ability to share a mental link with loved ones was destroyed in the process. We were completely drained of emotions. We only felt a terrible numbness. We lost our joy for life." Tears escaped my eyes. I could imagine the desperation my ancestors had felt, now that I had experienced what it was being whole with Gaia. I couldn't imagine going back to not having it, even after just a few hours. Kam was pale and couldn't speak, but Areel was visibly trembling. I knew he was thinking of Sara.

"And the worst part of it is that we volunteered. We wanted to help them. The Pures on Solo were good people, and they were suffering some sort of painful withdrawal. They explained how they were going to milk our auras to distill the feelings they were addicted to but couldn't produce by themselves. They never stopped. We never recovered. Our emotions were their opium, but their minds couldn't safely process the overload of raw sentiments. They became mean. Then forgot who we were, what we had given them freely. They ended up annihilating their primary source of drug and then moved on to exploit other planets." I was still shaking, but I had managed to say almost everything. Now it was time for the questions.

"You never had the slightest idea that someone else was on Earth," Kam stated after several minutes of silent thinking.

I shook my head. "They sent researchers to every planet where an Observer was on duty. Ironically, we scouted for them." Maybe one day, talking about it would be easier, less painful.

"There was never a Solean community hiding on Earth, escaping from them?" Areel went to sit on the sofa opposite me.

"No, the three of us are the only Soleans who ever put foot on Earth."

Areel crossed his legs at the ankles and braced the two armrests on the sofa. "The Pures brought our artifacts to Earth."

"They brought our artifacts with them wherever they went." That part was the saddest of the whole story.

"Why?" Areel asked.

I felt the urge to cry but steadied my voice. "We were their first love, so to speak. Some of them felt something similar to guilt for what they had done to us. Those more sensitive Pures found consolation, or maybe even atonement, in bringing with them little mementoes that would remind them what their actions had created." I had seen the hate that the rest of their race felt toward that inner group of Pures who had inherited from us the quality of compassion. The prisoner's mind was full of rage for their careless actions. Actually, from his point of view, he was quite right since planting Solean material on Earth had ultimately been the reason why I discovered them. Their search team on Earth should have done a faster job of covering their traces.

"Eventually their minds, already damaged by the ingestion of our emotions, gave up, and they committed suicide. The ones that unluckily assisted that horror added another streak of insanity to their already corrupted minds and became the soulless addicts that have savaged civilization after civilization to obtain their fix. The same beings tortured Gaia for months, looking for a way to use the humans for their needs.

"My presence on the planet slowed their research; they didn't want to risk alerting an Observer, and the quality of the human emotions provided to be too intense for their immediate consumption. A series of incredible coincidences put me on their path, and when I disappeared and Areel started poking around, they lost their calm and, luckily for us, made several errors." I paused and gathered my thoughts to deliver the last piece of information. "There is more."

Areel's hands grabbed the armrests with renewed strength, and his knuckles went white before my eyes.

Kam sighed.

"Lex, my Ancestor Guide, the respected Wise in charge of deciding the fate of the Solean people, is not Solean at all. He is a Pure."

Areel gasped.

"He also tried to kill me." I wondered if the pain from Lex's betrayal would ever lessen.

Areel, his eyes wide, looked first at me and then at Kam, who slowly nodded and said, "Our prisoner had a psychic gun charged with his mental signature."

"That would be proof enough, but I also saw Lex giving the command in the prisoner's memories."

"It can't be." Areel held his head in his hands. "Nobody knew you were on Earth."

I moved on the sofa, trying to find a more comfortable spot, but my uneasiness wasn't physical. "I inadvertently warned Lex by sending a mental cry when I landed on Earth, and Saverio, the human they forced to collaborate, had seen me."

"And he was at the castle where he and the Pure ambushed us," Kam added, ending the conversation.

They both left the main room a few minutes later, needing time to think alone. I stayed behind and decided to discover if I could use the kitchen gadgets to prepare a meal. When they came back an hour later, I had managed to learn the basics of how the kitchen worked.

"We have to decide what to do with our prisoner." I addressed them without preamble.

Kam scowled. "I feel such rage toward him. I can't even tolerate his presence on this ship."

"We aren't able to think rationally at the moment, not after what we discovered." Areel was visibly tired.

"I suggest we keep the prisoner in deep sleep for the whole length of the trip. It will be easier for the three of us to handle the situation." It was the ethical way; I was ashamed to think that probably wasn't my preference. But I was stronger than that. I couldn't succumb to my darker instincts again.

"I agree with you; this is the only way to save our consciences." Areel's voice shook.

"Yes, I don't see any other solution." Kam put the final word on the topic, to my great relief.

18

Having survived the heart-to-heart with Kam and Areel, my only desire was to go back to Gaia. "I'm exhausted. If there isn't anything else you'd like to talk—"

"Go." Areel smiled.

"Yes, please, go." Kam pointed at the hallway.

I blushed. "Was I so obvious?"

"Even without the sharing, you are not very hard to read," Kam said.

"Lately… say in the last day or two, your aura has been broadcasting quite loudly." Areel too waved his hand toward the hallway.

"Keep it quiet." Kam's request accompanied me outside of the control room.

I heard the two of them laughing from the hallway. They were still having fun at my expense when I reached the med-bay. I passed several hours watching Gaia sleep peacefully. I double checked that her body temperature was warm enough, and then I relaxed beside her, careful to not disturb her rest. I let the health-bot take her vitals when she started sweating, and I cradled her while she went through a detox from the substances the Pures had injected her with. Once she stopped sweating, I raised the linen sheet and the blanket covering her, then I summoned the water present in the room, added some pine and eucalyptus scents to refresh her senses, and gave her a shower. I warmed the water until it became a misty vapor all around her. Perfumed dew covered her naked skin, and I was overwhelmed by the sight of her.

Gaia was more than a beautiful addiction for me. She was my religion. Her body was the temple into which I desired admittance, to pray.

She was aware of my presence, and her aura let me know how much she liked being cleaned. She moved in the narrow bed until comfortable on her side, her wet hair covering the pillow and her throat exposed. I bent to kiss the unruly mass of her hair; the blonde shades had faded during the long, dark imprisonment. Gaia sighed pleasantly in her sleep, giving me permission to continue. I moved her hair out of the way and kissed the base of her neck while I changed the molecules in the air once again and hot light dried her body. I caressed her arm and perfumed the air with the scents of cotton and lilac. "Sleep well, my love."

I was tired myself but could barely close my eyes. I couldn't relax in that bed, which was too small for the two of us. Her naked proximity drove me crazy. Finally, I decided I had to do something to fix that situation. I ran to Areel's and Sara's room, and he told me to come in at the first knock. "May I?" My eyes went to the women's clothes on the nightstand, and he handed the whole heap to me. I chose two items, thanked him, and ran back to Gaia. I reverently touched her, unable to resist the urge to leave a trail of kisses on her body, but I finally found peace when she was dressed in shorts and a tank top.

We spent the rest of the night in a light slumber, dreaming our communal dreams, and we kissed while caressing each other.

"Hi." I waited until I was sure she was fully awake, but I had been waiting for a while, and I was getting anxious to talk to her.

"Hi to you."

Her eyes were bright in the half-light of the room, and I couldn't help but kiss her.

"What happened while I was sleeping?"

"I talked to Areel and Kam—"

"Kam?"

"Kam is a friend of mine."

"Is he Solean?"

I nodded. "He left Solo when Areel disappeared off the face of the earth and instead found me. It's only thanks to him that I discovered where you were kept." I paused for a moment. "You'll meet him soon enough." Then I showed her the salient facts of what she had missed while resting. This second time around, it was more pleasant to go through the conversation I had had with Kam and Areel. Firstly, I didn't struggle for words that time but streamed my thoughts directly to her mind. And secondly, she was Gaia.

She wanted to know about Sara, and I showed her my visit to her room. She smiled at Pallino's presence in my memory. I mentioned Areel's worries about possible side effects, being that she was human and the medical technology was meant for an alien race. On the tail of that thought, she wondered how she was faring so well compared to her friend.

"It's us. Together, we're stronger than we are alone. When we touched the first time and shared our souls, we went through a process that changed us. We healed our emotional wounds with the act of sharing. We're different now. We've changed even at a molecular level. I don't know the extent of our transformation, but I guess we'll know soon enough." I rearranged my body on the bed to give her some space.

"I do feel calm and in control. The experience I had should've been harder to deal with, but I feel fine. I'm almost worried that it's going to bite me back later. I thought that maybe the happiness of seeing you had temporarily blinded my other feelings, but I don't feel I'm going to crumble anytime soon. I think you're right. We did heal our minds." She stretched, and her stomach made some noise.

We both laughed. "I went down this path before. I learned the hard way that this body... *I* need to eat." I took her in my arms, and she looked so small, so fragile.

Like a kitten, she snuggled closer to me. "I'm not easily breakable."

"You're stronger than me, in so many ways, but I can't stop fretting about you." I raised her face and smiled when I saw her mischievous eyes staring back at mine.

"I love being pampered."

I don't know what possessed me, but for some unexpected reason, I read her words in a general meaning, and something deep inside me produced a painful emotion I could barely shield in time.

She smiled at my reaction. I hadn't been fast enough in concealing my jealousy. "By you," she added.

I felt like an idiot and hid my shame behind a kiss. "Sorry, sorry. Human emotions drive me crazy."

"And I also love this new aspect of you."

We spent a few minutes in silence, basking in each other's presence, then she noticed she wasn't naked anymore and wondered when she had dressed herself.

"You haven't…" I wanted to hide in a deep hole to prevent this conversation from happening.

"Thanks." Gaia raised an eyebrow, perplexed by my uneasiness.

"I had to—" I carefully moved my body away from her touch, which in the narrow space was quite an accomplishment, but I was feeling terribly shy at the moment. "I couldn't sleep in the same bed with you—"

"Oh… oh… oh!" Gaia's facial expressions ranged from puzzled to offended to uncertain. Finally, comprehension dawned in her eyes, and she blushed as deeply as I had.

"Would you like some breakfast?" Her stomach was rumbling more loudly, and so was mine.

"I'm starving." Gaia brushed my mouth with her lips and cunningly let me know what she thought about the topic we hadn't discussed. *And not just for food.*

"Not fair, Gaia. Breakfast, please." I brushed her lips back. *This is not the best moment to start that conversation, but I want to talk about it. A lot.*

Her eyes lit up at my suggestion. "Surprise me with your cooking expertise. I'm really hungry."

I pushed her out of the room before she could say anything else. I led her slowly through the short hallway, giving Gaia the time to get accustomed to the different gravity.

"The gravity inside the ship is lighter. It makes long trips more comfortable. My guess is that your body was healed in record time by the same power that healed your mind: our sharing." I answered her silent question about her quick recovery while we were walking to the kitchen.

"Give me the grand tour."

The place was empty, and I played host for a while, showing her how the kitchen worked—something I had just discovered myself.

Not a long conversation since it was easier than operating most of the appliances on Earth. I cooked silently, just content to be in the same room with her in such a domestic setting.

Gaia didn't break the silence and spent some time looking at the ship for the first time. By now, I was used to the monochromatic ambience, but I was curious to know what she thought about it. "Let me pamper you some more." I took a chair from one of the two tables for her.

She sat, gave a thorough look at the furniture, and knocked on the surface. "What kind of material is the furniture made of?"

I went back to the kitchen counter to load a tray with the food I had just prepared. "Not sure. We don't have anything like it on Solo."

She stood, met me halfway, took the two cups with the red beverage Areel had mixed for me earlier, and went back to her seat. "We sure don't have anything like that on Earth. This material looks so fragile—"

"It's sturdy enough to have survived a crash." I laid the tray on the table, sat by her, and started serving her.

She looked around one more time. "What happened there?"

"You'd call it a miracle. When I thought everything was lost, this ship appeared in the sky of Silenzio to give me new hope."

"Silenzio—Areel told me about it. Was it really silent?"

"Yes, it was. I couldn't communicate with anybody. At first, I thought I would lose my sanity. But then I started seeing you. I lived for our dates." I leaned to kiss her and felt her erratic hearbeats.

"What happened when this ship crashed?"

"I walked across Silenzio to reach the wreckage, hoping the ship was salvageable." I let her experience through my memories the moment I inadvertently awakened Reah. "I felt the new life inside her, a small, pulsating light demanding to be."

"Who would want to harm an innocent?"

"According to their society's rules, their union was considered blasphemous."

"I hope they're fine now."

"I think they found their haven on Silenzio."

"And you found a way out of it, thanks to them." *And for that, I will be forever in debt to the alien couple.*

"Me too." I nudged her nose with mine. "Let's eat now."

She nodded and relaxed back on the chair, her eyes sweeping the table.

I let her be for a few minutes, then I waved my hand before her. "Elios to Gaia." She finally came back to me. "What would you like to eat?" I pointed at the feast on the table.

"Everything looks good. Surprise me."

I cut a small piece from a red fruit and fed her, gently opening her lips: something I had dreamed of doing for so long, and it felt extremely intimate. "How is it?"

She savored the morsel. "Good as it smells. Salty and meaty, with the consistency of soft tofu."

I motioned for her to drink the juice resembling boiling blood, and I watched while Gaia, with a mistrusting look on her eyes, put the rim of the cup at her mouth. She smiled. "What is it?" I asked.

"This is my first meal in…" She shook her head. "I don't know when I ate last."

"Six months."

"I was kept prisoner for six months?"

I took her hand in mine and showed her what we had both gone through during that time.

"Thanks… for everything." She brought my hand to her lips.

"Anything for you." I kissed her. "I'd do anything for you." For a moment, memories of what I had done during her rescue at the alien facility emerged from the deepest recesses of my mind. I hastily pushed them back. "I'm sorry. I didn't mean for you to see that."

She squeezed my hand and then pressed it to her heart. "I know. Nothing is going to happen to me."

"I know… because I won't let it." I pulled her onto my lap, and we enjoyed the rest of our breakfast together, making small talk. When we were done eating, I decided it was time for her surprise. "I want to show you our room." I circled her waist.

"Okay." She had already taken one step toward the hallway, but a sudden doubt made me stop.

"Is it okay with you if we sleep together? In the same bed?"

"I think we just did."

"That was done under more dramatic circumstances." I released her. "I'm not sure you want me around day and night."

She laid one hand over my heart, and the other reached for my neck. "It is exactly what I want. Forever." She caressed me with slow circles while looking at me with her hazel eyes. I was lost in those bright lights, and I gasped when she thought, *And sleeping with you is the least of my concerns at the moment.*

Before she could read my own thoughts on the topic, I removed her hand from my neck and kept her at a safe distance. *I want you more than air. I want you more than food or water. I want you now.*

"Sooner or later, I'll discover what you were thinking." A mischievous light was in her eyes. "You'll see; I'm a fast learner."

"Believe me, you'll know it soon enough if you don't stop teasing me so." I resumed our little stroll through the ship and reached the room I had earlier chosen and decorated for us.

Gaia stopped beside the door, which was now completely transparent, and gave me an inquisitive glance.

"It becomes opaque at a vocal command." Suddenly, I was nervous. I had rehearsed that moment in my mind countless times, but now I felt inadequate.

"I love you, Gaia." I bent to kiss her softly while scooping her up, and I entered our room with her cradled in my arms. She hid her face against my chest, and for a moment, I thought I'd botched it. Then I listened to her thoughts and breathed in relief. I loved the way her body curled up against mine, almost weightless. I liked the feeling of surprising her, and I had gone the extra step to ensure that. The sparkle in her eyes when Gaia saw her little painting on the wall was the best gift she could give me. "I couldn't leave it behind. When I saw it in your apartment in Tarquinia, it spoke to me." On a wall full of colorful canvases, the hydrangeas and geraniums had stood out. I lowered her to her feet. "While you were sleeping, I arranged the room. I hope you like it."

"You edited your memories." Gaia looked at me with an intensity that sent shivers through my body.

"Yes, I did. I wanted to surprise you." I felt slightly guilty at having used my newfound ability of shielding my memories from her, but her joy was worth the trouble.

"Thanks." Gaia took two or three steps around the room and noticed the window on the wall.

"It's a screen that can project any image you want." I gave the screen a vocal command, and a green forest with a waterfall appeared outside the window. I waited expectantly for Gaia to recognize the place I had chosen.

"Oh, this is the trail I showed you on Mount Rainier." She planted an enthusiastic kiss on my mouth.

"It is now." I heard her thinking the picture looked realistic, and I added, "The image you're looking at is being taken right now. It's a live broadcasting of the location I chose." I turned my back to the screen to better look at her. "I still can't believe we are here, now." Holding her hand, I sat on the bed.

"I can't wrap my head around all of this." She smiled and sat by me. "I'm worried you're going to disappear." She raised my hand to her lips for a peck and then pressed it to her heart. The recent memory of us entering the room sped her heartbeats.

It means exactly what you think. "We already exchanged our vows. We did it the first time we saw each other. I will wed you in any form you think is most proper, but our union transcends any human or Solean form of companionship." I leaned to kiss her nose and passed my free hand through her hair. *You are my wife, my companion, my soul mate.*

She choked.

"Oh, it wasn't my intention—"

"No, no. You didn't say anything wrong. The opposite. You're perfect. This moment is perfect." She softly cried. "I'm just terrified it's going to end."

I lay on the bed and pulled her down with me, kissing her tears away.

She chuckled. "I'm being silly. I know."

I kept kissing her.

"I don't know what just happened to me." She shivered. "Just don't let me go."

"Never again."

"I love you."

"My love." I showed her images of wedding ceremonies, some from Earth, some from other planets. She liked it and thought of outlandish rites involving us, and we laughed at the idea of getting married in that fashion.

Between kissing and laughing, the need to be closer to Gaia became an imperative I couldn't ignore, and I covered her with my body. A silvery light from the nocturnal view of the forest cast a dreamlike atmosphere over the room. Reality blurred while my hands searched for her face and then lower for her throat. I was vaguely aware of the riot of colors and music keeping us company.

"Do you realize the effect you have on me?" Gaia's voice was a hoarse whisper.

"You have the same effect on me. I'm defenseless in your hands." I was trembling, and I could barely breathe.

"I love you. I love you. I love you."

Gaia's words sounded like singing to me, and I kissed her with renewed intensity, a primordial longing guiding my body. With my lips, I followed the contour of her jaw down to the hollow of her throat, and then my hands found the strap of her top, and I freed her shoulder. I shivered when I felt Gaia's hands under my shirt, moving it out of the way, caressing my chest in slow patterns. My mind reached for hers, in a deep sharing that brought us even closer. Our auras combined, expressing our emotions with a hint of exotic spices that matched the scent emanating from our warm bodies. I was lost in that beautiful chaos when I caught one of Gaia's fleeting thoughts. Physical pain ran through my hypersensitive skin. I slowly rolled to lie on my back and closed my eyes, but even the moonlight provided to be too bright. Gaia reached for my hand, and once again I was in her mind.

Why did I have to think of that? What does it change if we have our first time here or somewhere else?

"Because the first time is a memory that lasts forever. And I agree with you." It was so difficult to articulate words in meaningful sentences. We deserved to take our time to make it truly special. "I love you. I want that perfect memory."

"I need you. In every possible way. We've been through a lot to waste time now."

I smiled. "The fact you had *that* thought *then* means a lot."

She frowned. "It doesn't mean I'm not ready."

"I know you are, as you well know that I am." I propped up on my elbow to keep a minimum of distance from her; otherwise, I wouldn't have found the strength to keep on talking. "But I want to give you the gift of an unforgettable memory. My wedding present to you." I sat and brought her up with me. "Would you accept me? Would you do me the honor of accepting my gift?"

"Thank you." She hugged me tightly. *You just did it. You just made it perfect. I'm the luckiest girl alive.*

"I'm the lucky one, my love. You would've found happiness. Even without me." She made a face at my statement, and I smiled.

"I'd never—"

I shushed her by putting a finger on her lips. "But I would never have understood what it is to be alive without you." I left a trail of soft kisses on her face. "I wasn't meant for love. My destiny was to spend my life alone. You changed me."

She pushed me away. "Without you, I would never have found happiness." *With time, I might have started a family with someone, but I never would have found real love.*

I felt a pang of sadness at her thought.

"My heart can't belong to anybody else." She kissed me, and soon her hands moved up and down my body.

I felt her shivering with me, and then she lowered herself onto the bed and pulled me down on top of her. *Gaia?*

She answered my question by removing my shirt. I lowered both straps of her top, and then we helped each other get rid of what was left of our clothes. I caressed her naked body, savoring the silkiness of her skin under my hands. I kissed her, and our auras exploded. I explored places in her body I hadn't dared before. I was fascinated by the way she reacted to my touch. The planes and valleys of her body beckoned me. The hollowness of her collarbone. The softness of the sides of her breasts. When I reached her hipbone, Gaia arched toward me.

I stopped, my need to be one with her no longer deniable. She nodded. I let my body take control, and she opened to me. Our minds reached a higher awareness while we moved in the same rhythm, kissing and caressing each other. Within her, I found bliss.

Later, we lay intertwined, the moonlight from the faraway scene illuminating us, our auras pulsating in soothing colors.

19

We holed up in our room until the next day. Before venturing outside, Gaia said, "I'd love to see the place where I lived in Rome."

I froze.

"Just the outside of my parents' building."

"I don't think it's a great idea."

"Please, just a moment."

"You don't know what you're asking for."

"Please…"

In the end, I couldn't deny her. I watched as she stared at the screen. Her whole family showed up for a private view, probably exiting and entering their building in between errands.

I kissed her shoulder. "They think you are back in Seattle."

"I know, but I need to talk to them, to hear their voices," she whispered.

"It's too dangerous right now. The same power behind your abduction could get hold of your family if you contacted them. They would do anything to stop us from reaching Solo."

"What can I do, then?" She turned to look at me.

I reached for her. "We have to wait. We can't leave any crumbs for our enemies to follow." I cradled her to me. "I'm working on something."

"What—"

"You must trust me for now." I brushed her face with small kisses.

She stood and pulled me up with her then reached for her clothes, which lay discarded on the floor. "Let's go visit Sara."

I hastily grabbed mine from the same heap and donned them. We walked to Areel and Sara's room and knocked at the door. After a single knock on the door, Areel told us to enter.

"How is she?"

He barely looked at us, his focus on Sara lying peacefully on the bed. "She looks more alert today."

"Are you still trying to reach for her mind?" I walked to the headrest.

Areel nodded. "I feel she can hear me now."

Gaia patted Areel's shoulder. "It worked for us. I'm sure it will work for you as well." She bent to leave a kiss on Sara's forehead. "What is it?"

He stirred at Gaia's question. "I wash her skin twice a day with an infusion I make."

"What's in it?"

"Herbs and minerals to help with her skin regeneration."

"Jasmine?" Gaia asked.

He smiled. "And a hint of freesias."

Gaia looked at her friend. "She'll be fine."

"I know she will." Areel turned to look at Sara as well.

I felt my friend's desire to be alone with his beloved, and I accompanied Gaia outside but stopped at the door for a moment. "Dinner is going to be ready in a few minutes."

His eyes on Sara, Areel answered, "Thanks. Coming later."

I directed Gaia to the kitchen. I needed to release some energy and gathered the fresh ingredients Kam had picked from the small hydroponic pod and left by the sink. Gaia and I worked in amiable silence, chopping the vegetables into small cubes that we tossed in a pan and cooked. Satisfied by the sizzling sound of the meal sautéing over the radiating heat of the stove, I brewed two cups of tea and led Gaia to sit at the table.

"Hi there," she said, and I turned to see Kam had entered the room.

"Hi." He gave me a look, and I nodded, then he turned toward Gaia. "Pleasure to finally meet you."

"Likewise." She smiled softly. "Thank you. I owe you my life and Elios's."

"I would've done anything for him."

"I know."

Kam's eyes widened in surprise, and he gave me a questioning look.

I answered, "We're one."

He thought about it for a moment then relaxed his frown. "Better this way. I know nothing of Earthly pleasantries." He smiled at Gaia. "We don't have to waste time explaining things. I like it."

As promised, an hour later, Areel joined us in the kitchen. I served him something to eat, but he was too distracted to enjoy the food. He was leaving when Kam stopped him.

"So, has she given any sign she knows you're there?" Kam paused, and when Areel turned on his heels to look at him, he asked, "Anything at all?"

It happened so quickly I didn't realize what Areel's intention was before it was too late. Without asking permission, he touched Kam's hand. Gaia and I gasped. Kam paled, and his eyes went wide, his attempt to dislodge Areel's hold failing.

"Areel, please stop." I was at his back, ready to touch him if necessary and exercise my power.

He released Kam before I had to intervene, and Kam stormed out of the room.

The situation defused for the moment, I sat back at the table and offered a chair to Areel, who stood still and looked ready for a fight. "Kam didn't mean to be cruel. He doesn't know—"

"Now he does." He turned on his heels and left.

I looked at his retreating shape and sighed inwardly.

Gaia stroked my arm. "Everything will be okay. Don't worry."

Much later, Gaia and I were back in the kitchen for a night snack when Kam came for a glass of water.

Soon after, Areel arrived and walked directly to Kam. "I'm sorry for touching you without permission."

Kam shrugged. "You have a lot on your mind."

"It's inexcusable." Areel shook his head.

"No, you were right to force me to see through your eyes. I wouldn't know what you're going through otherwise. I'm sorry."

At Kam's words, Areel sat on a chair and took his head between his hands. "What if she wakes and doesn't recognize me? What if—"

"Don't think about that," Gaia whispered.

* * *

Time on the ship passed slowly.

Then, one morning, Sara woke from her medically induced slumber.

Gaia and I had just emerged from our room when we heard voices coming from Areel's and headed that way. Sara sat on her bed, having breakfast, Areel and Pallino guarding her closely.

"Sara!" Gaia left my side to run to her friend. "I missed you so much—"

Sara smiled. "I'm back."

"You look… good," Gaia said while I raised my eyebrow at Areel, who smiled back at me in response.

Sara motioned toward Areel. "He was with me the whole time."

Gaia nodded. "I know."

Areel lowered his eyes to the bed.

Sara looked over Gaia's shoulders at me. "Elios."

"It's nice to see you again." Gaia stepped back into my shade, and I took her hand.

Sara nodded. "It is. Thank you for coming back for us."

The memories of that night still painful to me, I remained silent.

Sara focused on a spot behind us. "And you must be Kam. Nice to meet you, and thanks to you too."

"Nice meeting you too." Kam stopped at the door. "You'll probably want to get used to"—he gestured at the room—"all of this."

"Yes, I think she needs to rest now. You can come back later." Areel stood and resolutely herded the three of us outside the room.

Before Areel closed us outside, Gaia managed to say, "As soon as your mastiff goes to sleep, I'm back."

Sara laughed. "Later."

"Later." Gaia waved her hand as the door became opaque.

Kam gave the two of us a puzzled look and then tilted his head toward Areel and Sara's now off-limits room. "You're all like that?"

"Pretty much." I dropped a kiss on Gaia's crown, and Kam left us rather abruptly.

"Was that necessary?" Despite her question, she sought my mouth for a breathtaking kiss.

"Yes." Already dizzy, I took her hand and ran back to our room to finish what we had started.

A few hours later, Kam timidly knocked at our door. "Elios? We need to talk."

I groaned, but Gaia laughed and mouthed it was okay at the same time I asked, "It must be now?"

"Yes. Otherwise I wouldn't have come to disturb you."

I dropped one last kiss on Gaia's lips. "I won't be long. I promise." I put on my shirt and pants with annoyed movements.

"I'll go fix something to eat." She reached for her top and donned it over a skirt then left the room with a smile.

I heard her greet Kam, but when I went to the door, she had already rounded the corner. I gave my friend an irritated stare. "What's so important it can't wait?"

Kam matched my stare with one of his own. "It's time to leave Earth, and we haven't talked about what's next."

His words had an immediate cooling effect. "I'm sorry. You're right. I've been so caught up with finally being able to be with Gaia—"

He tilted his head and and raised one eyebrow. "That you don't want to think about anything else. I get it."

I sighed inwardly. "Actually, I do think about everything else. I'm just exhausted by shielding my thoughts from Gaia. I don't want her to worry about me. And I don't want her to find out what I'm planning before it's time to reveal it." I looked at the corner where she had disappeared.

Kam stepped out and stood before me. "What are you talking about?"

I passed my right hand through my hair, then I pointed my chin in the direction of Areel's room. "I think it's better if we ask him to join us."

"Okay." Kam moved out of the way and followed me.

A few steps later, I knocked at Areel and Sara's door. Nobody answered. I checked the auras inside, found only Areel's, then proceeded to open the door and enter the room. "Wake up." I gently nudged the snoring shape cuddled under the blanket. Sara must have tucked him in before leaving.

"Areel," Kam called in a low voice.

The shape shifted, then a black head of hair appeared from under the blanket, followed by the rest of Areel, who blinked several times. "I'm tired."

"I know, and I'm sorry, but this talk can't wait." I felt slightly guilty at disturbing him. Areel had barely rested while taking care of Sara. "You can go back to sleep later."

"Do you mind?" Kam gestured toward the only chair by the bed.

Areel muttered his sleepy assent to Kam, and I leaned against the wall. I was too nervous to sit anyway.

"What is it?" Areel propped himself up and then took his face between his hands and roughly caressed his jaws.

I hesitated, and Kam spoke first. "We must decide what to do in case the girls want to go back to their families."

I saw Areel flinch, and I half smiled at him in sympathy. "It's a possibility."

He made a choked sound and then nodded.

"I thought about something." I pushed myself off the wall. "We could erase their memories so they would be safe." I felt sick to the stomach just saying it out loud. I had carried that idea deep inside me, being careful to shield it from Gaia, and now that it was in the open it terrified me.

Areel gasped and Kam nodded.

I paced a few steps back and forth. "It's the only way for them to go back to Earth. Both the Pures and the Soleans would be after their memories."

"It makes sense." Kam turned to face our companion.

Areel blinked twice before saying, "It does, but I don't like it."

"Me neither, but I want Gaia to be free to decide what she wants to do. Don't you want the same for Sara?"

Areel opened his mouth then closed it and finally nodded. "Of course I want Sara to have that choice."

"Well, now that we have agreed on that, we should talk about us." Kam's eyes zeroed in on me.

I frowned. "Nothing has changed. I will go back to Solo to testify."

"But you know the consequences of such an act—" Areel lowered his chin to his bent knees. "Maybe you could leave us there and fly away with Gaia."

"Where to? If not the Pures, Solo will be looking for me to track me down, and with me, Gaia as well. No, I won't put her in danger."

"Then after the girls have decided, we'll fly back home and try our luck." Kam stood up. "I'll go check the astral charts for the best time for departure."

Areel waited for our friend to be out of the room. "I've only had a few days with Sara."

"It's unfair, I know." My heart already ached at the prospect of having that conversation with Gaia. "But it's for their best." I couldn't stand to talk about it a moment longer. "I'm going for a quick shower." I waved at him and left his room, deep in thought already.

I stood under scalding water for several minutes, but the uneasiness didn't leave me. Back in my room, I tried to meditate, but my will to focus was lacking. Eventually, I decided to go to the kitchen to see what Gaia was up to. I heard her laughing from the hallway, and my mood lifted. She wasn't alone. Areel's and Sara's voices echoed from the kitchen. The scene I found upon entering the common room was one of joy, and my mind clouded at the thought that soon I could be losing all of that. I went to Gaia's side. "How do you feel, Sara?" She and Areel had moved to the sitting area and called the couch. I moved two chairs from the kitchen area for Gaia and me.

"I feel well, like in a dream." Sara smiled.

"Sometimes, I feel I'm dreaming too," Gaia said.

I took her hand in mine and caressed her wrist in lazy circles. She shivered at the contact. *Good.*

We're not alone. Gaia blushed mentally then hastily looked at our friends.

I kept tracing her sensitive skin. *We could be.*

Gaia stood up, and I was following her when Kam entered the common area, his face promising nothing good. "We'll approach the critical point of no return in less than two days."

At his words, my heart slammed against my ribcage.

Gaia sat again. "But I thought we had more time."

"Can't we wait for Sara to get used to things?" Areel kept his eyes on Sara.

Kam shook his head. "The conditions for the jump are ideal only for the next forty-two hours. Past that limit, we'll have to wait another full Earth revolution." He took a chair from the kitchen table and joined our circle.

"We can't wait another year in orbit. It's too dangerous," I said out loud and then I asked Gaia, *Are you okay?* Her silence was answer enough.

"We're lucky Sara woke up just now." Kam turned to face Areel. "We should've left already... with Lex turning out to be a Pure—"

Kam's words were out of his mouth before I could stop him, but he must have felt my stare piercing through his back because he turned again to give me an apologetic shrug.

"What is he talking about?" Gaia asked.

I didn't want to have this conversation before the others. I had meant to talk to her once all the decisions had been made. "He's the one who betrayed all of us. He isn't Solean—"

She acknowledged my words, then I saw her eyes widen when she put the pieces together.

Areel said, "He's one of the Pures in charge of hiding the truth about what happened before the Dark."

Gaia touched me.

I can't accept what Lex did. Had to keep those memories buried. It's still too painful. Later...

She applied gentle pressure on my arm. *Don't worry. We don't have to talk about it.*

Kam coughed, demanding our attention. "I hate to interrupt, but we should get back to the problem at hand. We must leave, and we must leave now. You"—he looked at Sara and then at Gaia—"have to decide what you want to do."

"They need a moment to digest the news." I felt Gaia falter beside me, the thoughts crowding her mind so loudly I would have heard them even without physical contact. She was devastated by the idea of having to leave her family without saying goodbye.

You don't have to.

I don't have a choice.

But you do.

No, I really don't.

I switched to voice to say what had to be said. "Yes, you and Sara have to decide now whether you want to follow us to Solo or go back to Earth." After one look at her wet eyes, my shield crumbled for the briefest of moments, and all my deepest thoughts and fears surfaced. I cursed myself and immediately put a heavy lid on my feelings. I wasn't fast enough.

"You can't go back to Solo," Gaia said.

"We are not talking about my decision." It took all my training not to crumble to pieces before her and beg her to stay with me. "I won't force you into a life of constant running and hiding. I want to have a chance for us."

"We can go somewhere else."

It seemed only a moment ago I had just had the same conversation with Kam and Areel. "You have to decide. Please."

Kam spoke, interrupting our private conversation. "I think we should discuss pros and cons since neither Gaia nor Sara seems to grasp all the consequences of taking this journey."

"Kam's right. Let's talk about it." Again, I forced the words out of my mouth. "You can travel with us and ask for asylum on Solo, independently from our fate." She looked at me in astonished silence. "Or we can take you back to Earth."

"But what about the Pures?" Sara asked.

"We'll take care of that." Areel held her closer to him.

I wished we were alone, Gaia and I. "If you decide to go back to Earth, you'll be safe, and you'll be able to rejoin your families."

"But what about endangering our families?" Gaia shifted on the chair.

I wasn't ready to tell her, and I cowardly shut her off from my thoughts. "You and your families will be safe."

"How can you be sure?" Sara moved out of Areel's embrace, and he pressed her back to himself while answering, "The Pures are after us. Once we leave Earth, they'll immediately follow—"

Gaia moved on the chair with restless energy. "Then you'll be endangering yourselves by taking us back to our families. The Pures must be waiting for you to make that exact move. They don't know where you are yet."

I wanted to kiss her and forget about all the rest. "It's a risk we are willing to take."

Gaia stared at me for a long moment. "It's a risk I won't take."

She reached out for me, but I kept shielding my thoughts. "But it's the only way for me to know you'd be left alone."

She shot me a confused look. "Why would you be so sure?" Then, before I could answer, she played my own words for me: *I'm working on something.*

I didn't answer.

She turned to Areel. "How?"

Sara echoed her question, one hand squeezing Areel's. "What are you planning to do?"

Neither Areel nor I uttered a word.

Kam took the initiative once again. "We'll manipulate your memories."

Gaia turned to face me. "What do you mean?"

I wished we had had more time. "It's the only way."

"Why?"

"Because the Pures won't have any use for you once you don't remember anything about us." I caressed her hand, needing the contact. "And Solo would never accept sending another replacement to finish the mission on Earth with you knowing about us all along."

Areel said to her, "It was part of my mission, if you remember."

Gaia remained speechless, her face expressing a turmoil of emotions.

Sara said, "You are asking us to make an impossible decision."

She took my hand and flooded me with her thoughts. "Is that what you really want?"

I couldn't tell her what I wanted.

My silence enraged her. "I can't believe you're asking me to forget you. And I can't believe you hid this from me."

Ache so raw I couldn't suppress it took hold of me, and she released my hand, cutting me off from her mind.

I barely saw Areel and Sara leaving the common room, and I barely heard Kam's parting words. "I'm sorry for all of you. I'll wait for your decision in my room." I was glad Gaia and I were finally alone.

She interrupted the prolonged silence first. "I have my family—"

A weight the size of the universe pressed on my ribcage. "I know. I understand."

"No, you don't." She caressed my jawline. "The mere idea of not remembering you breaks my heart."

I leaned against her hand. "It could all be for nothing."

"How can you say that?"

"You are leaving everything behind for me, because of me, and I don't know what's going to happen once we reach Solo. We could be separated." Scenario after scenario played before my eyes.

"Then we'll have now." She brushed my lips. "Now, it's worth it."

I put some distance between us and lowered my eyes. "I want you to be truly, completely happy."

She put a finger under my chin and forced me to look at her. "I choose you."

"I want you to choose *you.*"

"I did."

I took her by the waist and pulled her onto my lap. My body and my soul rejoiced at her proximity, and I forced myself to ask one more time, "Would you reconsider? Please?"

"Stop it. Now." Her voice was icy and cut me deeply. "I'm selfish. I'd give up anything just to have a moment with you. Don't you understand?" She stood up, looking down at me, her hazel eyes cold for the first time. Gaia stormed out of the kitchen, and I followed her a few minutes later.

I knocked on the door of our room and waited for her to acknowledge me. Then I knocked again, but she still didn't answer. I couldn't stand to be separated from her any longer, and I entered. Gaia was on the floor, the head resting on the bed, silently crying, her eyes open, staring at the window screen that was now black.

Gaia had reprogrammed the screen not to show her neighborhood in Rome.

"Sorry." I stepped inside and stopped by her. "I'll do everything in my power to make you happy." I sat on the floor.

"Just tell me everything will be fine."

"We'll be fine." I hugged her and let my body and my aura speak for me for the rest of the night. I didn't want any words to mar the sweetness of those moments.

Kam woke us up early the next morning and told us to join him in the common room. We found Areel and Sara in the kitchen, dark circles under their eyes. They were talking softly and waiting for us with a breakfast ready on the table.

"I'll go with Areel."

That was Sara's greeting, and I saw in the corner of my eye a tear escaping the well-guarded mask Gaia was wearing.

* * *

Twenty hours later, we had left Earth behind, traveling toward the first of five wormholes we had to jump through to reach Solo. Before entering deep sleep—and leaving the rest of the couples alone—Kam had calculated that the fastest route would take eight months. I was happy our ship couldn't travel any faster; it would give Gaia and me precious time together, time we spent basking in each other's presence, in a constant state of Sharing. For Gaia's sake, I tried to keep all my fears at bay, but I constantly worried about being separated once we reached my planet. Each night, I held onto her, unable to imagine a life in which she wasn't there to hold me also. I made love to her as if it were the first and the last time. I kissed her as if my life depended on it.

The eight months passed too quickly.

20

"I deeply regret it has come to this, my son." Lex had sent me a message before the first blast hit our ship and had then shut off the communication channel.

"I knew it was too simple." My words drowned in the noise. My eyes and everybody else's were glued to the screen. A ship-day away from the Solean atmosphere, we were attacked. Our vessel was meant for speed and could probably dodge fire better than the ship in front of us, but it couldn't fire back with anything more than a blast of light.

"We can't retreat. One of the engines has just been hit." Areel read the message on the control panel. He was trying to hide his emotions from Sara, but she was too scared already.

"I knew it was *way* too simple," I repeated for Areel's sake. "The Pures' facility was deserted, and we managed to get in and out with three people and encountered almost no resistance." When the first fire grazed our bow without a single warning, my mind finally put all the pieces together. Lex was simply biding his time.

"That's not completely true. You did mow down a lot of enemies." Gaia was standing next to me and had one hand on my arm.

She knew what I was going through. Again. My Ancestor Guide wanted me dead, and somehow that stung more than the fact that he wasn't Solean and that he had betrayed my whole race. I couldn't shrug off the feeling that it was personal. I should have seen the bigger picture, but I couldn't. "I should've thought he'd know my plans. Of course he'd be here waiting for me to come back home."

"It was the only decision we could make."

Kam intervened in the conversation without leaving the console he was operating. We had to go manual as soon as we realized what was happening.

"I should have seen this coming." I kept looking at Gaia and felt ashamed. "I should've done better by you." I choked on the words while another blast rumbled the hull.

She lost her balance and was thrown onto the floor. I ended up against a wall but scrambled to my feet immediately to help her.

"We're together. It's going to be okay," Gaia whispered when I embraced her.

"I'm sorry. It's all my fault. I was so naïve."

Another blast divided us. As soon as my feet found the floor, I reached for Gaia again and saw blind faith looking back at me.

"We have to find a way out of here." I squeezed her hand and went to the radio panel. "I'll send another distress call." At the moment, we didn't have lots of options. We couldn't outrun the enemy's ship, and we couldn't fire back. We couldn't jump since the closest wormhole was one day away. We were stuck.

"Lex is counting on a fast kill," I explained to four astonished faces. "We can't let that happen. If we stall the other ship long enough, sooner or later a Solean vessel will notice us. This is a busy stretch of space." It wasn't even the shadow of the plan, but we didn't have anything else. I opened the communication channel and after asking for help, I let out my rage. "Lex, have the courage to show your face." I talked to the thin air for all I knew. I had trusted him with my most intimate thoughts. I had put my life in his hands. I had accepted his verdict as just when he sent me to Silenzio. But I couldn't accept that he wasn't going to explain his reasons to me. I was trembling in unison with the ship.

"Elios?" Gaia touched my elbow softly, and the ship was rocked by another hit. We all lost our positions, and it took several seconds to stand up.

"Lex is probably not even on that ship," Kam said, and Sara shot him a terrified glance.

Somehow, Kam's words awoke me from my apathy, and a sudden idea sprang to life. "I'll use his own teachings against him again." I kissed Gaia and let her know my plan.

"Yes." She hugged me and then released me with another kiss. "It will work."

I reached for the control panel where Kam was piloting the ship.

"Are you sure?" He looked at me, and a sparkle of hope was reflected in his eyes. "Are you sure?" he asked Gaia.

"Everything's going to be okay." Gaia looked at the others, gave me her hand, and closed her eyes.

At the beginning, only darkness surrounded us.

I let our minds link together and find the right path toward the light, where there was a tiny speck of white beckoning far away. It was the light Gaia had followed when she was communicating with me during the long months of her abduction. We moved slowly at first then faster, and we left the light behind. Myriad little bright points dotted the pitch black, and we moved again until the stars in the sky were close to us. Finally, we saw the ship and the dark aura surrounding it. The ship moved increasingly more slowly. It almost stopped, and we could see the blasts coming toward our vessel frozen in space. We moved our ship from one point to another, avoiding hits as we went. We were our spacecraft, and we enjoyed our new freedom. The other ship, malevolent and dark, grew impatient and started attacking with its entire arsenal. We simply moved, lazily enjoying the dance, escaping their hatred with fluid and joyous jumps.

Irritated by our perseverance in escaping them, the Pures' ship threw an energy net to block our progress to freedom. We let the net close toward our hull, but at the last second we skirted away. Our maneuver prevented them from attacking one more time. They had felt victory close and had underestimated our resilience. Soon they were angry and couldn't maintain an analytical point of view. They opened fire one more time without realizing we weren't alone anymore.

A stern voice resonated in the control room, breaking the mental link between Gaia's mind and mine. We opened our eyes to confront reality speeding at regular time again. I realized with disappointment that it was just me again, and I looked for Gaia's hand. I wanted to be alone with her, but there wasn't time now. Words echoed in the air, and a smile stretched my lips.

"Cease fire immediately and surrender." Never was an authoritative order more welcome.

"Identify yourselves," the voice demanded as soon as Kam, who had gently moved me out of the console, put our engines in neutral. Kam was already giving our data when a conflagration of colors blinded our view of the space for a second.

"They are flying away." Areel was the first to talk.

"It doesn't matter anymore. Their attack is proof enough. Our memories will incriminate Lex." Kam's relief was contagious.

"We are free!" Gaia couldn't contain her happiness now that the ramifications of what just happened were clearer.

"I still have to face a Court judgment…" I tried to put things in perspective although I was feeling hopeful that Lex's crimes and the rest of the truth were going to play a role in my absolution. And then another voice intruded upon our cheerfulness.

"I will not be betrayed by one of my own. Never." Lex was on that ship after all. I should have been flattered that even while escaping for his freedom, he had thought to send me a last message.

"I was never one of yours. You never deserved my affection and my loyalty," I answered back, knowing Lex had already closed the channel. His ship was disappearing, pursued by the Solean vessel. I didn't care what was going to happen to him. I cared only about the person holding my hand. I breathed slowly and smiled at Gaia.

* * *

A Superior Officer I had never met before entered the hull, two cadets accompanying him. "Elios, the College of Superior Observers requests your presence. Follow us."

Gaia and I stepped forward at once, but the officer raised one hand. "Both humans will remain onboard."

I instinctively brought Gaia closer to me. "I won't leave her behind."

"It isn't for you to decide." The officer's eyes moved from me to Gaia and back. "You well know we have the means to ensure your cooperation. Don't force me to use them." Then his face softened. "Please, Elios. Be reasonable."

I didn't want to leave Gaia on the ship. I wasn't sure I was ever coming back to it.

The officer raised one hand, requesting a Share. "Trust me."

My first instinct was to deny it, but I knew it would come to a Share sooner or later, and the man had had the decency to ask me politely. As soon as his hand touched mine, I was inside his mind and relieved that he hadn't meant to read my memories. Instead, he showed me what had happened on my planet soon after the attack against our ship had become public knowledge. Solo was outraged by Lex's betrayal and had demanded swift retribution for all the people involved in the Wise Ancestor's plan. By the time our ship had landed on Solo, the truth about him, who he was, and what he had done had already come out. I interrupted the sharing with renewed hope. I looked at Gaia and took her in my arms. "I must go with him." *Everything is going to be fine.*

* * *

I followed the men outside the ship, Areel and Kam beside me. The runway was paved with crushed quartzes and volcanic rocks, and the black tarmac shone with unexpected brilliance. The air was warm in the late afternoon, and I breathed in the scent that was Solo, savoring the tanginess of the summer blooms and the distant exhaust fumes from the megalopolis. Ahead were the spires of Kartena and in the distance the Observers' Academy, also my future and Gaia's future. I looked over my shoulder at the ship. I hated having to leave Gaia behind, but it would be over soon. I smiled reassuringly at Areel, whose aura sent waves of dark colors.

"The Court has already gathered." The officer led us to an air-cab, one of the models with the passengers' space open in the center, the seats distributed around the glass wall, while the driver sat in a separate cubicle. "Sit where you like."

The cadets—who hadn't said a word—kept close to the officer, and Kam, Areel, and I took the seats on the other side. We were airborne a moment later.

I spent the one-hour ride looking outside, nose to the transparent wall of the cab. Below, field after field of red katin, one of the Solean grains, alternated with the blue-violet stripes of water canals running parallel to the fields. I wished Gaia were with me to see how beautiful my planet was. I committed to memory all the details to show her later. Soon, dwellings appeared, scattered and isolated at first; then a small village was replaced by a bigger settlement. A moment later, the imposing buildings of Kartena obscured the plain, and despite the reassurance I had given Gaia, dread gripped my heart. I was a renegade. That hadn't changed.

"Elios?" Areel gave me a half smile.

I reciprocated, but I pressed a hand to my chest to keep the anxiety firmly inside my ribcage. Kam remained silent.

The officer stirred and pointed his chin over his shoulder. The tower of the Observers' Academy was rising toward us. "You'll testify separately."

"Of course." I stared at the building that represented the innocence of my youth, and I wondered about my future.

After descending in a lazy spiral, the air-cab landed on the balcony my friends and I knew so well, and I saw both Kam and Areel smile at the same time, their eyes lingering a moment on the spot where we had challenged the winds and our luck countless times.

The passenger door opened with a *whoosh*, and cold air hit my face. I shivered and hugged myself, the shirt I was wearing barely shielding me from the icy draft battering the balcony. The officer nodded at the cadets. Two of them stood and positioned themselves before Areel and Kam. The third waited for his superior to stand, then they both approached me. "Follow your designated escort."

My friends looked at me, and I hoped I could reassure them everything would be okay, but I was numb. I waved at them. "See you soon."

Kam waved back. "Soon." He exited the cab after his escort.

Areel followed his cadet with his eyes trained on the slate floor. They were both out of my sight in the blink of an eye.

I nodded at the officer and at my escort. "I got special treatment."

"It doesn't happen every day, a highly decorated Observer breaking his oath, escaping from his prison, and uncovering a truth that will change Solo's history." The officer signed for me to step inside the Academy from the antechamber opening onto the balcony.

The cadet opened the door, and the officer entered the building. I walked in behind him, then the young man followed. I looked for my friends, but they had already left the antechamber for their destinations. I looked at the empty room, devoid of furniture or decorations—white ceiling, white walls, and white-tiled floor—and it felt like all that blankness mirrored my mind. *It will be over soon.*

"This way." The officer pressed his palm against the elevator's panel. The wall before him parted, and a small room made entirely of glass was revealed.

I couldn't enjoy the ride down to the core of the Academy and trained my eyes on the only opaque wall, to keep dizziness at bay. Regulating my breathing, I focused on happy memories.

"We've arrived." The officer's voice intruded on my tentative meditation.

The wall opened before us, and we were welcomed by a small posse. I was taken aback by the multitude of auras loudly projecting discordant emotions. The officer shouted several commands to the cadet who tried to fend off the crowd. People asked me questions.

"Do not answer." The officer gave me a warning look, and I nodded. "I thought we had kept their presence a secret," he told the cadet, who blanched and stammered, "I don't know how that happened…" They escorted me through the crowd, my eyes blinded by the pulsating auras all around me. They were too many, and I felt like drowning in the multitude of colors even though I knew nobody would have dared to come any closer.

"Finally." The officer gave me one last push, and I found myself inside a big chamber full of Superior Observers sitting on several rows of benches lying in a semicircle.

A sense of déjà vu possessed me, and although the air was warm and moist, I shivered. I was led to the center of the room where a single chair stood.

"Sit and relax." The officer patted the chair and then stepped aside.

I sat and waited, but I didn't relax. I looked at him, silently asking for guidance.

"There will be a Share, and then you'll be judged," he answered, pointing at the pool opening on the floor I hadn't noticed at first. "You know the drill."

I knew the drill. Mirroring my previous experience with the mermaid beings, the Share was over soon. One of the Superior

Observers sitting among the crowd rose from the bench and addressed me. "I am the new appointed Wise Ancestors' Guide. I am known as Carolus." He paused, looked around as if asking for consensus, and then focused back on me. "In other, simpler circumstances I would've taken the place of your Ancestor Guide. However, new measures are required in dealing with your exceptional case."

He was not an Observer then, the new Lex for everybody but me. Pain flared anew in my heart.

"I'm saddened to inform you that you've been found guilty, again, of breaking your oath—"

My hopes crashed, and I was waiting for the rest of the sentence when the roar from the crowd outside burst inside the chamber. At first I only heard a cacophony of sounds, then a word, a name, emerged, and I wept.

"Elios!" the people chanted.

"As you see, we are experiencing an unprecedented situation." Carolus smiled at me. "And as such, we have decided to take a different approach to your punishment." He motioned toward the officer who was still standing by my side. "Let them in."

The officer walked toward the wall beside the pool and pressed his palm over a rectangle. A door appeared on the wall and opened to reveal Kam and Areel behind. As they reached me at the center of the chamber, they looked as bewildered as I felt.

Carolus acknowledged my friends with a nod and then sat back on the bench. "Let the judgment begin."

* * *

Areel and I were approaching our ship when the cargo bay door opened and a whirlwind of lips and arms got hold of me and didn't let me go. I carried Gaia to our bedroom, where I cradled her to me, washing away her tears with my kisses.

"What happened?" she finally whispered.

"Areel and I were found guilty of breaking our oaths." I caressed her. "We're not allowed to come back to Solo." I passed my fingers through her hair. "It's one life sentence on Silenzio." I opened my mind and shared my recent memories with her.

She took a moment before connecting with me, but when she did, a gasp escaped her mouth. "Is it true?"

I smiled, my face buried in her hair. "The College of Superior Observers unanimously decided you and Sara must follow us. You know of our existence."

Her joy was irresistible, and for a long while there was no talking but only caresses and shivers. Then, she propped herself on an elbow and looked at me with a puzzled expression. "What did you mean by *one* life sentence?"

"Once on Silenzio, I won't have access to another body. I'll grow old in this one." I caressed her jawline. *With you.*

"I'm sorry…"

I put a finger under her chin. "Look at me." I wiped the tears marring her face. "It's the most beautiful gift my superiors could give me."

"But—"

I smiled. "I asked for it."

"You asked for it?"

"Areel, Kam, and I are considered heroes. Our memories proved our role in unmasking the truth about Lex."

She slowly caressed my face. "But you said you were found guilty."

"We are guilty of breaking our oaths of chastity, but we came back knowing our fate once we reached Solo."

"The College of Superior Observers realized your sacrifice?"

I heard her disbelief in her thoughts. "They asked us to decide our own sentence."

"They did what?"

I couldn't help but laugh at her reaction. "Heroes must be rewarded." I left a small kiss on the tip of her nose. "And Earth is safe."

"Earth is safe." Her eyes widened. "Your superiors decided to send someone else to finish your mission?"

"Yes."

"Is it going to be Kam?"

"No, Kam wouldn't be objective. The Council has decided on a veteran. And he has been ordered to alter your families' memories. At least your parents won't suffer from your absence."

Her eyes were unfocused for a long moment, but then she blinked, tears falling down her face.

I cradled her and brushed away the tears. "You do know if there had been even the slightest chance for us to go back to Earth, I would have fought for it."

She put some distance between us and severed our mental contact. "I know." She put a finger on my lips. "I know."

* * *

Before we left Solo, Kam came to say goodbye.

"Take care of him," he said to Gaia.

"He's my whole life."

From the corner where I was checking our provisions, I heard her answer and my heart did a somersault in my chest.

Kam and I didn't need words to express our feelings, and we just nodded at each other on his way out, after he had talked to Areel and Sara. Still, Areel and I stared outside from the cockpit window. When we were given permission to take off, I wiped my eyes. I would miss my friend.

* * *

I draped a blanket over Gaia's shoulders. She was shivering. The salty breeze from Silenzio's ocean ruffled her hair. "Ready?"

She nodded.

I cradled her in my arms. "Welcome home."

Dear Reader, if you liked this book, please consider writing a review. As an indie author, I rely solely on word of mouth to promote my stories. Just a few words from you will ensure my work is discovered by other readers.

Monica

To keep up to date with Monica's new releases and promotions scan the QR code with your smartphone or mobile device.

Backstory and Acknowledgments

I have been writing Elios's and Gaia's stories for so long, it doesn't seem possible I am finally at the stage of thanking everybody who was involved in the project. But here we are, four years later and several books already published.

Thanks, Mom. You would have loved both *Elios* and *Gaia*. Thanks, Dad, for reading my books in English and not having asked, not even once, I translate them in Italian.

Thanks, Maria Luisa. You were the very first one to read the rough draft of both stories. I can't forget how you took the time out of your schedule to send me mails full of notes.

Thanks, Claudia. You too were there at the beginning of my journey, and your enthusiasm about my writing endeavors was contagious then, and it is contagious now.

Thanks, Gaia and Giuseppe. As usual, just because.

Thanks, Roberto. Without you, none of this would be possible at all.

PERSONS OF INTEREST

I wrote this book

Red Adept Publishing edited and proofread it

Roberto Ruggeri patiently formatted it

You, dear reader, hopefully enjoyed reading it as much as I did writing it

BIO

Monica La Porta landed in Seattle several years ago, where she lives with her family. Despite popular feelings about the Northwest weather, she finds the mist and the rain the perfect conditions to concoct new universes. When Monica isn't writing or reading, she can be found painting on her digital tablet or sculpting. Whenever the sun shines, she comes out of her cave and treats her beloved beagle, Nero, to long walks into the Washington wild.

You can find Monica La Porta here:
Blog: http://www.monicalaporta.com
Facebook: https://www.facebook.com/monicalaportaauthor/
Goodreads: https://www.goodreads.com/MonicaLaPorta
Twitter: https://twitter.com/momilp
BookBub: https://www.bookbub.com/authors/monica-la-porta
wattpad: https://www.wattpad.com/user/momilp

OTHER BOOKS BY MONICA LA PORTA

To keep up to date with Monica's new releases and promotions scan the QR code with your smartphone or mobile device.

The Priest – Book One of the Ginecean Chronicles

Mauricio is a slave. Like any man born on Ginecea, he is but a number to the pure breed women who rule over him with cruel hands. Imprisoned inside the Temple since birth, Mauricio has never been outside, never felt the warmth of the sun on his skin. He lives a life devoid of hopes and desires. Then one day, he hears Rosie sing. He risks everything for one look at her and his life is changed forever. An impossible friendship blossoms into affection deemed sinful and perverted in a society where the only rightful union is between women. Love is born where only hate has roots and leads Mauricio to uncover a truth that could destroy Ginecea.

Pax in the Land of Women – Book Two of the Ginecean Chronicles

Love doesn't obey preordained rules. Sometimes, social status and gender mean nothing. The purest of affections can be born between two people living in different worlds. In a society where women rule over an enslaved race of men and love between a woman and man is considered a perversion, Pax's and Prince's union is destined for a tragic end. Coming from an existence of privilege, Pax has never endured harshness. She has never had any reason to doubt the rules Ginecea was built on. Everything changes when she is sent to spend her summer on a desolate farm and is exposed to the ongoing brutalities against defenseless men. A wrong turn leads her to witness Prince's thrashing at the hands of the guards. One look from him and Pax's perfect life is shattered, the memory of his dark eyes haunting her night and day. As a pure breed, born to one of the most prestigious family in Ginecea, she would have never thought it possible to fall in love with a man. Marked as a sinner, Pax abjures her ancestry to save Prince's life. She hopes they can disappear into the desert, but social prejudice and political schemes give them no respite. The Priestess, the ruler of all Ginecea, has other plans for Pax Layan and her family. Second in The Ginecean Chronicles, Pax in the Land of Women is a dystopian tale set on the planet Ginecea.

Prince at War – Book Three of the Ginecean Chronicles

The City of Men has been destroyed. The pure breeds want him dead. Prince is still running for his life. This time, he's not alone. Pax and the rest of the survivors count on him to keep them alive in the unforgiving desert. Pursued by the heartless Priestess and the President of Ginecea, Prince and Pax fight to find a haven for their unborn child. He knows the two women won't stop at anything to achieve their goal. But he can't fathom the true reasons behind their motives. Ginecea wants the heads of anyone who helped the fugitive men and nobody is safe. Not even the fathered women, slaughtered by a Priestess crazed by hate. The world is in an uproar and Pax and Prince stand in the eye of the storm. Prince at War is the third book in The Ginecean Chronicles, a series set in the dystopian world of Ginecea where women rule over enslaved men, and heterosexual love is the ultimate sin.

Elios – Elios and Gaia Series

He had no name until she gave him one. Elios has existed for eons, yet he has never lived. As a Solean Observer, his latest assignment is to study human nature. When Earth reaches its final days, he will be the one judging whether humanity's memory deserves to be preserved. This is not his first mission, and he is confident that he will make Lex, his Ancestor Guide, proud once again. Then, in Athens, Elios locks eyes with Gaia, and for the first time in his long life, he develops feelings he doesn't have a name for. An impulse stronger than any he has ever felt will drive him to follow Gaia first to Rome, where she lives, and then across the ocean to the United States when she goes to study abroad. In Seattle, unable to fight his sentiments any longer, Elios finally approaches Gaia. What starts as an innocent desire to talk to her just once, soon becomes a fire Elios can't quench. And yet, bound by his oath as an Observer, he can't have any physical contact with her. Struggling between his duties to Solo, the planet that gave him birth, and Gaia, who has become the only reason for his existence, Elios must decide. But fate, in the form of an archeological finding discovered inside an Etruscan tomb, decides for him and Gaia, separating them. Although Elios is a companion novel to Gaia, they can be read in either order. They are both stand-alone stories from different points of view. You met Gaia and Elios in her book; now hear his story.

Gaia – Elios and Gaia Series

While vacationing in Greece, Gaia locks eyes with a stranger, twice. Two years later, back in Rome, she should be enjoying college life; instead, the memories of his lapis lazuli eyes and Mona Lisa smile still haunt her. Gaia longs to meet him again and unwittingly sabotages her romantic life by refusing to move on. Only her anthropological studies about the mysterious Etruscans make her feel alive. A chance to breathe new air is presented to her when she wins a full scholarship to study abroad at the University of Washington. In rainy Seattle, Gaia finally meets the man of her dreams, but he proves to be... otherworldly. Meanwhile, in her field of studies, what starts as an interesting archeological finding about a six-fingered human image, soon evolves into the discovery of the millennium, but not where Earth is concerned. Although Gaia is a companion novel of Elios, you can read these in either order. They are both stand-alone stories from different points of view. You met Gaia and Elios in his book; now hear her story.

The Prince's Day Out

Once upon a time, in a faraway land, there was a young prince who lived confined to his bedroom. Accompanied by his sister, he traveled to the most incredible places thanks to his imagination. Follow the Prince and the Princess's fantastic journey through a magic kingdom where seagulls transport cities and ships sail on pearl necklaces instead of waves. Twelve whimsical drawings illustrate the story.

Linda of the Night

Linda was born with hair the color of the mature grain and eyes of the lightest shade of blue. Tall and willowy, she's the ugliest girl alive. Kept inside her house by her parents for fear of being ridiculed for her hideous appearance, Linda dreams of being like the dark-haired, curvaceous girls who live just outside her walls. One night, she dares the inconceivable and leaves the safety of her home. For the first time alone, Linda walks for hours until she is lost— only to find her destiny in the arms of a mysterious stranger.